VOICES FROM THE VAULTS

VOICES FROM THE VAULTS

AUTHENTIC TALES OF VAMPIRES AND GHOSTS

EDITED BY
DEVENDRA P. VARMA

KEY PORTER·BOOKS

Canadian Cataloguing in Publication Data

Main entry under title:

Voices from the vaults

ISBN 1-55013-054-4

1. Vampires – Fiction. 2. Ghost stories. I. Varma, Devendra P., 1923–

PN6120.95.V3V65   1987   808.83'9375   C87-094127-5

Key Porter Books Limited
70 The Esplanade
Toronto, Ontario
Canada   M5E 1R2

Illustrations: Tibor Kovalik
Typesetting: Computer Composition of Canada
Printed and bound in Canada
87 88 89 90 6 5 4 3 2 1

*For Madame Régine de Parquet
of Le Havre, France
who enlightened me on many
sepulchral secrets*

TABLE OF CONTENTS

INTRODUCTION

DEVENDRA P. VARMA

HE DREAM OF IMMORTALITY and the concept of returning from the dead have ever haunted mankind. The purgatorial lore and antedeluvial legends always conjectured the return of departed spirits. The vampire motif is a human-animal, life-death configuration. The vampire kills and recreates. He is the Destroyer and the Preserver.

The vampire myth is a fascinating but unsolved enigma, but its origins point to the mystic cults of the ancient East, the carved vampire-fangs and canine-teeth of oriental images of gods, and those legends of weird deities who slaked their thirst by drinking the blood of sleeping mortals. Those horrifying figures of demons symbolizing the sinister side of the aspects of fertility and salvation in the Himalayan Kingdoms of Tibet, Nepal and Outer Mongolia, supposedly nourishing themselves on flesh, bones and blood, and engaging in various styles of worship, mirror the primordial urges of primitive peoples to explore the hell of the soul.

The Indian Kali, the goddess of epidemics, war and death, her ebony complexion symbolic of black magic, like the dark Egyptian Isis, clad in skins of the dead, scooping brains from human skulls, and the awesome figures of Tantric Buddhism in remote mountain shrines, stimulated the mystics to comprehend that man can achieve heaven only when he wades right through hell.

The vampire remains a fascinating manifestation of the occult, inextricably woven in strands of mystery, terror and fantasy. Such legends originated in the East with the ancient Egyptians and the Chinese, the Tibetans and in the mountain shrines of India. By way of the trade caravans, and through pilgrims traversing the great silk route from China to the Mediterranean, the vampire superstition crossed over the steppes and spread to the ancient cities nestling on the northern Black Sea coast. Passed on to the Arabs, the vampire legend arrived in Greece and then into the Balkan peninsula, the eastern Carpathians, the basin of Hungary and the Transylvanian Alps.

1

There is a subterranean philosophy in this legend, which symbolizes ancient mystic belief in existence beyond the grave, the decay of the physical body, and the strange passions and the everlasting conflict between powers of darkness and light. In that realm of twilight between consciousness and sleep, when the will and moral senses are bemused, the impact of the vampire theme appears subtle and meaningful. Besides the delicious delights of the sublime and the supernatural, and wider concern with folklore and the occult, the vampire belief lends itself very well to an exploration of relationships which involve the exercise of power — political and social, as well as psychological.

In the grim abodes of terror, the vampire stands alone in the twilight zone betwixt life and death. Does the perturbed spirit from its sepulchre's verge return with retributive power as an avenging spirit to disturb the quiet calm of the loved one, and solicit the consecrated rites of interment, pointing to the mouldering relics of its bones? Or do these cold creatures of beyond have their sway upon warm and mortal flesh, to awaken a shudder and half-remembered consciousness by the hint of a touch on the vulnerable body, by a breath or a kiss?

Do the invisible demons lust after the flesh of mortals? Lilith, the fabled first bride of Adam, when expelled from Eden, had turned into the queen of succubi. She is referred to, in *Isaiah* 34: 14, as the "screech-owl" or "night monster". According to *Genesis*, the "sons of God" often gazed upon the loveliness of mortal maidens and took them as consorts. Classical myths tell us of gods who often consorted with the daughters of men. Zeus approached the imprisoned Danae in a shower of gold. Transforming himself into a swan he ravished Leda, mother of Helen of Troy; and impregnated Semele, the mother of Dionysus, who died of shock when she beheld her lover in effulgent glory. Eros, the god of love, took Psyche as bride, but met her only under the mantle of darkness, so that she could never observe his face.

The unearthly lovers appeared as ravishing demons. Venus, the goddess of love, was also a succubus. Once a jesting young knight placed a ring on the finger of her statue. The voluptuous goddess paid him nocturnal visits to claim him as lover. When he got married, the ethereal mistress thrust herself in between his physical body and that of his spouse.

The witchcraft mania identified women with rituals and lusts of the flesh. And in the atmosphere of ecclesiastical repression, sexual licence came to be associated with worship of the Devil. The incubi and succubi hovered around every bed. In several cases, the demon ravisher was imagined as a vampire — such as the Nosferat in Romania and the Mara of Scandinavia — whose very embrace presaged death.

Subjected to manifold interpretations, this frightening lore got nourished and ornamented in the course of centuries by hints of Satanism, necrophilia and sado-masochism. Often equated with plague, pestilence and sickness of the soul in the past, under recent psychological examination some have discovered sexual undertones in the vampire myth. The vampire stories contain scenes in which fiends hover over white-clad, reclining heroines. By ancient sanction of the romantic mode, this erotic content became an intrinsic manifestation in the European tradition.

The handsome vampire slobbering blood over the exposed throats of his beautiful victims — the demon lover who dies and yet loves — the stake pierced through the naked body of a beauteous vampire, and the nocturnal scenes drenched in gory detail, are all susceptible to a Freudian or Jungian interpretation.

The concept of the dead rising from the tomb to feed upon the blood of innocent virgins, is not a macabre, but a voluptuous idea. The vampire tales are set in Gothic landscapes of gloomy castles, wind-washed valleys or crumbling ruins nestling on a wooded hillside. The vampire rises from the moist and damp earth in a glowing mist. The dim radiance of the rising moon, the naked branches of leafless trees, establish a psychololgical mood of anguish and foreboding.

The vampire is not always a ghastly figure. Tall and handsome, well-groomed despite his waxen pallor, he has hypnotic eyes and vivid red lips curled into a smile. As the Undead, he casts no shadow and has no reflection, but what is prominent are his canine teeth. The shadow beneath his lids adds to his romantic expression of melancholy and lonesome sadness. He glides along empty corridors as the wind rustles through shroudlike, ghostly curtains.

There is yearning, hunger and thirst, an aching longing in his heart. A rueful agony makes him a magnetic figure transcending time and space. His victim has been lying awake in her bed awaiting his coming as the night wind rustles the decayed autumnal leaves. Her reclining body is bathed in moonlight until an aura of silver mist clings about her. Her golden tresses cloak the beauty of her tender figure in a luxuriant voluptuousness. She lies in an occult swoon for her midnight visitor, and awakens in languorous stillness at the break of dawn, like a sensuous maid after a night of love.

It is, indeed, a sensuous, romantic situation — the victim falling into a soothing unconsciousness, drifting into the realm of sleep, falling into a territory of the unknown, in an uncharted blackness! And what an experience it is to be embraced by a female vampire! She is a bewitching beauty, a lady of lovely countenance, full cheeks, straight nose, lush Italianate lips, and teeth of sparkling whiteness. What an experience to look at her large, luminous eyes, to listen to the rustle of silk and tinkle of bracelets or pendant ear-rings, before swooning into oblivion!

Sin follows temptation, and evil is terrible but also irresistible. Even a loathsome embrace marks the naked cruelty of passion. The vampire's embrace plumbs the bottomless pit of damnation; yet it ravages the heights of heaven with rage and rapture.

In the European concept, the vampire is odious yet still attractive. The creation of a delirious imagination sprinkled with gossamer fantasy, he is a symbol of love transcending time and space. The vampire does not destroy but dehumanizes. He creates a state in which emotional life gets suspended, and the victim is deprived of individual emotions, freedom of will or moral judgment. He gives a new dimension to concepts of love, tenderness and autumnal light. That is why, perhaps, the Surrealists, in their quest for the absolute in love and freedom, were attracted to Gothic romance.

Under glacial mountain peaks and storm-laden thunder-clouds, across the tempestuous lake in Geneva during the summer of 1816, in that sublime and awful setting of Villa Diodati, the first spell was cast to raise the undead demon that continues to haunt English literature — the vampire! That necromancer was Dr. John Polidori, the young and handsome "gentleman who travelled with Lord Byron, as physician", whose well-groomed hair, dark flashing eyes and continental, unctuous complexion, added a strange fascination to the Mediterranean charm of his personality.

Although Polidori did complete the first vampire tale, the original idea of presenting this ancient legend must be credited to Byron, whose mind was brimming with the walking dead of German tales that he and the Shelleys were perusing together. Polidori, in the meanwhile, was having nightmares arising from a terrible idea about "a skull-headed lady".

Byron had planned a vampire tale on the death of a mysterious, melancholy man, Augustus Darvell, and of his resurrection as a vampire. The story, however, was never completed. Tracing Byron's abandoned plot and drawing from anecdotes and fugitive suggestions which Byron had spilled in various conversations, Polidori published *The Vampyre* in 1819. This, in turn, gave rise to a full-fledged literary genre. In Germany and France this satanic, folkloric figure stalked into the pages of Tieck, Hoffman, Merimée, Gautier, Baudelaire, Lautréamont, Maupassant, Gogol and Tolstoy. And the theme came to be exploited by authors like Charles Nodier, James Planché and Alexandre Dumas. *The Vampyre* was reincarnated in the French and English melodramas of the 1820s and in long-running penny-dreadfuls of the 1840s. However, its real value lay in the enrichment of imagination bestowed upon subsequent writers like Thomas Preskett Prest, Joseph Sheridan Le Fanu and Bram Stoker, who created their own undying concepts of the undead.

Polidori's tale contained a pattern and formula which adapted well to popular taste. Ruthven was reincarnated in Greece, Italy, the Balkans, rural England and Scotland, but the essence of the story remained the same. Its long-term sequels can still be viewed on the television and cinema screens at midnight.

Polidori's tale was an outstanding success. An admirably-told story with the right admixture of thrills, the mysterious figure of the risen dead, the fearfully pallid and clay-cold Ruthven, gave currency to a rumour that this character was no figment of fancy but a real individual. It transposed the description of Ruthven to the popular image of Byron as destructive libertine. Lord Ruthven, the vampire, came to be actually identified with the poet. The theme was not only the epitomized metamorphosis of Satan in the Gothic romance, but also represented the haunting Byronic vampire. People glanced around crowded ball-rooms to spy, at a safe distance, the figure with "gaunt face", "piercing eyes" and "crimson lips".

Belief in vampires is often dismissed as a delusion of superstitious and primitive countries, or rationalized as evidence of premature burial. The

German romantics thought it part of black magic to invoke spirits of the dead. The vampire myth has also been attributed to those Christians who professed to have solved the mysteries of Christ's resurrection, and who, when exiled from Palestine, had emigrated to central Europe to become despotic rulers.

According to the Hindu mythology, *Ralarati* was both a witch and a vampire. In Assyrian demonology, the *Ekimmu* was a vampire demon. The Singalese called him *Katakhanes*, while the Burmese worshipped their *Swawmx*. The classical Greeks were afraid of the bisexual demon *Lamia*, who stole children and sucked their blood. In Solomonic legend, *Ornias* was a handsome vampire. A Slavic expression for vampire is *Vikodlak*, while in Poland these are called *Upirs*. Even in remote valleys and clustering villages of Greece the vampire stalks, unquestioned and accepted as *Brucolacas*.

During the eighteenth century, epidemics of vampirism emanating from eastern Europe had swept over Istria, East Prussia, Hungary, Austrian Serbia, Silesia, Wallachia, Russia and several Balkan countries. There were duly attested, formal government reports on these visitations, compiled on the orders of Emperor Charles VI.

Horace Walpole mentions that King George II of Britain and Louis XV of France were stirred by the strange case of Arnold Paole (1731-2) who was smitten by a vampire near Cassowa in Turkish Persia. Before his death he confessed that he might become a vampire. Some seventeen people died within a couple of days without any symptoms of a previous ailment. The Austrian government launched a full enquiry on December 12, 1731.

A woman, Stanjoika, in perfect health, one night awoke screaming. She stated that she had been touched on the neck by a man who had been dead. Gradually her strength ebbed away and she died within a week. Under her left ear there was a bluish scar from which blood had apparently been sucked.

It was reported that Arnold Paole did turn into a vampire and infected others. His body was disinterred forty days after burial, but his flesh had not decomposed. His eyes were besmirched with fresh blood which streamed from his ears and nose, and trickled over his shirt and funeral shroud. The stake, when driven through his heart, produced a piercing shriek followed by spurting blood. After cremation his ashes were consigned to his tomb.

This information, contained in a government despatch, caused a sensation: at the annual Leipzig fair in 1732 a cheap version of the Arnold Paole story turned into an instant best-seller. *The Dutch Gleaner* and *The London Journal* published an embellished version. *The Gentleman's Magazine*, May 1732, noted that "this account, of *Vampyres*, you'll observe, comes from the Eastern Part of the World . . . ." It referred to the state of Hungary and noted that, "these *Vampyres* are said to torment and kill the *living* by *sucking out* their *Blood*."

Augustin Calmet (1672-1757) and Montague Summers (1880-1948), both holy fathers in the Christian faith, were true investigators of vampire phenomena. Calmet followed the reports mentioned with a *Treatise* which aroused interest amongst intellectuals. Subsequently, there were four dissertations and involved debates amongst enlightened scholars like Voltaire, Rousseau, and Van Swieten, the personal physician and advisor of the Empress Maria Theresa.

In our times, Montague Summers examined many factual cases very scrupulously. Commenting upon vampirism he said:

> Not that they do not occur but that they are carefully hushed and stifled. More than one such instance has come to my notice . . . . Such cases, in truth, are happening every day, and I have met with not a few instances in my own experience.

Last year in Pitesti, Romania, wooden stakes were driven through the hearts of a family of five. For several years there had been widespread rumours of sanguinary scenes and bizarre attacks, and people claimed to have witnessed vampires sipping human blood. The authorities who investigated the cases of Ion Andrei (41), and his wife Jana (39), reported that they were impaled by hysterical neighbours who suspected them of being vampires.

Dr. Stephen Kaplan of the Vampire Research Center of Elmhurst, New York, estimates that there are 80 to 100 vampires living in the United States. Two psychiatrists in Cape Town, writing in a South African medical journal, suggest that one of the murder incentives is the uncanny desire to drink blood. Dr. R. E. Hemphill and Dr. T. Zabow report three cases in which white, middle-class males, not apparently of Transylvanian origin, have had this craving, satisfied only by taking blood from living animals, or by sucking blood from the necks and shoulders of their lovers. Denied these sources, they have cut their own arms and wrists to drink blood. The doctors add that although women are inclined to be auto-vampires, usually drinking their own blood, men are tempted to feast on others. They cite Haigh, the acid bath murderer, as a classic case; he murdered nine people, slit their throats, and drank a cupful of blood from each.

Professor Walter Storkie of California, an authority on vampire lore in Hungary, Romania, Yugoslavia and Greece, has written to me:

> We certainly have the subject of vampires in common, for I too, have been interested in them for many years since my first visit to Hungary in 1929 where I had a vampire experience.

From the very dawn of history, vampire cases have been reported in far-off cultures of the world: in Babylonia, China, India, and especially in the Slavic countries. Talented writers have woven chilling fantasies based on old folk-tales and legends. The modern revival of interest in vampire lore chimes with the escalation of violence and terror in modern civilization and curiosity about the occult. The vampire belief deciphers the symbols of larger conflict, the romantic agony pulsating within the social forces.

The vampire theme is perennially popular, and in skilful hands it never ceases to chill and inspire readers. Tales of the undead, terror-stricken tombs and haunted castles, stories in which readers experience creeping shudders and freezing, sleep-destroying nocturnal fears, often lurk on the edges of even sophisticated minds. There remains an irresistible attraction of the living dead. We may drive a stake through his heart and scatter his ashes unto the elements, but the vampire cannot die. As long as man cherishes dreams of immortality, his peering eyes will recognize the phantoms in the darkness.

Here are voices from the vaults, an anthology of vampire stories and tales of haunting from different climes by authors of various nationalities. There are authentic stories of modern vampire visitations as well as classic tales of ghostly lore. Some are historical accounts, others literary inventions.

Here are some first-rate vampire tales from the masters of the macabre. F. G. Loring's "The Tomb of Sarah" originally appeared, in October 1900, in the pages of *Pall Mall Magazine*. With his vast antiquarian and archaelogical erudition, M.R. James created "Count Magnus". F. Marion Crawford, an American, lived and studied Sanskrit in India where he delved deeply into the occult. He also sojourned a long time in Italy. His beautifully told vampire story, "For the Blood is the Life" is garnished with atmosphere and folklore.

Then there are vampire classics, like Joseph Sheridan Le Fanu's "Schalken the Painter" and Thomas Preskett Prest's "Varney, the Vampire". Le Fanu's powerfully-told story first appeared in the *Dublin University Magazine* in 1839 as one of the "Purcell Papers". Fr. Francis Purcell, an old Irish priest who collected legends and tales of the supernatural, left behind a large quantity of notes and manuscripts on his researches. Le Fanu's story centres on Rose, an artist's niece, in medieval Holland, who mysteriously disappears after being betrothed to a wealthy and sinister suitor.

Thomas Preskett Prest injected new life into the vampire theme. *Varney, the Vampire*, the long-popular penny-dreadful, unravels the tale of the seduction of an innocent heroine in a series of scenes set in haunted castles, country churchyards and charnel houses, all full of atmospheric details. Always revived by the moon's rays, the disillusioned vampire leaps into Vesuvius in the end.

Alexis Tolstoy's "The Family of the Vourdalak" is the curious story of an ailing and sinful father whose miserable doom was to bestow the kiss of death on members of his ill-fated house. He suddenly leaves home on a hunt and instructs his children that if he doesn't return at the appointed hour, they should hold a funeral for him — and if he does come back, they must drive a stake into his heart, for he will have turned into a vampire.

"The Italian Count" is based upon the true experience of the Reverend Montague Summers, the pre-eminent authority on vampires, who had probed deeply into this quaint lore. The account of "Nellie's Grave" brings us nearer home, to the vampire manifestations in Rhode Island. In 1969 its author had seen the villagers of Rodna in Romania plunge a stake through the heart of the corpse of a girl. They weren't taking any chances of her rising from the grave.

There cannot be any compendium of the supernatural without a specimen from Bram Stoker, and a story from Robert Bloch, the acclaimed modern craftsman of the macabre. We have them here, and also Tagore of India and Sung-Ling of China are represented. We have Tolstoy and Gautier. The malevolent mystery solved by Amelia B. Edwards, also famed for Egyptian researches, and the malefic hauntings of Perceval Landon appear in these pages. The effective Scottish scenario by Peter Allan, and the poetic lyricism of Margaret L. Carter linked to the vampire theme, are among the masterpieces offered.

An impressive vampire tale has to be skilfully contrived. The descriptive details must create the requisite air of that vague, mysterious border-land, where reality melts into shadows and material guilt is punished by supernatural avengers. Suspense and apprehension should create a spiritual terror on a far higher, more awful plane, beyond spectral forms and fading corners of dim twilit rooms. The atmosphere created by deft touches, and by soft tender strokes of imperceptible lightness, brings the nature of undefined horror and haunting in tune with the loneliness and a dark brooding melancholy. The most valuable ingredients in a vampire story are the atmosphere and the nicely managed crescendo.

This anthology offers truly original and timeless creations. Stories in this collection have once again risen, vampire-like, for a new lease of life, and are being offered for your enjoyment. They may take us a little closer to solving this romantic mystery.

THE COUNT'S SOLILOQUY

MARGARET L. CARTER

Days of endless dreamless sleep,
Nights of crimson waking dreams,
Winging where the chill moon gleams
    Beneath the somber clouds
    Of Transylvania.

There she lies: a peasant maid
Wearing a cross upon her breast,
And garlic blooms to guard her rest;
    In the misty woodlands
    Of Transylvania.

My thirsty lips still are parched
For virgins sweet whose throats I rend —
This ruined tower I must defend
    On the wind-swept cliffs
    Of Transylvania.

DOMDANIEL

PETER ALLAN

T TAKES A LONG TIME to reconcile oneself to living in a foreign country but for years now I have almost regarded myself as an Englishman; in reality I am one of those fortunate refugees who escaped from Eastern Europe when the troubles began there some thirty years ago, and I have never been back.

The years have passed peacefully enough and I have become so settled that I have never been sufficiently interested to establish whether or not I still have any relatives alive on the continent. It is unlikely, and long ago I settled in to the life of the English.

I have spoken English for so long that I now look upon it as my native tongue — well, almost anyway. I married an English girl soon after I came here and two lovely daughters completed our family.

I have become fascinated by the English and over the years I have spent hours of enjoyment at my desk, poring over volumes of ancient legend, folklore and myth for the various superstitions, odd customs and strange beliefs of the inhabitants of these islands. This has become an absorbing interest with me and I never miss an opportunity to note down local legends whenever I visit any part of Britain. Often, I fear, I have driven my family almost to distraction when they would have much preferred we drive on past some dreary little church and village, to a larger town with shops. But they have respected my interests and even on our holidays they have become accustomed to our route invariably wandering here and there to visit some obscure mound, stone circle or ancient burial place, some old building or reputed site of some long-forgotten event.

They were not surprised therefore, after we decided on a touring holiday in Scotland, to find that I had devised a route that bypassed most of the towns! However, we compromised; little thinking that we were to find ourselves in the middle of an adventure so strange that in writing it down it sounds more like fiction than fact. Yet it happened; yes, it's all only too true . . .

After visiting the Lake District on our way north from the outskirts of Oxford where we had lived for the past fifteen years, we made our way towards Edinburgh, our ancient black Ford only grumbling occasionally at the steepest hill. It was evening when we approached Edinburgh and since none of us had visited the city before, we decided to spend the night outside and enter and explore by daylight after a night's rest.

We noticed a sign advertising accommodation and succeeded in obtaining an evening meal and bed and breakfast for ourselves at a farmhouse where the friendly but cautious inhabitant fed us well. In the morning we set off in sunshine, refreshed and excited at the prospect of exploring Scotland's finest city.

I had read a lot about the legends and stories of strange happenings that abound in Edinburgh and while my wife and my daughters, Joan and Julia, went window-shopping, I explored the older parts of the city. I found the Museum of Antiquities with its Treasure of Traprain: that collection of church plate discovered in a crushed and broken condition after a raid into Gaul in the fifth century; the Cinerary urns; the flag carried by Douglas at the Battle of Otterburn in 1388; the strange stones carved with peculiar designs that no one has succeeded in interpreting; the seventeenth-century thumbscrews and manacles; the guillotine by which so many notables lost their heads. I visited too the curious stone graves at the corner of Castle Hill; Brodie's Close, the habitat of Brodie, a reputable citizen by day and burglar by night who was eventually hanged by a drop improved by himself; the Witches' Walk haunted by the ghost of Robert Louis Stevenson — and the hours flew by and it was time to meet my family and resume our journey into Scotland.

We had intended to make our way up the east side (taking in a visit to historic Glamis Castle with its ghosts and rooms of mystery), crossing somewhere in the vicinity of Loch Ness, hoping to catch a glimpse of the legendary monster, and then make our way back down the west coast with visits to some of the Western Isles; but a few hours after we left Edinburgh the weather changed so we turned off west in the hope of leaving the bad weather behind us.

Having the best part of a fortnight before us we were not worried by the fact that as I turned first south towards lighter skies and north towards a break in the lowering clouds, we had virtually no idea of where we were.

It was now late afternoon and in appalling weather we topped the crest of a hill in a heavily-wooded stretch of countryside and were relieved to see far below a few houses clustered together around a winding river. By some freak of nature a shaft of sunlight from the setting sun covered the little community, sheltering at the foot of the hills — mountains almost — on every side and we decided that we would see whether we could put up there for the night.

Several times we lost sight of the hamlet for the rain lashed against the windscreen of the car and now and again we would encounter what seemed to be banks of fog. Twice we almost gave up and decided to turn back but then one or other of us would catch sight of the village again and off we would go, slipping and slithering along the pitted and narrow road that twisted and turned ahead of us in the failing light.

Oddly enough each time we saw the village, it seemed just as far away as when we had first seen it and that was hours earlier. Then suddenly, after none of us had seen anything but the blinding rain lashing the trees and hedges bordering the road, until we expected at any moment to find our path blocked by a fallen tree, we seemed to pass out of the storm into a calmness that had an unreal quality after the fury of the rain. We found ourselves among the houses that we had seen from afar.

Now that we were close at hand we could see in the gathering dusk that the houses were very old indeed. As we slowly made our way past the silent, shadow-ridden cottages, we saw no trace of life other than the lighted windows that told us there were in fact inhabitants in this seemingly deserted place.

We had passed perhaps half a dozen houses when I decided that we ought to see whether we could find accommodation so I stopped the car, told my family to wait, and approached the stone doorway of the nearest cottage.

There was still just enough light to make out the stout wooden door set in the deep walls of the cottage. I noticed a niche above the doorway and could dimly make out a figure of some kind set into the stone.

Inside the cottage I could hear the sound of muffled speech and I banged on the door with my fist for I could see no knocker. Immediately there was complete silence. I waited a moment and when there was still no sound, I knocked again. Again only silence answered me.

I knocked a third time and called out 'Is anyone there?' I heard more muffled talking and the sound of someone shuffling towards the door so I stood back and waited. Although I judged the occupant must have reached the door no effort was made to open it, so I knocked yet again and called out, 'Is anyone there? I've lost my way.'

I heard the sound of a bolt being withdrawn and a heavy latch being lifted. The door creaked open a few inches and I saw half a face, including one wide-open eye, a shock of red hair and a ragged red beard silhouetted against a dimly-lit interior.

'I'm sorry to trouble you,' I explained. 'But I seem to have lost my way and as it is getting dark I wondered whether you might know where my family and I could stop for the night?'

'No — no room,' replied the man. 'Best move on — move on . . .' and the door was shut in my face and I heard the latch fastened and the bolt shot home.

I turned and made for the next cottage, about fifty yards away. As I passed the window of the cottage I had knocked at, I noticed several faces pressed against the windowpane, watching me. As I walked towards the second dark and squat dwelling in that silent hamlet I again noticed a stone figure set in a niche above the doorway and I made a mental note to find out the reason for those odd appendages; something I had never seen before in Britain.

The reaction to my arrival at the second cottage was almost identical to my original experience. At my initial knock the murmur of voices within ceased abruptly. At the second knock I heard footsteps approach the door followed by more silence and on my third knock I heard bolts withdrawn. The latch was lifted and the door was carefully opened a few inches to reveal the apprehensive face of a wiry and elderly Scot who looked at me enquiringly without saying a word.

I smiled and said as pleasantly as I could that I seemed to be lost and wondered whether there was any chance of finding accommodation for my family and myself for the night. This time I was not even rewarded by a word of refusal. Only a curt shake of the head before the door was closed and the bolts shot home.

I returned to the car and, having related my experiences, decided to proceed a little further and see whether I could find a less inhospitable inhabitant. I was on the point of suggesting that we press on through the village until we reached somewhere else but my wife and daughters looked so exhausted after the tiring journey through the storm that I decided to try and find somewhere to stop as soon as possible.

We passed a few more cottages, none of which looked more inviting than those I had already tried, and then we came upon a corner house, a little larger than most of the cottages we had seen so far, and there the door was open and someone was standing with his back to the road reaching up over the door. I quickly pulled up but by the time I was out of the car the person had disappeared and the door was shut.

I hastened up the little path and knocked at the door. All was quiet within. I knocked again and almost immediately the door was opened. The man who now faced me must have been standing just inside. He was a big man, dressed in a collarless striped shirt and thick working trousers. Although he looked as though he would be a match in strength for any two ordinary men of my size, he seemed nervous and looked anxiously at me and beyond me to the car containing my family.

'I'm terribly sorry to trouble you,' I began. 'But I seem to have lost my way. My family is fatigued and I wonder whether you could possibly suggest where we might find accommodation just for the night?'

As I spoke the man had been surveying me from head to toe. His glance returned to my face. 'Come far?' he asked, almost rudely.

I was grateful to receive an answer. 'Oh, we're touring,' I said hurriedly. 'But there was a storm and we lost our way. We'd be so grateful for a night's lodging. We'd be off first thing in the morning. Can you possibly help? I have money,' I added, pulling out my wallet.

The man looked at the money and then back at my face. He seemed to be trying to decide whether I could be trusted. After a moment he evidently made up his mind.

'Sorry — no room . . .' and he made to close the door. 'Oh, I see,' I spoke hurriedly again, before the door closed completely. 'That's alright . . . er . . . could you suggest where I might be more fortunate? Is there an inn here, or a big house where you think they might have room?'

The man stood looking at me through the half-closed door. 'The big house . . .' he said slowly, a waver in his voice. 'The big house . . .' he said again slowly. 'Yes, they've got room, but I don't think . . .' he seemed at a loss for words. 'Try the inn, The Full Moon, round the corner there but I don't know, I don't know . . . why don't you go on through the pass . . .?' And the door closed.

As I turned to go something touched my head and looking up I saw yet another niche over the doorway. This time the light from our car head-lamps gave me a better view and I saw that the stone figure set in the niche seemed to be a male figure in a hood carrying a stake in one hand and a curious and inappropriately large cross in the other. Hanging from the figure I saw a bunch of leaves that the occupant had evidently been putting in place when I had arrived and this was what had brushed my head. I looked closely and was surprised to find the narrow leaves and ball of flowers that I had often seen growing wild in Southern Europe. It was garlic.

I was puzzled for a moment; but the plight of my family, anxiously peering at me from the interior of the car reminded me that it was accommodation we were looking for and I hastened to tell them there was an inn nearby.

The Full Moon looked deserted when we eventually found it. I could see no lights at all but when I reached the door, I found it opened at my touch and I stepped inside. The sound of talking that had reached my ears as I opened the door ceased abruptly as I entered and I found myself being surveyed with something more than idle curiosity by the landlord, leaning on the bar, and half a dozen or so occupants, dotted about the sparsely-furnished room.

I nodded to the men staring at me silently over their drinks and walked towards the bar. The innkeeper gave no smile of welcome and gazed steadfastly at me.

'Good evening,' I began. 'Could I have a pint of bitter, please?' The innkeeper took a glass and filled it, still keeping his eyes fixed upon me. I put my money on the bar and took the glass. After a long drink I replaced the half-empty glass on the bar and smiled at the landlord. He seemed more relaxed now and actually nodded at me.

'Lovely countryside hereabouts,' I ventured, by way of an opening. 'We're touring and seem to have lost our way.' The landlord made no comment and I thought it best to continue. 'Actually, we were wondering whether you could accommodate us for a night — then we can be on our way first thing in the morning,' I added hurriedly as I saw him begin to shake his head.

'No room,' he said at last, after what seemed an age of pregnant silence. 'I'd get on if I were you.'

'Yes, well,' I began again. 'My wife is very tired and we've come a fair way. We'd like to stop here just for the night, if we could. Anywhere would do, just for the night. Couldn't you possibly find somewhere . . . I'd be most grateful,' I added, pulling out my wallet.

'No — no — no room at all here,' the innkeeper replied, almost too quickly.

I took another drink as he spoke, waiting for him to suggest an alternative. When he said no more I put the empty glass down and asked: 'Well, what about the big house — do you think they might take us for one night?'

The landlord stared visibly. 'The big house — oh, I wouldn't think so. No, I'd not recommend that!' I was beginning to feel that I was taking part in a film; it all seemed so unreasonable, so unreal and so unwelcoming.

'I say, but look here,' I said with a little more spirit. 'We're visitors and surely there must be somewhere we can stop for a night. We seem to be miles from anywhere and we need to rest before going on. If you're sure you can't help us, tell me the way to the big house and I'll try there.'

The innkeeper thought for a moment. He looked at the others in the room. 'He's away, isn't he?' he asked, of no one in particular. I looked round at the nearest couple of men but they sat silent with their drinks in front of them. Then both gave a brief nod to the landlord, whereupon he turned back to me.

'Well, try the big house if you like. You'll find the drive a quarter of a mile along the road here, on your left. The gate will be fastened so you'll have to leave your car and walk up to the house. Old Henrock will be there, but don't say I sent you . . .'

He turned abruptly and went to the other end of the bar and began to fill a glass for himself. 'Thank you,' I said, turning to go. 'And goodnight,' I received no reply and made my way out of the inn.

By this time my wife and daughters were beginning to be tired of my repeatedly saying that I could find no sympathy wherever I called, in what I was beginning to think must be the most unwelcoming village in Scotland, and when I said that I was going to try the big house as a last resort, my wife insisted that she would accompany me and see whether she could persuade 'old Henrock' to take us in for the night.

By now it was quite dark and my wife and I climbed over the gate — there was no other way for us to enter for the massive gate was fastened with a heavy chain wound several times round the gate and gatepost before being locked with a padlock that looked rusted as if it had been unused for years.

As we made our way along the overgrown drive the wind rose and we found ourselves labouring against great gusts of wind that blew the low-hanging branches of the mass of trees bordering the drive, into our faces. We pressed on to the accompaniment of occasional hootings of owls and swirling bats that frightened the life out of my wife who was afraid, like so many women, that they would get caught in her hair. Now and again we caught sight of the dark outline of a house ahead of us and, to our relief, we saw a light in one of the upper windows.

We were about twenty yards from the door, set in a massive arch with wide steps leading to it, when we realised that the door was open and as we drew nearer we could distinguish someone standing in the deep shadow of the doorway. Hand in hand we hurried across the last few yards and into the doorway out of the driving wind and swirling leaves.

'Sorry to trouble you . . .' I began. The figure of a man, tall and forbidding in the dim light, detached itself from the shadows and stood looking down at us. He was dressed in black or very dark clothing, unrelieved even by a white shirt for he wore a dark high-necked sweater under a black velvet jacket. By contrast his face, clean-shaven and unwrinkled although he was certainly not a young man, was almost chalk-white. His piercing dark eyes flashed from my face to that of my wife, and stayed there. Hardly moving his lips he said in a faraway voice with a foreign accent, 'How did you get in? What do you want? This is private property. The master is away.'

I put an arm around my wife's waist and we pressed towards the doorway. 'May we come in for a moment, please? We've lost our way and seeing the drive, we climbed over the gate in the hope that someone could help us.'

Henrock, for he it was we later learned, stood to one side and with a theatrical gesture, bade us enter. Doing so we found ourselves in a large hall with an enormous sweeping staircase ahead of us. So much we could make out in the dim light before we heard the door crash to behind us and, startled for a moment, we turned to find Henrock bolting and chaining the heavy door before turning and striking a match. He passed us and lit two candles that were mounted on each side of the staircase in wrought-iron holders decorated with dragons' heads. He placed himself carefully just behind one candle and looked down on us.

'The master is away,' he said again as if that statement would answer all our problems.

'Yes . . .' I said unable to think of the best line of approach. My wife came to my rescue. Brushing her long hair back from her face, she faced him with her most attractive smile and said, demurely: 'We *are* sorry to trouble you but we are at our wits' end. We've been lost for ages and just can't go any further. If you could possibly see your way to allowing us to spend the night here, we'll be extremely grateful and we promise to be no trouble at all. We really are tired out. We'll gladly recompense you for your kindness and we'll be away first thing in the morning. Please . . .' she hesitated to allow full emphasis to her words. 'Please — we'd be so grateful.'

Henrock hadn't taken his eyes from my wife's face as she spoke and now he answered, still staring at her. 'The master is away,' he said yet again. 'I don't know when he will be back. He is not accustomed to visitors. We have no food.' He hesitated for a moment and my wife, pressing her advantage, pleaded: 'Please, oh, please, just let us rest until the morning . . .'

Henrock said nothing for a moment, half-smiled, revealing two appallingly ugly upper side teeth, and then he abruptly turned and walked away from us up the stairs. 'Follow me,' he called over his shoulder.

With a glance of relief at each other we followed him up the stairway and into a room where candles were burning in a low-slung chandelier. He indicated that we should enter and pointed to a wooden seat by the window. Taking up a position with his back to the door he said, hesitatingly: 'I don't know whether the master would approve, but stay the night in this room if you wish; now I will leave you,' and he was almost gone before I called out: 'Oh, our daughters are in the car at the end of the drive. Do you think you could unlock the gate so that we can bring the car up to the house?'

Henrock turned, his dark eyes flashing for a moment. 'You said nothing of any children?' 'Er — well, no . . .' my wife interjected. 'We were just going to say that we hoped you would extend your hospitality to them. They are not children, actually, they're nearly twenty. They won't be any trouble though — they just need somewhere to sleep. You don't mind, do you?'

Henrock stood silent for what must have been the best part of a minute. 'They can sleep in the master's room,' he said at last. 'But I can't open the drive gates,' he added quickly. 'You must leave the car where it is. It will be quite safe,' he added. 'No one comes here.' The next moment he was gone.

I looked at my wife. 'Stay here; I'll fetch the girls and lock the car,' I told her. 'I'll bring the little suitcase. We'll be off early in the morning . . .' When I was halfway down the staircase I heard a door open behind me and Henrock appeared carrying a candle in a long brass holder. He stood in the doorway of the room at the end of the stairs. 'This is the master's room,' he said in a reverent tone. 'I'll leave the door open.' I was about to answer when I realised that he had gone.

Half an hour later we had said 'goodnight' to the girls and they were in their room. We prepared ourselves for the night and before long were thankfully tucked up, close together for comfort, in the brass bedstead in the corner of the room, having extinguished the candles. There were no curtains to the windows and for a while we lay awake, thinking our own thoughts, and watching the clouds scurry across the moonlit sky.

We both awakened with a start as a clap of thunder seemed to shake the house. The storm we had travelled through seemed to have reached the village and lightning streaked across the sky lighting up our shadowy room; the wind howled; the uncurtained window rattled and shook as it was beaten by gusts of wind, the pouring rain, and what looked like branches; and for some time we were unable to get back to sleep. At length the storm passed and we resumed our rest — only to wake again with sickening suddenness at the sound of a piercing shriek — Joan's voice!

I leapt from the bed and pulled at the door. It was shut fast and seemed to be locked! I shouted, I banged at the door. I shouted and kicked but all to no avail. All was now quiet and in fact there were no more screams after that first awful one. I listened intently but could hear no sound whatever. The house might have been empty. I tried the door again for one last time but it was closed fast and nothing I could do would shift it. There was nothing for it but to go back to bed and wait for morning.

We tossed and turned for some hours until I could stand it no longer. I looked at my watch and saw to my astonishment that it was barely three o'clock, but I knew that I should not sleep any more. My wife too was wide awake. 'I'm going to get up,' I said. I looked out of the window. It was still dark.

I began to get dressed when suddenly the door of the bedroom opened and Henrock stood there. He was dressed exactly as we had seen him the previous night but he seemed agitated.

'The master returned last night,' he said simply. 'As your daughters have his room he is downstairs. I think you had all better leave as soon as you can.' I was about to question him about the fastened door and the scream, but he had gone. 'I'll see about the girls,' I said to my wife. 'Get dressed quickly.' I ran out of the room and saw Henrock turn the handle of the master's room; he just opened the door, closed it again and then went downstairs.

I dashed into the room occupied by our daughters. They were awake and looked wide-eyed at my sudden entry. 'Are you all right?' I enquired, breathlessly. 'Henrock says his master has returned and we must leave. Get dressed as quickly as you can and we'll be on our way. Oh, and what was that scream in the night?'

'Oh! my God! what a night,' replied Julia. 'Joan had a nightmare or something and nearly frightened the life out of me. We'll tell you all about it later. Hey, come on Joan, you look awful — it was only a dream after all . . .'

Shortly afterwards we all gathered at the head of the stairs with our belongings. Joan did look pale and she seemed quite weak but her mother said it was all the travelling and the disturbed night, so I did not take too much notice.

We made our way down the stairs and had reached the door without seeing anyone when I caught sight of Henrock standing in the shadow of a doorway leading off the hall. He didn't move out of the shadows as he spoke.

'Ah! we're just off,' I said. 'Please accept this for your trouble.' I handed him the ten pound note I had ready. 'We were grateful for the night's shelter. I do hope your master was not too inconvenienced by our being here?'

Henrock still did not move and he made no attempt to take the money. 'The master wishes to see you,' he said flatly and opening a door behind him he stood to one side. I took a step towards him while my wife and daughters remained by the front door. 'All of you,' Henrock added, and directed us inside the room.

With some trepidation we walked together into the room. It was as sparsely furnished as the rest of the house that we had seen but seated at a grand piano was a man whose appearance defies an adequate description.

I never saw anyone like him before. He seemed old yet there was a sprightliness and magnetism about him that belied the long white hair and the scraggy neck for his face was unlined and full, bloated even. His dark eyes were overshadowed by bushy black eyebrows that looked like tufts of feathers, eyebrows that seemed to run from one side of his face to the other. He looked intently at each of us and then his eyes returned with piercing intensity to the girls. Suddenly he seemed to remember his manners and he turned to my wife and me with a charming old-world courtesy, rising from the piano with outstretched hand.

'Welcome to Domdaniel,' he said in a deep voice, almost without moving his lips, much as Henrock had spoken, and I remembered wondering whether this was a family idiosyncrasy and whether Henrock and his master were related for there was a similar bearing and sense of dignity about both of them — yet this seemed most unlikely; and the master was if anything even taller than the servant.

'Welcome to Domdaniel,' he said again, indicating a long seat by the window, which was uncurtained, although it was still dark outside. 'Forgive me,' he went on. 'I was forgetting, it is dark in here.' And he lit a candle on the piano. 'I'm afraid I enjoy the dark,' he said, with a ghost of a smile. Having lit the candle he came towards me with outstretched hand. 'My name is Domain, Damon Domain and I apologise for my inadequate hospitality. I have long ago forgotten the pleasures of company and am a poor host . . . but I have sent Henrock out for some food. He will not be long. Visitors are a luxury we have almost forgotten and we have no provisions available. I trust your charming daughters slept well?' he added, turning to Joan and Julia.

The hand I shook seemed icy cold and although I only held it for a second I had the impression that there was something in the hand for my own palm seemed to touch something soft that tickled; but I forgot it a moment later for in turning to my daughters he had smiled and I saw that he too was afflicted by two gigantic and pointed eyeteeth! No wonder the poor man tried to keep his lips closed.

A second later he had closed his lips and I almost thought I must have been mistaken for now there was no hint of any abnormality as he stood, bending forward slightly, his tall figure clothed in a dark, close-fitting suit, a high black roll-collared pullover hiding some of the scragginess of his long and powerful neck. Even his shoes were black I noticed, slip-on boots with elastic sides, highly-polished.

'Well, yes,' replied Julia with some hesitancy. 'We were certainly tired and very grateful for the use of your bed but Joan had a nightmare and she doesn't seem to have recovered yet . . . are you all right Joan, you do look pale?'

'Yes, yes, I'm all right,' replied Joan dreamily. 'Well, actually, I'd like to lie down. Oh, sorry, we're just off aren't we? Mummy, could we go? I do feel a bit washed-out . . .'

'But my dear, I wouldn't think of it,' broke in our host. 'What would you think of me if I sent you away from this humble abode unwell? No, no, you must all be my guests until you are fit again for the journey.' 'No,' he insisted as I rose from my seat in protest. 'You will all consider yourselves my guests; and now,' he glanced towards the window where the first streaks of dawn were just beginning to show. 'Now I must ask you to excuse me. I too am tired after my journey and must rest; but Henrock will see that I am comfortable downstairs. Joan, you must return to bed and the rest of you please enjoy your day in our little village; I shall look forward to seeing you this evening . . .'

He turned abruptly and left us before we could say a word in reply.

Joan did look exhausted and needed little persuasion to return to bed. Her mother said she would stay with her so Julia and I returned our things upstairs and then thought we would go for a walk round the village.

As we left the house we met Henrock in the hall. 'The master tells me you are all staying for a while. I shall try to make you comfortable but I hope you will forgive the eccentricities of a lonely man and his servant of many years?'

I said we were very grateful for the kindness they were showing us and hoped we would not be too much trouble.

'Not at all,' replied Henrock. 'It will be pleasant to have guests again — but would you do one thing for us?'

'Yes, of course,' I replied and Julia nodded her consent. 'I'm very serious,' went on Henrock, almost stepping out of the shadows in his anxiety. 'It is a small thing but I want you to promise me something, nay I want you to swear by everything you hold dear, your wife and the girl upstairs. Swear you will do this one thing I ask.' Henrock's voice rose in fierce intensity.

We looked at each other. There was nothing we could do but agree. 'Of course, if it is within our power, we swear to do what you say,' I said, as lightly and evenly as I could. Henrock made us swear for my wife and Joan too and we wondered what on earth it could be that he was going to ask us to do; we were more than a little relieved when he said:

'It's very simple, but I'm serious. You must not talk to anyone in the village about us or this house, under any circumstances. You see they are a silly and superstitious people; they dislike my master and we have sworn never to have anything to do with anyone living there. You understand?' he concluded. 'You have solemnly sworn . . .'

'Yes, we understand,' I replied. 'We will not breathe a word.' With a bow of relief Henrock opened the door and we stepped out into the fresh morning air.

'Oh, we dine at night,' Henrock called to us from the doorway. 'There will be a good meal waiting for you then; conserve your appetite and you will enjoy the meal all the more, I promise you.'

Julia and I set off down the drive. We were both silent for a time, each occupied with our own thoughts — and fears. The weather was glorious after the stormy night and we soon arrived in sight of the drive gates when we both stopped dead in our tracks. Our car, which we had left parked on the outside of the locked gates, now stood within the gates!

I hurried forward but could find no explanation for the move. The drive gate was closed and the chain still secured. The lock still looked rusted and I would have said it had been unopened for months; the gate was quite immovable, and apparently the lock was rusted solid inside.

I turned my attention to the car. How on earth could it have been driven through anyway, since I had the keys? I unlocked and opened the car door. I tried the motor several times before it would turn over so I decided that some of the rain during the night's downpour must have found its way into the engine. There seemed little point in trying to get the car started just then in any case and I decided to leave it for the present, hoping it would dry out and start without difficulty later on.

As Julia and I climbed over the gate I saw to my amazement the clear tyre marks where I had left the car, now filled with water — but there were no traces of any marks through the gates and no signs of any marks where the car had been driven to its present position. If it had not been impossible I would have said the car had been lifted bodily over the gate and placed where it now stood!

With yet another problem to think about we set off up the hill away from the village in the direction of the hills, steaming in the morning sun.

For a time we walked side by side, silent and thoughtful. After a while I remembered that Julia had said she would tell me about Joan's nightmare. I asked her to tell me about it.

Julia looked at me for a moment. 'Well, it was very strange really. I was awakened by Joan's piercing scream but when I started up in alarm and asked what in heaven's name was the matter, she looked at me in surprise and asked what I meant. She hadn't realised that she had screamed but she said she felt sick and faint and thought she must have had a nightmare. She couldn't remember anything clearly but recalled the impression of an awful smell, like mouldy flesh, and said her neck felt sore. I thought she must have fallen asleep in an awkward position, and then she found her neck was bleeding. There seemed to be some pin-pricks at the side of her neck and when we found an open safety-pin in the bed we decided that the combination of an accidental prick while she was asleep had triggered off her nightmare and scream. She was very quiet and listless but insisted that she was all right and told me to go back to sleep. Then you came in.'

We walked for hours, climbing most of the time. We stopped from time to time and at one point ate a bar of chocolate I had in my pocket. We could hardly believe it when we found that it was mid-afternoon, and we turned back. Far below us in the distance we could see the village we had left and we made our leisurely way back, weary but refreshed by the hours in the open air.

The sun had set and it was getting dark when we walked down the hill towards the big house and there we were met at the drive gate by my distressed wife who gasped out that she had been looking for us for hours but had no idea which direction we had taken. In frantic, broken sentences, she told us what had happened.

Soon after Joan had been put to bed she had fallen into a deep slumber. For a time my wife had sat by her side but she became frightened when Joan's breathing had quietened to such a degree that she had seemed to be hardly breathing at all. Uncertain what to do, among strangers in a strange house, she had run downstairs but had been unable to find anyone. Most of the doors she had tried had been locked; she could see no telephone and, thinking that Henrock must be somewhere in the grounds, she had gone out of the front door and made her way all round the house. She had discovered another drive that led to the rear of the house, a drive that disappeared among trees, high shrubs and bushes, but of Henrock there was no sign.

Frantic by this time, she had returned to the front of the house to find the door shut fast. She received no answer to her repeated knocking. She rushed down the front drive hoping to meet us returning and had tripped or stumbled in her hurry. She said she must have hit her head as she fell and knocked herself unconscious for the next thing she remembered she was waking to find it was nearly dark. Her ankle was twisted and she was bleeding from the neck where she thought a briar must have caught her as she fell.

There were two neat punctures in her neck but little blood and I comforted her and told her we would find Joan and leave at once. As I held her to me she suddenly slumped into unconsciousness and I realised that the fall must have been a heavy one and she had hurt herself more than she had thought.

Between us Julia and I carried my wife up the drive and we were relieved to see a light in the room over the front door. At any rate someone was now at home. As we reached the door it was opened by Henrock who seemed genuinely alarmed and worried by the condition of my wife who was still unconscious.

With hardly a word of explanation we carried her upstairs and put her to bed in the room we had occupied; Henrock assisting and then standing watching us until she seemed as comfortable as we could make her.

'I must find a doctor at once,' I said to Henrock. 'Do you have a telephone? And how is Joan?'

Henrock motioned us to be quiet for the sake of my wife and led the way downstairs and into the room where we had earlier talked with his master. Once inside he guided us to the long seat by the window and took up a position himself by the piano.

The gist of the story he then related was that after he had assisted his master to retire and refresh himself, he had hurried out to fetch a doctor for Joan. When he returned with the doctor my wife was nowhere in sight but Joan was so ill that the doctor said she must go to hospital immediately and he would take her in his car, which he did.

Julia and I listened, wide-eyed and almost unbelieving, to all this but Henrock went on to say that the doctor was returning to talk to us about Joan and he expected him in fact at any moment, so he could look at my wife when he arrived. 'In the meantime,' concluded Henrock, 'my master hopes you will join him in the Long Room where a meal has been prepared for you . . .'

How could we eat at such a time! But, as in a dream, Julia and I followed Henrock across the hall where he unlocked a door and led us down a short passage and into a room where a table was laden with food. Sitting in a massive carved chair at the far end of the Long Room, away from the table, sat our host Damon Domain.

He rose from the chair in welcome but he did not move from the shadowy corner. 'My friends . . . I hope you will forgive me but I have already dined. I am sure all your troubles will soon be over but in the meantime please eat a little of the food that Henrock has prepared and sample my vintage Romanian red wine. I think you will find it palatable . . .'

'You are most kind,' I managed to say, although food and drink were far from my thoughts at that moment. 'But I would like to see that my wife is comfortable first.' 'Of course,' the tall dark figure of the owner of this strange household agreed. 'Henrock, take our guest upstairs while I encourage his charming daughter to begin. You must be famished, my dear, after your long walk,' he added, turning to Julia.

I followed Henrock out of the room, back along the corridor and up the main staircase. At the door of the bedroom he halted for a moment and then threw open the door. The bedclothes were disarrayed but of my wife there was no sign! I turned aghast to Henrock for an explanation. He stood in the doorway, silent and sympathetic.

'I think it would be best not to mention this matter to your daughter,' he began. 'Not mention it . . .' I almost shouted. He looked pained at my tone. 'I'm afraid your wife was more seriously hurt than you thought . . . I was able to arrange for her immediate removal . . . you may see her soon,' he added, as I started towards him.

'She is quite safe,' he assured me. 'But she could not stay here without attention. You shall see her soon, I promise you. Now, please, the master is waiting.'

This *must* all be a dream I told myself as I started down the stairs ahead of Henrock; no, a nightmare. Surely I will wake up soon. I must.

Never shall I forget the scene that met my eyes when I walked into the Long Room which I had left only minutes before. Julia was slumped across the table, apparently unconscious, on her side, and over her bent Domain, his back towards me, his arms raised, drawing outwards the odd, dated, jacket-cape that he wore so that he looked for all the world like a great bat about to feed.

I darted forward and at my approach he turned. For a second I thought I saw again those awful fang-like teeth and a flash of some powerful and evil thing showed itself in the flashing eyes; but it all happened so quickly that immediately afterwards I thought I might have been mistaken; the look had gone and in its place the concerned and quiet man we knew as Damon Domain hurried towards me, his mouth almost closed but slightly smiling, spreading his hands in apology. 'My dear sir, a thousand apologies; there has been a little accident. Your daughter cut herself with a chipped wineglass and I was just doing what I could to assist. She seems to have fainted from shock but I am sure she will recover in a moment. Look — it really is a very little accident, the skin is just pricked on her neck — that's all.'

As I leaned over Julia her eyelids fluttered and I was about to ask her what had happened when she gave me a look so full of agonised hopelessness, the like of which I hope never to see again, and then lapsed back into unconsciousness.

She looked so terribly pale and lifeless that I was alarmed and taking her in my arms I laid her on the big settee by the wall where I felt she would be more comfortable. Having covered her with a thick woollen wrap that lay nearby, I turned to find that our host had hardly moved. He stood by the side of the table, drawn up to his full height; a commanding and forbidding figure. His eyes gleamed in the candlelight and his face seemed more bloated than when I had seen him previously. I turned towards the door where Henrock still stood, gazing in a hypnotic way at his master. I was in a quandary and for the first time I felt really frightened in this strange house with its stranger inmates.

'I must find a doctor,' I said at last. 'And I insist on seeing my wife. What on earth is going on?' I raised my voice but it had no effect upon my two hearers who remained motionless and silent.

Suddenly Damon Domain seemed to recover himself and looked at me afresh: 'Yes, yes, of course. We must make your daughter comfortable; but have no fear for she is a fine, healthy girl and will soon be quite fit again. Henrock: prepare a place for her to rest, near to her mother.'

Henrock turned and left the room but I was disturbed. What had Domain meant when he suggested Julia be put somewhere near my wife? Something told me that all was far from well with my wife and my daughters and I ran after Henrock and caught him by the arm at the top of the stairs. I swung him round to face me. 'Now, look here. I've had about enough of all this. Take me to my wife at once.' He stared coldly at me. 'I think you should wait with the master. I will prepare somewhere for your daughter to rest and recover.'

So saying he turned to leave but in my anger, frustration and distress I lunged at him to swing him round again. Instead I knocked him off balance and before I could prevent it happening, he had crashed through the banister and fallen some twenty-five feet to the hall below!

Horror-stricken, I watched him fall and land with a sickening thud onto the stone floor. I knew that he must be terribly injured if not killed and I was about to rush down the stairs when, to my amazement, I saw him turn over on to his side, get up off the floor and walk across the hall and through the doorway, as though nothing untoward had happened!

Aghast I staggered back and, intending (I think) to make my way back to our host, I turned to find him at my shoulder. His face blazed with anger and fiendish power. Almost before I realised what was happening his powerful hands had seized me, my head was thrust sharply back and sideways and I caught a glimpse of those horrible fangs before I felt the sharp double-pain as he bit deep into the jugular vein, and I knew no more.

I AWOKE, I know not how long afterwards, to find myself lying on my back. It was dark and yet I found that I could see tolerably well. I seemed to be lying in some kind of box and on earth! Good God! I was in a coffin of earth!

I started up but found myself weak beyond description. I felt drained of every drop of blood — as well I might be, I told myself.

In a way I had half-suspected the awful truth and looking back I realised that I should have known much sooner that we had stumbled into the retreat of a vampire!

What a fool I had been! It all seemed so obvious now that I couldn't think how I had not known almost as soon as we had arrived. I suppose (like most people) I unconsciously refused to believe that such things existed in the 1970s, but with my interest in the strange and the unusual I surely should have known.

The hostility of the villagers and their terror of the dark; the niches over each doorway that must have been some kind of protective amulet; even the garlic which no vampire can face. The fearsome fangs of Henrock and of his master who arrived at night in that terrible storm. The way their eyebrows met over the nose and of course it was hair in the palm that I had felt when I had shaken hands. My skin shivered at the thought. The way both of them had always positioned themselves so that they did not reveal the tell-tale fact that they cast no shadows. The absence of any mirror in the house; and no cross of any kind; why even their shoes had no laces! *They* had never partaken of any food or drink in our presence. Superhuman strength that could lift a car over a gate. A heavy fall had not harmed Henrock for he was invincible except against garlic, a cross or a stake through the heart!

While all this was passing through my mind I lay, exhausted, gazing up at the ceiling; but gradually I felt a little stronger and at length I pulled myself up and looked around me. Even as I had dreaded yet knew in my heart, there were other boxes similar to that wherein I lay. Five more were spread about the room or dungeon, I knew not what it was.

A little longer and I felt able to rise and lift my weary limbs. I forced myself to climb out of the box and leave the sickeningly damp and earthy bed.

Slowly I crawled over to the nearest box. There lay my dear wife, pale and hardly breathing with the tell-tale trickle of blood from the two pricks in her white neck. I tried to wake her, uncontrollable tears running down my cheeks, but she seemed to be in a deep coma of some kind. I stepped across the room and found my dear daughters in a similar condition. They looked so pale but so beautiful. I wept unashamedly, found myself slipping to the floor, and must have lost consciousness.

I AWAKENED AGAIN in darkness. This was no dream! I was still in this accursed room with the unconscious bodies of my dear family. I pulled myself upright and tried to think what I could do. There might not be much time. In fact there was no time to help any of us. We were already doomed but if only I could stop this nest of vampires.

I pumped my brain to recollect what I could of vampires and vampirism. They could not face a cross, I knew that. But how could that help me now. At least, perhaps, I could protect my family from further assaults if only I could fashion some crosses. How, oh heavens, how?

I forced myself to reach the other two occupied boxes or coffins. They were empty but the impressions in them left no doubt in my mind that they were the resting places of Henrock and his master. Soon, I guessed, it would be dawn and then they would come to take their rest — perhaps they would even come for a final feed — before remaining imprisoned in their boxes during the hours of daylight. I had no time to lose.

How could I manufacture three crosses, even four? Frantically I looked around me. There were no windows and, apart from the boxes, nothing but a few odds and ends in the room. Broken furniture, newspapers, some petrol cans, an old mattress — nothing that I could see would help me, and yet . . .

I seized a broken chair and a leg came off in my hand. I looked again at the unoccupied boxes. Could I perhaps conjure up some crosses from the wood of the boxes? It seemed worth a try.

Using the chair leg as a hammer I broke off the ends of one box, one piece of wood after the other; then the other end. By now I felt weak with fatigue but I forced myself to attack the other unoccupied box in the same way. This done I took two narrow pieces of wood and placing one across the other in the form of a cross, I placed it gently over the dear pale face of my sleeping wife. Then I did the same for my daughters. Taking two of the larger pieces of wood from the side of one box I succeeded in forming a huge cross which I balanced against the box I had lain in so that it faced the door and might discourage whoever or whatever came through the door.

Really exhausted now I slumped to the floor in an agony of despair. What would I do to save my family? Oh God! Must I fashion stakes and pierce their lovely bodies? And what could I do to stop these fiends forever?

Suddenly I remembered fire. Vampires cannot withstand fire! Could I set fire to this cursed place and rid the world of these wretched creatures?

I struggled to my feet again and made my way across the room to where the rubbish lay. There was paper and it was dry. The mattress, too, might burn. I looked carefully around me. The door was wooden and the posts, which looked very old and dry should burn if only I could get them well alight. Then I saw the petrol cans. I pulled one out. It was empty. Then another; that was empty too. A third had some petrol in it! A fourth was full! And a fifth!

I hesitated for only a moment. I knew what I had to do. I took more pieces of wood from the sides of the broken boxes; split the wood by bending it against itself with the help of the chair leg, and so I fashioned three stakes.

I tore the mattress apart, crumpled the paper against the door and doorposts, spread the contents of the mattress over and around the paper, piled the rest of the wood from the broken boxes and the remains of the chair and the bits and pieces of furniture in a conical shape against the door. I poured all the petrol I could find over it. I found my pocket lighter and was about to set light to the paper when I stopped. The whole house was as quiet as death. To ensure the destruction of Henrock and his master I must at least be sure that they were in the house. Dare I wait until I could be sure that they were both at home?

I sat back on the floor and rested. Yes, I decided I would try to delay setting light to the rubbish and, hopefully, to the house, until I heard some sound that suggested that 'they' were within the walls of Domdaniel. 'Domdaniel,' I thought, how aptly named, 'an infernal dwelling.'

Author's Note. The above account, in a minute hand, was written in a pocket notebook which was discovered in a remote Scottish village in an empty petrol can in the cellar of an isolated house which had been completely destroyed by fire. Also in the cellar the remains were found of three female bodies in earth-filled coffins and the remains of a man lay on the floor, on his back with legs straight together and arms outstretched at right angles, in the form of a cross. Outside what had been the door of the cellar police reported finding two huge piles of thick dust that stank abominably. When disturbed the dust disintegrated and disappeared.

THE TOMB OF SARAH

F.G. LORING

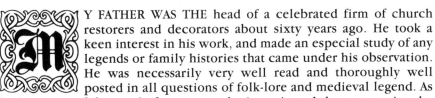Y FATHER WAS THE head of a celebrated firm of church restorers and decorators about sixty years ago. He took a keen interest in his work, and made an especial study of any legends or family histories that came under his observation. He was necessarily very well read and thoroughly well posted in all questions of folk-lore and medieval legend. As he kept a careful record of every case he investigated the manuscripts he left at his death have a special interest. From amongst them I have selected the following, as being a particularly weird and extraordinary experience. In presenting it to the public I feel it is superfluous to apologize for its supernatural character.

My Father's Diary
1841 17th June. Received a commission from my old friend, Peter Grant, to enlarge and restore the chancel of his church at Hagarstone, in the wilds of the west country.

5th July. Went down to Hagarstone with my head man, Somers. A very long and tiring journey.

7th July. Got the work well started. The old church is one of special interest to the antiquarian, and I shall endeavor while restoring it to alter the existing arrangements as little as possible. One large tomb, however, must be moved bodily ten feet at least to the southward. Curiously enough there is a somewhat forbidding inscription upon it in Latin, and I am sorry that this particular tomb should have to be moved. It stands amongst the graves of the Kenyons, an old family which has been extinct in these parts for centuries. The inscription on it runs thus:

SARAH 1630
FOR THE SAKE OF THE DEAD AND THE WELFARE OF THE
LIVING, LET THIS SEPULCHRE REMAIN UNTOUCHED
AND ITS OCCUPANT UNDISTURBED UNTIL
THE COMING OF CHRIST.
IN THE NAME OF THE FATHER, THE SON
AND THE HOLY GHOST.

8th July. Took counsel with Grant concerning the "Sarah Tomb." We are both very loath to disturb it, but the ground has sunk so beneath it that the safety of the church is in danger; thus we have no choice. However, the work shall be done as reverently as possible under our own direction.

Grant says there is a legend in the neighborhood that it is the tomb of the last of the Kenyons, the evil Countess Sarah, who was murdered in 1630. She lived quite alone in the old castle, whose ruins still stand three miles from here on the road to Bristol. Her reputation was an evil one even for those days. She was a witch or were-woman, the only companion of her solitude being a familiar in the shape of a huge Asiatic wolf. This creature was reputed to seize upon children, or failing these, sheep and other small animals, and convey them to the castle, where the countess used to suck their blood. It was popularly supposed that she could never be killed. This, however, proved a fallacy, since she was strangled one day by a mad peasant woman who had lost two children, she declaring that they had both been seized and carried off by the countess's familiar. This is a very interesting story, since it points to a local superstition very similar to that of the vampire, existing in Slavonic and Hungarian Europe.

The tomb is built of black marble, surmounted by an enormous slab of the same material. On the slab is a magnificent group of figures. A young and handsome woman reclines upon a couch; round her neck is a piece of rope, the end of which she holds in her hand. At her side is a gigantic dog with bared fangs and lolling tongue. The face of the reclining figure is a cruel one; the corners of the mouth are curiously lifted, showing the sharp points of long canine or dog teeth. The whole group, though magnificently executed, leaves a most unpleasant sensation.

If we move the tomb it will have to be done in two pieces, the covering slab first and then the tomb proper. We have decided to remove the covering slab tomorrow.

9th July. 6 p.m. A very strange day.

By noon everything was ready for lifting off the covering stone, and after the men's dinner we started the jacks and pulleys. The slab lifted easily enough, though it fitted closely into its seat and was further secured by some sort of mortar or putty, which must have kept the interior perfectly air-tight.

None of us was prepared for the horrible rush of foul, moldy air that escaped as the cover lifted clear of its seating. And the contents that gradually came into view were more startling still. There lay the fully dressed body of a woman, wizened and shrunk and ghastly pale as if from starvation. Round her neck was a loose cord, and, judging by the scars still visible, the story of death by strangulation was true enough.

The most horrible part, however, was the extraordinary freshness of the body. Except for the appearance of starvation, life might have been only just extinct. The flesh was soft and white, the eyes were wide open and seemed to stare at us with a fearful understanding in them. The body itself lay on mold, without any pretense to coffin or shell.

For several moments we gazed with horrible curiosity, and then it became too much for my workmen, who implored us to replace the covering slab. That, of course, we would not do; but I set the carpenters to work at once to make a temporary cover while we moved the tomb to its new position. This is a long job, and will take two or three days at least.

9 p.m. Just at sunset we were startled by the howling of, seemingly, every dog in the village. It lasted for ten minutes or a quarter of an hour, and then ceased as suddenly as it had begun. This, and a curious mist that has risen round the church, makes me feel rather anxious about the "Sarah Tomb." According to the best established traditions of the vampire-haunted countries, the disturbance of dogs or wolves at sunset is supposed to indicate the presence of one of these fiends, and local fog is always considered to be a certain sign. The vampire has the power of producing it for the purpose of concealing its movements near its hiding-place at any time.

I dare not mention or even hint my fears to the rector, for he is, not unnaturally perhaps, a rank disbeliever in many things that I know, from experience, are not only possible but even probable. I must work this out alone at first, and get his aid without his knowing in what direction he is helping me. I shall now watch till midnight at least.

10.15 p.m. As I feared and half expected. Just before ten there was another outburst of the hideous howling. It was commenced most distinctly by a particularly horrible and blood-curdling wail from the vicinity of the churchyard. The chorus lasted only a few minutes, however, and at the end of it I saw a large dark shape, like a huge dog, emerge from the fog and lope away at a rapid canter towards the open country. Assuming this to be what I fear, I shall see it return soon after midnight.

12.30 a.m. I was right. Almost as midnight struck I saw the beast returning. It stopped at the spot where the fog seemed to commence, and, lifting up its head, gave tongue to that particularly horrible long-drawn wail that I had noticed as preceding the outburst earlier in the evening.

Tomorrow I shall tell the rector what I have seen; and if, as I expect, we hear of some neighboring sheepfold having been raided, I shall get him to watch with me for this nocturnal marauder. I shall also examine the "Sarah Tomb" for something which he may notice without any previous hint from me.

10th July. I found the workmen this morning much disturbed in mind about the howling of the dogs. "We doan't like it, zur," one of the men said to me, "we doan't like it; there was summat abroad last night that was unholy." They were still more uncomfortable when the news came round that a large dog had made a raid upon a flock of sheep, scattering them far and wide, and leaving three of them dead with torn throats in the field.

When I told the rector of what I had seen and what was being said in the village, he immediately decided that we must try and catch or at least indentify the beast I had seen. "Of course," he said, "it is some dog lately imported into the neighborhood, for I know of nothing about here nearly as large as the animal you describe, though its size may be due to the deceptive moonlight."

This afternoon I asked the rector, as a favor, to assist me in lifting the temporary cover that was on the tomb, giving as an excuse the reason that I wished to obtain a portion of the curious mortar with which it had been sealed. After a slight demur he consented, and we raised the lid. If the sight that met out eyes gave me a shock, at least it appalled Grant.

"Great God!" he exclaimed; "the woman is alive!" And so it seemed for a moment. The corpse had lost much of its starved appearance and looked hideously fresh and alive. It was still wrinkled and shrunken, but the lips were firm, and of the rich red hue of health. The eyes, if possible, were more appalling than ever, though fixed and staring. At one corner of the mouth I thought I noticed a slight dark-colored froth, but I said nothing about it then.

"Take your piece of mortar, Harry," gasped Grant "and let us shut the tomb again. God help me! Parson though I am, such dead faces frighten me!"

Nor was I sorry to hide that terrible face again; but I got my bit of mortar, and I have advanced a step towards the solution of the mystery.

This afternoon the tomb was moved several feet towards its new position, but it will be two or three days yet before we shall be ready to replace the slab.

10.15 p.m. Again the same howling at sunset, the same fog enveloping the church, and at ten o'clock the same great beast slipping silently out into the open country. I must get the rector's help and watch for its return. But precautions we must take, for if things are as I believe, we take our lives in our hands when we venture out into the night to waylay the — *vampire.* Why not admit it at once? For that the beast I have seen is the vampire of that evil thing in the tomb I can have no reasonable doubt.

Not yet come to its full strength — thank Heaven! — after the starvation of nearly two centuries, for at present it can only maraud as a wolf apparently. But, in a day or two, when full power returns, the dreadful woman in new strength and beauty will be able to leave her refuge. Then it would not be sheep merely that would satisfy her disgusting lust for blood, but victims that would yield their lifeblood without a murmur to her caressing touch — victims that, dying of her foul embrace, themselves must become vampires in their turn to prey on others.

Mercifully my knowledge gives me a safeguard; for that little piece of mortar that I rescued today from the tomb contains a portion of the sacred host, and who holds it, humbly and firmly believing in its virtue, may pass safely through such an ordeal as I intend to submit myself and the rector to tonight.

12.30 a.m. Our adventure is over for the present, and we are back safe.

After writing the last entry recorded above, I went off to find Grant and tell him that the marauder was out on the prowl again. "But, Grant," I said, "before we start out tonight I must insist that you will let me conduct this affair in my own way; you must promise to put yourself completely under my orders without asking any questions as to the why and wherefore."

After a little demur, and some excusable chaff on his part at the serious view I was taking of what he called a "dog hunt," he gave me his promise. I then told him that we were to watch tonight and try to track the mysterious beast, but not to interfere with it in any way. I think, in spite of his jests, that I impressed him with the fact that there might be, after all, good reason for my precautions.

It was just after eleven when we stepped out into the still night.

Our first move was to try to penetrate the dense fog round the church, but there was something so chilly about it, and a faint smell so disgustingly rank and loathsome, that neither our nerves nor our stomachs were proof against it. Instead, we stationed ourselves in the dark shadow of a yew-tree that commanded a good view of the wicket entrance to the churchyard.

At midnight the howling of the dogs began again, and in a few minutes we saw a large grey shape, with green eyes shining like lamps, shamble swiftly down the path towards us.

The rector started forward, but I laid a firm hand upon his arm and whispered a warning: "Remember!" Then we both stood very still and watched as the great beast cantered swiftly by. It was real enough, for we could hear the clicking of its nails on the stone flags. It passed within a few yards of us, and seemed to be nothing more nor less than a great grey wolf, thin and gaunt, with bristling hair and dripping jaws. It stopped where the mist commenced, and turned round. It was truly a horrible sight, and made one's blood run cold. The eyes burned like fires, the upper lip was snarling and raised, showing the great canine teeth, while round the mouth clung and dripped a dark-colored froth.

It raised its head and gave tongue to its long wailing howl, which was answered from afar by the village dogs. After standing for a few moments it turned and disappeared into the thickest part of the fog.

Very shortly afterwards the atmosphere began to clear, and within ten minutes the mist was all gone, the dogs in the village were silent, and the night seemed to reassume its normal aspect. We examined the spot where the beast had been standing and found, plainly enough upon the stone flags, dark spots of froth and saliva.

"Well, rector," I said, "will you admit now, in view of the things you have seen today, in consideration of the legend, the woman in the tomb, the fog, the howling dogs, and, last but not least, the mysterious beast you have seen so close, that there is something not quite normal in it all? Will you put yourself unreservedly in my hands and help me, *whatever I may do,* first to make assurance doubly sure, and finally to take the necessary steps for putting an end to this horror of the night?'' I saw that the uncanny influence of the night was strong upon him, and wished to impress it as much as possible.

"Needs must," he replied "when the Devil drives; and in the face of what I have seen I must believe that some unholy forces are at work. Yet, how can they work in the sacred precincts of a church? Shall we not call rather upon Heaven to assist us in our need?"

"Grant," I said solemnly, "that we must do, each in his own way. God helps those who help themselves, and by His help and the light of my knowledge we must fight this battle for Him and the poor lost soul within."

We then returned to the rectory and to our rooms, though I have sat up to write this account while the scene is fresh in my mind.

11th July. Found the workmen again very much disturbed in their minds, and full of a strange dog that had been seen during the night by several people, who had hunted it. Farmer Stotman, who had been watching his sheep (the same flock that had been raided the night before), had surprised it over a fresh carcass and tried to drive it off, but its size and fierceness so alarmed him that he had beaten a hasty retreat for a gun. When he returned the animal was gone, though he found that three more sheep from his flock were dead and torn.

The "Sarah Tomb" was moved today to its new position; but it was a long, heavy business, and there was not time to replace the covering slab. For this I was glad as in the prosaic light of day the rector almost disbelieves the events of the night, and is prepared to think everything to have been magnified and distorted by our imagination.

As, however, I could not possibly proceed with my war of extermination against this foul thing without assistance, and as there is nobody else I can rely upon, I appealed to him for one more night — to convince him that it was no delusion, but a ghastly, horrible truth, which must be fought and conquered for our own sakes, as well as that of all those living in the neighborhood.

"Put yourself in my hands, rector," I said, "for tonight at least. Let us take those precautions which my study of the subject tells me are the right ones. Tonight you and I must watch in the church; and I feel assured that tomorrow you will be as convinced as I am, and be equally prepared to take those awful steps which I know to be proper, and I must warn you that we shall find a more startling change in the body lying there than you noticed yesterday."

My words came true; for on raising the wooden cover once more the rank stench of a slaughterhouse arose, making us feel positively sick. There lay the vampire, but how changed from the starved and shrunken corpse we saw two days ago for the first time! The wrinkles had almost disappeared, the flesh was firm and full, the crimson lips grinned horribly over the long pointed teeth, and a distinct smear of blood had trickled down one corner of the mouth. We set our teeth, however, and hardened our hearts. Then we replaced the cover and put what we had collected into a safe place in the vestry. Yet even now Grant could not believe that there was any real or pressing danger concealed in that awful tomb, as he raised strenuous objections to any apparent desecration of the body without further proof. This he shall have tonight. God grant that I am not taking too much on myself! If there is any truth in old legends it would be easy enough to destroy the vampire now; but Grant will not have it.

I hope for the best of this night's work, but the danger in waiting is very great.

6 p.m. I have prepared everything: the sharp knives, the pointed stake, fresh garlic, and the wild dog-roses. All these I have taken and concealed in the vestry, where we can get at them when our solemn vigil commences.

If either or both of us die with our fearful task undone, let those reading my record see that this is done. I lay it upon them as a solemn obligation. "That vampire be pierced through the heart with the stake, then let the burial service be read over the poor clay at last released from its doom. Thus shall the vampire cease to be, and a lost soul rest."

12th July. All is over. After the most terrible night of watching and horror, one vampire at least will trouble the world no more. But how thankful should we be to a merciful Providence that that awful tomb was not disturbed by anyone not having the knowledge necessary to deal with its dreadful occupant! I write this with no feelings of self-complacency, but simply with a great gratitude for the years of study I have been able to devote to this subject.

And now to my tale.

Just before sunset last night the rector and I locked ourselves into the church, and took up our position in the pulpit. It was one of those pulpits, to be found in some churches, which is entered from the vestry, the preacher appearing at a good height through an arched opening in the wall. This gave us a sense of security, which we felt we needed, a good view of the interior, and direct access to the implements which I had concealed in the vestry.

The sun set and the twilight gradually deepened and faded. There was, so far, no sign of the usual fog, nor any howling of the dogs. At nine o'clock the moon rose, and her pale light gradually flooded the aisles, and still no sign of any kind from the "Sarah Tomb." The rector had asked me several times what he might expect, but I was determined that no words or thought of mine should influence him, and that he should be convinced by his own senses alone.

By half-past ten we were both getting very tired, and I began to think that perhaps after all we should see nothing that night. However, soon after eleven we observed a light mist rising from the "Sarah Tomb." It seemed to scintillate and sparkle as it rose, and curled in a sort of pillar or spiral.

I said nothing, but I heard the rector give a sort of a gasp as he clutched my arm feverishly. "Great Heaven!" he whispered, "it is taking shape."

And, true enough, in a very few moments we saw standing erect by the tomb the ghastly figure of the Countess Sarah!

She looked thin and haggard still, and her face was deadly white; but the crimson lips looked like a hideous gash in the pale cheeks, and her eyes glared like red coals in the gloom of the church.

It was a fearful thing to watch as she stepped unsteadily down the aisle, staggering a little as if from weakness and exhaustion. This was perhaps natural, as her body must have suffered much physically from her long incarceration, in spite of the unholy forces which kept it fresh and well.

We watched her to the door, and wondered what would happen; but it appeared to present no difficulty, for she melted through it and disappeared.

"Now, Grant," I said, "do you believe?"

"Yes," he replied, "I must. Everything is in your hands, and I will obey your commands to the letter, if you can only instruct me how to rid my poor people of this unnameable terror."

"By God's help I will," said I; "but you shall be yet more convinced first, for we have a terrible work to do, and much to answer for in the future, before we leave the church again this morning. And now to work, for in its present weak state the vampire will not wander far, but may return at any time, and must not find us unprepared."

We stepped down from the pulpit, and taking dog-roses and garlic from the vestry, proceeded to the tomb. I arrived first and, throwing off the wooden cover cried: "Look! it's empty!" There was nothing there! Nothing except the impress of the body in the loose damp mold!

I took the flowers and laid them in a circle round the tomb for legend teaches us that vampires will not pass over these particular blossoms if they can avoid it.

Then, eight or ten feet away, I made a circle on the stone pavement, large enough for the rector and myself to stand in, and within the circle I placed the implements that I had brought into the church with me.

"Now," I said, "from this circle, which nothing unholy can step across, you shall see the vampire face to face, and see her afraid to cross that other circle of garlic and dog-roses to regain her unholy refuge. But on no account step beyond the holy place you stand in, for the vampire has a fearful strength not her own, and, like a snake, can draw her victim willingly to his own destruction."

Now so far my work was done, and, calling the rector, we stepped into the holy circle to await the vampire's return.

Nor was this long delayed. Presently a damp, cold odor seemed to pervade the church, which made our hair bristle and flesh creep. And then, down the aisle with noiseless feet, came That which we watched for.

I heard the rector mutter a prayer, and I held him tightly by the arm, for he was shivering violently.

Long before we could distinguish the features we saw the glowing eyes and the crimson sensual mouth. She went straight to her tomb, but stopped short when she encountered my flowers. She walked right round the tomb seeking a place to enter, and as she walked she saw us. A spasm of diabolical hate and fury passed over her face; but it quickly vanished, and a smile of love, more devilish still, took its place. She stretched out her arms towards us. Then we saw that round her mouth gathered a bloody froth, and from under her lips long pointed teeth gleamed and champed.

She spoke: a soft soothing voice, a voice that carried a spell with it, and affected us both strangely, particularly the rector. I wished to test as far as possible, without endangering our lives, the vampire's power.

Her voice had a soporific effect, which I resisted easily enough, but which seemed to throw the rector into a sort of trance. More than this: it seemed to compel him to her in spite of his efforts to resist.

"Come!" she said, "come! I give sleep and peace — sleep and peace — sleep and peace."

She advanced a little towards us; but not far, for I noted that the sacred circle seemed to keep her back like an iron hand.

My companion seemed to become demoralized and spellbound. He tried to step forward and, finding me detain him, whispered: "Harry, let go! I must go! She is calling me! I must! I must! Oh, help me! help me!" And he began to struggle.

It was time to finish.

"Grant!" I cried, in a loud, firm voice, "in the name of all that you hold sacred, have done and play the man!" He shuddered violently and gasped: "Where am I?" Then he remembered, and clung to me convulsively for a moment.

At this a look of damnable hate changed the smiling face before us, and with a sort of shriek she staggered back.

"Back!" I cried: "back to your unholy tomb! No longer shall you molest the suffering world! Your end is near."

It was fear that now showed itself in her beautiful face (for it was beautiful in spite of its horror) as she shrank back, back and over the circlet of flowers, shivering as she did so. At last, with a low mournful cry, she appeared to melt back again into her tomb.

As she did so the first gleams of the rising sun lit up the world, and I knew all danger was over for the day.

Taking Grant by the arm, I drew him with me out of the circle and led him to the tomb. There lay the vampire once more, still in her living death as we had a moment before seen her in her devilish life. But in the eyes remained that awful expression of hate, and cringing, appalling fear.

Grant was pulling himself together.

"Now," I said, "will you dare the last terrible act and rid the world forever of this horror?"

"By God!" he said solemnly, "I will. Tell me what to do."

"Help me lift her out of the tomb. She can harm us no more," I replied.

With averted faces we set to our terrible task, and laid her out upon the flags.

"Now," I said, "read the burial service over the poor body, and then let us give it its release from this living hell that holds it."

Reverently the rector read the beautiful words, and reverently I made the necessary responses. When it was over I took the stake and, without giving myself time to think, plunged it with all my strength through the heart.

As though really alive, the body for a moment writhed and kicked convulsively, and an awful heart-rending shriek rang through the silent church; then all was still.

Then we lifted the poor body back; and, thank God! the consolation that legend tells is never denied to those who have to do such awful work as ours came at last. Over the face stole a great and solemn peace; the lips lost their crimson hue, the prominent sharp teeth sank back into the mouth, and for a moment we saw before us the calm, pale face of a most beautiful woman, who smiled as she slept. A few minutes more, and she faded away to dust before our eyes as we watched. We set to work and cleaned up every trace of our work, and then departed for the rectory. Most thankful were we to step out of the church, with its horrible associations, into the rosy warmth of the summer morning. [With the above end the notes in my father's diary, though a few days later this further entry occurs]:

15th July. Since the 12th everything has been quiet and as usual. We replaced and sealed up the "Sarah Tomb" this morning. The workmen were surprised to find the body had disappeared, but took it to be the natural result of exposing it to the air.

One odd thing came to my ears today. It appears that the child of one of the villagers strayed from home the night of the 11th inst., and was found asleep in a coppice near the church, very pale and quite exhausted. There were two small marks on her throat, which have since disappeared.

What does this mean? I have, however, kept it to myself, as, now the vampire is no more, no further danger either to that child or to any other is to be apprehended. It is only those who die of the vampire's embrace that become vampires at death in their turn.

THE ROOM IN THE TOWER

E.F. BENSON

T IS PROBABLE THAT everybody who is at all a constant dreamer has had at least one experience of an event or a sequence of circumstances which have come to his mind in sleep being subsequently realized in the material world. But, in my opinion, so far from this being a strange thing, it would be far odder if this fulfilment did not occasionally happen, since our dreams are, as a rule, concerned with people whom we know and places with which we are familiar, such as might very naturally occur in the awake and daylit world. True, these dreams are often broken into by some absurd and fantastic incident, which puts them out of court in regard to their subsequent fulfilment, but on the mere calculation of chances, it does not appear in the least unlikely that a dream imagined by anyone who dreams constantly should occasionally come true. Not long ago, for instance, I experienced such a fulfilment of a dream which seems to me in no way remarkable and to have no kind of psychical significance. The manner of it was as follows.

A certain friend of mine, living abroad, is amiable enough to write to me about once in a fortnight. Thus, when fourteen days or thereabouts have elapsed since I last heard from him, my mind, probably, either consciously or subconsciously, is expectant of a letter from him. One night last week I dreamed that as I was going upstairs to dress for dinner I heard, as I often heard, the sound of the postman's knock on my front door, and diverted my direction downstairs instead. There, among other correspondence, was a letter from him. Thereafter the fantastic entered, for on opening it I found inside the ace of diamonds, and scribbled across it in his well-known handwriting, "I am sending you this for safe custody, as you know it is running an unreasonable risk to keep aces in Italy." The next evening I was just preparing to go upstairs to dress when I heard the postman's knock, and did precisely as I had done in my dream. There, among other letters, was one from my friend. Only it did not contain the ace of diamonds. Had it done so, I should have attached more weight to the matter, which, as it stands, seems to me a perfectly ordinary coincidence. No doubt I consciously or subconsciously expected a letter from him, and this suggested to me my dream. Similarly, the fact that my friend had not written to me for a fortnight suggested to him that he should do so. But occasionally it is not so easy to find such an explanation, and for the following story I can find no explanation at all. It came out of the dark, and into the dark it has gone again.

All my life I have been a habitual dreamer: the nights are few, that is to say, when I do not find on awaking in the morning that some mental experience has been mine, and sometimes, all night long, apparently, a series of the most dazzling adventures befall me. Almost without exception these adventures are pleasant, though often merely trivial. It is of an exception that I am going to speak.

It was when I was about sixteen that a certain dream first came to me, and this is how it befell. It opened with my being set down at the door of a big red-brick house, where, I understood, I was going to stay. The servant who opened the door told me that tea was being served in the garden, and led me through a low dark-panelled hall, with a large open fireplace, on to a cheerful green lawn set round with flower beds. There were grouped about the tea-table a small party of people, but they were all strangers to me except one, who was a schoolfellow called Jack Stone, clearly the son of the house, and he introduced me to his mother and father and a couple of sisters. I was, I remember, somewhat astonished to find myself here, for the boy in question was scarcely known to me, and I rather disliked what I knew of him; moreover, he had left school nearly a year before. The afternoon was very hot, and an intolerable oppression reigned. On the far side of the lawn ran a red-brick wall, with an iron gate in its center, outside which stood a walnut tree. We sat in the shadow of the house opposite a row of long windows, inside which I could see a table with cloth laid, glimmering with glass and silver. This garden front of the house was very long, and at one end of it stood a tower of three stories, which looked to me much older than the rest of the building.

Before long, Mrs. Stone, who, like the rest of the party, had sat in absolute silence, said to me, "Jack will show you your room: I have given you the room in the tower."

Quite inexplicably my heart sank at her words. I felt as if I had known that I should have the room in the tower, and that it contained something dreadful and significant. Jack instantly got up, and I understood that I had to follow him. In silence we passed through the hall, and mounted a great oak staircase with many corners, and arrived at a small landing with two doors set in it. He pushed one of these open for me to enter, and without coming in himself, closed it after. Then I knew that my conjecture had been right: there was something awful in the room, and with the terror of nightmare growing swiftly and enveloping me, I awoke in a spasm of terror.

Now that dream or variations on it occurred to me intermittently for fifteen years. Most often it came in exactly this form, the arrival, the tea laid out on the lawn, the deadly silence succeeded by that one deadly sentence, the mounting with Jack Stone up to the room in the tower where horror dwelt, and it always came to a close in the nightmare of terror at that which was in the room, though I never saw what it was. At other times I experienced variations on this same theme. Occasionally, for instance, we would be sitting at dinner in the dining-room, into the windows of which I had looked on the first night when the dream of this house visited me, but, wherever we were, there was the same silence, the same sense of dreadful oppression and foreboding. And the silence I knew would always be broken by Mrs. Stone saying to me, "Jack will show you your room: I have given you the room in the tower." Upon which (this was invariable) I had to follow him up the oak staircase with many corners, and enter the place that I dreaded more and more each time that I visited it in sleep. Or, again, I would find myself playing cards still in silence in a drawing-room lit with immense chandeliers, that gave a blinding illumination. What the game was I have no idea; what I remember, with a sense of miserable anticipation, was that soon Mrs. Stone would get up and say to me, "Jack will show you your room: I have given you the room in the tower." This drawing-room where we played cards was next to the dining-room, and, as I have said, was always brilliantly illuminated, whereas the rest of the house was full of dusk and shadows. And yet, how often, in spite of those bouquets of lights, have I not pored over the cards that were dealt me, scarcely able for some reason to see them. Their designs, too, were strange: there were no red suits, but all were black, and among them there were certain cards which were black all over. I hated and dreaded those.

As this dream continued to recur, I got to know the greater part of the house. There was a smoking-room beyond the drawing-room, at the end of a passage with a green baize door. It was always very dark there, and as often as I went there I passed somebody whom I could not see in the doorway coming out. Curious developments, too, took place in the characters that peopled the dream as might happen to living persons. Mrs. Stone, for instance, who, when I first saw her, had been black-haired, became gray, and instead of rising briskly, as she had done at first when she said, "Jack will show you your room: I have given you the room in the tower," got up very feebly, as if the strength was leaving her limbs. Jack also grew up, and became a rather ill-looking young man, with a brown moustache, while one of the sisters ceased to appear, and I understood she was married.

Then it so happened that I was not visited by this dream for six months or more, and I began to hope, in such inexplicable dread did I hold it, that it had passed away for good. But one night after this interval I again found myself being shown out onto the lawn for tea, and Mrs. Stone was not there, while the others were all dressed in black. At once I guessed the reason, and my heart leaped at the thought that perhaps this time I should not have to sleep in the room in the tower, and though we usually all sat in silence, on this occasion the sense of relief made me talk and laugh as I had never yet done. But even then matters were not altogether comfortable, for no one else spoke, but they all looked secretly at each other. And soon the foolish stream of my talk ran dry, and gradually an apprehension worse than anything I had previously known gained on me as the light slowly faded.

Suddenly a voice which I knew well broke the stillness, the voice of Mrs. Stone, saying, "Jack will show you your room: I have given you the room in the tower." It seemed to come from near the gate in the red-brick wall that bounded the lawn, and looking up, I saw that the grass outside was sown thick with gravestones. A curious grayish light shone from them, and I could read the lettering on the grave nearest me, and it was, "In evil memory of Julia Stone." And as usual Jack got up, and again I followed him through the hall and up the staircase with many corners. On this occasion it was darker than usual, and when I passed into the room in the tower I could only just see the furniture, the position of which was already familiar to me. Also there was a dreadful odor of decay in the room, and I woke screaming.

The dream, with such variations and developments as I have mentioned, went on at intervals for fifteen years. Sometimes I would dream it two or three nights in succession; once, as I have said, there was an intermission of six months, but taking a reasonable average, I should say that I dreamed it quite as often as once in a month. It had, as is plain, something of nightmare about it, since it always ended in the same appalling terror, which so far from getting less, seemed to me to gather fresh fear every time that I experienced it. There was, too, a strange and dreadful consistency about it. The characters in it, as I have mentioned, got regularly older, death and marriage visited this silent family, and I never in the dream, after Mrs. Stone had died, set eyes on her again. But it was always her voice that told me that the room in the tower was prepared for me, and whether we had tea out on the lawn, or the scene was laid in one of the rooms overlooking it, I could always see her gravestone standing just outside the iron gate. It was the same, too, with the married daughter; usually she was not present, but once or twice she returned again, in company with a man, whom I took to be her husband. He, too, like the rest of them, was always silent. But, owing to the constant repetition of the dream, I had ceased to attach, in my waking hours, any significance to it. I never met Jack Stone again during all those years, nor did I ever see a house that resembled this dark house of my dream. And then something happened.

I had been in London in this year, up till the end of July, and during the first week in August went down to stay with a friend in a house he had taken for the summer months, in the Ashdown Forest district of Sussex. I left London early, for John Clinton was to meet me at Forest Row Station, and we were going to spend the day golfing, and go to his house in the evening. He had his motor with him, and we set off, about five of the afternoon, after a thoroughly delightful day, for the drive, the distance being some ten miles. As it was still so early we did not have tea at the club house, but waited till we should get home. As we drove, the weather, which up till then had been, though hot, deliciously fresh, seemed to me to alter in quality, and become very stagnant and oppressive, and I felt that indefinable sense of ominous apprehension that I am accustomed to before thunder. John, however, did not share my views, attributing my loss of lightness to the fact that I had lost both my matches. Events proved, however, that I was right, though I do not think that the thunderstorm that broke that night was the sole cause of my depression.

Our way lay through deep high-banked lanes, and before we had gone very far I fell asleep, and was only awakened by the stopping of the motor. And with a sudden thrill, partly of fear but chiefly of curiosity, I found myself standing in the doorway of my house of dream. We went, I half wondering whether or not I was dreaming still, through a low oak-panelled hall, and out onto the lawn, where tea was laid in the shadow of the house. It was set in flower beds, a red-brick wall, with a gate in it, bounded one side, and out beyond that was a space of rough grass with a walnut tree. The façade of the house was very long, and at one end stood a three-storied tower, markedly older than the rest.

Here for the moment all resemblance to the repeated dream ceased. There was no silent and somehow terrible family, but a large assembly of exceedingly cheerful persons, all of whom were known to me. And in spite of the horror with which the dream itself had always filled me, I felt nothing of it now that the scene of it was thus reproduced before me. But I felt intensest curiosity as to what was going to happen.

Tea pursued its cheerful course, and before long Mrs. Clinton got up. And at that moment I think I knew what she was going to say. She spoke to me, and what she said was: "Jack will show you your room: I have given you the room in the tower."

At that, for half a second, the horror of the dream took hold of me again. But it quickly passed, and again I felt nothing more than the most intense curiosity. It was not very long before it was amply satisfied.

John turned to me.

"Right up at the top of the house," he said, "but I think you'll be comfortable. We're absolutely full up. Would you like to go and see it now? By Jove, I believe that you are right, and that we are going to have a thunderstorm. How dark it has become."

I got up and followed him. We passed through the hall, and up the perfectly familiar staircase. Then he opened the door, and I went in. And at that moment sheer unreasoning terror again possessed me. I did not know for certain what I feared: I simply feared. Then like a sudden recollection, when one remembers a name which has long escaped the memory, I knew what I feared. I feared Mrs. Stone, whose grave with the sinister inscription, "In evil memory," I had so often seen in my dream, just beyond the lawn which lay below my window. And then once more the fear passed so completely that I wondered what there was to fear, and I found myself, sober and quiet and sane, in the room in the tower, the name of which I had so often heard in my dream, and the scene of which was so familiar.

I looked round it with a certain sense of proprietorship, and found that nothing had been changed from the dreaming nights in which I knew it so well. Just to the left of the door was the bed, lengthways along the wall, with the head of it in the angle. In a line with it was the fireplace and a small bookcase; opposite the door the outer wall was pierced by two lattice-paned windows, between which stood the dressing-table, while ranged along the fourth wall was the washing-stand and a big cupboard. My luggage had already been unpacked, for the furniture of dressing and undressing lay orderly on the wash-stand and toilet-table, while my dinner clothes were spread out on the coverlet of the bed. And then, with a sudden start of unexplained dismay, I saw that there were two rather conspicuous objects which I had not seen before in my dreams: one a life-sized oil painting of Mrs. Stone, the other a black-and-white sketch of Jack Stone, representing him as he had appeared to me only a week before in the last of the series of these repeated dreams, a rather secret and evil-looking man of about thirty. His picture hung between the windows, looking straight across the room to the other portrait, which hung at the side of the bed. At that I looked next, and as I looked I felt once more the horror of nightmare seize me.

It represented Mrs. Stone as I had seen her last in my dreams: old and withered and white-haired. But in spite of the evident feebleness of body, a dreadful exuberance and vitality shone through the envelope of flesh, an exuberance wholly malign, a vitality that foamed and frothed with unimaginable evil. Evil beamed from the narrow, leering eyes; it laughed in the demon-like mouth. The whole face was infused with some secret and appalling mirth; the hands, clasped together on the knee, seemed shaking with suppressed and nameless glee. Then I saw also that it was signed in the left-hand bottom corner, and wondering who the artist could be, I looked more closely, and read the inscription, "Julia Stone by Julia Stone."

There came a tap at the door, and John Clinton entered.

"Got everything you want?" he asked.

"Rather more than I want," said I, pointing to the picture. He laughed.

"Hard-featured old lady," he said. "By herself, too, I remember. Anyhow she can't have flattered herself much."

"But don't you see?" said I. "It's scarcely a human face at all. It's the face of some witch, of some devil."

He looked at it more closely.

"Yes, it isn't very pleasant," he said. "Scarcely a bedside manner, eh? Yes; I can imagine getting the nightmare if I went to sleep with that close by my bed. I'll have it taken down if you like."

"I really wish you would," I said. He rang the bell, and with the help of a servant we detached the picture and carried it out onto the landing, and put it with its face to the wall.

"By Jove, the old lady is a weight," said John, mopping his forehead. "I wonder if she had something on her mind."

The extraordinary weight of the picture had struck me too. I was about to reply, when I caught sight of my own hand. There was blood on it, in considerable quantities, covering the whole palm.

"I've cut myself somehow," said I.

John gave a little startled exclamation.

"Why, I have too," he said.

Simultaneously the footman took out his handkerchief and wiped his hand with it. I saw that there was blood also on his handkerchief.

John and I went back into the tower room and washed the blood off; but neither on his hand nor on mine was there the slightest trace of a scratch or cut. It seemed to me that, having ascertained this, we both, by a sort of tacit consent, did not allude to it again. Something in my case had dimly occurred to me that I did not wish to think about. It was but a conjecture, but I fancied that I knew the same thing had occurred to him.

The heat and oppression of the air, for the storm we had expected was still undischarged, increased very much after dinner, and for some time most of the party, among whom were John Clinton and myself, sat outside on the path bounding the lawn, where we had had tea. The night was absolutely dark, and no twinkle of star or moon ray could penetrate the pall of cloud that overset the sky. By degrees our assembly thinned, the women went up to bed, men dispersed to the smoking or billiard room, and by eleven o'clock my host and I were the only two left. All the evening I thought that he had something on his mind, and as soon as we were alone he spoke.

"The man who helped us with the picture had blood on his hand, too, did you notice?" he said.

"I asked him just now if he had cut himself, and he said he supposed he had, but that he could find no mark of it. Now where did that blood come from?"

By dint of telling myself that I was not going to think about it, I had succeeded in not doing so, and I did not want, especially just at bedtime, to be reminded of it.

"I don't know," said I, "and I don't really care so long as the picture of Mrs. Stone is not by my bed."

He got up.

"But it's odd," he said. "Ha! Now you'll see another odd thing."

A dog of his, an Irish terrier by breed, had come out of the house as we talked. The door behind us into the hall was open, and a bright oblong of light shone across the lawn to the iron gate which led on to the rough grass outside, where the walnut tree stood. I saw that the dog had all his hackles up, bristling with rage and fright; his lips were curled back from his teeth, as if he was ready to spring at something, and he was growling to himself. He took not the slightest notice of his master or me, but stiffly and tensely walked across the grass to the iron gate. There he stood for a moment, looking through the bars and still growling. Then of a sudden his courage seemed to desert him: he gave one long howl, and scuttled back to the house with a curious crouching sort of movement.

"He does that half-a-dozen times a day." said John. "He sees something which he both hates and fears."

I walked to the gate and looked over it. Something was moving on the grass outside, and soon a sound which I could not instantly identify came to my ears. Then I remembered what it was: it was the purring of a cat. I lit a match, and saw the purrer, a big blue Persian, walking round and round in a little circle just outside the gate, stepping high and ecstatically, with tail carried aloft like a banner. Its eyes were bright and shining, and every now and then it put its head down and sniffed at the grass.

I laughed.

"The end of that mystery, I am afraid." I said. Here's a large cat having Walpurgis night all alone."

"Yes, that's Darius," said John. "He spends half the day and all night there. But that's not the end of the dog mystery, for Toby and he are the best of friends, but the beginning of the cat mystery. What's the cat doing there? And why is Darius pleased, while Toby is terror-stricken?"

At that moment I remembered the rather horrible detail of my dreams when I saw through the gate, just where the cat was now, the white tombstone with the sinister inscription. But before I could answer the rain began, as suddenly and heavily as if a tap had been turned on, and simultaneously the big cat squeezed through the bars of the gate, and came leaping across the lawn to the house for shelter. Then it sat in the doorway, looking out eagerly into the dark. It spat and struck at John with its paw, as he pushed it in, in order to close the door.

Somehow, with the portrait of Julia Stone in the passage outside, the room in the tower had absolutely no alarm for me, and as I went to bed, feeling very sleepy and heavy, I had nothing more than interest for the curious incident about our bleeding hands, and the conduct of the cat and dog. The last thing I looked at before I put out my light was the square empty space by my bed where the portrait had been. Here the paper was of its original full tint of dark red: over the rest of the walls it had faded. Then I blew out my candle and instantly fell asleep.

My awaking was equally instantaneous, and I sat bolt upright in bed under the impression that some bright light had been flashed in my face, though it was now absolutely pitch dark. I knew exactly where I was, in the room which I had dreaded in dreams, but no horror that I ever felt when asleep approached the fear that now invaded and froze my brain. Immediately after a peal of thunder crackled just above the house, but the probability that it was only a flash of lightning which awoke me gave no reassurance to my galloping heart. Something I knew was in the room with me, and instinctively I put out my right hand, which was nearest the wall, to keep it away. And my hand touched the edge of a picture-frame hanging close to me.

I sprang out of bed, upsetting the small table that stood by it, and I heard my watch, candle, and matches clatter onto the floor. But for the moment there was no need of light, for a blinding flash leaped out of the clouds, and showed me that by my bed again hung the picture of Mrs. Stone. And instantly the room went into blackness again. But in that flash I saw another thing also, namely a figure that leaned over the end of my bed, watching me. It was dressed in some close-clinging white garment, spotted and stained with mold, and the face was that of the portrait.

Overhead the thunder cracked and roared, and when it ceased and the deathly stillness succeeded, I heard the rustle of movement coming nearer me, and, more horrible yet, perceived an odor of corruption and decay. And then a hand was laid on the side of my neck, and close beside my ear I heard quick-taken, eager breathing. Yet I knew that this thing, though it could be perceived by touch, by smell, by eye and by ear, was still not of this earth, but something that had passed out of the body and had power to make itself manifest. Then a voice, already familiar to me, spoke.

"I knew you would come to the room in the tower," it said. "I have been long waiting for you. At last you have come. Tonight I shall feast; before long we will feast together."

And the quick breathing came closer to me; I could feel it on my neck.

At that the terror, which I think had paralyzed me for the moment, gave way to the wild instinct of self-preservation. I hit wildly with both arms, kicking out at the same moment, and heard a little animal-squeal, and something soft dropped with a thud beside me. I took a couple of steps forward, nearly tripping up over whatever it was that lay there, and by the merest good-luck found the handle of the door. In another second I ran out on the landing, and had banged the door behind me. Almost at the same moment I heard a door open somewhere below, and John Clinton, candle in hand, came running upstairs.

"What is it?" he said. "I sleep just below you, and heard a noise as if — Good heavens, there's blood on your shoulder."

I stood there, so he told me afterwards, swaying from side to side, white as a sheet, with the mark on my shoulder as if a hand covered with blood had been laid there.

"It's in there," I said, pointing. "She, you know. The portrait is in there, too, hanging up on the place we took it from."

At that he laughed.

"My dear fellow, this is mere nightmare," he said.

He pushed by me, and opened the door, I standing there simply inert with terror, unable to stop him, unable to move.

"Phew! What an awful smell," he said.

Then there was silence; he had passed out of my sight behind the open door. Next moment he came out again, as white as myself, and instantly shut it.

"Yes, the portrait's there," he said, "and on the floor is a thing — a thing spotted with earth, like what they bury people in. Come away, quick, come away."

How I got downstairs I hardly know. An awful shuddering and nausea of the spirit rather than of the flesh had seized me, and more than once he had to place my feet upon the steps, while every now and then he cast glances of terror and apprehension up the stairs. But in time we came to his dressing-room on the floor below, and there I told him what I have here described.

The sequel can be made short; indeed, some of my readers have perhaps already guessed what it was, if they remember that inexplicable affair of the churchyard at West Fawley, some eight years ago, where an attempt was made three times to bury the body of a certain woman who had committed suicide. On each occasion the coffin was found in the course of a few days again protruding from the ground. After the third attempt, in order that the thing should not be talked about, the body was buried elsewhere in unconsecrated ground. Where it was buried was just outside the iron gate of the garden belonging to the house where this woman had lived. She had committed suicide in a room at the top of the tower in that house. Her name was Julia Stone.

Subsequently the body was again secretly dug up, and the coffin was found to be full of blood.

THE BEAUTIFUL VAMPIRE

THÉOPHILE GAUTIER

Translated by Paul Hookham

OU ASK ME, brother, if I have loved ; yes. It is a strange and terrible story, and although I am sixty-six years old, I scarcely dare to stir the ashes of that memory. I am reluctant to refuse any request of yours, but I would not tell such a story to any soul less tempered by experience.

The events are so strange that I cannot believe that they ever happened to me. For more than three years I was the victim of an extraordinary, diabolical obsession. I, a poor country priest, led every night in a dream (pray God it was a dream!) the life of a lost soul, a voluptuary, a Sardanapalus. One single glance thrown at a woman nearly cost me the loss of my soul; but in the end, with the help of God and my patron saint, I was able to drive out the malignant spirit that possessed me. My life was complicated with a nocturnal existence of quite a different nature. During the day I was a priest of the Lord, chaste, occupied in prayer and holy works; at night, from the moment I closed my eyes, I became a young nobleman, a connoisseur of women, dogs and horses, dicing, drinking, blaspheming; and when I awoke at daybreak, it seemed as if I fell asleep and dreamed I was a priest.

Of that nocturnal life I have preserved memories of things and of words which I cannot banish from my mind; and although I have never left the walls of my presbytery, one would say, to hear me talk, that I was a man who had tasted every experience and turned his back on the world, one who had sought refuge in religion and desired to end his troubled days in the bosom of the Church, rather than a humble priest grown old in an obscure parish in the depths of a wood, wholly cut off from the life of the day.

Yes, I have loved as no one in the world has loved, with a mad furious passion, so violent that I wonder it did not burst my heart. Ah! what nights! what nights!

From my earliest childhood I felt that the priesthood was my vocation;

all my studies were therefore directed to that end, and my life up to the age of twenty-four was nothing but a long novitiate. Having finished my theological training, I took all the minor orders in turn, and my superiors thought me fit, despite my youth, to receive the last and most serious degree. The day of my ordination was appointed for Easter week.

I had never gone into society; for me the world was bounded by the limits of college and seminary. I knew vaguely that there was something which was called woman, but I gave no thought to it; I was perfectly innocent. I saw my old and infirm mother twice a year only. That was the only link I had with the outside world.

I felt no regret, not the slightest hesitation, in face of this irrevocable pledge; I was full of joy and impatience. Never did a young bridegroom count the hours with more feverish eagerness; I could not sleep for thinking of it; I dreamt that I was saying mass. To be a priest seemed to me to be the most wonderful thing in the world; I would have refused to be a king or a poet. My ambition knew no higher flight.

I am telling you this to show you that I was the last person in the world to whom such a thing should have happened, and of what inexplicable fascination I was the victim.

When the great day came, I walked to the church with so light a step that I seemed to tread on air or to have wings on my shoulders. I felt as if I were an angel, and I was astonished at the serious and preoccupied faces of my companions; for there were several of us. I had passed the night in prayer and was in a frame of mind that bordered on ecstasy. The bishop, a venerable old man, seemed to be God the Father contemplating His eternity, and I saw heaven through the vaulted roof of the sacred building.

You know the details of the ceremony: the benediction, the communion, the anointing of the palms of the hands with the oil of the catechumens, and lastly the holy sacrifice offered together with the bishop. I will not dwell upon this. Oh! how right Job is when he says that the man is imprudent who does not close a bargain with his eyes!

I chanced to raise my head, which till then I had held bowed down, and saw her before me — so near that I could have touched her, although in reality she was some distance away and on the other side of the railing — I saw, I say, a young woman of rare beauty and dressed with regal splendour. It was as though scales had fallen from my eyes. I experienced the sensation of a blind man who suddenly recovers his sight. The bishop, so radiant a moment before, faded out all of a sudden; the tapers grew pale in their gold sconces like the stars at daybreak, and the whole church became quite dark. The lovely creature stood out against the background of shadow like an angelic vision; she seemed to be illuminated of herself, to create rather than to receive light.

I lowered my eyelids, firmly resolved not to lift them again, so as to be free from the influence of external objects; for my thoughts wandered more and more, and I hardly knew what I was doing.

A minute later I opened my eyes again, for through my lashes I saw her,

glittering with all the colours of the prism, and in a roseate twilight, as when one looks at the sun.

Oh! how beautiful she was! The greatest painters, searching for ideal beauty in heaven and bringing down to earth the divine portrait of the Madonna, do not approach this fabulous reality. Neither poet's verse nor painter's palette can give an idea of it.

She was fairly tall, with the figure and carriage of a goddess. Her soft hair was parted and flowed over her temples like two waves of gold; a queen with her diadem, one might fancy; her forehead of a bluish, transparent whiteness, spread broad and serene over almost brown eyebrows, a peculiarity which still further enhanced the effect of sea-green eyes that shone with a sparkle and brilliance that were unbearable. What eyes! With one flash they decided the fate of a man; they had a life, a limpidity, a liquid brightness, which I have never seen in a human eye; rays like arrows darted from them straight to the heart. I know not whether the flame that illuminated them came from heaven or hell, but of a surety it came from one or the other. This woman was an angel or a demon, perhaps both: certainly she did not spring from the womb of Eve, the common mother. Teeth of purest Oriental pearl gleamed through the red of her smiling lips, and at each movement of her mouth little dimples showed in the roseate softness of her adorable cheeks. The nose was well-cut and of truly royal pride, and betokened the most noble descent. Bright agates wantoned on the smooth, shining skin of her half-revealed shoulders, and rows of large pearls, nearly as white as her neck, fell on her breast. From time to time she raised her head with the undulating motion of a snake or of a bridling peacock, which sent a movement through the high open-work ruff that encircled her throat like a silver trellis.

She wore a dress of red velvet, and from the broad ermine-trimmed sleeves emerged patrician hands of infinite delicacy, with long rounded fingers, so translucent that the light shone through them, like those of Aurora.

All these details are still as present to my eyes as if they dated from yesterday, for though my mind was extremely troubled, nothing escaped me: the minutest details, the tiny black spot on the side of the chin, the scarcely perceptible down at the corners of the lips, the velvet softness of the brow, the quivering shadow of the eyelashes on the cheeks — I took everything in with an astonishing clearness.

As I looked at her, I felt doors which hitherto had been closed open within me: it was as if little windows were unshuttered in every direction to open up unknown vistas; life appeared to me in a wholly new aspect. I had just been born into another world of thought and feeling. A frightful anguish gripped my heart; each minute that passed seemed a second and an age.

Meanwhile, the ceremony proceeded, and carried me far away from the world the entrance to which my growing desires were furiously besieging. I said yes when I wanted to say no, while everything in me revolted and protested against the wrong my tongue was doing to my soul; in spite of myself, some mysterious power tore the words from my throat. Thus it is, perhaps, that so many young women go to the altar with the fixed intention of refusing emphatically the husbands forced upon them, and not one carries out her project. It is thus, doubtless, that poor novices take the veil, for all their determination to tear it in shreds at the moment of uttering their vows. One dares not cause such a scandal in public, or disappoint the expectations of so many people; the wishes of all, the looks of all, seem to weigh on one like a casque of lead; and then the procedure has been so well arranged, everything so completely regulated in advance, in a manner so manifestly irrevocable, that thought yields to the weight of facts and becomes completely impotent.

The gaze of the beautiful stranger changed its expression as the ceremony proceeded. Tender and caressing at first, it took the air of disdain and dissatisfaction of one misunderstood.

I made an effort, violent enough to uproot a mountain, to cry out that I did not wish to be a priest; but I could not do it; my tongue clove to the roof of my mouth, and I could not translate my desire into the faintest movement of refusal. Wide awake, I was in a condition like that of nightmare, when you want to utter the word upon which your life depends, and cannot do it.

She seemed to be aware of the torture I was suffering, and, as if to give me courage, cast upon me a look full of divine promise. Her eyes were a poem, of which each look was a verse. They said:

'If you will be mine, I will make you happier than God Himself in His paradise; the angels will envy you. Tear off that funeral winding-sheet in which you are about to wrap yourself. I am Beauty, I am Youth, I am Life; come to me, and we will be Love. What could Jehovah offer you in exchange for that? Our life will glide by like a dream, and be but a kiss prolonged to eternity.

'Dash that cup from your lips, and you are free. I will transport you to unknown isles; you shall sleep upon my breast in a bed of pure gold under a canopy of silver. For I love you, and would take you from your God, before Whom so many noble hearts melt into floods of love that reach Him not.'

I seemed to hear these words in a rhythm of infinite sweetness; for her look all but had sound, and the sentences her eyes sent to me echoed in the depths of my heart as if invisible lips had breathed them into my soul. I felt myself ready to renounce God, yet my lips went mechanically through the formalities of the ceremony. The beautiful one flung me a second glance so beseeching, so despairing, that steel blades went through my heart, and I felt more darts in my breast than the Mother of Sorrows.

It was done; I was a priest.

Never did human countenance portray such poignant anguish. The girl who sees her betrothed die suddenly at her side, the mother beside the empty cradle of her child, Eve sitting on the threshold of Paradise, the miser who finds a stone in the place of his treasure, the poet who has dropped into the fire the only manuscript of his finest work — none of these could seem more prostrated by grief, more inconsolable. The blood fled from her lovely cheeks and she became as white as marble; her beautiful arms fell beside her body; as though the muscles had lost their power, and she leaned against a pillar as if her legs were weakening and slipping from under her.

As for me — livid, my forehead bathed in a bloodier sweat than that of Calvary, I tottered to the door of the church; I was suffocated; it seemed as if the vaulted roof above was falling upon my shoulders and that my head alone was supporting the whole weight of the dome.

As I was about to cross the threshold a hand suddenly grasped mine — a woman's hand! I had never touched one. It was cold as a snake's skin, and its impress remained, burning into my flesh like the brand of a red-hot iron. It was she. 'Unhappy man! unhappy man! what have you done?' she said to me in a low voice; then she disappeared in the crowd.

The old bishop passed by; he looked at me with a severe expression. My demeanour must have been strange; I paled, I flushed, my vision was clouded. One of my companions took compassion on me and led me away; alone, I could not have found my way back to the seminary. At a turn of a street, while the young priest's head was turned another way, a negro page, fantastically dressed, came towards me and handed me, without stopping, a little pocket-book with gilt-edged corners, signing to me to hide it.

I slipped it into my sleeve and kept it there until I was alone in my cell. I undid the clasp. There were but two leaves with the words: 'Clarimonde, Concini Palace.' I was then so little conversant with life that I had never heard of Clarimonde, in spite of her celebrity, and had no idea where the Concini Palace was. I made a thousand conjectures, each one more extravagant than the last, but to tell the truth, provided I could see her again, I cared little what she might be, great lady or courtesan.

This love, just born, had taken root imperishably; I did not even think of attempting to eradicate it. I felt so strongly that it was impossible. This woman had taken complete possession of me; one look had sufficed to work the change in me; she had breathed her will into me; my life was no more my own, but hers, drawing its breath from her. I committed a thousand extravagances; I kissed the place on my hand which she had touched, and repeated her name for hours together. I had only to close my eyes to see her as clearly as if she had really been present, and I kept repeating the words she had spoken at the church door: 'Unhappy man! unhappy man! what have you done?'

I realized all the horror of the situation, and the funeral and dreadful aspects of the state into which I had just been initiated were clearly revealed to me. To be a priest! That is to say, to be chaste, not to love, to make no distinction of sex or age, to turn aside from all beauty, to cower beneath the icy shadow of a monastery or a church, to see only the dying, to keep watch beside unknown corpses, to wear your own mourning in the shape of your black cassock, until at last your priest's robe shall be your own coffin-cloth!

And I felt life rising within me like an underground lake that fills and overflows; my blood throbbed violently in my arteries; my youth, so long repressed, burst out all at once like the aloe that takes a hundred years to flower and blossoms with a clap of thunder.

What should I do to see Clarimonde again? I had no pretext for leaving the seminary, knowing no one in the town; I was not even to remain there, was only waiting until the parish which was to be my charge should be allotted to me. I tried to loosen the bars of the window; but it was a fearful height, and descent without a ladder was not to be dreamed of. Besides, it could only be made at night; and how find my way in the intricate maze of the streets? All these difficulties, which would have been nothing to others, were immense to me, a poor seminarist, a lover without experience, without money, without clothes.

If I had not been a priest I might have seen her every day; I should have been her lover, her husband, I told myself in my infatuation. Instead of being wrapped in my dismal shroud, I should have clothes of silk and velvet, gold chains, a sword at my side and a feather in my cap, like handsome young cavaliers. My hair, instead of being spoilt by a large tonsure, would play about my neck in wavy curls. I should have a beautiful waxed moustache and be a gallant. But an hour passed before an altar, a few scarcely articulated words, had cut me off for ever from the number of the living; I had myself sealed the stone of my tomb, pushed with my own hand the bolt of my prison!

I went to the window. The sky was beautifully blue, the trees were clad in their spring dress; Nature seemed to make parade of an ironic gaiety. The square was full of people; they came and went; young sparks and young beauties, couple by couple, made their way towards gardens and arbours. Boon companions passed by arm-in-arm singing drinking-songs. There was movement, life, bustle; liveliness that contrasted sadly with my mourning and my loneliness. A young mother on the doorstep played with her child, kissed the rosy little mouth still beaded with drops of milk, teased it with a thousand of those divine childishnesses which mothers alone can invent. The father, who stood at a distance, smiled quietly on the charming group, and with folded arms hugged his happiness to his heart. I could not bear the sight; I closed the windows and threw myself on my bed, my heart filled with hatred and fearful jealousy, gnawing my fingers and my blanket like a tiger that has hungered for three days.

I do not know how long I remained thus; but, turning with a convulsive movement, I saw the Abbé Sérapion standing in the middle of the room and watching me with fixed attention. I was overcome with shame, and letting my head fall on my breast, I covered my eyes with my hands.

'Romauld, my friend, something extraordinary is taking place in you,' said Sérapion, after a few minutes' silence; 'your behaviour is truly unaccountable! You, so pious, so calm, so gentle, you rage in your cell like a wild beast. Be on your guard, my brother, and do not listen to the promptings of the devil; the evil spirit, incensed because you are for ever consecrated to the Lord, is prowling round you like a ravenous wolf and making a last effort to draw you to him. Instead of letting yourself be downcast, my dear Romauld, make yourself a breastplate of prayers, a buckle of mortifications, and valiantly do battle with the enemy; you will conquer him. Virtue must be put to the test; gold comes out of the cupel finer than before. Do not be afraid or discouraged; the most watchful and steadfast souls have had moments such as these. Pray, fast, meditate, and the evil spirit will leave you.'

The words of the Abbé Sérapion recalled me to myself, and I regained something of my composure.

'I came,' he continued, 'to announce to you your nomination to the living of C —. The priest who had it has just died, and Monseigneur the Bishop has directed me to install you there; be ready to start tomorrow.'

I replied with a movement of the head that I would be ready, and the Abbé withdrew. I opened my missal and began to read prayers; but the lines soon became confused; the sequence of thoughts in my brain became tangled, and the book dropped from my hand without my noticing it.

I must leave tomorrow without seeing her again! Add another obstacle to all this that already lay between us! Lose for ever the hope of meeting her except by a miracle! Should I write to her? By whom could I send a letter? Considering the sacred character with which I was invested, to whom should I unbosom myself, in whom could I confide? I was distracted with doubts and fears. Then, what the Abbé Sérapion had said about the wiles of the devil came back to my mind. The strangeness of the adventure, the unearthly beauty of Clarimonde, the phosphorescent brilliance of her eyes, the burning impress of her hand, the trouble of mind into which she had thrown me, the sudden change which had taken place in me, my pious aspirations dispelled in a moment — all this proved clearly the presence of the devil, and that soft hand was perhaps only the glove with which he had sheathed his claw.

These ideas threw me into a great terror; I picked up the missal which had fallen from my knees and betook myself again to prayer.

The next day Sérapion came to fetch me. Two mules awaited us before the door laden with our scanty baggage; he mounted one and I the other. As we traversed the streets of the town I glanced at all the windows and balconies in the hope of seeing Clarimonde; but it was too early; and the town was not yet awake. My eyes tried to penetrate the blinds and curtains of all the mansions before which we passed. Sérapion, doubtless, attributed this curiosity to the admiration which the beauty of the architecture excited in me, for he slackened his mount's pace in order to give me time to look. At length we reached the town gate and began to climb the hill. When I was at the top, I turned to take a last look at the place where Clarimonde lived. The shadow of a cloud completely covered the town; its blue and red roofs were merged in a general half-tone over which the morning smoke floated here and there, like white wisps of foam. By a curious optical effect, one edifice stood out shining and golden under a single ray of light, a house higher than the buildings near it, which were completely lost in the mist; although more than a league distant, it seemed quite near. The smallest details could be distinguished — turrets, leads, windows, even its swallow-tailed weathercocks.

'What is that palace I see down there lit up by a sunbeam?' I asked Sérapion.

He shaded his eyes with his hand, and, looking towards it, answered:

'It is the ancient palace which the Prince Concini has given to the courtesan Clarimonde; fearful things take place there.'

At that moment — I do not know even now whether it was reality or an illusion — I thought I saw a slim white figure glide on to the terrace; it sparkled there for a moment and faded out. It was Clarimonde!

Oh! did she know that at that very moment, from the top of the steep road that was leading me away from her, and which I was never more to descend, I was gazing, ardent and troubled, on the palace where she lived, and which a mocking play of light seemed to bring close to me, as if to bid me enter it as master? Without doubt she knew it, for her soul was linked to mine in too intimate a sympathy not to feel its faintest vibrations; and it was this consciousness that had impelled her, still arrayed in her night-robe, to ascend the terrace in the shining dews of morning.

The shadow enveloped the palace, and there was now only a motionless sea of roofs and summits, in which nothing could be distinguished but an undulating expanse. Sérapion urged his mule forward, my own immediately fell into pace, and a bend in the road placed the town of S— for ever beyond my view, for I was never to return to it. After three days of travel through rather dreary country, we saw peeping out from among the trees the weather-cock of the church at which I was to officiate; and after passing along a few crooked roads between thatched cottages and crofts, we found ourselves before its front, which was not magnificent. A porch adorned with a few flutings and two or three roughly-sculptured columns of sandstone, a tiled roof and buttresses of the same sandstone as the pillars; to the left the churchyard, overgrown with rank herbage, with a large iron cross in the middle; to the right, overshadowed by the church, the presbytery. It was a dwelling of extreme simplicity and severe cleanliness.

We went in. Some fowls were pecking the ground in search of scantily strewn grains of oats; apparently accustomed to the black robes of priests, they were not at all disconcerted at our intrusion, and barely disturbed themselves to allow us to pass. A cracked and husky barking reached our ears, and we saw an old dog come running towards us.

It was my predecessor's dog. He had the dimmed eye, grey jowl, and all the signs of the most advanced age a dog can live to. I patted him gently, and he at once began to walk by my side with an air of inexpressible satisfaction. An oldish woman, who had been housekeeper to the old curé, also came out to meet us, and after showing us into a low-ceilinged room, asked me if it was my intention to keep her. I said that I would keep her, the dog, the fowls, and all the furniture that her master had left her at his death, which threw her into transports of joy; the Abbé Sérapion paid her on the spot the price she asked.

My installation complete, the Abbé Sérapion returned to the seminary. I was left alone with no one but myself to rely on. The thought of Clarimonde began again to obsess me, and, strive to banish it as I might, I did not always succeed. One evening, as I strolled along the box-bordered walks of my little garden, I fancied I saw through the trimmed hedge the figure of a woman, who was following all my movements, her two sea-green eyes shining through the leaves; but it was only an illusion, for on reaching the further end of the walk, I found nothing but a footprint on the sand, so small that one would have pronounced it the footmark of a child. The garden was surrounded by very high walls; I searched every nook and corner of it, but no one was there. I have never been able to explain this occurrence, which indeed was nothing compared with the strange things which were to happen to me.

I lived thus for a year, fulfilling punctually all the duties of my state, praying, fasting, exhorting, ministering to the sick, giving so much in alms as to be deprived of the most indispensable necessities. But I felt that all was barren within me, and that the fountains of grace had dried up. I did not enjoy the happiness that the fulfilment of a holy mission gives; my thoughts were elsewhere; and Clarimonde's words often returned to my lips like a kind of involuntary refrain. Brother, meditate well on this! For having once raised my eyes to a woman, for a fault apparently so trifling, I have suffered for years the most grievous torment; my whole life has been troubled, always and for ever.

I will not detain you longer with these secret defeats, the victories always followed by a deeper relapse, but will pass at once to a decisive event. One night the door-bell rang violently. The old housekeeper went to open it, and a man of swarthy appearance, richly but outlandishly dressed and wearing a long sword, stood revealed in the light of Barbara's lantern. Her first feeling was one of fear, but the man reassured her and told her that he must see me immediately on a matter that concerned me as a priest. Barbara brought him upstairs to me. I was just going to bed. The man informed me that his mistress, a very great lady, was at the point of death and wished to see a priest. I replied that I was ready to accompany him; I took with me the requisites for extreme unction, and went down as quickly as I could.

Before the door, two horses, black as night, their chests streaked with two long waves of foam, were impatiently pawing the ground. The man held the stirrup for me and helped me to mount one of them; then, resting his hand upon the pommel of the saddle, vaulted on to the other. He gripped his horse with his knees, gave it free rein, and it shot forward like an arrow. Mine, the bridle of which he held, set off at a gallop also, and kept exactly abreast of the other. We tore over the ground; the earth swept beneath us grey and streaked, and the dark outline of the trees fled past like a routed army. We passed through a forest of such dense and chilly darkness that I felt my flesh creep with a thrill of superstitious terror. The showers of sparks that our horses' hoofs beat from the stones left a trail of fire in our wake; and if anyone had seen my guide and me at that hour of the night, he would have taken us for two phantom horsemen careering through a nightmare. Will-o'-the-wisps crossed our path from time to time, and jackdaws squawked piteously in the depths of the wood, where the phosphorescent eyes of wild cats gleamed now and then. The manes of our horses streamed more and more wildly, the sweat poured down their sides, the breath came from their nostrils panting and laboured. But when he saw them failing, the groom, to rally them, uttered a guttural cry such as human lips never uttered, and the furious pace was resumed.

At last the whirlwind subsided; a black mass, dotted with a few points of light, rose suddenly before us; our horses' hoofs rang more sharply on an iron causeway, and we passed under a vaulted passage which opened its dark jaws between two gigantic towers. Great excitement prevailed in the castle; servants with torches in their hands were hurrying through the courtyard in all directions, and lights were going up and down from landing to landing. I had a confused view of a vast structure, columns, arcades, and stairways, an architectural splendour altogether regal and fantastic. A negro page, the same who had brought me Clarimonde's pocket-book, whom I recognized immediately, came to help me dismount, and a major-domo dressed in black velvet, with a gold chain about his neck and an ivory staff in his hand, advanced to meet me. Tears flowed from his eyes, and trickled down his cheeks on to his white beard.

'Too late!' he said, shaking his head. 'Too late, sir Priest! But if you have not been able to save her soul, come and watch by the poor body.'

He took my arm and led me to the chamber of death. I wept as bitterly as he, for I knew now that the dead woman was no other than Clarimonde, loved so much and so madly.

A *prie-Dieu* was placed at the bedside; a bluish flame flickering over a bronze cup threw a feeble and uncertain light through the room and brought into twinkling prominence here and there some projecting angle of furniture or moulding. On the table, in a vase of chased silver, was a faded white rose, whose petals, save one which still clung to its stem, had fallen at the foot of the vase like fragrant tears. A broken black mask, a fan, fancy dresses of every kind lay about on the chairs, and showed that Death had come into this sumptuous dwelling unexpected and unannounced. I knelt down without daring to look towards the bed, and began to recite psalms with fervour, thanking God for having placed the tomb between the thought of this woman and myself, so that I might add to my prayers her name, henceforth sanctified.

But little by little my enthusiasm abated, and my thoughts wandered. There was nothing of the death-chamber about this room. Instead of the fetid, corpse-infected atmosphere which I was accustomed to breathe in these funereal vigils, a languishing vapour of Eastern perfumes, an indefinable feminine, love-inspiring scent floated gently on the warm air. The pale light suggested rather a twilight arranged for voluptuous pleasure than the yellow rays of the night-light that flickers beside a corpse. I reflected on the strange chance by which I had found Clarimonde again at the moment when I was losing her for ever, and a sigh of regret escaped my breast. It seemed as if someone sighed behind me also, and I turned involuntarily. It was an echo. As I turned, my eyes fell upon the death-bed they had till then avoided. The red damask curtains, embroidered with large flowers and relieved by spiral fringes of gold, showed the dead woman lying at full length, her hands joined on her breast. It was covered with linen drapery of dazzling whiteness, a whiteness accentuated by the dark purple of the tapestry, and so fine in texture that it in no way concealed the exquisite form of the body, and permitted the eye to follow the beautiful outlines, undulous as a swan's neck, which death itself had not been able to stiffen. One would have said it was an alabaster statue, wrought by a clever sculptor for the tomb of a queen, or, still better, a young girl asleep with snow fallen on her.

I could contain myself no longer: the atmosphere intoxicated me, the feverish scent of half-faded roses went to my brain; and I strode up and down the room, pausing each time before the bed to look upon the beauty that lay dead under its transparent burial robe. Strange thoughts passed through my mind; I pictured to myself that she was not really dead at all, that it was only a stratagem which she had employed to draw me to her castle and tell me of her love. For a moment I even imagined that I saw her foot move under the whiteness of her coverings, and the straight folds of the shroud change their outline.

And then I said to myself: 'Is this really Clarimonde? What proof of it have I? May not that black page have entered the service of another woman? I must be mad so to distress and agitate myself.' But my beating heart replied: 'It is she, it is she!' I approached the bed again, and gazed with redoubled attention at the object of my uncertainty. Shall I confess it? That perfection of form, although purified and sanctified by the shadow of death, affected me more pleasurably than it should have done, and that repose was so like sleep as to deceive the onlooker.

I forgot that I had come to discharge a funereal rite, and imagined myself a young bridegroom entering the chamber of his bride, who hides her face in modesty and will not let her charms be seen. Torn with grief, mad with joy, shivering with fear and delight, I bent towards her and took hold of the corner of the sheet; I raised it gently, holding my breath for fear of waking her. My heart beat so wildly that I felt a rushing noise in my temples, and my forehead streamed with sweat as though I had moved a slab of marble.

It was indeed Clarimonde, as I had seen her in the church on the day of my ordination; she was just as charming, and death, with her, seemed but one form of coquetry the more. The pallor of her cheeks, the fuller rose of her lips, the long drooping lashes that made a brown fringe on the whiteness of the face, gave her an expression of melancholy chastity and pensive suffering that was inexpressively seductive; her long loosened hair, in which a few little blue flowers were still mingled, made a pillow for her head and covered her bare shoulders with its curls; her beautiful hands, purer, more transparent than the sacrificial wafer, were crossed in an attitude of pious repose and mute prayer — an attitude that counter-balanced the too great seduction, it might have been, even in death, of the exquisite moulding and ivory whiteness of her bare arms, from which the bracelets of pearls had not been taken.

I remained for a long time absorbed in silent contemplation, and the longer I looked, the less could I believe that life had for ever deserted that beautiful body. I do not know if it was an illusion or a reflection from the lamp, but it seemed that the blood began to flow again under that dull pallor. I touched her arm lightly; it was cold, but no colder than was her hand on the day that it had touched mine under the portal of the church. I resumed my former position, bending my face over hers, and letting the warm dew of my tears rain upon her cheeks. Ah! what a bitter sensation of despair and impotence I felt! What an agony that vigil was! I should have liked to be able to gather together all my life that I might give it to her and breathe into those icy relics the fire that consumed me. The night was advancing; and feeling that the moment of eternal separation was at hand, I could not deny myself the last and supreme pleasure of leaving a kiss upon the dead lips of her who had all my love.

Oh, miracle! light breath mingled with my breath, and Clarimonde's mouth replied to the pressure of mine: her eyes opened and regained a little brilliance: she sighed, and uncrossing her arms, put them round my neck with a look of inexpressible bliss.

'Ah! it is you, Romuald,' she said, in a voice as languishing and sweet as the last vibration of a harp; 'what have you been doing? I have waited for you so long that I have died; but now that we are betrothed, I shall be able to see you and come to you. Farewell, Romuald, farewell! I love you; that is all I wished to tell you, and I give you back the life which you recalled in me for a minute by your kiss. Farewell, for a little while!'

Her head fell back, but she still held me in her arms as if to keep me with her. A furious gust of wind blew through the window and swept into the room; the last petal of the white rose quivered for a moment like a wing at the end of its stalk, then it broke away and flew out through the open window, bearing with it the soul of Clarimonde. The light went out, and I fell senseless on the bosom of the beautiful corpse.

When I came to myself I was lying on my bed in my little room at the presbytery, and the former curé's old dog was licking my hand, which lay outside the blanket. Barbara was busying herself about the room with the trembling movements of old age, opening and shutting drawers or stirring powders in glasses. On seeing me open my eyes, the old woman uttered a cry of joy, and the dog barked and wagged his tail; but I was so weak that I could not speak a word or make the least movement.

I learned afterwards that I had been in this condition for three days, giving no sign of life except an almost imperceptible breathing. Those three days were a blank in my life, and I do not know whither my spirit had gone during the whole of that time; I remember nothing at all about it. Barbara told me that the same man of swarthy aspect, who had come to fetch me in the night, had brought me back the next morning in a closed litter, and had immediately taken his departure. As soon as I could collect my thoughts, I went over in my mind all the events of that fatal night. At first I believed that I had been the plaything of a magical illusion; but actual and tangible circumstances soon demolished that supposition. I could not think that I had been dreaming, since Barbara as well as myself had seen the man with the two black horses and accurately described their trappings and appearance. At the same time, no one in the neighbourhood had any knowledge of a castle answering the description of the castle where I had found Clarimonde.

One morning the Abbé Sérapion entered my room. Barbara had sent to tell him that I was ill, and he had lost no time in coming to me. Although this promptitude was a proof of his affection and concern for me, his visit did not give me the pleasure that it ought to have given me. There was something searching and inquisitorial in the Abbé Sérapion's look that made me uncomfortable. I felt embarrassed and guilt-stricken in his presence. He had been the first to discover that something was preying on my mind, and I was angry with him for his perception.

Even while he was inquiring about my health in hypocritically honeyed tones, he fixed his two yellow lion's eyes on mine and plunged his gaze into my soul like a plummet. Then he asked me a few questions about the way I managed my parish, asked whether I took pleasure in my work, how I passed the time my duties left free, if I had made any acquaintances among the inhabitants of the place, what were my favourite books, and a thousand other details of the kind. I replied to all this as briefly as possible, and he, without waiting till I had finished speaking, passed on to something else. This conversation had evidently nothing to do with what he wished to say. Then, without the least preface, and as if he were giving me a piece of news which he had just remembered and was afraid of forgetting, he said, in a clear and ringing voice that sounded in my ears like the trumpets of the Last Judgment:

'The famous courtesan Clarimonde died lately, after an orgy that lasted eight days and eight nights. It was something hellishly splendid. The abominations of Balthazar's and Cleopatra's feasts were revived. Good God! in what an age we live! The guests were served by copper-complexioned slaves who spoke an unknown language, and who, I believe, were real demons; the livery of the lowest among them might have served as the gala dress of an emperor. There have always been very strange stories about this Clarimonde; and all her lovers have come to a miserable and violent end. The tale went that she was a ghoul, a female vampire; but I believe she was Beelzebub in person.'

He ceased speaking, and watched me more narrowly than ever to see the effect of his words upon me. I could not prevent myself from starting on hearing the name of Clarimonde, and this news of her death, besides the grief it caused me, by its strange coincidence with the night scene I had witnessed, threw me into a state of agitation and fear which was reflected in my face, do what I would to control it. Sérapion cast an anxious and severe glance on me; then he said:

'My son, I must do my duty and warn you that you are on the brink of a precipice; beware lest you fall. Satan has long claws, and tombs are not always secure. The stone that covers Clarimonde should be sealed with a triple seal; for according to what men say, this is not the first time she has died. May God watch over you, Romauld!'

When he had uttered these words, Sérapion went slowly to the door, and I did not see him again; for he set out for S— immediately.

I had now entirely recovered and had resumed my accustomed duties. The memory of Clarimonde and the old Abbé's words were always in my mind; however, no extraordinary event had occurred to confirm Sérapion's gloomy forebodings, and I began to think that his fears and my own terrors had been exaggerated; but one night I had a dream. I had hardly fallen asleep when I heard the rings of my bed-curtains slide along the rods with a loud clatter; I raised myself sharply upon my elbow and saw the shadowy form of a woman standing before me.

At once I recognized Clarimonde.

She held in her hand a small lamp like those which are placed in tombs, and its rays gave her slender fingers a rosy transparence which spread upward, fading by insensible degrees into the dull, milky white of her bare arm. She had no other garment than the linen shroud that covered her on her death-bed, the folds of which she held to her breast as if ashamed of being so scantily clothed, but her little hand was too small for the task; she was so pale that the colour of the drapery, under the faint rays of the lamp, was confused with that of her flesh. Wrapped in this fine tissue which revealed all the outlines of her body, she looked like a marble statue of an antique bather rather than a woman, endowed with life. Dead or living, statue or woman, shade or body, her beauty was always the same; only the green sparkle of her eyes was a little dulled, and her mouth, before so vermilion, was now only tinged with a soft faint rose almost as pale as that of her cheeks. The little blue flowers I had noticed in her hair were quite withered and had lost nearly all their petals; but none the less she was charming, so charming that, despite the strangeness of the adventure and the mysterious manner in which she had entered my room, I was not for one moment afraid.

She placed the lamp on the table and seated herself on the foot of my bed; then, leaning towards me, she spoke in that voice, at once silvery and soft as velvet, which I had never heard from any lips but hers:

'I have kept you waiting a long time, dear Romauld, and you must have thought that I had forgotten you. But I have come a very long way, from a place from which no one has ever yet returned; there is neither sun nor moon in the country I come from; nothing but space and shadow; neither road nor pathway; no earth for the foot, no air for the wings; and yet I am here, for love is stronger than death and will conquer it in the end. Ah! what gloomy faces, what terrible things I have seen on my journey! How difficult it has been for my soul, come back to this world by the power of my will, to find its body and take up its abode there! What efforts I had to make before I could lift the stone with which they had covered me! See! the inside of my poor hands is all bruised. Kiss them and heal them, dear love!'

She pressed the cold palms of her hands, in turn, to my lips; I did indeed kiss them again and again, and she watched me do so with a smile of inexpressible content.

I confess to my shame that I had wholly forgotten the Abbé Sérapion's advice and the sacred character I had assumed. I had fallen without resistance and at the first assault. I had not even made an effort to repel the tempter; the coolness of Clarimonde's hand penetrated mine, and I felt voluptuous shivers run over my body. Poor child! In spite of all that I have seen of her, I can still hardly believe that she was a demon; at least she had not the appearance of one, and never has Satan better hidden his claws and hoofs. She had tucked her heels under her and sat on the edge of my couch in an attitude full of unstudied coquetry. Now and again she passed her little hand through my hair and rolled it into curls, as if to try how new ways of arranging it would suit me. I submitted to this with a most guilty satisfaction, and she kept up an accompaniment of the most charming prattle.

It is remarkable that I felt no astonishment at such an extraordinary adventure, and with that faculty which one has in dreams of accepting the most bizarre events as quite ordinary, I saw in it nothing that was not perfectly natural.

'I loved you long before I saw you, dear Romuald, and sought you everywhere. You were my ideal, and when I saw you in the church at the fatal moment, I said at once "It is he!" I gave you a look into which I put all the love that I had, and that I was to have for you; a look to damn a cardinal, to bring a king to his knees at my feet before all his court. You remained obdurate and preferred your God to me.

'Ah! how jealous I am of God, Whom you loved and still love better than me!

'How unhappy I am! I shall never have your heart for my very own; I, whom you recalled to life with a kiss; I, the dead Clarimonde, who, for your sake, has broken the doors of the tomb, and has come to devote to you the life which she has only resumed to make you happy!'

These words were broken by intoxicating caresses which benumbed my senses and my reason to such a point that I did not fear, in order to console her, to utter a frightful blasphemy and tell her that I loved her as much as God.

New life came into her eyes; they shone like chrysoprases.

'Truly? truly? as much as God!' she said, clasping me in her beautiful arms. 'If it is so, you will come with me, you will follow me where I wish. You will leave your ugly black robes. You will be the proudest, the most envied of cavaliers; you will be my lover. To be the acknowledged lover of Clarimonde, who has refused a Pope, think of it! Ah! the happy life, the golden existence that we shall lead! When shall we start, my gallant?'

'Tomorrow! Tomorrow!' I cried in my delirium.

'Tomorrow, then!' she replied. 'I shall have time to change my clothes, for these are a little scanty and not suited for travelling. I must also tell my servants, who believe me to be dead in good earnest and are broken-hearted. Money, clothes, carriages, everything will be ready. I will come and fetch you at this time tomorrow. Farewell, dear heart.'

She touched my forehead with her lips. The lamp went out, the curtains closed again, and I saw no more; a leaden, dreamless sleep weighed me down and held me torpid until next morning. I woke later than usual, and the recollection of that strange vision disturbed my mind through the day; I persuaded myself at last that it was a mere product of a heated imagination. Yet the sensations had been so vivid that it was difficult to believe that they were not real, and it was not without fear of what was going to happen that I went to bed, after praying God to banish evil thoughts from my mind and to watch over my sleep.

I was soon fast asleep, and my dream continued. The curtains were drawn apart, and I saw Clarimonde, not, as the first time, pale in her white shroud and with the hues of death upon her cheeks, but gay, lively and elegant, in a magnificent travelling-dress of green velvet edged with gold and looped up on one side to show a satin skirt. Her fair hair escaped in large curls under a large black felt hat trimmed with white feathers fancifully twisted; she held in her hand a little riding-whip, the handle of which ended in a golden whistle. She touched me lightly with it and said:

'Well, fair sleeper, is this how you make your preparations? I counted on finding you waiting. Get up quickly; we have no time to lose.'

I jumped out of bed.

'Come, dress and let us be off,' she said, pointing to a small parcel she had brought; 'the horses are impatient and are champing their bits at the door. We ought to be ten leagues from here already.'

I dressed myself in haste, and she herself handed me the articles of clothing, going into fits of laughter at my awkwardness and showing me how to put them on when I made mistakes. She dressed my hair with a light touch and, when this was done, put into my hand a little pocket mirror of Venetian crystal framed in silver filigree, saying:

'What do you think of yourself? Would you take me into your service as valet?'

I was no longer the same person. I did not recognize myself. I was no more like my old self than a finished statue is like a block of stone. The face I knew seemed but a coarse sketch of the face the mirror reflected. I was handsome; and my vanity was roused by the transformation. The fine clothes, the rich embroidered waistcoat, made quite another man of me;

and I marvelled at the power of a few ells of cloth cut in a certain fashion. The spirit of my costume found its way under my skin, and in ten minutes I was a passable coxcomb.

I walked round the room several times to give myself an easy bearing. Clarimonde watched me with an air of motherly pride, and seemed well pleased with her work.

'Come, we have been childish long enough; we must be off, dear Romauld! We have far to go and we shall not get there in time.'

She took me by the hand and led me away. All the doors opened to her immediately she touched them, and we passed the dog without waking him.

At the door we found Margheritone, the groom who had already been my guide; he held by their bridles three horses, black like the first, one for me, one for himself, and one for Clarimonde. Those horses must have been Spanish jennets out of mares by Zephyr; for they went as fast as the wind, and the moon, which had risen at our departure to light us on our way, rolled through the sky like a wheel broken loose from its chariot; we saw it on our right leaping from tree to tree as if it lost breath in pursuit of us. Soon we came to a plain where, by a clump of trees, a carriage drawn by four powerful beasts was waiting for us; we got into it, and the postilions set off at a furious gallop. I had one arm round Clarimonde and I held one of her hands clasped in mine; she laid her head on my shoulder, and I felt her half-uncovered bosom against my arm. I had never known such perfect happiness. In that moment I forgot everything, and I no more remembered having been a priest than I remembered what I had done in my mother's womb, so great was the fascination the malignant spirit exercised over me.

From that night onward my nature was in some way doubled; there were within me two men, neither of whom knew the other. Sometimes I thought I was a priest who dreamed every night that he was a nobleman, sometimes that I was a nobleman who dreamed that he was a priest. I could no longer distinguish dreams from real life; I did not know where reality began and illusion ended. The dissolute, supercilious young lord jeered at the priest, and the priest abhorred the dissipations of the young lord. Two spirals, entwined and confused, yet never actually touching, would give a good idea of this two-headed existence of mine. Despite the strangeness of the situation, I do not believe that I was ever insane. I always retained quite clearly the perception of my two existences. Only, there was one absurd fact that I could never explain to myself; this was that the feeling of the same identity should exist in two such different men. It was an anomaly I could not account for, whether I believed myself to be the curé of the little parish of C— or Signor Romauldo, the acknowledged lover of Clarimonde.

I was always, or at least imagined myself to be, in Venice; even now I cannot properly disentangle illusion from reality in this bizarre adventure. We lived in a great marble palace on the Canaleio, full of frescoes and statues, with two Titians of the best period in Clarimonde's bedroom, a palace fit for a king. We had each our own gondola with gondoliers in our livery, our own music-room and our own poet.

Clarimonde understood life in the grand style; she had a little of Cleopatra in her nature. As for me, I adopted the airs of a prince's son, and was as arrogant as if I had been descended from one of the twelve apostles or the four evangelists of the Most Serene Republic; I would not have turned aside to make way for the Doges, and I do not believe that there has been anyone more insolent since Satan fell from heaven. I went to the Ridotto and played the devil's own game. I frequented the best society, sons of ruined noble houses, actresses, swindlers, parasites and cut-throats.

Yet, in spite of the dissipated life I led, I remained faithful to Clarimonde. I loved her to distraction. She would have awakened satiety itself from its slumbers, and kept inconstancy inconstant. To possess Clarimonde was to possess twenty mistresses, it was to possess all the women in the world, so versatile was she, so changeable, so unlike herself; a veritable chameleon! An infidelity you would have committed with someone else, she made you commit with her by completely assuming the character, the style and the type of beauty of the woman you seemed to admire.

She returned my love a hundredfold; and it was in vain that young nobles and even elders of the Council of Ten made her most magnificent offers. A Foscari even went so far as to propose to marry her. She refused everything. She had money enough; she wanted nothing but love, a young love, a pure love, a love awakened by her, a love that must be the first and the last. I should have been perfectly happy but for an accursed nightmare that returned every night, in which I fancied myself a village curé mortifying the flesh and doing penance for my excesses of the day. Reassured by being with her, I hardly thought any more of the strange manner in which I had made her acquaintance. But the Abbé Sérapion's words still returned to my mind at times, and did not cease to make me uneasy.

For some time Clarimonde's health had not been so good; her colour faded day by day. The doctors who were sent for did not understand what her illness was or what treatment to give. They prescribed a few medicines that could do neither good nor harm, and did not come again. Meanwhile she grew visibly paler and became colder and colder. She was almost as white and as dead as on the memorable night in the mysterious castle. I was heartbroken to see her thus slowly fading away. Touched by my grief, she smiled upon me softly and sadly, with the resigned smile of those who know they are going to die.

One morning I was sitting at her bedside, eating my breakfast at a little table, so as not to leave her for a minute. As I was cutting some fruit, I happened to make a rather deep gash in my finger. The blood spurted out immediately in crimson jets, and some of the drops were sprinkled upon Clarimonde. Her eyes lit up, her features assumed an expression of fierce, wild joy that I had never seen in them before. She leapt out of bed with the agility of an animal, a monkey or a cat, flew at my wound, and began to suck it with an air of unspeakable delight. She swallowed the blood in small draughts, slowly and grudgingly, like an epicure tasting Xeres and

Syracuse wine; she half closed her eyes, and the pupils of her green eyes became elongated instead of round. Now and again she stopped to kiss my hand, then she began again to press the wound with her lips, to coax out a few more red drops. When she saw that no more blood was coming, she stood up with moist and shining eyes, rosier than a May dawn, her face full, her hand warm and soft, lovelier than ever and in perfect health.

'I shall not die! I shall not die!' she cried, half mad with joy, and hanging on my neck; 'I shall be able to love you for a long time still. My life is in yours, and all that is me comes from you. A few drops of your rich and noble blood, more precious and more potent than all the elixirs in the world, have given me back my life.'

This scene made a deep impression upon me and filled me with strange doubts concerning Clarimonde; and that very evening, when sleep had taken me back to my presbytery, I saw the Abbé Sérapion, graver and more anxious than ever. He observed me attentively and said: 'Not content with destroying your soul, you wish to destroy your body also. Unhappy young man, into what a snare you are fallen!' The tone in which he uttered these words struck me sharply, but in spite of its vividness, the impression was soon dispelled, and a thousand other cares effaced it from my mind.

One evening, however, looking in my mirror, the treacherous position of which she had not taken count of, I saw Clarimonde drop a powder into the cup of spiced wine which she used to prepare after the meal. I took the cup and pretended to sip from it; then I put it down on a table as if to finish it later at my leisure, and taking advantage of a moment when her back was turned, I threw the contents under the table; after which I retired to my room and went to bed, resolved to keep awake and see what would happen. I had not long to wait; Clarimonde came in and, having taken off her wrap, lay down in bed by my side. When she felt sure that I was asleep, she bared my arm and drew a golden pin from her hair; then she began to murmur in a low voice:

'One drop, just one little red drop, a ruby on the point of my needle!. . . Since you love me still, I must not die . . . . Ah! poor love! his beautiful blood, so red, I am going to drink it! Sleep, my only treasure; sleep, my god, my child; I will not hurt you, I will only take from your life what I need to keep mine from going out. If I did not love you so much, I could bring myself to have other lovers, whose veins I would drain dry; but since I have known you, I have held all other men in abhorrence . . . . Ah! what a lovely arm! how round it is! how white it is! I shall never dare to prick that pretty blue vein.'

And as she said this she wept, and I felt her tears rain upon my arm as she held it. At length she decided to act; she made a little prick in my arm with her needle, and began to sip the blood that flowed from it. Before she had taken more than a few drops she was seized with the fear of exhausting me; she carefully bound my arm with a little bandage, after smearing the wound with an ointment that closed it at once.

I could no longer be in doubt, the Abbé Sérapion was right. But in spite of this conviction, I would not suppress my love for Clarimonde, and I would willingly have given her all the blood she needed to maintain her artificial existence. Besides, I was not really frightened; to me, the woman made up for the vampire, and what I had heard and seen reassured me; I had then rich veins that would not quickly be exhausted, and I was not bargaining away my life drop by drop. I would have opened my arm myself and said to her: 'Drink! let my love enter your body with my blood!' I avoided making the least allusion to the powder she had poured out for me, or to the scene with the needle, and we went on living in the most perfect harmony.

Nevertheless, my priest's scruples tormented me more than ever, and I was always seeking new penances to tame and mortify my flesh. Although all this visionary existence was involuntary, and my other self took no part in it, I dared not touch the Christ with hands so contaminated and a soul polluted by such debaucheries, real or imagined. To avoid falling into these fatiguing hallucinations, I tried to prevent myself from sleeping; I held my eyelids open with my fingers and stood upright against the wall, struggling against sleep with all my strength; but my eyes were soon full of drowsiness, and finding that the struggle was in vain, I let my arms fall in discouragement and weariness, and the tide swept me back towards the treacherous shores.

Sérapion remonstrated with me with the greatest vehemence, and reproached me bitterly for my supineness and lack of fervour. One day, when I had been more agitated than usual, he said to me:

'There is only one way to rid you of this obsession, and although it is an extreme measure, it must be taken; for desperate ills, desperate remedies. I know where Clarimonde was buried; we must dig up her body, and let you see in what a wretched state the object of your love now is; you will not be tempted to lose your soul for a filthy corpse, devoured by worms and ready to fall to dust; it will surely bring you to your right mind.'

For my own part, I was so worn out with this double life that I agreed, wishing to learn, once for all, whether the priest or the nobleman was the victim of an illusion; I was prepared to kill one of these two men who were in me for the benefit of the other, whichever it might be, or to kill them both, for such a life could not last. The Abbé Sérapion provided himself with a mattock, crow-bar and lantern, and at midnight we set out for the cemetery of —, the arrangement of which, below and above ground, he knew perfectly.

After turning the light of the dark lantern on the inscriptions on several tombstones, we came at last to a stone half buried in long grass and covered with moss and parasitic plants, on which we deciphered the beginning of an epitaph:

> Here lies Clarimonde
> Beautiful beyond
> All that earth could . . .

'This is it,' said Sérapion, and placing the lantern on the ground, he slipped the crowbar into the interstice of the stone and began to lift it. The stone gave way, and he set to work with the mattock. I watched him, gloomier and more silent than the night itself; he himself, bent over her dismal work, dripped sweat and panted; his laboured breath sounded like a death-rattle.

It was a strange sight, and anyone who had seen us from outside would have taken us for sacrilegious shroud-stealers rather than for priests of God. There was something hard and savage in Sérapion's zeal that gave him the look more of a demon than that of an apostle or angel, and his face, with its large austere features accentuated by the rays of the lantern, was not reassuring. I felt an icy sweat gathering in beads on my limbs, and my hair stood up on my head with a tingling sensation; in my heart I looked upon the action of the pitiless Sérapion as an abominable desecration, and would have been glad if, from the flank of the dark clouds that rolled heavily over us, a triangle of flame had shot out and reduced him to ashes. The owls perched in the cypresses, disturbed by the light of the lantern, came flapping heavily against the glass with their dusty wings and uttering plaintive cries; foxes yelped in the distance, and a thousand sinister sounds broke the silence.

At length Sérapion's mattock struck against the coffin, the boards of which echoed with a hollow, sonorous sound, that awful sound which nothingness gives when touched; he lifted the lid, and I saw Clarimonde, pale as marble, with clasped hands; her white shroud made only one single fold from head to feet. A little red drop gleamed like a rose at the corner of her discoloured mouth.

Sérapion, on seeing this, burst into a fury:

'Ah! there you are, demon, shameless harlot, drinker of blood and gold!' and he sprinkled with holy water the corpse and the coffin also, tracing upon it the figure of a cross.

No sooner had poor Clarimonde been touched by the sacred dew than her lovely body crumbled into dust; nothing remained but a horrible, shapeless heap of ashes, flesh and half-calcined bones.

'Behold your mistress, my lord Romuald!' said the pitiless priest, pointing to the miserable relics. 'Will you ever again be tempted to go walking with your beautiful lady at Lido and Fusine?'

I bowed my head; a great change had taken place in me. I returned to my presbytery, and the lord Romuald, lover of Clarimonde, took leave of the poor priest with whom he had so long and so strangely kept company. I only saw Clarimonde once more; the following night she appeared and said to me, as at our first meeting under the portal of the church:

'Unhappy man! unhappy man! what have you done? Why did you listen to that idiot priest? Were you not happy? And what had I done to you, that you should violate my poor grave and strip bare the horror of my annihilation? All communication between our souls and our bodies is broken. Farewell, you will regret me.'

She vanished into the air like smoke, and I never saw her again.

Alas, she spoke the truth! I have regretted her more than once, and I still regret her. My soul's peace has been very dearly bought; the love of God was not too great a thing to replace hers.

There, brother, is the story of my youth. Never look on a woman, but go with your eyes fixed on the ground, for chaste and steadfast as you may be, one minute may make you lose Eternity.

NELLIE'S GRAVE

VLAD KINKOPF

LEARNED OF NELLIE VAUGHN in a letter from a former student of mine which I read on a late October afternoon in Boston while savoring a glass of Sam Adams beer. It seemed that Nellie's body was buried in the Rhode Island Historical Cemetery No. 2, located on the outskirts of West Greenwich town. Nellie was suspected of being a vampire. I felt compelled to visit her graveyard, especially when I learned of the following inscription etched on her gravestone: "I AM WAITING AND WATCHING FOR YOU!"

Rhode Island has long been famed as the vampire capital of America. Bram Stoker, the author of *Dracula*, had been fascinated with newspaper reports about New England vampires, and that Irish author read and noted the incidents during his frequent trips to the States. Stoker preserved the clipping of a newspaper account entitled "Vampires in New England" from the February 2, 1896 issue of the now defunct newspaper *New York World*, which is in the files of his private papers now housed at the Rosenbach Foundation in Philadelphia. The newspaper story related to Rhode Island vampires. The article stated that belief in vampires was "rampant in a district which includes the towns of Exeter, Foster, Kingston, East Greenwich and many scattered hamlets." It described six cases of vampirism in a small village near Newport, all within a few years: the most recent case involved a mother and her four children who had all died in rapid succession. The villagers considered that the children were infected by vampires and had thereby turned into vampires themselves. So they dug up the last child's body and did what is done in such cases: they extracted the heart and burned it. The article also referred to another case in a Rhode Island seaside town, where a mason by trade, an educated man, had lost two brothers due to tuberculosis. After the second death, the mason's father warned him that he had to dig up the bodies of his brothers and carve out their hearts to burn them. The mason refused, and soon after got sick

75

and died. Only then did the villagers feel compelled to take matters in their own hands. They dug up the mason's body, cut the heart out and burned it to stop the plague from spreading. They knew that vampires first attack members of their own family and near relations. And then the rampage widens.

On All Hallow's Eve I arrived in West Greenwich by car from Boston. Rhode Island Cemetery No. 2 is not marked on any map. I stopped at the local fire station to ask for directions. Two men and a young lady were on duty. I was told that there were many cemeteries in the area. No one knew for certain about the location of No. 2. One of the men was about to telephone an old lady who was knowledgeable in these matters when, by chance, I asked the young girl if she knew anything about Nellie Vaughn. Her eyes lit up, and she exclaimed, "Oh, you mean the vampire?" She proceeded to tell me that she knew where the graveyard was; that no grass could grow over the grave; and that Nellie's tombstone kept sinking deeper and deeper into the earth. She told me that people believe that there are other vampires in that graveyard, and that at night, particularly on Hallowe'en, strange sights are seen there.

She directed me to drive down Plain Meeting House Road to an abandoned Baptist Church. Behind the church stretches the cemetery containing Nellie's tomb. So I drove on and on, way down Plain Meeting House Road, but found nothing but stretching wilderness. Along the way I spotted a young girl riding a bicycle. I hailed her from my car, and she stopped. I asked her if she knew where the nearest cemetery was, and she replied that there were several in the area. I said: "I'm looking for the grave of Nellie Vaughn." "Oh!" the girl smiled: "The vampire!" And she directed me further down the road.

It was getting dark when I finally arrived at the cemetery at the corner of Plain Meeting House Road and Liberty Road. The old Baptist church was boarded up, no more in use. Behind the church was the small graveyard, so small that I had no trouble locating Nellie's grave. On the top of the stone were the words "AT REST", and below that "Nellie L., Daughter of George B. & Ellen Vaughn, Died Mar. 31, 1889, in the 19th Year of Her Age." Under that were inscribed the words: "I AM WAITING AND WATCHING FOR YOU."

As I stood there contemplating the gravesite, where the grass did not grow and the stone seemed to be sinking into the ground, a young couple arrived. They were holding hands. I asked the young man if he knew anything about Nellie. He answered that the original gravestone had been damaged by vandals, and replaced. They strolled away while I lingered on.

Darkness slowly closed in. The old stones in the cemetery stood up like leprous, livid decaying fingers. They pointed towards an empty sky, as if they had been nailed to the dank earth and were trying to escape. Eventually, I heard muffled sounds coming from Nellie's grave. I felt like running away, but I was numbed and immobile. Out of the tomb rose the faint outline of a young woman. She glided towards me with a smile on her pock-marked face, and outstretched her arms. I remembered my Homer:

one must offer blood to the returning dead, like Tiresias, in order for the dead to gain the power of speech. With a pen-knife I slashed my right forearm and within seconds drops of blood spattered the ground, followed by a trickle which continued to flow over my palm and fingers. Nellie rushed to drink the gore. In her haste, the excess blood dripped from her lips. Once Nellie had finished drinking, she said: "You have come in search of the vampires of Rhode Island. Well, my dear, you shall have your fill . . . .

"Little Rhody may be the smallest of the states, but it has had more vampires than there are coals in Newcastle. The Wampanoag and Narragansett Indians who settled here long before Roger Williams came in 1636, had vampires. You can tell from the evidence of their burial mounds. They tied the feet and hands of the corpses together with rope in order to prevent the dead from walking. Sometimes they slit the feet of the corpses . . . .

"The white man was aware of vampires here before the Revolution. A young farmer named Snuffy Stukeley, who was called that because of his butternut brown jacket made of homespun, lived on a farm in a remote corner of Rhode Island. This place is full of remote corners! Snuffy's wife bore him fourteen children in fairly rapid succession. Sarah was the eldest of them all. When Sarah had just become a teenager, her father had a nightmare. He saw half of his orchard decay and die. He felt that this nightmare was a warning about his children's fate. The nightmare recurred. It troubled Snuffy greatly.

"Soon after having had these nightmares, Snuffy saw his eldest daughter Sarah become very ill. She wasted away with severe anemia. Doctors were unable to help her and she died. Then Snuffy's second daughter complained that dead Sarah was visiting her every night. Sarah had a strange grin on her face. The second daughter contracted consumption and passed away. And so, one after another, all six of the Stukeley daughters died under mysterious circumstances. Before their deaths, each complained that Sarah kept visiting them night after night, sitting on their beds, and causing aches and pains to parts of their bodies.

"At last, when Stukeley's son became ill, the father recalled his nightmare. The prophecy had come true — half of his family had died. Action had to be taken. He consulted members of the village. They advised him to exhume all the female bodies in order. His neighbors the Wilcoxes, Reynolds, Whitfords, Mooneys and Gardiners all helped him to perform the ghoulish task. The bodies of all the girls were exhumed.

"Five of the bodies were found badly decomposed. Their stinking odor rose to high heaven. But, weirdly enough, Sarah's body was in good condition, despite the fact that she had died long before others. Her eyelids were open. Her body was found turned in the grave. Her hair and nails had grown: the signs of a vampire. The villagers cut the heart out from her body and fresh blood streamed forth. They burned the heart on a rock. Despite these measures, Stukeley's ailing son died. The folks around explained it away: the ritual had been performed too late — he was already too far gone.

"A hundred years after Sarah, I came down with a strange disease. It was consumption — tuberculosis as it's called today. I simply wasted away. Severe anemia. Doctors were powerless. After my death in 1889, my three brothers and two sisters followed me to the grave, all within one year. The villagers dug up my corpse. Rigor mortis had not set in. My skin was still pliable. Fresh blood flowed from my mouth. Some learned men thought that I was merely in a state of catalepsy, but this was not so. I was dead but yet not dead, *un-dead*. I should have stayed in my coffin. They cut out my heart and burned it. But they were too late. I had already infected another.

"My childhood girlfriend, Mercy Brown, the same age as I, from the neighboring town of Exeter was my victim. She and I had played together. We read old books hidden by my father George in the attic. You see, my father dabbled in the occult. He and William Rose from nearby Kingston practised old rituals. With the help of John Hazard, the unholy three built a Druid altar. There were rumors of blood sacrifices. Among my father's notes I found an account of a small group of Jewish sectarians who had discovered the secret of Jesus Christ's resurrection from the dead. This sect had carried the knowledge and practice to the Balkans when they were forced to emigrate from the Holy Land. Another group had passed the secret on to some Sephardic Jews who carried it to the New World when they established the Truro synagogue in Newport. I now had in my hands the secret of the rituals. I enticed Mercy Brown into those unholy practices. Before my death, she came to know the occult science of resurrection.

"Three years after my death Mercy Brown died. She preyed upon her mother and Mary Olive, her sister. All died within a short period of time. A son of the Brown family, Edwin, who was living in West Wickford at the time, became ill. The symptoms were the familiar ones associated with consumption. Edwin was dispatched to Colorado for a cure. However, as soon as he came home, he got ill again. His relatives in Exeter tried their best to save Edwin. They concluded that he was a victim of vampires. So, on a gusty March day in 1892 the locals marched into the Chestnut Hill Cemetery armed with shovels and pick-axes.

"Under the watchful direction of a certified medical practitioner, Dr. Harold Metcalf of Wickford, the bodies of the three women were disinterred in broad daylight. The bodies of Mrs. Brown and her eldest daughter, Mary Olive, had decayed. But the corpse of my friend and confidante, 19-year-old Mercy Brown, buried some nine weeks before, had not decomposed at all.

"Dr. Metcalf, who was quick with the knife, cut out the heart and the liver from Mercy's body. Fresh blood dripped from the severed organs, which some of the villagers took as proof that she was a vampire. They found a stone and burned her heart on it. Dr. Metcalf took the liver, ground it up, dissolved it in his own home-made medicine and gave it to Edwin to drink as an antidote. Edwin drank the dreadful potion but died on May 2, 1892, and his body joined those of his mother and sisters in the family plot behind the old Baptist church in Exeter.

"Now, one hundred years later, I am ready to begin again," Nellie continued. "The old ways are still the best . . . ."

Her narrative was interrupted by the glare of headlights of an approaching automobile near the abandoned Baptist Church. The firemen, having become apprehensive, had come to look for me. I got back to the station where I dressed my self-inflicted wound. Later, when I drove past the church, on the little bridge which spans a culvert near the cemetery, I saw the figure of a girl wrapped in a shawl, with long tresses of golden hair and a strange glint in her eyes.

Nellie is still out there.

THE ITALIAN COUNT

PETER UNDERWOOD

HE REVEREND ALPHONSUS Joseph-Mary Augustus Montague Summers MA, FRSL, spent much of his life abroad in Italy, although he passed his last years in an antique and strangely quiet home in Richmond Green, Surrey, England. It was in that abode in 1947 that I talked with him about some of his remarkable experiences with ghosts, vampires and denizens of the uncanny world. One particular story, concerning his personal encounter with a vampire in northern Italy intrigued me. That terrifying incident had happened several years ago.

Summers held that evil is a reality but goodness is overpowering, and one must be always prepared and armed for the struggle. He knew of the existence of vampires, wrote treatises on the subject, and claimed to have encountered them himself.

Summers told me this story in his resonant voice. His limpid eyes and cherubic face seemingly recalled the awesome incidents and people he actually encountered. To repeat that tale of horror and write about it after the passage of many years causes me to shudder and look over my shoulder. I ask myself whether there could ever have existed such a being as the Italian Count, for that was how Summers always referred to him. He knew the real name of that infamous individual, but he had sworn in dire peril not to divulge his identity, nor ever to write about him. Doubtless, the Reverend Summers, with all his knowledge, power and influence, was more than a little afraid of the Count, who might yet be able in some strange way to get him.

In 1909, Summers was visiting northern Italy where he heard strange tales of vampires. Rumours had reached him concerning several unexpected deaths, where bodies were found drained of blood. More stories followed and still more, all from the same area, until Summers was convinced that the dead were victims of a vampire, and decided to visit the affected area equipped with his famous Vampire Talisman.

81

Summers showed me the talisman. It had been made in the 17th-century in eastern Europe, and had been used with considerable effect — to his certain knowledge — in several vampire infestations.

Both sides of the medal contain lettering in the old Slavonic or Romanian and incorporate both Roman and Cyrillic characters, but even Summers, with his not inconsiderable scholarship, was unable to translate it. In the centre of the medal, the obverse side bears the head of a man who has a distinctive nose, staring eyes and a long face that can be seen on all reputed etchings of Dracula or Vlad Tepes, "Vlad the Impaler", the historical Wallachian prince. The figure appears to be clothed in and the head protected by some kind of chain-mail. The figure, as becomes a prince or ruler, wears what appears to be a seven-jewelled crown. Around the neck there is a row of seven circular stones. On the left-hand side of the head is a circle over a cross, the age-old talisman against vampires, etched like a brand of fire. The reverse of the medallion depicts a curious, man-like figure, with a bird-like head wearing a conical cap, while some form of mail encases the whole body. In one hand the figure grasps a sword, and with the other hand holds a pointed stake, both, however, pointing downwards. The traditional method of ridding the world of a vampire is to put a stake through his heart and cut off his head.

Armed with this formidable talisman, Summers set out to look for the vampire in the area where there were daily reports of bodies being found drained of blood. He already knew that in some parts of Europe there was a prevalent belief that passive vampires in life become active after death; that those whose blood has been sucked in life by vampires will turn into vampires after death, and that the only way to prevent this calamity from spreading is for the threatened victim to eat some earth from the grave of the attacking vampire, and to smear his own body with the blood from the vampire's corpse.

As he drew near the wild and mountainous countryside that was the centre of the reputed visitation, Summers told me that he had an over-whelming impression of entering a bewitched area, a part of the world where rational belief and natural law had been suspended. He felt a curious coldness and an awareness that he was utterly alone, that forces over which he had no control were closing upon him. Although it was still daylight, a large bat swooped above him as he trudged along a dusty and deserted path.

As dusk fell, he arrived at a solitary and silent dwelling that had the appearance of an inn and, thinking that here he at least could lodge for the night and perhaps make his headquarters for further investigations, he banged on the heavy door. His knocking echoed in the emptiness and was followed by a strange stillness. He knocked again, but there was only the echo. He banged repeatedly, louder and louder. Surely, someone would answer . . . .

Suddenly he heard a muffled shuffling, a dragging sound which he could not comprehend. It made his blood run cold. The sound ceased and then again resumed, coming a little nearer. Silence prevailed once more. Summers banged again, and the door suddenly swung open. Slumped on the floor at his feet lay a young girl, her whole body curiously thin, the skin a strange white colour and hanging loosely on the bones. Her face was dead-white. Her open mouth was gasping for air. Her body was spattered with blood, and a bloody trail led back into the hallway where the girl had dragged herself to the door to answer his knocking.

Summers, touched to the quick by the terrible, fear-filled wide eyes that looked up at him, lifted the girl in his arms and asked who or what had done this terrible thing. The girl seemed to summon her last waning strength; her white and thin hand dropped to the blood-stained floor, and slowly with her bony finger she wrote in blood the following words: T H E C O U N T. As she finished, she drew her hand to her side. Her tortured eyes closed and Summers found that he was holding a dead body in his arms.

Summers laid the body on an ancient ottoman and covered it as best he could. Then he saw to his horror that her eyes had opened again. He forced himself to close them and he knew that, to the end of his days, he would be haunted by her lifeless stare. Shaking himself, he took out the Vampire Talisman and holding it before him, he warily explored the empty inn. It was completely deserted. In two bedrooms he found such disorder and chaos that it was obvious that violent struggles had taken place there. The bedroom windows were swinging loosely, but all other entrances and doors were closed, fastened and heavily shuttered. Some casements, Summers noticed, were hung with sprigs of garlic, and this convinced him that his worst fears were justified.

Looking out through one of the windows Summers saw, away in the distance, the silhouette of a castle perched on the side of a mountain. He noted the glimmer of a single light burning high up in what appeared to be its topmost tower. Night had fallen. A full moon lit the desolate countryside and cast eerie shadows whenever Summers moved. He looked out of the window again. The darkness seemed almost to pulsate as he stared at the twisting roadway and the boulders bordering it. The scant bushes and quietly waving spindly trees seemed like eyes watching his every movement.

Holding his medallion in front of him, Summers entered a small, undisturbed and garlic-protected room at the back of the inn and, weary from his journey, lay down and was soon fast asleep.

He was awakened at dawn by the sound of knocking. He made his way quietly into one of the front bedrooms and was about to look out the window when he was struck in the face by a window which was swinging open and shut. It must have been caught by a sudden gust of wind — yet there was no wind. As Summers touched his painful nose, an enormous bat flew out from behind the window, fluttered for a moment in the air in front of him, its unblinking little eyes fixed on his, its tiny blood-stained teeth clearly visible — and then with a sudden swirl it swung away and flew with incredible speed in the direction of the castle he had noticed the night before.

Then Summers heard the knocking again, louder this time and definitely from downstairs. He leaned out of the window and looked down. In the cobbled courtyard of the inn stood an ancient coach, its single horse snorting and pawing as though anxious to be on its way. Standing at the door of the inn Summers could just discern the figures of two people. As he watched, they knocked again and looked up. Summers darted back into the bedroom but a guttural voice called and beseeched him to open the door. "My daughter . . . my daughter . . . what have you done to my daughter . . .?" the voice wailed.

Montague Summers hurried to the door to admit two poorly-dressed villagers, a man and a woman. Summers quickly showed them his clerical vestments and the heavy crucifix he wore around his neck and he hurriedly explained how he had stumbled upon the inn the night before. He told them of the awful discovery that he had made. They eyed the crucifix and the vestments and looked at each other. A vampire would not — could not — possess and handle such things, especially a crucifix. Then Summers showed to them the pathetic corpse of their daughter.

They told him that she had worked at the inn before the sudden spate of unexplained deaths. They had implored her to return home but she had refused, even when the owners and everyone else packed off and left. The girl had said she was safe. Did she not have a picture of a saint, blessed by the Pope himself, hanging above her bed? And she wore a crucifix round her neck, another round her waist and one on each wrist; and she had sealed her room with garlic — was ever anyone so protected? Somehow she must have been persuaded to leave her room, to remove her protective amulets and so become a victim. She wore no crucifix when she was found, and it seemed likely that she had been deceived by the vampire, if vampire it was, appearing to her in another form. At all events, once she was unprotected, she met an awful end. But she had managed to write the words "The Count" in blood on the floor. The old people looked to where Summers pointed and saw the last message their daughter had written. "What does this mean?" asked Summers. They hurriedly crossed themselves and pointed in the direction of the castle. "It must be the Count," they muttered. "Oh, God save us . . . ."

The dead girl was hurriedly buried in the garden and they rolled a heavy stone on to her grave and covered it with a cross and garlic. Summers then decided to call on the Count. The couple warned him that the Count saw no one. Over the whole region he was the lord whose word was law. The only people who ever saw him were those he sent for, usually the young and pretty girls as they grew up, and many of them were never seen again once they entered the portals of the castle. The Count found excellent work for them in other parts of his kingdom!

The old couple, devastated by the awful death of their only daughter, were all for mustering the villagers and local people to storm the castle by night and set it alight for, they said, vampires cannot withstand fire. But Summers was dubious, for the Count, if he was a vampire, might metamorphose or transform himself into a bat or a wolf and escape the flames.

Summers first wanted to have tangible proof. He possessed a deep and wide knowledge of architecture, and he sent a message to the Count saying that he had travelled many miles to explore the architectural monuments in northern Italy. More than any other building in his travels, this one, with its unique shape, structure and location fascinated him, and he would consider it a privilege to call on the Count for the purpose of discussing his remarkable castle. The ploy was successful, and Summers received a reply stating that the Count would receive the visitor in his castle at dusk the following day. But, he added, "I am an old man and you must forgive my eccentric ways. Many years ago I was attacked with a crucifix. It appears impolite, but I must ask you not to carry a crucifix of any kind on your person during your visit, and I must warn you that I shall know immediately if you have a crucifix with you."

As the dusk fell, Summers approached the castle, having trudged along the deserted path up the steep and rugged incline. He noticed on the journey a bat of unusual size above him, then behind him, then around him. Doubtless, he told himself, the Count was making sure that his visitor carried no crucifix. As he made his way up the last flight of stone steps, the bat flew off and disappeared.

Arriving at the dark door with its heavy surround in the shape of a bat with outspread wings, Summers reached for the bell-pull, a plaited rope which felt suspiciously like human hair, and at the end of which hung what could have been a baby's skull . . . but before he touched it, the heavy door swung open. Summers peered into the dim interior. He could just discern a wealth of period furniture and fitments and an immense circular stairway that faced the door. As he entered, a strikingly beautiful woman appeared from nowhere. She was dressed in a long black velvet dress that clung to her figure. She hardly opened her lips, but Summers heard her say: "The Master will see you in his study, at the top of the stairs." It was such an odd voice, almost as though the speaker had a mouthful of thick liquid, but already the girl had turned away. He noticed her entrancing figure in clinging velvet, and her long blonde hair hanging to her waist.

She paused at the foot of the stairs and pointed the way to Summers, up the stairs. He nodded to her, and began to mount and then, on an impulse, he turned to glance at her again. But she had not expected him to look back, and now she stood boldly glaring at him, her eyes gleaming and mouth open — revealing enormous blood-stained fangs!

Summers shuddered, but continued to mount the stairway. On and on it seemed to spiral, round and round. Now and then he passed doorways which presumably led to different floors, but he continued, and the stairs became narrower and narrower until he arrived at the top. He felt as though he was on a precipice, and when he looked down the stairs he could hardly see anything, for it was so dark, or perhaps the circular steps had made him giddy. He proceeded towards a large door, all covered with some material like dark skin or leather, and studded with what looked like human teeth. As he peered at the door it slowly opened, and before him stood a tall, singular figure.

The Count was impeccably dressed in a dinner suit and wore an enormous red decoration of some principality around his neck. "Welcome to my home," he said in a deep voice. "Forgive my dress, but I shall be dining shortly and the hours of darkness pass quickly; I only dine at night. But do come in."

He led the way into his circular study. It was lined with bookshelves, and there were divans placed about, all covered with rich brocade. Black candles burned in tall silver candlesticks in each of the windows round the room.

The Count seated himself, in an elaborately-carved ebony chair, behind a deeply carved desk which Summers longed to examine. But the Count looked straight at Summers and said: "Let me tell you Montague Summers that I know who you are. Let us not waste any time. What do you want?"

Summers began asking the Count about the architecture of the castle and was just getting into his stride when the sound of a shouting and clamouring mob drifted up through the window. Summers stopped speaking, and the Count listened for a moment and then crossed over to open the window. The babble of voices grew louder, and Summers was about to approach the window himself to see what was happening when the Count turned round and faced him, livid with rage.

"So, you planned to trick me," he roared, "you stupid fool . . . You thought of engaging me in a conversation while the rustics set fire to my castle! But you forget that I am able to alter myself and escape unseen. Even a crucifix cannot stop me."

"No," replied Summers with fear rising to a pitch of bravery. "But I have this . . ." and he produced the Vampire Talisman and held it out in front of him at arm's length, straight in the face of the Count. There was an awful scream, as though a flaming brand had been pressed on the face of the Count, who sank upon the floor. Summers approached the Count and unthinkingly allowed his arm to drop. The Count suddenly recovered, and again rose to his feet. Summers found himself looking into the hypnotic eyes of a cornered vampire. Summers felt his own strength ebbing away and the will to struggle with his adversary fading but, summoning every ounce of his strength and intellect, he again lifted his hand and thrust the medallion towards the Count. The stricken vampire cringed, but reached out to tug fiercely on the hanging bell-rope.

Almost immediately the door was flung wide open, and the same beautiful woman appeared. Her lips were closed to hide her terrible fangs, so that she looked again full of sweetness and life. Smoke curled up the stairs behind her. "The Count orders you to leave at once," she said in a tone that brooked no opposition. Summers pocketed the medallion, and made his way past the girl, down the smoke-laden stairway and out of the castle. As he passed through the doorway he waded through fire and smoke on every side in the darkness. He looked back, but the door of the castle had been slammed shut. Through the haze he saw the old couple whose daughter was the Count's last victim, and they helped him through the fire to safety.

By early dawn the ancient castle was gutted, a smouldering ruin, its irreplaceable artifacts destroyed forever and with them its occupants. As Montague Summers later said to me: "No vampire could possibly withstand the sight of the medallion and fire on a single night!"

The last time I met Montague Summers he gave me the Vampire Talisman. I treasure it and look at it sometimes and wonder whether it really has the power of which he was convinced. Pray God I may never have to test its efficacy myself.

THE HUNGRY STONES

RABINDRANATH TAGORE

Y KINSMAN AND MYSELF were returning to Calcutta from our Puja trip when we met the man in a train. From his dress and bearing we took him at first for an up-country Mahomedan, but we were puzzled as we heard him talk. He discoursed upon all subjects so confidently that you might think the Disposer of All Things consulted him at all times in all that He did. Hitherto we had been perfectly happy, as we did not know that secret and unheard-of forces were at work, that the Russians had advanced close to us, that the English had deep and secret policies, that confusion among the native chiefs had come to a head. But our newly acquired friend said with a sly smile: "There happen more things in heaven and earth, Horatio, than are reported in your newspapers." As we had never stirred out of our homes before, the demeanour of the man struck us dumb with wonder. Be the topic ever so trivial, he would quote science, or comment on the *Vedas,* or repeat quatrains from some Persian poet; and as we had no pretence to a knowledge of science or the *Vedas* or Persian, our admiration for him went on increasing, and my kinsman, a theosophist, was firmly convinced that our fellow-passenger must have been supernaturally inspired by some strange 'magnetism' or 'occult power,' by an 'astral body' or something of that kind. He listened to the tritest saying that fell from the lips of our extraordinary companion with devotional rapture, and secretly took down notes of his conversation. I fancy that the extraordinary man saw this, and was a little pleased with it.

When the train reached the junction, we assembled in the waiting-room for the connection. It was then 10 p.m., and as the train, we heard, was likely to be very late, owing to something wrong in the lines, I spread my bed on the table and was about to lie down for a comfortable doze, when the extraordinary person deliberately set about spinning the following yarn. Of course, I could get no sleep that night.

When, owing to disagreement about some questions of administrative policy, I threw up my post at Junagarh, and entered the service of the Nizam of Hyderabad, they appointed me at once, as a strong young man, collector of cotton duties at Barich.

Barich is a lovely place. The *Susta* 'chatters over stony ways and babbles on the pebbles,' tripping, like a skilful dancing girl, in through the woods below the lonely hills. A flight of 150 steps rises from the river, and above that flight, on the river's brim and at the foot of the hills, there stands a solitary marble palace. Around it there is no habitation of man — the village and the cotton mart of Barich being far off.

About 250 years ago the Emperor Mahmud Shah II had built this lonely palace for his pleasure and luxury. In his days jets of rose-water spurted from its fountains, and on the cold marble floors of its spray-cooled rooms young Persian damsels would sit, their hair dishevelled before bathing, and, splashing their soft naked feet in the clear water of the reservoirs, would sing, to the tune of the guitar, the *ghazals* of their vineyards.

The fountains play no longer; the songs have ceased; no longer do snow-white feet step gracefully on the snowy marble. It is but the vast and solitary quarters of cess — collectors like us, men oppressed with solitude and deprived of the society of women. Now, Karim Khan, the old clerk of my office, warned me repeatedly not to take up my abode there. "Pass the day there, if you like," said he, "but never stay the night." I passed it off with a light laugh. The servants said that they would work till dark, and go away at night. I gave my ready assent. The house had such a bad name that even thieves would not venture near it after dark.

At first the solitude of the deserted palace weighed upon me like a nightmare. I would stay out, and work hard as long as possible, then return home at night jaded and tired, go to bed and fall asleep.

Before a week had passed, the place began to exert a weird fascination upon me. It is difficult to describe or to induce people to believe; but I felt as if the whole house was like a living organism slowly and imperceptibly digesting me by the action of some stupefying gastric juice.

Perhaps the process had begun as soon as I set my foot in the house, but I distinctly remember the day on which I first was conscious of it.

It was the beginning of summer, and the market being dull I had no work to do. A little before sunset I was sitting in an arm-chair near the water's edge below the steps. The *Susta* had shrunk and sunk low; a broad patch of sand on the other side glowed with the hues of evening; on this side the pebbles at the bottom of the clear shallow waters were glistening. There was not a breath of wind anywhere, and the still air was laden with an oppressive scent from the spicy shrubs growing on the hills close by.

As the sun sank behind the hill-tops a long dark curtain fell upon the stage of day, and the intervening hills cut short the time in which light and shade mingle at sunset. I thought of going out for a ride, and was about to get up when I heard a footfall on the steps behind. I looked back, but there was no one.

As I sat down again, thinking it to be an illusion, I heard many footfalls, as if a larger number of persons were rushing down the steps. A strange thrill of delight, slightly tinged with fear, passed through my frame, and though there was not a figure before my eyes, methought I saw a bevy of joyous maidens coming down the steps to bathe in the *Susta* in that summer evening. Not a sound was in the valley, in the river, or in the palace, to break the silence, but I distinctly heard the maidens' gay and mirthful laugh, like the gurgle of a spring gushing forth in a hundred cascades, as they ran past me, in quick playful pursuit of each other, towards the river, without noticing me at all. As they were invisible to me, so I was, as it were, invisible to them. The river was perfectly calm, but I felt that its still, shallow, and clear waters were stirred suddenly by the splash of many an arm jingling with bracelets, that the girls laughed and dashed and spattered water at one another, that the feet of the fair swimmers tossed the tiny waves up in showers of pearl.

I felt a thrill at my heart — I cannot say whether the excitement was due to fear or delight or curiosity. I had a strong desire to see them more clearly, but naught was visible before me. I thought I could catch all that they said if I only strained my ears; but however hard I strained them, I heard nothing but the chirping of the cicadas in the woods. It seemed as if a dark curtain of 250 years was hanging before me, and I would fain lift a corner of it tremblingly and peer through, though the assembly on the other side was completely enveloped in darkness.

The oppressive closeness of the evening was broken by a sudden gust of wind, and the still surface of the *Susta* rippled and curled like the hair of a nymph, and from the woods wrapt in the evening gloom there came forth a simultaneous murmur, as though they were awakening from a black dream. Call it reality or dream, the momentary glimpse of that invisible mirage reflected from a far-off world, 250 years old, vanished in a flash. The mystic forms that brushed past me with their quick unbodied steps, and loud, voiceless laughter, and threw themselves into the river, did not go back wringing their dripping robes as they went. Like fragrance wafted away by the wind they were dispersed by a single breath of the spring.

Then I was filled with a lively fear that it was the Muse that had taken advantage of my solitude and possessed me — the witch had evidently come to ruin a poor devil like myself making a living by collecting cotton duties. I decided to have a good dinner — it is the empty stomach that all sorts of incurable diseases find an easy prey. I sent for my cook and gave orders for a rich, sumptuous *moghlai* dinner, redolent of spices and *ghi*.

Next morning the whole affair appeared a queer fantasy. With a light heart I put on a *sola* hat like the *sahebs,* and drove out to my work. I was to have written my quarterly report that day, and expected to return late; but before it was dark I was strangely drawn to my house — by what I could not say — I felt they were all waiting, and that I should delay no longer. Leaving my report unfinished I rose, put on my *sola* hat, and startling the dark, shady, desolate path with the rattle of my carriage, I reached the vast silent palace standing on the gloomy skirts of the hills.

On the first floor the stairs led to a very spacious hall, its roof stretching wide over ornamental arches resting on three rows of massive pillars, and groaning day and night under the weight of its own intense solitude. The day had just closed, and the lamps had not yet been lighted. As I pushed the door open a great bustle seemed to follow within, as if a throng of people had broken up in confusion, and rushed out through the doors and windows and corridors and verandas and rooms, to make its hurried escape.

As I saw no one I stood bewildered, my hair on end in a kind of ecstatic delight, and a faint scent of *attar* and unguents almost effaced by age lingered in my nostrils. Standing in the darkness of that vast desolate hall between the rows of those ancient pillars, I could hear the gurgle of fountains splashing on the marble floor, a strange tune on the guitar, the jingle of ornaments and the tinkle of anklets, the clang of bells tolling the hours, the distant note of *nahabat,* the din of the crystal pendants of chandeliers shaken by the breeze, the song of *bulbuls* from the cages in the corridors, the cackle of storks in the gardens, all creating round me a strange unearthly music.

Then I came under such a spell that this intangible, inaccessible, unearthly vision appeared to be the only reality in the world — and all else a mere dream. That I, that is to say, Srijut So-and-so, the eldest son of So-and-so of blessed memory, should be drawing a monthly salary of Rs. 450 by the discharge of my duties as collector of cotton duties, and driving in my dog-cart to my office every day in a short coat and *sola* hat, appeared to me to be such an astonishingly ludicrous illusion that I burst into a horse-laugh, as I stood in the gloom of that vast silent hall.

At that moment my servant entered with a lighted kerosene lamp in his hand. I do not know whether he thought me mad, but it came back to me at once that I was in very deed Srijut So-and-so, son of So-and-so of blessed memory, and that, while our poets, great and small, alone could say whether inside or outside the earth there was a region where unseen fountains perpetually played and fairy guitars, struck by invisible fingers, sent forth an eternal harmony, this at any rate was certain, that I collected duties at the cotton market at Barich, and earned thereby Rs. 450 per mensem as my salary. I laughed in great glee at my curious illusion, as I sat over the newspaper at my camp-table, lighted by the kerosene lamp.

After I had finished my paper and eaten my *moghlai* dinner, I put out the lamp, and lay down on my bed in a small side-room. Through the open window a radiant star, high above the Avalli hills skirted by the darkness of their woods, was gazing intently from millions and millions of miles away in the sky at Mr. Collector lying on a humble camp-bedstead. I wondered and felt amused at the idea, and do not know when I fell asleep or how long I slept; but I suddenly awoke with a start, though I heard no sound and saw no intruder — only the steady bright star on the hilltop had set, and the dim light of the new moon was stealthily entering the room through the open window, as if ashamed of its intrusion.

I saw nobody, but felt as if some one was gently pushing me. As I awoke she said not a word, but beckoned me with her five fingers bedecked with rings to follow her cautiously. I got up noiselessly, and, though not a soul save myself was there in the countless apartments of that deserted palace with its slumbering sounds and waking echoes, I feared at every step lest any one should wake up. Most of the rooms of the palace were always kept closed, and I had never entered them.

I followed breathless and with silent steps my invisible guide — I cannot now say where. What endless dark and narrow passages, what long corridors, what silent and solemn audience-chambers and close secret cells I crossed!

Though I could not see my fair guide, her form was not invisible to my mind's eye, — an Arab girl, her arms, hard and smooth as marble, visible through her loose sleeves, a thin veil falling on her face from the fringe of her cap, and a curved dagger at her waist! Methought that one of the thousand and one Arabian Nights had been wafted to me from the world of romance, and that at the dead of night I was wending my way through the dark narrow alleys of slumbering Bagdad to a trysting-place fraught with peril.

At last my fair guide stopped abruptly before a deep blue screen, and seemed to point to something below. There was nothing there, but a sudden dread froze the blood in my heart — methought I saw there on the floor at the foot of the screen a terrible negro eunuch dressed in rich brocade, sitting and dozing with outstretched legs, with a naked sword on his lap. My fair guide lightly tripped over his legs and held up a fringe of the screen. I could catch a glimpse of a part of the room spread with a Persian carpet — some one was sitting inside on a bed — I could not see her, but only caught a glimpse of two exquisite feet in gold-embroidered slippers, hanging out from loose saffron-coloured *paijamas* and placed idly on the orange-coloured velvet carpet. On one side there was a bluish crystal tray on which a few apples, pears, oranges, and bunches of grapes in plenty, two small cups, and a gold-tinted decanter were evidently awaiting the guest. A fragrant intoxicating vapour, issuing from a strange sort of incense that burned within, almost overpowered my senses.

As with trembling heart I made an attempt to step across the outstretched legs of the eunuch, he woke up suddenly with a start, and the sword fell from his lap with a sharp clang on the marble floor.

A terrific scream made me jump, and I saw I was sitting on that camp-bedstead of mine sweating heavily; and the crescent moon looked pale in the morning light like a weary sleepless patient at dawn; and our crazy Meher Ali was crying out, as is his daily custom, "Stand back! Stand back!!" while he went along the lonely road.

Such was the abrupt close of one of my Arabian Nights; but there were yet a thousand nights left.

Then followed a great discord between my days and nights. During the day I would go to my work worn and tired, cursing the bewitching night and her empty dreams, but as night came my daily life with its bonds and shackles of work would appear a petty, false, ludicrous vanity.

After nightfall I was caught and overwhelmed in the snare of a strange intoxication. I would then be transformed into some unknown personage of a bygone age, playing my part in unwritten history; and my short English coat and tight breeches did not suit me in the least. With a red velvet cap on my head, loose *paijamas,* an embroidered vest, a long flowing silk gown, and coloured handkerchiefs scented with *attar,* I would complete my elaborate toilet, sit on a high-cushioned chair, and replace my cigarette with a many-coiled *narghileh* filled with rose-water, as if in eager expectation of a strange meeting with the beloved one.

I have no power to describe the marvellous incidents that unfolded themselves as the gloom of the night deepened. I felt as if in the curious apartments of that vast edifice the fragments of a beautiful story, which I could follow for some distance, but of which I could never see the end, flew about in a sudden gust of the vernal breeze. And all the same I would wander from room to room in pursuit of them the whole night long.

Amid the eddy of these dream-fragments, amid the smell of *henna* and the twanging of the guitar, amid the waves of air charged with fragrant spray, I would catch like a flash of lightning the momentary glimpse of a fair damsel. She it was who had saffron-coloured *paijamas,* white ruddy soft feet in gold-embroidered slippers with curved toes, a close-fitting bodice wrought with gold, a red cap, from which a golden frill fell on her snowy brow and cheeks.

She had maddened me. In pursuit of her I wandered from room to room, from path to path among the bewildering maze of alleys in the enchanted dreamland of the nether world of sleep.

Sometimes in the evening, while arraying myself carefully as a prince of the blood-royal before a large mirror, with a candle burning on either side, I would see a sudden reflection of the Persian beauty by the side of my own. A swift turn of her neck, a quick eager glance of intense passion and pain glowing in her large dark eyes, just a suspicion of speech on her dainty red lips, her figure, fair and slim, crowned with youth like a blossoming creeper, quickly uplifted in her graceful tilting gait, a dazzling flash of pain and craving and ecstasy, a smile and a glance and a blaze of jewels and silk, and she melted away. A wild gust of wind, laden with all the fragrance of hills and woods, would put out my light, and I would fling aside my dress and lie down on my bed, my eyes closed and my body thrilling with delight, and there around me in the breeze, amid all the perfume of the woods and hills, floated through the silent gloom many a caress and many a kiss and many a tender touch of hands, and gentle murmurs in my ears, and fragrant breaths on my brow; or a sweetly-perfumed kerchief was wafted again and again on my cheeks. Then slowly a mysterious serpent would twist her stupefying coils about me; and heaving a heavy sigh, I would lapse into insensibility, and then into a profound slumber.

One evening I decided to go out on my horse — I do not know who implored me to stay — but I would listen to no entreaties that day. My English hat and coat were resting on a rack, and I was about to take them down when a sudden whirlwind, crested with the sands of the *Susta* and the dead leaves of the Avalli hills, caught them up, and whirled them round and round, while a loud peal of merry laughter rose higher and higher, striking all the chords of mirth till it died away in the land of sunset.

I could not go out for my ride, and the next day I gave up my queer English coat and hat for good.

That day again at dead of night I heard the stifled heart-breaking sobs of some one — as if below the bed, below the floor, below the stony foundation of that gigantic palace, from the depths of a dark damp grave, a voice piteously cried and implored me: "Oh, rescue me! Break through these doors of hard illusion, deathlike slumber and fruitless dreams, place me by your side on the saddle, press me to your heart, and, riding through hills and woods and across the river, take me to the warm radiance of your sunny rooms above!"

Who am I? Oh, how can I rescue thee? What drowning beauty, what incarnate passion shall I drag to the shore from this wild eddy of dreams? O lovely ethereal apparition! Where didst thou flourish and when? By what cool spring, under the shade of what date-groves, wast thou born — in the lap of what homeless wanderer in the desert? What Bedouin snatched thee from thy mother's arms, an opening bud plucked from a wild creeper, placed thee on a horse swift as lightning, crossed the burning sands, and took thee to the slave-market of what royal city? And there, what officer of the Badshah, seeing the glory of thy bashful blossoming youth, paid for thee in gold, placed thee in a golden palanquin, and offered thee as a present for the seraglio of his master? And O, the history of that place! The music of the *sareng,* the jingle of anklets, the occasional flash of daggers and the glowing wine of Shiraz poison, and the piercing flashing glance! What infinite grandeur, what endless servitude! The slave-girls to thy right and left waved the *chamar,* as diamonds flashed from their bracelets; the Badshah, the king of kings, fell on his knees at thy snowy feet in bejewelled shoes, and outside the terrible Abyssinian eunuch, looking like a messenger of death, but clothed like an angel, stood with a naked sword in his hand! Then, O, thou flower of the desert, swept away by the blood-stained dazzling ocean of grandeur, with its foam of jealousy, its rocks and shoals of intrigue, on what shore of cruel death wast thou cast, or in what other land more splendid and more cruel?

Suddenly at this moment that crazy Meher Ali screamed out: "Stand back! Stand back!! All is false! All is false!!" I opened my eyes and saw that it was already light. My *chaprasi* came and handed me my letters, and the cook waited with a *salam* for my orders.

I said: "No, I can stay here no longer." That very day I packed up, and moved to my office. Old Karim Khan smiled a little as he saw me. I felt nettled, but said nothing, and fell to my work.

As evening approached I grew absent-minded; I felt as if I had an appointment to keep; and the work of examining the cotton accounts seemed wholly useless; even the *Nizamat* of the Nizam did not appear to be of much worth. Whatever belonged to the present, whatever was moving and acting and working for bread seemed trivial, meaningless, and contemptible.

I threw my pen down, closed my ledgers, got into my dog-cart, and drove away. I noticed that it stopped of itself at the gate of the marble palace just at the hour of twilight. With quick steps I climbed the stairs, and entered the room.

A heavy silence was reigning within. The dark rooms were looking sullen as if they had taken offence. My heart was full of contrition, but there was no one to whom I could lay it bare, or of whom I could ask forgiveness. I wandered about the dark rooms with a vacant mind. I wished I had a guitar to which I could sing to the unknown: "O fire, the poor moth that made a vain effort to fly away has come back to thee! Forgive it but this once, burn its wings and consume it in thy flame!"

Suddenly two tear-drops fell from overhead on my brow. Dark masses of clouds overcast the top of the Avalli hills that day. The gloomy woods and the sooty waters of the *Susta* were waiting in terrible suspense and in an ominous calm. Suddenly land, water, and sky shivered, and a wild tempest-blast rushed howling through the distant pathless woods, showing its lightning-teeth like a raving maniac who had broken his chains. The desolate halls of the palace banged their doors, and moaned in the bitterness of anguish.

The servants were all in the office, and there was no one to light the lamps. The night was cloudy and moonless. In the dense gloom within I could distinctly feel that a woman was lying on her face on the carpet below the bed — clasping and tearing her long dishevelled hair with desperate fingers. Blood was trickling down her fair brow, and she was now laughing a hard, harsh, mirthless laugh, now bursting into violent wringing sobs, now rending her bodice and striking at her bare bosom, as the wind roared in through the open window, and the rain poured in torrents and soaked her through and through.

All night there was no cessation of the storm or of the passionate cry. I wandered from room to room in the dark, with unavailing sorrow. Whom could I console when no one was by? Whose was this intense agony of sorrow? Whence arose this inconsolable grief?

And the mad man cried out: "Stand back! Stand back!! All is false! All is false!!"

I saw that the day had dawned, and Meher Ali was going round and round the palace with his usual cry in that dreadful weather. Suddenly it came to me that perhaps he also had once lived in that house, and that, though he had gone mad, he came there every day, and went round and round, fascinated by the weird spell cast by the marble demon.

Despite the storm and rain I ran to him and asked: "Ho, Meher Ali, what is false?"

The man answered nothing, but pushing me aside went round and round with his frantic cry, like a bird flying fascinated about the jaws of a snake, and made a desperate effort to warn himself by repeating: "Stand back! Stand back!! All is false! All is false!!"

I ran like a mad man through the pelting rain to my office, and asked Karim Khan: "Tell me the meaning of all this!"

What I gathered from that old man was this: That one time countless unrequited passions and unsatisfied longings and lurid flames of wild blazing pleasure raged within that palace, and that the curse of all the heart-aches and blasted hopes had made its every stone thirsty and hungry, eager to swallow up like a famished ogress any living man who might chance to approach. Not one of those who lived there for three consecutive nights could escape these cruel jaws, save Meher Ali, who had escaped at the cost of his reason.

I asked: "Is there no means whatever of my release?" The old man said: "There is only one means, and that is very difficult. I will tell you what it is, but first you must hear the history of a young Persian girl who once lived in that pleasure-dome. A stranger or a more bitterly heart-rending tragedy was never enacted on this earth."

JUST AT this moment the coolies announced that the train was coming. So soon? We hurriedly packed up our luggage, as the train steamed in. An English gentleman, apparently just aroused from slumber, was looking out of a first-class carriage endeavouring to read the name of the station. As soon as he caught sight of our fellow-passenger, he cried, "Hallo," and took him into his own compartment. As we got into a second-class carriage, we had no chance of finding out who the man was nor what was the end of his story.

I said: "The man evidently took us for fools and imposed upon us out of fun. The story is pure fabrication from start to finish." The discussion that followed ended in a lifelong rupture between my theosophist kinsman and myself.

A CALL IN THE BLOOD

MARGARET L. CARTER

THE SUMMONS DRAGGED HER up from sleep. Sleep and a single clammy sheet weighed her down like six feet of earth. Her body felt like a statue carved from ice. Her heart thawed first. Little by little, heat seeped from the center of her chest through veins and nerves. Inch by inch, she changed from ice to flesh. The reviving process hurt, like plunging a frozen limb into warm water. But she had to wake up. Something in the night was calling her, something she needed.

Laura flexed her fingers and toes, feeling needle-pricks shoot through them. Stretching arms and legs, she sat up. The window in the one bedroom of her cabin was open. No screen — in this somewhat ramshackle resort, most of the cabins seemed to be missing at least one screen. November in the Blue Ridge Mountains meant chilly nights. The first frost had fallen earlier this week, and soon the snows would come. Yet as Laura, in her sleeveless, V-necked gown, pulled herself to her feet, one hand clutching the brass bedpost, she stood by the open window without shivering. The chill outside was nothing compared to the cold within her. She recognized the anomaly, knew she ought to feel cold. Most of the cabins were already empty, tourists having fled the autumn weather. At Thanksgiving the resort would close for the season. But Laura couldn't leave as long as he was here. The one she needed.

She made her way onto the porch, stumbling from one piece of furniture to the next, clutching for support like an invalid rising from a coma of weeks or months. What was calling her? Why couldn't she remember? Rough edges of planks on the weather-worn porch scraped her feet, but numbness insulated her against discomfort. She leaned on a wooden post, inhaling the sharp, pine-scented air, trying to draw in strength. She faced the moon, newly risen, swollen. Its yellow orb reminded her of the closed eye of a sleeping beast of prey, a monstrous cat. In a moment that eye would open, and its glow would mesmerize her, awaiting the predator's leap.

Shutting her own eyes, behind the lids she saw the image of another pair, staring into the darkness. Now she remembered. Victor — he was lying awake, his eyes burning into the night, calling her. She stepped off the porch. The rustle of leaves underfoot jarred her more fully awake. Why was she preparing to grope through the woods half-naked on a cold night? Shame flooded her. Squeezing both arms tightly across her chest, she stood rigid, resisting the call. She felt it as wires constricting her neck and breasts. Pain burned in her parched throat, her loins, the pit of her stomach. She took a step away from the house, and the pain slackened. The call was like a fiery cord drawing her to him, hurting only if she pulled against it.

Superimposed upon the black columns of tree trunks she saw his eyes staring into the night, willing her to come. The image faded into a vision of his face as she'd seen it that first night. She had met Victor before that end-of-season Halloween costume dance, but only to wave casual greetings down a path or across a room. At the lodge that night he'd worn evening dress with a black cape, as had at least a dozen other men at the party. Only Victor's eyes, though, snared and held hers as he surveyed her costume. She, too, had been draped in black and scarlet, vaguely intending a seductive modernization of traditional witch's garb; her flame-hued hair, the legendary Devil's mark, reinforced the motif. The harmony of their disguises had struck her as an omen. He remarked on the splashes of red punctuating her black velvet, asking whether she was a black widow spider, hunting for men to drain of their life-force. Yet Laura felt that he was the one spinning a web to enmesh her. She'd laughed at his wit and riposted with the old verse, "Come into my parlor, said the spider to the fly." Now, this night, she felt still more like a gauze-winged creature being reeled in by silky but unbreakable tendrils.

Damp leaves and pine needles slipped under her bare feet. She clambered, half the time on all fours, over hilly ground, seeking the most direct route to Victor's cabin. Her need wouldn't allow the luxury of the long way around, by cleared, gravel-strewn trails. When bushes, already leafless, screened her path, she ripped them aside with both hands. Though her strength was growing as she drew nearer her goal, her breath still came fast and shallow, and she had to steady herself now and then against the rough trunks of pine trees. Whenever she dared stop to rest, the need burned hotter. A constriction in her loins wrung a moan from her. She pushed on.

As Laura shoved vines out of her way, a thorn scraped the back of her hand. Barely feeling the pain, she raised her arm to gaze dully at the scratch. A thin red slash blossomed across her skin. Her breasts tightened and tingled at the scent of blood. For a moment she forgot to move, as the vivid color held her eyes. Had she always seen this well in the dark? Or only since Victor? She couldn't remember. In fact, when she strained her memory, she could recall nothing about her life before arriving at the mountain cabin. Memory teased like the tune of a song humming in her head, the lyrics irrecoverable. She knew that by day she recollected a family, a job, a life outside — but by day she was not fully alive. Sunlight made her head ache, driving her indoors. She slept more and more between dawn and dusk, to leave the nights free for Victor. How many times had she visited him? Trying to recall specifics was like trying to catch the scraps of a dream, blowing away like skeletal leaves shredded by a late autumn wind.

As she raked through the rubbish heap of her thoughts, she managed to seize one detail. This evening — or was it last night or the night before? — she'd ventured into the lodge dining hall for the first time in at least a week. Hunger had driven her to order the beef stew she'd enjoyed so much during her early days at the resort. (Or had she? That was part of the blur before Victor.) When the bowl had been set before her, though, the rich, brown smell of broth had abruptly metamorphosed to a stench of decay. She'd found herself staring down at charred fragments of dead animals. Swallowing nausea, she'd fled from the oak-beamed room, with the sweltering heat of its stone hearth, into the chill twilight.

How long since she'd eaten solid food? She thought she'd had nothing more substantial than milk since the night of the dance. She remembered stale egg sandwiches, pumpkin-faced cookies, and champagne punch. At midnight Victor had walked her to his cabin, her first visit there. She recalled having the inane notion that he, not champagne, was bubbling through her veins. Though his arm had encircled her, the contact between his fingers and her bare shoulder searing like dry ice, she hadn't needed the support. She'd felt herself gliding above the earth like an astral body released from its flesh, her perception heightened so that mundane objects pulsed with a firefly glow. A tantalizing contrast to her present tortuous advance.

An owl hooted as she blundered into the lower branches of its tree. Like the bird, memory flitted out of reach when she grasped at it. What had happened that night at Victor's cottage? Why did the need for him grip her vitals like a taloned fist, coil through her veins like the craving for a drug? She remembered the smooth shedding of his cloak, her dress. She relived lying on his narrow bed, side by side, her full length pressed to his. And then — only disconnected snapshots viewed through a crimson fog. Sparks flashing behind her eyelids like lightning leaping across a summer night sky. A scarlet drop suspended like a ruby on pale flesh. And their two bloodstreams melting into one, like a pair of flames fusing.

Her vision cleared, unfolding the sight of Victor's cabin a few hundred feet away. Trees had been thinned here to make space for the house. By shutting her eyes she could see his, wide open, gleaming with impatience as they summoned her to renew the bond he had shared with her every night since that first embrace. Dizziness surged over her. When it ebbed, she stumbled down the hillside to the porch of the cabin. Once there, she had to lean against the door and wait for his nearness to restore her strength. Her legs ached from the hike over uneven ground, but the ache in her breast and entrails yearned more insistently. She scrabbled at the door. The knob resisted her struggle to twist it open. Locked. Her fingernails raked the peeling paint from the wood. She hardly heard the groans rising in her own throat.

At last she gathered her wits and walked around the house. At the back she found an open window, unscreened, that she immediately recognized as Victor's. His breathing rose and fell in her ears like waves on rock. She rested her forehead against the window frame, drinking in the rhythm of his heart. That sound grew to thunderous volume, engulfing and obliterating all else. Her own heart began to throb in unison with it, until she could no longer distinguish the two. Irresistibly lured, she climbed over the windowsill, hardly noticing either the splinters in her hand or the ripping sound as her nightgown snagged on a nail.

Now she stood at his bedside. His eyes were not open, after all. Though his breathing was heavy with sleep, even his sleeping mind called to her. She glimpsed the filmy pastel of her gown, ghostlike, in the mirror across the room. She gently lowered herself to the mattress, reclining over him. His eyes opened then, to stare unmoving into hers. Enthralled, she leaned closer. Her hands came to rest on his shoulders. The contact set electricity vibrating in the centers of her palms.

His passion blazed up to fuse with hers. Every cell of her body was flooded, filled, and revitalized by him. She tasted the hot, sweet tang of some potent liquor. Delirious, she drew back to look down at Victor. Their minds merging along with their blood, she experienced an instant of double vision. Not only did she see him lying immobile, his head thrown back to reveal a crimson gash just above his collarbone. She also saw herself through his eyes — heavy-lidded, intoxicated with lust, brows grown together, hair tangled with flakes of dead leaves, mouth smeared with dark wetness. Laura touched her bloodstained face, and the tiny hairs on her palm bristled.

She pulled back into herself and found memory there. She recalled what her self-loathing had made her forget — that she had spun the web for him, that he was the thrall and she the demon who had drained his life, night after night, her thirst so fixed on him that she could not resist returning over and over, no matter what the cost. She turned from her entranced prey to the mirror. She caught only a glimpse of red-stained lips curled back from voracious teeth, before her image faded into nothingness.

THE CLOAK

ROBERT BLOCH

HE SUN WAS DYING, and its blood spattered the sky as it crept into its sepulchre behind the hills. The keening wind sent the dry, fallen leaves scurrying toward the west, as though hastening them to the funeral of the sun.

'Nuts!' said Henderson to himself, and stopped thinking.

The sun was setting in a dingy red sky, and a dirty raw wind was kicking up the half-rotten leaves in a filthy gutter. Why should he waste time with cheap imagery?

'Nuts!' said Henderson, again.

It was probably a mood evoked by the day, he mused. After all, this was the sunset of Halloween. Tonight was the dreaded All-hallows Eve, when spirits walked and skulls cried out from their graves beneath the earth.

Either that, or tonight was just another rotten cold fall day. Henderson sighed. There was a time, he reflected, when the coming of this night meant something. A dark Europe, groaning in superstitious terror, dedicated this Eve to the grinning Unknown. A million doors had once been barred against the evil visitants, a million prayers mumbled, a million candles lit. There was something majestic about the idea, Henderson reflected. Life had been an adventure in those times, and men walked in terror of what the next turn of a midnight road might bring. They had lived in a world of demons and ghouls and elementals who sought their souls — and by Heaven, in those days a man's soul meant something. This new skepticism had taken a profound meaning away from life. Men no longer revered their souls.

'Nuts!' said Henderson again, quite automatically. There was something crude and twentieth-century about the coarse expression which always checked his introspective flights of fancy.

The voice in his brain that said 'nuts' took the place of humanity to Henderson — common humanity which would voice the same sentiment if they heard his secret thoughts. So now Henderson uttered the word and endeavoured to forget problems and purple patches alike.

He was walking down this street at sunset to buy a costume for the masquerade party tonight, and he had much better concentrate on finding the costumier's before it closed than waste his time daydreaming about Halloween.

His eyes searched the darkening shadows of the dingy buildings lining the narrow thoroughfare. Once again he peered at the address he had scribbled down after finding it in the phone book.

Why the devil didn't they light up the shops when it got dark? He couldn't make out numbers. This was a poor, run-down neighbourhood, but after all —

Abruptly, Henderson spied the place across the street and started over. He passed the window and glanced in. The last rays of the sun slanted over the top of the building across the way and fell directly on the window and its display. Henderson drew a sharp intake of breath.

He was staring at a costumier's window — not looking through a fissure into hell. Then why was it all red fire, lighting the grinning visages of fiends?

'Sunset,' Henderson muttered aloud. Of course it was, and the faces were merely clever masks such as would be displayed in this sort of place. Still, it gave the imaginative man a start. He opened the door and entered.

The place was dark and still. There was a smell of loneliness in the air — the smell that haunts all places long undisturbed; tombs, and graves in deep woods, and caverns in the earth, and —

'Nuts.'

What the devil was wrong with him, anyway? Henderson smiled apologetically at the empty darkness. This was the smell of the costumier's shop, and it carried him back to college days of amateur theatricals. Henderson had known this smell of moth balls, decayed furs, grease paint and oils. He had played amateur Hamlet and in his hands he had held a smirking skull that hid all knowledge in its empty eyes — a skull, from the costumier's.

Well, here he was again, and the skull gave him the idea. After all, Halloween night it was. Certainly in this mood of his he didn't want to go as a rajah, or a Turk, or a pirate — they all did that. Why not go as a fiend, or a warlock, or a werewolf? He could see Lindstrom's face when he walked into the elegant penthouse wearing rags of some sort. The fellow would have a fit, with society crowds wearing their expensive Elsa Maxwell take-offs. Henderson didn't greatly care for Lindstrom's sophisticated friends anyway; a gang of amateur Noel Cowards and horsy women wearing harnesses of jewels. Why not carry out the spirit of Halloween and go as a monster?

HENDERSON STOOD THERE in the dusk, waiting for someone to turn on the lights, come out from the back room and serve him. After a minute or so he grew impatient and rapped sharply on the counter.

'Say in there! Service!'

Silence. And a shuffling noise from the rear, then — an unpleasant noise

to hear in the gloom. There was a banging from downstairs and the heavy clump of footsteps. Suddenly Henderson gasped. A black bulk was rising from the floor!

It was, of course, only the opening of the trapdoor from the basement. A man shuffled behind the counter, carrying a lamp. In that light his eyes blinked drowsily.

The man's yellowish face crinkled into a smile.

'I was sleeping, I'm afraid,' said the man softly. 'Can I serve you, sir?'

'I was looking for a Halloween costume.'

'Oh yes. And what was it you had in mind?'

The voice was weary, infinitely weary. The eyes continued to blink in the flabby yellow face.

'Nothing usual, I'm afraid. You see, I rather fancied some sort of monster getup for a par — Don't suppose you carry anything in that line?'

'I could show you masks.'

'No. I mean, werewolf outfits, something of that sort. More of the authentic.'

'So. The *authentic*.'

'Yes.' Why did this old dunce stress the word?

'I might — yes, I might have just the thing for you, sir.' The eyes blinked, but the thin mouth pursed in a smile. 'Just the thing for Halloween.'

'What's that?'

'Have you ever considered the possibility of being a vampire?'

'Like Dracula?'

'Ah — yes, I suppose — Dracula.'

'Not a bad idea. Do you think I'm the type for that, though?'

The man appraised him with that tight smile. 'Vampires are all types, I understand. You would do nicely.'

'Hardly a compliment,' Henderson chuckled. 'But why not? What's the outfit?'

'Outfit? Merely evening clothes, or what you wear. I will furnish you with the authentic cloak.'

'Just a cloak — is that all?'

'Just a cloak. But it is worn like a shroud. It is shroudcloth, you know. Wait, I'll get it for you.'

The shuffling feet carried the man into the rear of the shop again. Down the trapdoor entrance he went, and Henderson waited. There was more banging, and presently the old man reappeared carrying the cloak. He was shaking dust from it in the darkness.

'Here it is — the genuine cloak.'

'Genuine?'

'Allow me to adjust it for you — it will work wonders, I'm sure.'

The cold, heavy cloth hung draped about Henderson's shoulders. The faint odour rose mustily in his nostrils as he stepped back and surveyed himself in the mirror. The light was poor, but Henderson saw that the cloak effected a striking transformation in his appearance. His long face seemed thinner, his eyes were accentuated in the facial pallor heightened by the somber cloak he wore. It was a big, black shroud.

'Genuine,' murmured the old man. He must have come up suddenly, for Henderson hadn't noticed him in the glass.

'I'll take it,' Henderson. 'How much?'

'You'll find it quite entertaining, I'm sure.'

'How much?'

'Oh. Shall we say five dollars?'

'Here.'

The old man took the money, blinking, and drew the cloak from Henderson's shoulders. When it slid away he felt suddenly warm again. It must be cold in the basement — the cloth was icy.

The old man wrapped the garment, smiling, and handed it over.

'I'll have it back tomorrow,' Henderson promised.

'No need. You purchased it. It is yours.'

'But— '

'I am leaving business shortly. Keep it. You will find more use for it than I, surely.'

'But— '

'A pleasant evening to you.'

Henderson made his way to the door in confusion, then turned to salute the blinking old man in the dimness.

Two eyes were burning at him from across the counter — two eyes that did not blink.

'Good night.' said Henderson, and closed the door quickly. He wondered if he were going just a trifle mad.

AT EIGHT, HENDERSON nearly called up Lindstrom to tell him he couldn't make it. The cold chills came the minute he put on the cloak, and when he looked at himself in the mirror his blurred eyes could scarcely make out the reflection.

But after a few drinks he felt better about it. He hadn't eaten, and the liquor warmed his blood. He paced the floor, attitudinizing with the cloak — sweeping it about him and scowling in what he thought was a ferocious manner. He was going to be a vampire all right! He called a cab, went down to the lobby. The driver came in, and Henderson was waiting, black cloak furled.

'I wish you to drive me,' he said, in a low voice.

The cabman took one look at him in the cloak and turned pale.

'Whazzat?'

'I ordered you to come,' said Henderson gutturally, while he quaked with inner mirth. He leered ferociously and swept the cloak back.

'Yeah, yeah. OK.'

The driver almost ran outside. Henderson stalked after him.

'Where to, boss — I mean, sir?'

The frightened face didn't turn as Henderson intoned the address and sat back.

The cab started with a lurch that set Henderson to chuckling deeply, in character. At the sound of the laughter the driver got panicky and raced his engine up to the limit set by the governor. Henderson laughed loudly, and the impressionable driver fairly quivered in his seat. It was quite a ride, but Henderson was entirely unprepared to open the door and find it slammed after him as the cabman drove hastily away without collecting a fare.

'I must look the part,' he thought complacently, as he took the elevator up to the penthouse apartment.

There were three or four others in the elevator; Henderson had seen them before at other affairs Lindstrom had invited him to attend, but nobody seemed to recognize him. It rather pleased him to think how his wearing of an unfamiliar cloak and an unfamiliar scowl seemed to change his entire personality and appearance. Here the other guests had donned elaborate disguises — one woman wore the costume of a Watteau shepherdess, another was attired as a Spanish ballerina, a tall man dressed as Pagliacci, and his companion had donned a toreador outfit. Yet Henderson recognized them all; knew that their expansive habiliments were not truly disguises at all, but merely elaborations calculated to enhance their appearance. Most people at costume parties gave vent to suppressed desires. The women showed off their figures, the men either accentuated their masculinity as the toreador did, or clowned it. Such things were pitiful; these conventional fools eagerly doffing their dismal business suits and rushing off to a lodge, or amateur theatrical, or mask ball, in order to satisfy their starving imaginations. Why didn't they dress in their garish colours on the street? Henderson often pondered the question.

Surely, these society folk in the elevator were fine-looking men and women in their outfits — so healthy, so red-faced, and full of vitality. They had such robust throats and necks. Henderson looked at the plump arms of the woman next to him. He stared, without realizing it, for a long moment. And then he saw that the occupants of the car had drawn away from him. They were standing in the corner, as though they feared his cloak and scowl, and his eyes fixed on the woman. Their chatter had ceased abruptly. The woman looked at him, as though she were about to speak, when the elevator doors opened and afforded Henderson a welcome respite.

What the devil was wrong? First the cab driver, then the woman. Had he drunk too much?

Well, no chance to consider that. Here was Marcus Lindstrom, and he was thrusting a glass into Henderson's hand.

'What have we here? Ah, a bogeyman!' It needed no second glance to perceive that Lindstrom, as usual at such affairs, was already quite bottle-dizzy. The fat host was positively swimming in alcohol.

'Have a drink, Henderson, my lad! I'll take mine from the bottle. That outfit of yours gave me a shock. Where'd you get the make-up?'

'Make-up? I'm not wearing any make-up.'

'Oh. So you're not. How . . . silly of me.'

Henderson wondered if he were crazy. Had Lindstrom really drawn back? Were his eyes actually filled with a certain dismay?

'I'll . . . I'll see you later,' babbled Lindstrom, edging away and quickly turning to the other arrivals. Henderson watched the back of Lindstrom's neck. It was fat and white. It bulged over the collar of his costume and there was a vein in it. A vein in Lindstrom's fat neck. Frightened Lindstrom.

Henderson stood alone in the ante-room. From the parlour beyond came the sound of music and laughter; party noises. Henderson hesitated before entering. He drank from the glass in his hand — Bacardi rum, and powerful. On top of his other drinks it almost made the man reel. But he drank, wondering. What was wrong with him and his costume? Why did he frighten people? Was he unconsciously acting his vampire role? That crack of Lindstrom's about make-up, now—

Acting on impulse, Henderson stepped over to the long panel mirror in the hall. He lurched a little, then stood in the harsh light before it. He faced the glass, stared into the mirror, and saw nothing.

He looked at himself in the mirror, and there was no one there!

Henderson began to laugh softly, evilly, deep in his throat. And as he gazed into the empty, unreflecting glass, his laughter rose in black glee.

'I'm drunk,' he whispered. 'I must be drunk. Mirror in my apartment made me blurred. Now I'm so far gone I can't see straight. Sure I'm drunk. Been acting ridiculously, scaring people. Now I'm seeing hallucinations — or not seeing them, rather. Visions. Angels.'

His voice lowered. 'Sure, angels. Standing right in back of me, now. 'Hello, angel.'

'Hello.'

Henderson whirled. There she stood, in the dark cloak, her hair a shimmering halo above her white, proud face; her eyes celestial blue, and her lips infernal red.

'Are you real?' asked Henderson, gently. 'Or am I a fool to believe in miracles?'

'This miracle's name is Sheila Darrly, and it would like to powder its nose if you please.'

'Kindly use this mirror through the courtesy of Stephen Henderson,' replied the cloaked man, with a grin. He stepped backwards, eyes intent.

The girl turned her head and favoured him with a slow, impish smile. 'Haven't you ever seen powder used before?' she asked.

'Didn't know angels indulged in cosmetics,' Henderson replied. 'But then there's a lot I don't know about angels. From now on I shall make them a special study of mine. There's so much I want to find out. So you'll probably find me following you around with a notebook all evening.'

'Notebooks for a vampire!'

'Oh, but I'm a very intelligent vampire — not one of those backwoods Transylvanian types. You'll find me charming, I'm sure.'

'Yes, you look like the sure type,' the girl mocked. 'But an angel and a vampire — that's a queer combination.'

'We can reform one another,' Henderson pointed out. 'Besides, I have a suspicion that there's a bit of the devil in you. That dark cloak over your angel costume; dark angel, you know. Instead of heaven you might hail from my home town.'

Henderson was flippant, but, underneath his banter, cyclonic thoughts whirled. He recalled discussions in the past; cynical observations he had made and believed.

Once, Henderson had declared that there was no such thing as love at first sight, save in books or plays where such a dramatic device served to speed up action. He asserted that people learned about romance from books and plays and accordingly adopted a belief in love at first sight when all one could possibly feel was desire.

And now this Sheila — this blonde angel — had to come along and drive out all thoughts of morbidity, all thoughts of drunkenness and foolish gazings into mirrors, from his mind; had to send him madly plunging into dreams of red lips, ethereal blue eyes and slim white arms.

Something of his feelings had swept into his eyes, and as the girl gazed up at him she felt the truth.

'Well,' she breathed, 'I hope the inspection pleases.'

'A miracle of understatement, that. But there was something I wanted to find out particularly about divinity. Do angels dance?'

'Tactful vampire! The next room?'

Arm in arm they entered the parlour. The merry-makers were in full swing. Liquor had already pitched gaiety at its height, but there was no dancing any longer. Boisterous little grouped couples laughed arm in arm about the room. The usual party gagsters were forming their antics in corners. The superficial atmosphere, which Henderson detested, was fully in evidence.

It was reaction which made Henderson draw himself up to full height and sweep the cloak about his shoulders. Reaction brought the scowl to his pale face, caused him to stalk along in brooding silence. Sheila seemed to regard this as a great joke.

'Pull a vampire act on them,' she giggled, clutching his arm. Henderson accordingly scowled at the couples, sneered horrendously at the women. And his progress was marked by the turning of heads, the abrupt cessation of chatter. He walked through the long room like Red Death incarnate. Whispers trailed in his wake.

'Who is that man?'

'We came up with him in the elevator, and he— '

'His eyes— '

'Vampire!'

'Hello, Dracula!' It was Marcus Lindstrom and a sullen-looking brunette in Cleopatra costume who lurched towards Henderson. Host Lindstrom could scarcely stand, and his companion in cups was equally at a loss. Henderson liked the man when sober at the club, but his behaviour at parties had always irritated him. Lindstrom was particularly objectionable in his present condition — it made him boorish.

'M'dear, I want you t'meet a very dear friend of mine. Yessir, it being Halloween and all, I invited Count Dracula here, t'gether with his daughter. Asked his grandmother, but she's busy tonight at the Black Sabbath — along with Aunt Jemima. Ha! Count, meet my little playmate.'

The woman leered up at Henderson.

'Oooh Dracula, what big eyes you have! Oooh, what big teeth you have! Oooo— '

'Really, Marcus,' Henderson protested. But the host had turned and shouted to the room.

'Folks, meet the real goods — only genuine living vampire in captivity! Dracula Henderson, only existing vampire with false teeth.'

In any other circumstances Henderson would have given Lindstrom a quick, efficient punch on the jaw. But Sheila was at his side, it was a public gathering; better to humour the man's clumsy jest. Why not be a vampire?

Smiling quickly at the girl, Henderson drew himself erect, faced the crowd, and frowned. His hands brushed the cloak. Funny, it still felt cold. Looking down he noticed for the first time that it was a little dirty at the edges; muddy or dusty. But the cold silk slid through his fingers as he drew it across his breast with one long hand. The feeling seemed to inspire him. He opened his eyes wide and let them blaze. His mouth opened. A sense of dramatic power filled him. And he looked at Marcus Lindstrom's soft, fat neck with the vein standing in the whiteness. He looked at the neck, saw the crowd watching him, and then the impulse seized him. He turned, eyes on that creasy neck — that wabbling, creasy neck of the fat man.

Hands darted out. Lindstrom squeaked like a frightened rat. He was a plump, sleek white rat, bursting with blood. Vampires liked blood. Blood from the rat, from the neck of the rat, from the vein in the neck of the squeaking rat.

'Warm blood.'

The deep voice was Henderson's own.

The hands were Henderson's own.

The hands that went round Lindstrom's neck as he spoke, the hands that felt the warmth, that searched out the vein. Henderson's face was bending for the neck, and, as Lindstrom struggled, his grip tightened. Lindstrom's face was turning purple. Blood was rushing to his head. That was good. Blood!

Henderson's mouth opened. He felt the air on his teeth. He bent down towards that fat neck, and then—

'STOP! THAT'S PLENTY!'

The voice, the cooling voice of Sheila. Her fingers on his arm. Henderson looked up, startled. He released Lindstrom, who sagged with open mouth.

The crowd was staring, and their mouths were all shaped in the instinctive O of amazement.

Sheila whispered, 'Bravo! Served him right — but you frightened him!'

Henderson struggled a moment to collect himself. Then he smiled and turned.

'Ladies and gentlemen,' he said, 'I have just given a slight demonstration to prove to you what our host said of me was entirely correct. I *am* a vampire. Now that you have been given fair warning, I am sure you will be in no further danger. If there is a doctor in the house I can, perhaps, arrange for a blood transfusion.'

The O's relaxed and laughter came from startled throats. Hysterical laughter, in part, then genuine. Henderson had carried it off. Marcus Lindstrom alone still stared with eyes that held utter fear. *He* knew.

And then the moment broke, for one of the gagsters ran into the room from the elevator. He had gone downstairs and borrowed the apron and cap of a newsboy. Now he raced through the crowd with a bundle of papers under his arm.

'Extra! Extra! Read all about it. Big Halloween Horror! Extra!'

Laughing guests purchased papers. A woman approached Sheila, and Henderson watched the girl walk away in a daze.

'See you later,' she called, and her glance sent fire through his veins. Still, he could not forget the terrible feeling that came over him when he had seized Lindstrom. Why?

Automatically, he accepted a paper from the shouting, pseudo newsboy. 'Big Halloween Horror,' he had shouted. What was that?

Blurred eyes searched the paper.

Then Henderson reeled back. That headline! It was an *Extra* after all. Henderson scanned the columns with mounting dread.

'Fire in costumier's . . . shortly after 8 p.m. firemen were summoned to the shop of . . . flames beyond control . . . completely demolished . . . damage estimated at . . . peculiarly enough, name of proprietor unknown . . . skeleton found in— '

'No!' gasped Henderson aloud.

He read, re-read *that* closely. The skeleton had been found in a box of earth in the cellar beneath the shop. The box was a coffin. There had been two other boxes, empty. The skeleton had been wrapped in a cloak, undamaged by the flames—

And in the hastily penned box at the bottom of the column were eyewitness comments, written up under scareheads of heavy black type. Neighbours had feared the place. Hungarian neighbourhood, hints of vampirism, of strangers who entered the shop. One man spoke of a cult believed to have held meetings in the place. Superstition about things sold there — love philters, outlandish charms and weird disguises.

Weird disguises — vampires — cloaks — his eyes!

'This is an authentic cloak.'

'I will not be using this much longer. Keep it.'

Memories of these words screamed through Henderson's brain. He plunged out of the room and rushed to the panel mirror.

A moment, then he flung one arm before his face to shield his eyes from the image that was not there — the missing reflection. *Vampires have no reflections.*

No wonder he looked strange. No wonder arms and necks invited him. He had wanted Lindstrom. Good God!

The cloak had done that, the dark cloak with the stains. The stains of earth, grave-earth. The wearing of the cloak, the cold cloak, had given him the feeling of a true vampire. It was a garment accursed, a thing that had lain on the body of one undead. The rusty stain along one sleeve was blood.

Blood. It would be nice to see blood. To taste its warmth, its red life, flowing.

No. That was insane. He was drunk, crazy.

'Ah! My pale friend the vampire.'

It was Sheila again. And above all horror rose the beating of Henderson's heart. As he looked at her shining eyes, her warm mouth shaped in red invitation, Henderson felt a wave of warmth. He looked at her white throat rising above her dark, shimmering cloak, and another kind of warmth arose. Love, desire, and a — hunger.

SHE MUST HAVE seen it in his eyes, but she did not flinch. Instead her own gaze burned in return.

Sheila loved him, too!

With an impulsive gesture, Henderson ripped the cloak from about his throat. The icy weight lifted. He was free. Somehow, he hadn't wanted to take the cloak off, but he had to. It was a cursed thing, and in another minute he might have taken the girl in his arms, taken her for a kiss and remained to—

But he dared not think of that.

'Tired of masquerading?' she asked. With a similar gesture she, too, removed her cloak and stood revealed in the glory of her angel robe. Her blonde, statuesque perfection forced a gasp to Henderson's throat.

'Angel' he whispered.

'Devil,' she mocked.

And suddenly they were embracing. Henderson had taken her cloak in his arm with his own. They stood with lips seeking rapture until Lindstrom and a group moved noisily into the ante-room.

At the sight of Henderson the fat host recoiled.

'You— ' he whispered. 'You are— '

'Just leaving,' Henderson smiled. Grasping the girl's arm, he drew her towards the empty elevator. The door shut on Lindstrom's pale, fear-filled face.

'Were we leaving?' Sheila whispered, snuggling against his shoulder.

'We were. But not for earth. We do not go down into my realm, but up — into yours.'

'The roof garden?'

'Exactly, my angelic one. I want to talk to you against the background of your own heavens, kiss you amidst the clouds, and — '

Her lips found his as the car rose.

'Angel and devil. What a match!'

'I thought so, too,' the girl confessed. 'Will our children have halos or horns?'

'Both, I'm sure.'

They stepped out on to the deserted rooftop. And once again it was Halloween.

Henderson felt it. Downstairs it was Lindstrom and his society friends, in a drunken costume party. Here it was night, silence, gloom. No light, no music, no drinking, no chatter which made one party identical with another; one night like all the rest. This night was individual here.

The sky was not blue but black. Clouds hung like the grey beards of hovering giants peering at the round orange globe of the moon. A cold wind blew from the sea, and filled the air with tiny murmurings from afar.

It was also quite cold.

'Give me my cloak,' Sheila whispered. Automatically, Henderson extended the garment, and the girl's body swirled under the dark splendour of the cloth. Her eyes burned up at Henderson with a call he could not resist. He kissed her, trembling.

'You're cold,' the girl said. ''Put on your cloak.'

Yes, Henderson, he thought to himself. Put on your cloak while you stare at her throat. Then, the next time you kiss her you will want her throat and she will give it in love and you will take it in — hunger.

'Put it on, darling — I insist,' the girl whispered. Her eyes were impatient, burning with an eagerness to match his own.

Henderson trembled.

Put on the cloak of darkness? The cloak of the grave, the cloak of death, the cloak of the vampire? The evil cloak, filled with a cold life of its own that transformed his face, transformed his mind?

'Here.'

The girl's slim arms were about him, pushing the cloak on to his shoulders. Her fingers brushed his neck, caressingly, as she linked the cloak about his throat.

Then he felt it — through him — that icy coldness turning to a more dreadful heat. He felt himself expanded, felt the sneer across his face. This was Power!

And the girl before him, her eyes taunting, inviting. He saw her ivory neck, her warm slim neck, waiting. It was waiting for him, for his lips.

For his teeth.

No — it couldn't be. He loved her. His love must conquer this madness. Yes, wear the cloak, defy its power, and take her in his arms as a man, not as a fiend. He must. It was the test.

'Sheila, I must tell you this.'

Her eyes — so alluring. It would be easy!

'Sheila, please. You read the paper tonight.'

'Yes.'

'I . . . I got my cloak there. I can't explain it. You saw how I took Lindstrom. I wanted to go through with it. Do you understand me? I meant to . . . to bite him. Wearing this thing makes me feel like one of those creatures. But I love you, Sheila.'

'I know.' Her eyes gleamed in the moonlight.

'I want to test it. I want to kiss you, wearing this cloak. I want to feel that my love is stronger than this — thing. If I weaken, promise me you'll break away and run, quickly. But don't misunderstand. I must face this feeling and fight it; I want my love for you to be that pure, that secure. Are you afraid?'

'No.' Still she stared at him, just as he stared at her throat. If she knew what was in his mind!

'You don't think I'm crazy? I went to this costumier's — he was a horrible little old man — and he gave me the cloak. Actually told me it was a real vampire's. I thought he was joking, but tonight I didn't see myself in the mirror, and I wanted Lindstrom's neck, and I want you. But I must test it.'

The girl's face mocked. Henderson summoned his strength. He bent forward, his impulses battling. For a moment he stood there under the ghastly orange moon, and his face was twisted in struggle.

And the girl lured.

Her odd, incredibly red lips parted in a silvery, chuckly laugh as her white arms rose from the black cloak she wore to circle his neck gently. 'I know — I knew when I looked in the mirror. I knew you had a cloak like mine — got yours where I got mine — '

Queerly, her lips seemed to elude his as he stood frozen for an instant of shock. Then he felt the icy hardness of her sharp little teeth on his throat, a strangely soothing sting and an engulfing blackness rising over him.

THE PAINTED SKIN

P'U SUNG-LING

Translated by Herbert A. Giles

A T T'AI-YUAN THERE lived a man named Wang. One morning he was out walking when he met a young lady carrying a bundle and hurrying along by herself. As she moved along with some difficulty, Wang quickened his pace and caught her up, and found she was a pretty girl of about sixteen. Much smitten, he inquired whither she was going so early, and no one with her. "A traveller like you," replied the girl, "cannot alleviate my distress; why trouble yourself to ask?" "What distress is it?" said Wang; "I'm sure I'll do anything I can for you." "My parents," answered she, "loved money, and they sold me as concubine into a rich family, where the wife was very jealous, and beat and abused me morning and night. It was more than I could stand, so I have run away." Wang asked her where she was going; to which she replied that a runaway had no fixed place of abode. "My house," said Wang, "is at no great distance; what do you say to coming there?" She joyfully acquiesced; and Wang, taking up her bundle, led the way to his house. Finding no one there, she asked Wang where his family were; to which he replied that that was only the library. "And a very nice place, too," said she; "but if you are kind enough to wish to save my life, you mustn't let it be known that I am here." Wang promised he would not divulge her secret and so she remained there for some days without anyone knowing anything about it. He then told his wife, and she, fearing the girl might belong to some influential family, advised him to send her away. This, however, he would not consent to do; when one day, going into the town, he met a Taoist priest, who looked at him in astonishment, and asked him what he had met. "I have met nothing," replied Wang. "Why," said the priest, "you are bewitched; what do you mean by not having met anything?" But Wang insisted that it was so, and the priest walked away, saying, "The fool! Some people don't seem to know when death is at hand." This startled Wang, who at first thought of the girl; but then he reflected that a pretty young thing as she was couldn't

117

well be a witch, and began to suspect that the priest merely wanted to do a stroke of business. When he returned, the library door was shut, and he couldn't get in, which made him suspect that something was wrong; and so he climbed over the wall, where he found the door of the inner room shut too. Softly creeping up, he looked through the window and saw a hideous devil, with a green face and jagged teeth like a saw, spreading a human skin upon the bed and painting it with a paint brush. The devil then threw aside the brush, and giving the skin a shake out, just as you would a coat, threw it over its shoulders, when lo! it was the girl. Terrified at this, Wang hurried away with his head down in search of the priest, who had gone he knew not whither; subsequently finding him in the fields, where he threw himself on his knees and begged the priest to save him. "As to driving her away," said the priest, "the creature must be in great distress to be seeking a substitute for herself; besides, I could hardly endure to injure a living thing." However, he gave Wang a flybrush, and bade him hang it at the door of the bedroom, agreeing to meet again at the Ch'ing-ti temple. Wang went home, but did not dare enter the library; so he hung up the brush at the bedroom door, and before long heard a sound of footsteps outside. Not daring to move, he made his wife peep out; and she saw the girl standing looking at the brush, afraid to pass it. She then ground her teeth and went away; but in a little while came back, and began cursing, saying, "You priest, you won't frighten me. Do you think I am going to give up what is already in my grasp?" Thereupon she tore the brush to pieces, and bursting open the door, walked straight up to the bed, where she ripped open Wang and tore out his heart, with which she went away. Wang's wife screamed out, and the servant came in with a light; but Wang was already dead and presented a most miserable spectacle. His wife, who was in an agony of fright, hardly dared cry for fear of making a noise; and next day she sent Wang's brother to see the priest. The latter got into a great rage, and cried out, "Was it for this that I had compassion on you, devil that you are?" proceeding at once with Wang's brother to the house, from which the girl had disappeared without anyone knowing whither she had gone. But the priest, raising his head, looked all round, and said, "Luckily she's not far off." He then asked who lived in the apartments on the south side, to which Wang's brother replied that he did; whereupon the priest declared that there she would be found. Wang's brother was horribly frightened and said he did not think so; and then the priest asked him if any stranger had been to the house. To this he answered that he had been out to the Ch'ing-ti temple and couldn't possibly say: but he went off to inquire, and in a little while came back and reported that an old woman had sought service with them as a maid-of-all-work, and had been engaged by his wife, "That is she," said the priest, as Wang's brother added she was still there; and they all set out to go to the house together. Then the priest took his wooden sword, and standing in the middle of the courtyard, shouted out, "Base-born fiend, give me back my flybrush!" Meanwhile the new maid-of-all-work was in a great state of alarm, and tried to get away by the door, but the priest struck her and down she fell flat, the human skin dropped off, and she became a hideous devil.

There she lay grunting like a pig, until the priest grasped his wooden sword and struck off her head. She then became a dense column of smoke curling up from the ground, when the priest took an uncorked gourd and threw it right into the midst of the smoke. A sucking noise was heard, and the whole column was drawn into the gourd; after which the priest corked it up closely and put it in his pouch. The skin, too, which was complete even to the eye-brows, eyes, hands, and feet, he also rolled up as if it had been a scroll, and was on the point of leaving with it, when Wang's wife stopped him, and with tears entreated him to bring her husband to life. The priest said he was unable to do that; but Wang's wife flung herself at his feet, and with loud lamentations implored his assistance. For some time he remained immersed in thought, and then replied, "My power is not equal to what you ask. I myself cannot raise the dead; but I will direct you to some one who can, and if you apply to him properly you will succeed." Wang's wife asked the priest who it was; to which he replied, "There is a maniac in the town who passes his time grovelling in the dirt. Go, prostrate yourself before him and beg him to help you. If he insults you, show no sign of anger." Wang's brother knew the man to whom he alluded, and accordingly bade the priest adieu, and proceeded thither with his sister-in-law.

They found the destitute creature raving away by the roadside, so filthy that it was all they could do to go near him. Wang's wife approached him on her knees; at which the maniac leered at her, and cried out, "Do you love me my beauty?" Wang's wife told him what she had come for, but he only laughed and said, "You can get plenty of other husbands. Why raise the dead one to life?" But Wang's wife entreated him to help her; whereupon he observed, "It's very strange: people apply to me to raise their dead as if I was king of the infernal regions." He then gave Wang's wife a thrashing with his staff, which she bore without a murmur, and before a gradually increasing crowd of spectators. After this he produced a loathsome pill which he told her she must swallow, but here she broke down and was quite unable to do so. However, she did manage it at last, and then the maniac, crying out, "How you do love me!" got up and went away without taking any more notice of her. They followed him into a temple with loud supplications, but he had disappeared, and every effort to find him was unsuccessful. Overcome with rage and shame, Wang's wife went home, where she mourned bitterly over her dead husband, grievously repenting the steps she had taken, and wishing only to die. She then bethought herself of preparing the corpse, near which none of the servants would venture, and set to work to close up the frightful wound of which he died.

While thus employed, interrupted from time to time by her sobs, she felt a rising lump in her throat, which by-and-by came out with a pop and fell straight into the dead man's wound. Looking closely at it, she saw it was a human heart; and then it began as it were to throb, emitting a warm vapour like smoke. Much excited, she at once closed the flesh over it, and held the sides of the wound together with all her might. Very soon, however, she got tired, and finding the vapour escaping from the crevices, she tore up a piece of silk and bound it round, at the same time bringing back circulation by rubbing the body and covering it up with clothes. In the night she removed the coverings, and found that breath was coming from the nose; and by next morning her husband was alive again, though disturbed in mind as if awaking from a dream, and feeling a pain in his heart. Where he had been wounded there was a cicatrix about as big as a cash, which soon after disappeared.

For the Blood Is the Life

F. MARION CRAWFORD

E HAD DINED AT sunset on the broad roof of the old tower, because it was cooler there during the great heat of summer. Besides, the little kitchen was built at one corner of the great square platform, which made it more convenient than if the dishes had to be carried down the steep stone steps, broken in places and everywhere worn with age. The tower was one of those built all down the west coast of Calabria by the Emperor Charles V early in the sixteenth century, to keep off the Barbary pirates, when the unbelievers were allied with Francis I against the Emperor and the Church. They have gone to ruin, a few still stand intact, and mine is one of the largest. How it came into my possession ten years ago, and why I spend a part of each year in it, are matters which do not concern this tale. The tower stands in one of the loneliest spots in Southern Italy, at the extremity of a curving rocky promontory, which forms a small but safe natural harbour at the southern extremity of the Gulf of Policastro, and just north of Cape Scalea, the birthplace of Judas Iscariot, according to the old local legend. The tower stands alone on this hooked spur of the rock, and there is not a house to be seen within three miles of it. When I go there I take a couple of sailors, one of whom is a fair cook, and when I am away it is in the charge of a gnome-like little being who was once a miner and who attached himself to me long ago.

My friend, who sometimes visits me in my summer solitude, is an artist by profession, a Scandinavian by birth, and a cosmopolitan by force of circumstances. We had dined at sunset; the sunset glow had reddened and faded again, and the evening purple steeped the vast chain of the mountains that embrace the deep gulf to eastward and rear themselves higher and higher toward the south. It was hot, and we sat at the landward corner of the platform, waiting for the night breeze to come down from the lower hills. The colour sank out of the air, there was a little interval of deep-grey twilight, and a lamp sent a yellow streak from the open door of the kitchen,

121

where the men were getting their supper.

Then the moon rose suddenly above the crest of the promontory, flooding the platform and lighting up every little spur of rock and knoll of grass below us, down to the edge of the motionless water. My friend lighted his pipe and sat looking at a spot on the hillside. I knew that he was looking at it, and for a long time past I had wondered whether he would ever see anything there that would fix his attention. I knew that spot well. It was clear that he was interested at last, though it was a long time before he spoke. Like most painters, he trusts to his own eyesight, as a lion trusts his strength and a stag his speed, and he is always disturbed when he cannot reconcile what he sees with what he believes that he ought to see.

"It's strange," he said. "Do you see that little mound just on this side of the boulder?"

"Yes," I said, and I guessed what was coming.

"It looks like a grave," observed Holger.

"Very true. It does look like a grave."

"Yes," continued my friend, his eyes still fixed on the spot. "But the strange thing is that I see the body lying on the top of it. Of course," continued Holger, turning his head on one side as artists do, "it must be an effect of light. In the first place, it is not a grave at all. Secondly, if it were, the body would be inside and not outside. Therefore, it's an effect of the moonlight. Don't you see it?"

"Perfectly; I always see it on moonlight nights."

"It doesn't seem to interest you much," said Holger.

"On the contrary, it does interest me, though I am used to it. You're not so far wrong, either. The mound is really a grave."

"Nonsense!" cried Holger, incredulously. "I suppose you'll tell me what I see lying on it is really a corpse!"

"No," I answered, "it's not. I know, because I have taken the trouble to go down and see."

"Then what is it?" asked Holger.

"It's nothing."

"You mean that it's an effect of light, I suppose?"

"Perhaps it is. But the inexplicable part of the matter is that it makes no difference whether the moon is rising or setting, or waxing or waning. If there's any moonlight at all, from east or west or overhead, so long as it shines on the grave you can see the outline of the body on top."

Holger stirred up his pipe with the point of his knife, and then used his finger for a stopper. When the tobacco burned well he rose from his chair.

"If you don't mind," he said, "I'll go down and take a look at it."

He left me, crossed the roof, and disappeared down the dark steps. I did not move, but sat looking down until he came out of the tower below. I heard him humming an old Danish song as he crossed the open space in the bright moonlight, going straight to the mysterious mound. When he was ten paces from it, Holger stopped short, made two steps forward, and then three or four backward, and then stopped again. I know what that meant. He had reached the spot where the Thing ceased to be visible — where, as he would have said, the effect of light changed.

Then he went on till he reached the mound and stood upon it. I could see the Thing still, but it was no longer lying down; it was on its knees now, winding its white arms round Holger's body and looking up into his face. A cool breeze stirred my hair at that moment, as the night wind began to come down from the hills, but it felt like a breath from another world.

The Thing seemed to be trying to climb to its feet, helping itself up by Holger's body while he stood upright, quite unconscious of it and apparently looking toward the tower, which is very picturesque when the moonlight falls upon it on that side.

"Come along!" I shouted. "Don't stay there all night!"

It seemed to me that he moved reluctantly as he stepped from the mound, or else with difficulty. That was it. The Thing's arms were still round his waist, but its feet could not leave the grave. As he came slowly forward it was drawn and lengthened like a wreath of mist, thin and white, till I saw distinctly that Holger shook himself, as a man does who feels a chill. At the same instant a little wail of pain came to me on the breeze — it might have been the cry of the small owl that lies among the rocks — and the misty presence floated swiftly back from Holger's advancing figure and lay once more at its length upon the mound.

Again I felt the cool breeze in my hair, and this time an icy thrill of dread ran down my spine. I remembered very well that I had once gone down there alone in the moonlight; that presently, being near, I had seen nothing; that, like Holger, I had gone and had stood upon the mound; and I remembered how, when I came back, sure that there was nothing there, I had felt the sudden conviction that there was something after all if I would only look behind me. I remembered the strong temptation to look back, a temptation I had resisted as unworthy of a man of sense, until, to get rid of it, I had shaken myself just as Holger did.

And now I knew that those white, misty arms had been round me too; I knew it in a flash, and I shuddered as I remembered that I had heard the night owl then too. But it had not been the night owl. It was the cry of the Thing.

I refilled my pipe and poured out a cup of strong southern wine; in less than a minute Holger was seated beside me again.

"Of course there's nothing there," he said, "but it's creepy, all the same. Do you know, when I was coming back I was so sure that there was something behind me that I wanted to turn round and look? It was an effort not to."

He laughed a little, knocked the ashes out of his pipe, and poured himself out some wine. For a while neither of us spoke, and the moon rose higher, and we both looked at the Thing that lay on the mound.

"You might make a story about that," said Holger after a long time.

"There is one," I answered. "If you're not sleepy, I'll tell it to you."

"Go ahead," said Holger, who likes stories.

OLD ALARIO WAS dying up there in the village behind the hill. You remember him, I have no doubt. They say that he made his money by selling sham jewellery in South America, and escaped with his gains when he was found out. Like all those fellows, if they bring anything back with them, he at once set to work to enlarge his house, and as there are no masons here, he sent all the way to Paola for two workmen. They were a rough-looking pair of scoundrels — a Neapolitan who had lost one eye and a Sicilian with an old scar half an inch deep across his left cheek. I often saw them, for on Sundays they used to come down here and fish off the rocks. When Alario caught the fever that killed him the masons were still at work. As he had agreed that part of their pay should be their board and lodging, he made them sleep in the house. His wife was dead, and he had an only son called Angelo, who was a much better sort than himself. Angelo was to marry the daughter of the richest man in the village, and, strange to say, though their marriage was arranged by their parents, the young people were said to be in love with each other.

For that matter, the whole village was in love with Angelo, and among the rest a wild, good-looking creature called Cristina, who was more like a gipsy than any girl I ever saw about here. She had very red lips and very black eyes, she was built like a greyhound, and had the tongue of the devil. But Angelo did not care a straw for her. He was rather a simple-minded fellow, quite different from his old scoundrel of a father, and under what I should call normal circumstances I really believe that he would never have looked at any girl except the nice plump little creature, with a fat dowry, whom his father meant him to marry. But things turned up which were neither normal nor natural.

On the other hand, a very handsome young shepherd from the hills above Maratea was in love with Cristina, who seems to have been quite indifferent to him. Cristina had no regular means of subsistence, but she was a good girl and willing to do any work or go on errands to any distance for the sake of a loaf of bread or a mess of beans, and permission to sleep under cover. She was especially glad when she could get something to do about the house of Angelo's father. There is no doctor in the village, and when the neighbours saw that old Alario was dying they sent Cristina to Scalea to fetch one. That was late in the afternoon, and if they had waited so long, it was because the dying miser refused to allow any such extravagance while he was able to speak. But while Cristina was gone matters grew rapidly worse, the priest was brought to the bedside, and when he had done what he could he gave it as his opinion to the bystanders that the old man was dead, and left the house.

You know these people. They have a physical horror of death. Until the priest spoke, the room had been full of people The words were hardly out of his mouth before it was empty. It was night now. They hurried down the dark steps and out into the street.

Angelo, as I have said, was away, Cristina had not come back — the simple woman-servant who had nursed the sick man fled with the rest, and the body was left alone in the flickering light of the earthen oil lamp.

Five minutes later two men looked in cautiously and crept forward toward the bed. They were the one-eyed Neapolitan mason and his Sicilian companion. They knew what they wanted. In a moment they had dragged from under the bed a small but heavy iron-bound box, and long before any one thought of coming back to the dead man they had left the house and the village under cover of the darkness. It was easy enough, for Alario's house is the last toward the gorge which leads down here, and the thieves merely went out by the back door, got over the stone wall, and had nothing to risk after that except the possibility of meeting some belated countryman, which was very small indeed, since few of the people use that path. They had a mattock and shovel, and they made their way here without accident.

I am telling you this story as it must have happened, for, of course, there were no witnesses to this part of it. The men brought the box down by the gorge, intending to bury it until they should be able to come back and take it away in a boat. They must have been clever enough to guess that some of the money would be in paper notes, for they would otherwise have buried it on the beach in the wet sand, where it would have been much safer. But the paper would have rotted if they had been obliged to leave it there long, so they dug their hole down there, close to that boulder. Yes, just where the mound is now.

Cristina did not find the doctor in Scalea, for he had been sent for from a place up the valley, halfway to San Domenico. If she had found him, he would have come on his mule by the upper road, which is smoother but much longer. But Cristina took the short cut by the rocks, which passes about fifty feet above the mound, and goes round that corner. The men were digging when she passed, and she heard them at work. It would not have been like her to go by without finding out what the noise was, for she was never afraid of anything in her life, and, besides, the fishermen sometimes come ashore here at night to get a stone for an anchor or to gather sticks to make a little fire. The night was dark, and Cristina probably came close to the two men before she could see what they were doing. She knew them, of course, and they knew her, and understood instantly that they were in her power. There was only one thing to be done for their safety, and they did it. They knocked her on the head, they dug the hole deep, and they buried her quickly with the iron-bound chest. They must have understood that their only chance of escaping suspicion lay in getting back to the village before their absence was noticed, for they returned immediately, and were found half an hour later gossiping quietly with the man who was making Alario's coffin. He was a crony of theirs, and had been working at the repairs in the old man's house. So far as I have been able to make out, the only persons who were supposed to know where Alario kept his treasure were Angelo and the one woman-servant I have mentioned. Angelo was away; it was the woman who discovered the theft.

It is easy enough to understand why no one else knew where the money was. The old man kept his door locked and the key in his pocket when he was out, and did not let the woman enter to clean the place unless he was there himself. The whole village knew that he had money somewhere, however, and the masons had probably discovered the whereabouts of the chest by climbing in at the window in his absence. If the old man had not been delirious until he lost consciousness, he would have been in frightful agony of mind for his riches. The faithful woman-servant forgot their existence only for a few moments when she fled with the rest, overcome by the horror of death. Twenty minutes had not passed before she returned with the two hideous old hags who are always called in to prepare the dead for burial. Even then she had not at first the courage to go near the bed with them, but she made a pretence of dropping something, went down on her knees as if to find it, and looked under the bedstead. The walls of the room were newly whitewashed down to the floor, and she saw at a glance that the chest was gone. It had been there in the afternoon, it had therefore been stolen in the short interval since she had left the room.

There are no carabineers stationed in the village; there is not so much as a municipal watchman, for there is no municipality. There never was such a place, I believe. Scalea is supposed to look after it in some mysterious way, and it takes a couple of hours to get anybody from there. As the old woman had lived in the village all her life, it did not even occur to her to apply to any civil authority for help. She simply set up a howl and ran through the village in the dark, screaming out that her dead master's house had been robbed. Many of the people looked out, but at first no one seemed inclined to help her. Most of them, judging her by themselves, whispered to each other that she had probably stolen the money herself. The first man to move was the father of the girl Angelo was to marry; having collected his household, all of whom felt a personal interest in the wealth which was to have come into the family, he declared it to be his opinion that the chest had been stolen by the two journeyman masons who lodged in the house. He headed a search for them, which naturally began in Alario's house and ended in the carpenter's workshop, where the thieves were found discussing a measure of wine with the carpenter over the half-finished coffin, by the light of one earthen lamp filled with oil and tallow. The search party at once accused the delinquents of the crime, and threatened to lock them up in the cellar till the carabineers could be fetched from Scalea. The two men looked at each other for one moment, and then without the slightest hesitation they put out the single light, seized the unfinished coffin between them, and using it as a sort of battering ram, dashed upon their assailants in the dark. In a few moments they were beyond pursuit.

That is the end of the first part of the story. The treasure had disappeared, and as no trace of it could be found the people naturally supposed that the thieves had succeeded in carrying it off. The old man was buried, and when Angelo came back at last he had to borrow money to pay for the miserable funeral, and had some difficulty in doing so. He hardly needed to be told that in losing his inheritance he had lost his bride. In this part of the world marriages are made on strictly business principles, and if the promised cash is not forthcoming on the appointed day the bride or the bridegroom whose parents have failed to produce it may as well take themselves off, for there will be no wedding. Poor Angelo knew that well enough. His father had been possessed of hardly any land, and now that the hard cash which he had brought from South America was gone, there was nothing left but debts for the building materials that were to have been used for enlarging and improving the old house. Angelo was beggared, and the nice plump little creature who was to have been his turned up her nose at him in the most approved fashion. As for Cristina, it was several days before she was missed, for no one remembered that she had been sent to Scalea for the doctor, who had never come. She often disappeared in the same way for days together, when she could find a little work here and there at the distant farms among the hills. But when she did not come back at all, people began to wonder, and at last made up their minds that she had connived with the masons and had escaped with them.

I paused and emptied my glass.

"That sort of thing could not happen anywhere else," observed Holger, filling his everlasting pipe again. "It is wonderful what a natural charm there is about murder and sudden death in a romantic country like this. Deeds that would be simply brutal and disgusting anywhere else became dramatic and mysterious because this is Italy and we are living in a genuine tower of Charles V built against genuine Barbary pirates."

"There's something in that," I admitted. Holger is the most romantic man in the world inside of himself, but he always thinks it necessary to explain why he feels anything.

"I suppose they found the poor girl's body with the box," he said presently.

"As it seems to interest you," I answered, "I'll tell you the rest of the story."

The moon had risen high by this time, the outline of the Thing on the mound was clearer to our eyes than before.

The village very soon settled down to its small, dull life. No one missed old Alario, who had been away so much on his voyages to South America that he had never been a familiar figure in his native place. Angelo lived in the half-finished house, and because he had no money to pay the old woman-servant she would not stay with him, but once in a long time she would come and wash a shirt for him for old acquaintance's sake. Besides the house, he had inherited a small patch of ground at some distance from the village; he tried to cultivate it, but he had no heart in the work, for he knew he could never pay the taxes on it and on the house, which would certainly be confiscated by the Government, or seized for the debt of the building material, which the man who had supplied it refused to take back.

Angelo was very unhappy. So long as his father had been alive and rich, every girl in the village had been in love with him; but that was all changed now. It had been pleasant to be admired and courted, and invited to drink wine by fathers who had girls to marry. It was hard to be stared at coldly, and sometimes laughed at because he had been robbed of his inheritance.

He cooked his miserable meals for himself, and from being sad became melancholy and morose.

At twilight, when the day's work was done, instead of hanging about in the open space before the church with young fellows of his own age, he took to wandering in lonely places on the outskirts of the village till it was quite dark. Then he slunk home and went to bed to save the expense of a light. But in those lonely twilight hours he began to have strange waking dreams. He was not always alone, for often when he sat on the stump of a tree, where the narrow path turns down the gorge, he was sure that a woman came up noiselessly over the rough stones, as if her feet were bare; and she stood under a clump of chestnut trees only half a dozen yards down the path, and beckoned to him without speaking. Though she was in the shadow he knew that her lips were red, and that when they parted a little and smiled at him she showed two small sharp teeth. He knew this at first rather than saw it, and he knew that it was Cristina, and that she was dead. Yet he was not afraid; he only wondered whether it was a dream, for he thought that if he had been awake he should have been frightened.

Besides, the dead woman had red lips, and that could only happen in a dream. Whenever he went near the gorge after sunset she was already there waiting for him, or else she very soon appeared, and he began to be sure that she came a little nearer to him every day. At first he had only been sure of her blood-red mouth, but now each feature grew distinct, and the pale face looked at him with deep and hungry eyes.

It was the eyes that grew dim. Little by little he came to know that some day the dream would not end when he turned away to go home, but would lead him down the gorge out of which the vision rose. She was nearer now when she beckoned to him. Her cheeks were not livid like those of the dead, but pale with starvation, with the furious and unappeased physical hunger of her eyes that devoured him. They feasted on his soul and cast a spell over him, and at last they were close to his own and held him. He could not tell whether her breath was as hot as fire or as cold as ice; he could not tell whether her red lips burned his or froze them, or whether her five fingers on his wrist seared scorching scars or bit his flesh like frost; he could not tell whether he was awake or asleep, whether she was alive or dead, but he knew that she loved him, she alone of all creatures, earthly or unearthly, and her spell had power over him.

When the moon rose high that night the shadow of that Thing was not alone down there upon the mound.

Angelo awoke in the cool dawn, drenched with dew and chilled through flesh, and blood, and bone. He opened his eyes to the faint grey light, and saw the stars still shining overhead. He was very weak, and his heart was beating so slowly that he was almost like a man fainting. Slowly he turned his head on the mound, as on a pillow, but the other face was not there. Fear seized him suddenly, a fear unspeakable and unknown; he sprang to his feet and fled up the gorge, and he never looked behind him until he reached the door of the house on the outskirts of the village. Drearily he went to his work that day, and wearily the hours dragged themselves after the sun, till at last it touched the sea and sank, and the great sharp hills above Maratea turned purple against the dove-coloured eastern sky.

Angelo shouldered his heavy hoe and left the field. He felt less tired now than in the morning when he had begun to work, but he promised himself that he would go home without lingering by the gorge, and eat the best supper he could get himself, and sleep all night in his bed like a Christian man. Not again would he be tempted down the narrow way by a shadow with red lips and icy breath; not again would he dream that dream of terror and delight. He was near the village now; it was half an hour since the sun had set, and the cracked church bell sent little discordant echoes across the rocks and ravines to tell all good people that the day was done. Angelo stood still a moment where the path forked, where it led toward the village on the left and down to the gorge on the right, where a clump of chestnut trees overhung the narrow way. He stood still a minute, lifting his battered hat from his head and gazing at the fast-fading sea westward, and his lips moved as he silently repeated the familiar evening prayer. His lips moved, but the words that followed them in his brain lost their meaning and turned into others, and ended in a name that he spoke aloud — Cristina! With the name, the tension of his will relaxed suddenly, reality went out and the dream took him again, and bore him on swiftly and surely like a man walking in his sleep, down, down, by the steep path in the gathering darkness. And as she glided beside him, Cristina whispered strange, sweet things in his ear, which somehow, if he had been awake, he knew that he could not quite have understood; but now they were the most wonderful words he had ever heard in his life. And she kissed him also, but not upon his mouth. He felt her sharp kisses upon his white throat, and he knew that her lips were red. So the wild dream sped on through twilight and darkness and moonrise, and all the glory of the summer's night. But in the chilly dawn he lay as one half dead upon the mound down there, recalling and not recalling, drained of his blood, yet strangely longing to give those red lips more. Then came the fear, the awful nameless panic, the mortal horror that guards the confines of the world we see not, neither know of as we know of other things, but which we feel when its icy chill freezes our bones and stirs our hair with the touch of a ghostly hand. Once more Angelo sprang from the mound and fled up the gorge in the breaking day, but his step was less sure this time, and he panted for breath as he ran; and when he came to the bright spring of water that rises halfway up the hillside, he dropped upon his knees and hands and plunged his whole face in and drank as he had never drunk before — for it was the thirst of the wounded man who has lain bleeding all night long upon the battle-field.

She had him fast now, and he could not escape her, but would come to her every evening at dusk until she had drained him of his last drop of blood. It was in vain that when the day was done he tried to take another turning and to go home by a path that did not lead near the gorge. It was in vain that he made promises to himself each morning at dawn when he climbed the lonely way up from the shore to the village. It was all in vain, for when the sun sank burning into the sea, and the coolness of the evening stole out as from a hiding-place to delight the weary world, his feet turned toward the old way, and she was waiting for him in the shadow under the chestnut trees; and then all happened as before, and she fell to kissing his white throat even as she flitted lightly down the way, winding one arm about him. And as his blood failed, she grew more hungry and more thirsty every day, and every day when he awoke in the early dawn it was harder to rouse himself to the effort of climbing the steep path to the village; and when he went to his work his feet dragged painfully, and there was hardly strength in his arms to wield the heavy hoe. He scarcely spoke to any one now, but the people said he was "consuming himself" for love of the girl he was to have married when he lost his inheritance; and they laughed heartily at the thought, for this is not a very romantic country. At this time, Antonio, the man who stays here to look after the tower, returned from a visit to his people, who live near Salerno. He had been away all the time since before Alario's death and knew nothing of what had happened. He has told me that he came back late in the afternoon and shut himself up in the tower to eat and sleep, for he was very tired. It was past midnight when he awoke, and when he looked out the waning moon was rising over the shoulder of the hill. He looked out toward the mound, and he saw something, and he did not sleep again that night. When he went out again in the morning it was broad daylight, and there was nothing to be seen on the mound but loose stones and driven sand. Yet he did not go very near it; he went straight up the path to the village and directly to the house of the old priest.

"I have seen an evil thing this night," he said; "I have seen how the dead drink the blood of the living. And the blood is the life."

"Tell me what you have seen," said the priest in reply.

Antonio told him everything he had seen.

"You must bring your book and your holy water tonight," he added. "I will be here before sunset to go down with you, and if it pleases your reverence to sup with me while we wait, I will make ready."

"I will come," the priest answered, "for I have read in old books of these strange beings which are neither quick nor dead, and which lie ever fresh in their graves, stealing out in the dusk to taste life and blood."

Antonio cannot read, but he was glad to see that the priest understood the business; for, of course, the books must have instructed him as to the best means of quieting the half-living Thing for ever.

So Antonio went away to his work, which consists largely in sitting on the shady side of the tower, when he is not perched upon a rock with a fishing-line catching nothing. But on that day he went twice to look at the mound in the bright sunlight, and he searched round and round it for some hole through which the being might get in and out; but he found none. When the sun began to sink and the air was cooler in the shadows, he went up to fetch the old priest, carrying a little wicker basket with him; and in this they placed a bottle of holy water, and the basin, and sprinkler, and the stole which the priest would need; and they came down and waited in the door of the tower till it should be dark. But while the light still lingered very grey and faint, they saw something moving, just there, two figures, a man's that walked, and a woman's that flitted beside him, and while her head lay on his shoulder she kissed his throat. The priest has told me that, too, and that his teeth chattered and he grasped Antonio's arm. The vision passed and disappeared into the shadow. Then Antonio got the leathern flask of strong liquor, which he kept for great occasions, and poured such a draught as made the old man feel almost young again; and he got the lantern, and his pick and shovel, and gave the priest his stole to put on and the holy water to carry, and they went out together toward the spot where the work was to be done. Antonio says that in spite of the rum his own knees shook together, and the priest stumbled over his Latin. For when they were yet a few yards from the mound the flickering light of the lantern upon Angelo's white face, unconscious as if in sleep, and on his upturned throat, over which a very thin red line of blood trickled down into his collar; and the flickering light of the lantern played upon another face that looked up from the feast — upon two deep, dead eyes that saw in spite of death — upon parted lips redder than life itself — upon two gleaming teeth on which glistened a rosy drop. Then the priest, good old man, shut his eyes tight and showered holy water before him, and his cracked voice rose almost to a scream; and then Antonio, who is no coward after all, raised his pick in one hand and the lantern in the other, as he sprang forward, not knowing what the end should be; and then he swears that he heard a woman's cry, and the Thing was gone, and Angelo lay alone on the mound unconscious, with the red line on his throat and the beads of deathly sweat on his cold forehead. They lifted him, half-dead as he was, and laid him on the ground close by; and then Antonio went to work, and the priest helped him, though he was old and could not do much; and they dug deep, and at last Antonio, standing in the grave, stooped down with his lantern to see what he might see.

His hair used to be dark brown, with grizzled streaks about the temples; in less than a month from that day he was as grey as a badger. He was a miner when he was young, and most of these fellows have seen ugly sights now and then, when accidents have happened, but he had never seen what he saw that night — that Thing which is neither alive nor dead, that Thing that will abide neither above ground nor in the grave. Antonio had brought something with him which the priest had not noticed. He had made it that afternoon — a sharp stake shaped from a piece of tough old driftwood. He had it with him now, and he had his heavy pick, and he had taken the lantern down into the grave. I don't think any power on earth could make him speak of what happened then, and the old priest was too frightened to look in. He says he heard Antonio breathing like a wild beast, and moving as if he were fighting with something almost as strong as himself; and he heard an evil sound also, with blows, as of something violently driven through flesh and bone; and then the most awful sound of all — a woman's shriek, the unearthly scream of a woman neither dead nor alive, but buried deep for many days. He, the poor old priest, could only rock himself as he knelt there in the sand, crying aloud his prayers and exorcisms to drown these dreadful sounds. Then suddenly a small iron-bound chest was thrown up and rolled over against the old man's knee, and in a moment Antonio was beside him, his face as white as tallow in the flickering light of the lantern, shovelling the sand and pebbles into the grave with furious haste, and looking over the edge till the pit was half full; and the priest said that there was much fresh blood on Antonio's hands and on his clothes.

I HAD COME to the end of my story. Holger finished his wine and leaned back in his chair.

"So Angelo got his own again," he said. "Did he marry the prim and plump young person to whom he had been betrothed?"

"No; he had been badly frightened. He went to South America, and has not been heard of since."

"And that poor thing's body is there still, I suppose," said Holger. "Is it quite dead yet, I wonder?"

I wonder, too. But whether it be dead or alive, I should hardly care to see it, even in broad daylight. Antonio is as grey as a badger, and he has never been quite the same man since that night.

SCHALKEN THE PAINTER

JOSEPH SHERIDAN LE FANU

HERE EXISTS, AT this moment, in good preservation a remarkable work of Schalken's. The curious management of its lights constitutes, as usual in his pieces, the chief apparent merit of the picture. I say *apparent,* for in its subject, and not in its handling, however exquisite, consists its real value. The picture represents the interior of what might be a chamber in some antique religious building; and its foreground is occupied by a female figure, in a species of white robe, part of which is arranged so as to form a veil. The dress, however, is not that of any religious order. In her hand the figure bears a lamp, by which alone her figure and face are illuminated; and her features wear such an arch smile, as well becomes a pretty woman when practising some prankish roguery; in the background, and, excepting where the dim red light of an expiring fire serves to define the form, in total shadow, stands the figure of a man dressed in the old Flemish fashion, in an attitude of alarm, his hand being placed upon the hilt of his sword, which he appears to be in the act of drawing.

There are some pictures, which impress one, I know not how, with a conviction that they represent not the mere ideal shapes and combinations which have floated through the imagination of the artist, but scenes, faces, and situations which have actually existed. There is in that strange picture, something that stamps it as the representation of a reality.

And such in truth it is, for it faithfully records a remarkable and mysterious occurrence, and perpetuates, in the face of the female figure, which occupies the most prominent place in the design, an accurate portrait of Rose Velderkaust, the niece of Gerard Douw, the first, and, I believe, the only love of Godfrey Schalken. My great grandfather knew the painter well; and from Schalken himself he learned the fearful story of the painting, and from him too he ultimately received the picture itself as a bequest. The story and the picture have become heir-looms in my family, and having described the latter, I shall, if you please, attempt to relate the tradition which has descended with the canvass.

There are few forms on which the mantle of romance hangs more ungracefully than upon that of the uncouth Schalken — the boorish but most cunning worker in oils, whose pieces delight the critics of our day almost as much as his manners disgusted the refined of his own; and yet this man, so rude, so dogged, so slovenly, in the midst of his celebrity, had in his obscure, but happier days, played the hero in a wild romance of mystery and passion.

When Schalken studied under the immortal Gerard Douw, he was a very young man; and in spite of his phlegmatic temperament, he once fell over head and ears in love with the beautiful niece of his wealthy master. Rose Velderkaust was still younger than he, having not yet attained her seventeenth year, and, if tradition speaks truth, possessed all the soft and dimpling charms of the fair, light-haired Flemish maidens. The young painter loved honestly and fervently. His frank adoration was rewarded. He declared his love, and extracted a faltering confession in return. He was the happiest and proudest painter in all Christendom. But there was somewhat to dash his elation; he was poor and undistinguished. He dared not ask old Gerard for the hand of his sweet ward. He must first win a reputation and a competence.

There were, therefore, many dread uncertainties and cold days before him; he had to fight his way against sore odds. But he had won the heart of dear Rose Velderkaust, and that was half the battle. It is needless to say his exertions were redoubled, and his lasting celebrity proves that his industry was not unrewarded by success.

These ardent labours, and worse still, the hopes that elevated and beguiled them, were however, destined to experience a sudden interruption — of a character so strange and mysterious as to baffle all inquiry and to throw over the events themselves a shadow of preternatural horror.

Schalken had one evening outstayed all his fellow-pupils, and still pursued his work in the deserted room. As the daylight was fast failing, he laid aside his colours, and applied himself to the completion of a sketch on which he had expressed extraordinary pains. It was a religious composition, and represented the temptations of a pot-bellied Saint Anthony. The young artist, however destitute of elevation, had, nevertheless, discernment enough to be dissatisfied with his own work, and many were the patient erasures and improvements which saint and devil underwent, yet all in vain. The large, old-fashioned room was silent, and, with the exception of himself, quite emptied of its usual inmates. An hour had thus passed away, nearly two, without any improved result. Daylight had already declined, and twilight was deepening into the darkness of night. The patience of the young painter was exhausted, and he stood before his unfinished production, angry and mortified, one hand buried in the folds of his long hair, and the other holding the piece of charcoal which had so

ill-performed its office, and which he now rubbed, without much regard to the sable streaks it produced, with irritable pressure upon his ample Flemish inexpressibles. "Curse the subject!" said the young man aloud; "curse the picture, the devils, the saint— "

At this moment a short, sudden sniff uttered close beside him, made the artist turn sharply round, and he now, for the first time, became aware that his labours had been overlooked by a stranger. Within about a yard and half, and rather behind him, there stood the figure of an elderly man in a cloak and broad-brimmed, conical hat; in his hand, which was protected with a heavy gauntlet-shaped glove, he carried a long ebony walking-stick, surmounted with what appeared, as it glittered dimly in the twilight, to be a massive head of gold, and upon his breast, through the folds of the cloak, there shone the links of a rich chain of the same metal. The room was so obscure that nothing further of the appearance of the figure could be ascertained, and his hat threw his features into profound shadow. It would not have been easy to conjecture the age of the intruder; but a quantity of dark haired escaping from beneath this sombre hat, as well as his firm and upright carriage served to indicate that his years could not yet exceed threescore, or thereabouts. There was an air of gravity and importance about the garb of this person, and something indescribably odd, I might say awful, in the perfect, stone-like stillness of the figure, that effectually checked the testy comment which had at once risen to the lips of the irritated artist. He, therefore, as soon as he had sufficiently recovered his surprise, asked the stranger, civilly, to be seated, and desired to know if he had any message to leave for his master.

"Tell Gerard Douw," said the unknown, without altering his attitude in the smallest degree, "that Minheer Vanderhausen, of Rotterdam, desires to speak with him on tomorrow evening at this hour, and if he please, in this room, upon matters of weight; that is all."

The stranger, having finished this message, turned abruptly, and, with a quick, but silent step quitted the room, before Schalken had time to say a word in reply. The young man felt a curiosity to see in what direction the burgher of Rotterdam would turn, on quitting the *studio,* and for that purpose he went directly to the window which commanded the door. A lobby of considerable extent intervened between the inner door of the painter's room and the street entrance, so that Schalken occupied the post of observation before the old man could possibly have reached the street. He watched in vain, however, There was no other mode of exit. Had the queer old man vanished, or was he lurking about the recesses of the lobby for some sinister purpose? This last suggestion filled the mind of Schalken with a vague uneasiness, which was so unaccountably intense as to make him alike afraid to remain in the room alone, and reluctant to pass through the lobby. However, with an effort which appeared very disproportioned to the occasion, he summoned resolution to leave the room, and, having locked the door and thrust the key in his pocket, without looking to the right or left, he traversed the passage which had so recently, perhaps still, contained the person of his mysterious visitant, scarcely venturing to breathe till he had arrived in the open street.

"Minheer Vanderhausen!" said Gerard Douw within himself, as the appointed hour approached, "Minheer Vanderhausen, of Rotterdam! I never heard of the man till yesterday. What can he want of me? A portrait, perhaps, to be painted; or a poor relation to be apprenticed; or a collection to be valued; or — pshaw! there's no one in Rotterdam to leave me a legacy. Well, whatever the business may be, we shall soon know it all."

It was now the close of day, and again every easel, except that of Schalken, was deserted. Gerard Douw was pacing the apartment with the restless step of impatient expectation, sometimes pausing to glance over the work of one of his absent pupils, but more frequently placing himself at the window, from whence he might observe the passengers who threaded the obscure by-street in which his studio was placed.

"Said you not, Godfrey," exclaimed Douw, after a long and fruitful gaze from his post of observation, and turning to Schalken, "that the hour he appointed was about seven by the clock of the Stadhouse?"

"It had just told seven when I first saw him, sir," answered the student.

"The hour is close at hand, then," said the master, consulting a horologe as large and as round as an orange. "Minheer Vanderhausen from Rotterdam — is it not so?"

"Such was the name."

"And an elderly man, richly clad?" pursued Douw, musingly.

"As well as I might see," replied his pupil; "he could not be young, nor yet very old, neither; and his dress was rich and grave, as might become a citizen of wealth and consideration."

At this moment the sonorous boom of the Stadhouse clock told, stroke after stroke, the hour of seven; the eyes of both master and student were directed to the door; and it was not until the last peal of the old bell had ceased to vibrate, that Douw exclaimed—

"So, so; we shall have his worship presently, that is, if he means to keep his hour; if not, you may wait for him, Godfrey, if you court his acquaintance. But what, after all, if it should prove but a mummery got up by Vankarp, or some such wag? I wish you had run all risks, and cudgelled the old burgomaster soundly. I'd wager a dozen of Rhenish, his worship would have unmasked, and pleaded old acquaintance in a trice."

"Here he comes, sir," said Schalken, in a low monitory tone; and instantly, upon turning towards the door, Gerard Douw observed the same figure which had, on the day before, so unexpectedly greeted his pupil Schalken.

There was something in the air of the figure which at once satisfied the painter that there was no masquerading in the case, and that he really stood in the presence of a man of worship; and so, without hesitation, he doffed his cap, and courteously saluting the stranger, requested him to be seated.

The visitor waved his hand slightly, as if in acknowledgement of the courtesy, but remained standing.

"I have the honour to see Minheer Vanderhausen of Rotterdam?" said Gerard Douw.

"The same," was the laconic reply of his visitor.

"I understand your worship desires to speak with me," continued Douw, "and I am here by appointment to wait your commands."

"Is that a man of trust?" said Vanderhausen, turning towards Schalken, who stood at a little distance behind his master.

"Certainly," replied Gerard.

"Then let him take this box, and get the nearest jeweller or goldsmith to value its contents, and let him return hither with a certificate of the valuation."

At the same time, he placed a small case about nine inches square in the hands of Gerard Douw, who was as much amazed at its weight as at the strange abruptness with which it was handed to him. In accordance with the wishes of the stranger, he delivered it into the hands of Schalken, and repeating his directions, despatched him upon the mission.

Schalken disposed his precious charge securely beneath the folds of his cloak, and rapidly traversing two or three narrow streets, he stopped at a corner house, the lower part of which was then occupied by the shop of a Jewish goldsmith. He entered the shop, and calling the little Hebrew into the obscurity of its back recesses, he proceeded to lay before him Vanderhausen's casket. On being examined by the light of a lamp, it appeared entirely cased with lead, the outer surface of which was much scraped and soiled, and nearly white with age. This having been partially removed, there appeared beneath a box of some hard wood; which also they forced open and after the removal of two or three folds of linen, they discovered its contents to be a mass of golden ingots, closely packed, and, as the Jew declared, of the most perfect quality. Every ingot underwent the scrutiny of the little Jew, who seemed to feel an epicurean delight in touching and testing these morsels of the glorious metal; and each one of them was replaced in its berth with the exclamation: "*Meinn Gott*, how very perfect! not one grain of alloy — beautiful, beautiful!" The task was at length finished, and the Jew certified under his hand the value of the ingots submitted to his examination, to amount to many thousand rix-dollars. With the desired document in his pocket, and the rich box of gold carefully pressed under his arm, and concealed by his cloak, he retraced his way, and entering the studio, found his master and the stranger in close conference. Schalken had no sooner left the room, in order to execute the commission he had taken in charge, than Vanderhausen addressed Gerard Douw in the following terms:—

"I cannot tarry with you to-night more than a few minutes, and so I shall shortly tell you the matter upon which I come. You visited the town of Rotterdam some four months ago, and then I saw in the church of St.

Lawrence your niece, Rose Velderkaust. I desire to marry her; and if I satisfy you that I am wealthier than any husband you can dream of for her, I expect that you will forward my suit with your authority. If you approve my proposal, you must close with it here and now, for I cannot wait for calculations and delays.''

Gerald Douw was hugely astonished by the nature of Minheer Vanderhausen's communication, but he did not venture to express surprise; for besides the motives supplied by prudence and politeness, the painter experienced a kind of chill and oppression like that which is said to intervene when one is placed in unconscious proximity with the object of a natural antipathy — an undefined but overpowering sensation, while standing in the presence of the eccentric stranger, which made him very unwilling to say anything which might reasonably offend him.

"I have no doubt," said Gerard, after two or three prefatory hems, "that the alliance which you propose would prove alike advantageous and honourable to my niece; but you must be aware that she has a will of her own, and may not acquiesce in what *we* may design for her advantage."

"Do not seek to deceive me, sir painter," said Vanderhausen; "you are her guardian — she is your ward — she is mine if *you* like to make her so."

The man of Rotterdam moved forward a little as he spoke, and Gerard Douw, he scarce knew why, inwardly prayed for the speedy return of Schalken.

"I desire," said the mysterious gentleman, "to place in your hands at once an evidence of my wealth, and a security for my liberal dealing with your niece. The lad will return in a minute or two with a sum in value five times the fortune which she has a right to expect from her husband. This shall lie in your hands, together with her dowry, and you may apply the united sum as suits her interest best; it shall be all exclusively hers while she lives: is that liberal?"

Douw assented, and inwardly acknowledged that fortune had been extraordinarily kind to his niece; the stranger, he thought, must be both wealthy and generous, and such an offer was not to be despised, though made by a humourist, and one of no very prepossessing presence. Rose had no very high pretensions, for she had but a modest dowry, which she owed entirely to the generosity of her uncle; neither had she any right to raise exceptions on the score of birth, for her own origin was far from splendid, and as to other objections, Gerard resolved, and, indeed, by the usages of the time, was warranted in resolving, not to listen to them for a moment.

"Sir," said he, addressing the stranger, "your offer is liberal, and whatever hesitation I may feel in closing with it immediately, arises solely from my not having the honour of knowing anything of your family or station. Upon these points you can, of course, satisfy me without difficulty?"

"As to my respectability," said the stranger, drily, "you must take that for granted at present; pester me with no inquiries; you can discover nothing more about me than I choose to make known. You shall have sufficient security for my respectability — my word, if you are honourable: if you are sordid, my gold.''

"A testy old gentleman," thought Douw, "he must have his own way; but, all things considered, I am not justified in declining his offer. I will not pledge myself unnecessarily, however.''

"You will not pledge yourself unnecessarily," said Vanderhausen, strangely uttering the very words which had just floated through the mind of his companion; "but you will do so if it *is* necessary, I presume; and I will show you that I consider it indispensable. If the gold I mean to leave in your hands satisfy you, and if you don't wish my proposal to be at once withdrawn, you must, before I leave this room, write your name to this engagement.''

Having thus spoken, he placed a paper in the hands of the master, the contents of which expressed an engagement entered into by Gerard Douw, to give to Wilken Vanderhausen of Rotterdam, in marriage, Rose Velderkaust, and soforth, within one week of the date thereof. While the painter was employed in reading this covenant, by the light of a twinkling oil lamp in the far wall of the room, Schalken, as we have stated, entered the studio, and having delivered the box and the valuation of the Jew, into the hands of the stranger, he was about to retire, when Vanderhausen called to him to wait; and, presenting the case and the certificate to Gerard Douw, he paused in the silence until he had satisfied himself, by an inspection of both, respecting the value of the pledge left in his hands. At length he said—

"Are you content?''

The painter said he would fain have another day to consider.

"Not an hour," said the suitor, apathetically.

"Well then," said Douw, with a sore effort, "I *am* content, it is a bargain.''

"Then sign at once," said Vanderhausen, "for I am weary.''

At the same time he produced a small case of writing materials, and Gerard signed the important document.

"Let this youth witness the covenant," said the old man; and Godfrey Schalken unconsciously attested the instrument which for ever bereft him of his dear Rose Velderkaust.

The compact being thus completed, the strange visitor folded up the paper, and stowed it safely in an inner pocket.

"I will visit you to-morrow night at nine o'clock, at your own house, Gerard Douw, and will see the object of our contract;" and so saying Wilken Vanderhausen moved stiffly, but rapidly, out of the room.

Schalken, eager to resolve his doubts, had placed himself by the window, in order to watch the street entrance; but the experiment served only to support his suspicions, for the old man did not issue from the door. This was *very* strange, odd, nay fearful. He and his master returned together, and talked but little on the way, for each had his own subjects of reflection, of anxiety, and of hope. Schalken, however, did not know the ruin which menaced his dearest projects.

Gerard Douw knew nothing of the attachment which had sprung up between his pupil and his niece; and even if he had, it is doubtful whether he would have regarded its existence as any serious obstruction to the wishes of Minheer Vanderhausen. Marriages were then and there matters of traffic and calculation; and it would have appeared as absurd in the eyes of the guardian to make a mutual attachment an essential element in a contract of the sort, as it would have been to draw up his bonds and receipts in the language of romance.

The painter, however, did not communicate to his niece the important step which he had taken in her behalf, a forbearance caused not by any anticipated opposition on her part, but solely by a ludicrous consciousness that if she were to ask him for a description of her destined bridegroom, he would be forced to confess that he had not once seen his face, and if called upon, would find it absolutely impossible to identify him. Upon the next day, Gerard Douw, after dinner, called his niece to him and having scanned her person with an air of satisfaction, he took her hand, and looking upon her pretty innocent face with a smile of kindness, he said:—

"Rose, my girl, that face of yours will make your fortune." Rose blushed and smiled. "Such faces and such tempers seldom go together, and when they do, the compound is a love charm, few heads or hearts can resist; trust me, you will soon be a bride, girl. But this is trifling, and I am pressed for time, so make ready the large room by eight o'clock to-night, and give directions for supper at nine. I expect a friend; and observe me, child, do you trick yourself out handsomely. I will not have him think us poor or sluttish."

With these words he left her, and took his way to the room in which his pupils worked.

When the evening closed in, Gerard called Schalken, who was about to take his departure to his own obscure and comfortable lodgings, and asked him to come home and sup with Rose and Vanderhausen. The invitation was, of course, accepted and Gerard Douw and his pupil soon found themselves in the handsome and, even then, antique chamber, which had been prepared for the reception of the stranger. A cheerful wood fire blazed in the hearth, a little at one side of which an old-fashioned table, which shone in the fire-light like burnished gold, was awaiting the supper, for which preparations were going forward; and ranged with exact regularity, stood the tall-backed chairs, whose ungracefulness was more than compensated by their comfort. The little party, consisting of Rose, her uncle, and the artist, awaited the arrival of the expected visitor with considerable impatience. Nine o'clock at length came, and with it a summons at the street door, which being speedily answered, was followed by a slow and emphatic tread upon the staircase; the steps moved heavily across the lobby, the door of the room in which the party we have described were assembled slowly opened, and there entered a figure which startled, almost appalled, the phlegmatic Dutchmen, and nearly made Rose scream with terror. It was the form, and arrayed in the garb of Minheer Vanderhausen; the air, the gait, the height were the same, but the features had never been seen by any of the party before. The stranger stopped at the door of the room, and displayed his form and face completely. He wore a dark-coloured cloth cloak, which was short and full, not falling quite to his knees; his legs were cased in dark purple silk stockings, and his shoes were adorned with roses of the same colour. The opening of the cloak in front showed the under-suit to consist of some very dark, perhaps sable material, and his hands were enclosed in a pair of heavy leather gloves, which ran up considerably above the wrist, in the manner of a gauntlet. In one hand he carried his walking-stick and his hat, which he had removed, and the other hung heavily by his side. A quantity of grizzled hair descended in long tresses from his head, and rested upon the plaits of a stiff ruff, which effectually concealed his neck. So far all was well; but the face! — all the flesh of the face was coloured with the bluish leaden hue, which is sometimes produced by metallic medicines, administered in excessive quantities; the eyes showed an undue proportion of muddy white, and had a certain indefinable character of insanity; the hue of the lips bearing the usual relation to that of the face, was, consequently, nearly black; and the entire character of the face was sensual, malignant, and even satanic. It was remarkable that the worshipful stranger suffered as little as possible of his flesh to appear, and that during his visit he did not once remove his gloves. Having stood for some moments at the door, Gerard Douw at length found breath and collectedness to bid him welcome, and with a mute inclination of the head, the stranger stepped forward into the room. There was something indescribably odd, even horrible, about all his motions, something undefinable, that was unnatural, unhuman; it was as if the limbs were guided and directed by a spirit unused to the management of bodily machinery. The stranger spoke hardly at all during his visit, which did not exceed half an hour; and the host himself could scarcely muster courage enough to utter the few necessary salutations and courtesies; and, indeed, such was the nervous terror which the presence of Vanderhausen inspired, that very little would have made all his entertainers fly in downright panic from the room. They had not so far lost all self-possession, however, as to fail to observe two strange peculiarities of their visitor. During his stay his eyelids did not once close, or, indeed, move in the slightest degree; and farther, there was a death-like stillness in his whole person, owing to the absence of the heaving motion of the chest, caused by the process of respiration. These two peculiarities, though when told they may appear trifling, produced a very striking and unpleasant effect when seen and observed. Vanderhausen at length relieved the painter of Leyden of his inauspicious presence; and with no trifling sense of relief the little party heard the street door close after him.

"Dear uncle," said Rose, "what a frightful man! I would not see him again for the wealth of the States."

"Tush, foolish girl," said Douw, whose sensations were anything but comfortable. "A man may be as ugly as the devil, and yet, if his heart and actions are good, he is worth all the pretty-faced perfumed puppies that walk the Mall. Rose, my girl, it is very true he has not thy pretty face, but I know him to be wealthy and liberal; and were he ten times more ugly, these two virtues would be enough to counter balance all his deformity, and if not sufficient actually to alter the shape and hue of his features, at least enough to prevent one thinking them so much amiss."

"Do you know, uncle," said Rose, "when I saw him standing at the door, I could not get it out of my head that I saw the old painted wooden figure that used to frighten me so much in the Church of St. Lawrence at Rotterdam."

Gerard laughed, though he could not help inwardly acknowledging the justness of the comparison. He was resolved, however, as far as he could, to check his niece's disposition to dilate upon the ugliness of her intended bridegroom, although he was not a little pleased, as well as puzzled, to observe that she appeared totally exempt from that mysterious dread of the stranger which, he could not disguise it from himself, considerably affected him, as also his pupil Godfrey Schalken.

Early on the next day there arrived, from various quarters of the town, rich presents of silks, velvets, jewellery, and soforth, for Rose; and also a packet directed to Gerard Douw, which on being opened, was found to contain a contract of marriage, formally drawn up, between Wilken Vanderhausen of the *Boom-quay,* in Rotterdam, and Rose Velderkaust of Leyden, niece to Gerard Douw, master in the art of painting, also of the same city; and containing engagements on the part of Vanderhausen to make settlements upon his bride, far more splendid than he had before led her guardian to believe likely, and which were to be secured to her use in the most unexceptionable manner possible — the money being placed in the hand of Gerard Douw himself.

I have no sentimental scenes to describe, no cruelty of guardians, no magnanimity of wards, no agonies, or transport of lovers. The record I have to make is one of sordidness, levity, and heartlessness. In less than a week after the first interview which we have just described, the contract of marriage was fulfilled, and Schalken saw the prize which he would have risked existence to secure, carried off in solemn pomp by his repulsive rival. For two or three days he absented himself from the school; he then returned and worked, if with less cheerfulness, with far more dogged resolution than before; the stimulus of love had given place to that of ambition. Months passed away, and, contrary to his expectation, and, indeed, to the direct promise of the parties, Gerard Douw heard nothing of his niece or her worshipful spouse. The interest of the money, which was to have been demanded in quarterly sums, lay unclaimed in his hands.

He began to grow extremely uneasy. Minheer Vanderhausen's direction in Rotterdam he was fully possessed of; after some irresolution he finally determined to journey thither — a trifling undertaking, and easily accomplished — and thus to satisfy himself of the safety and comfort of his ward, for whom he entertained an honest and strong affection. His search was in vain, however; no one in Rotterdam had ever heard of Minheer Vanderhausen. Gerard Douw left not a house in the Boom-quay untried, but all in vain. No one could give him any information whatever touching the object of his inquiry, and he was obliged to return to Leyden nothing wiser and far more anxious, than when he had left it.

On his arrival he hastened to the establishment from which Vanderhausen had hired the lumbering, though, considering the times, most luxurious vehicle, which the bridal party had employed to convey them to Rotterdam. From the driver of this machine he learned that having proceeded by slow stages, they had late in the evening approached Rotterdam; but that before they entered the city, and while yet nearly a mile from it, a small party of men, soberly clad, and after the old fashion, with peaked beards and moustaches, standing in the centre of the road, obstructed the further progress of the carriage. The driver reined in his horses, much fearing, from the obscurity of the hour, and the loneliness of the road, that some mischief was intended. His fears were, however, somewhat allayed by his observing that these strange men carried a large litter, of an antique shape, and which they immediately set down upon the pavement, whereupon the bridegroom, having opened the coach-door from within, descended, and having assisted his bride to do likewise, led her, weeping bitterly and wringing her hands, to the litter, which they both entered. It was then raised by the men who surrounded it, and speedily carried towards the city, and before it had proceeded very far, the darkness concealed it from the view of the Dutch coachman. In the inside of the vehicle he found a purse, whose contents more than thrice paid the hire of the carriage and man. He saw and could tell nothing more of Minheer Vanderhausen and his beautiful lady.

This mystery was a source of profound anxiety and even of grief to Gerard Douw. There was evidently fraud in the dealing with Vanderhausen with him, though what purpose committed he could not imagine. He greatly doubted how far it was possible for a man possessing such a countenance to be anything but a villain, and every day that passed without his hearing from or of his niece, instead of inducing him to forget his fears, on the contrary tended more and more to aggravate them. The loss of her cheerful society tended also to depress his spirits; and in order to dispel the gloom, which often crept upon his mind after his daily occupations were over, he was wont frequently to ask Schalken to accompany him home, and share his otherwise solitary supper.

One evening, the painter and his pupil were sitting by the fire, having accomplished a comfortable meal, and had yielded to the silent and delicious melancholy of digestion, when their ruminations were disturbed by a loud sound at the street door, as if occasioned by some person rushing and scrambling vehemently against it. A domestic had run without delay to ascertain the cause of the disturbance, and they heard him twice or thrice interrogate the applicant for admission, but without eliciting any other answer but a sustained reiteration of the sounds. They heard him then open the hall-door, and immediately there followed a light and rapid tread upon the staircase. Schalken advanced towards the door. It opened before he reached it, and Rose rushed into the room. She looked wild, fierce and haggard with terror and exhaustion, but her dress surprised them as much as even her unexpected appearance. It consisted of a kind of white woollen wrapper, made close about the neck, and descending to the very ground. It was much deranged and travel-soiled. The poor creature had hardly entered the chamber when she fell senseless on the floor. With some difficulty they succeeded in reviving her, and on recovering her senses, she instantly exclaimed, in a tone of terror rather than mere impatience:—

"Wine! wine! quickly, or I'm lost!"

Astonished and almost scared at the strange agitation in which the call was made, they at once administered to her wishes, and she drank some wine with a haste and eagerness which surprised them. She had hardly swallowed it, when she exclaimed, with the same urgency:

"Food, for God's sake, food, at once, or I perish."

A considerable fragment of a roast joint was upon the table, and Schalken immediately began to cut some, but he was anticipated, for no sooner did she see it than she caught it, a more than mortal image of famine, and with her hands, and even with her teeth, she tore off the flesh, and swallowed it. When the paroxysm of hunger had been a little appeased, she appeared on a sudden overcome with shame, or it may have been that other more agitating thoughts overpowered and scared her, for she began to weep bitterly and to wring her hands.

"Oh, send for a minister of God," said she; "I am not safe till he comes; send for him speedily."

Gerard Douw despatched a messenger instantly, and prevailed on his niece to allow him to surrender his bedchamber to her use. He also persuaded her to retire to it at once to rest; her consent was extorted upon the condition that they would not leave her for a moment.

"Oh that the holy man were here," she said; "he can deliver me: the dead and the living can never be one: God has forbidden it."

With these mysterious words she surrendered herself to their guidance, and they proceeded to the chamber which Gerard Douw had assigned to her use.

"Do not, do not leave me for a moment," said she; "I am lost for ever if you do."

Gerard Douw's chamber was approached through a spacious apartment, which they were now about to enter. He and Schalken each carried a candle, so that a sufficiency of light was cast upon all surrounding objects. They were now entering the large chamber, which as I have said, communicated with Douw's apartment, when Rose suddenly stopped, and, in a whisper which thrilled them both with horror, she said:—

"Oh, God! he is here! he is here! See, see! there he goes!"

She pointed towards the door of the inner room, and Schalken thought he saw a shadowy and ill-defined form gliding into that apartment. He drew his sword, and, raising the candle so as to throw its light with increased distinctness upon the objects in the room, he entered the chamber into which the shadow had glided. No figure was there — nothing but the furniture which belonged to the room, and yet he could not be deceived as to the fact that something had moved before them into the chamber. A sickening dread came upon him, and the cold perspiration broke out in heavy drops upon his forehead; nor was he more composed, when he heard the increased urgency and agony of entreaty, with which Rose implored them not to leave her for a moment.

"I saw him," said she; "he's here. I cannot be deceived; I know him; he's by me; he is with me; he's in the room. Then, for God's sake, as you would save me, do not stir from beside me."

They at length prevailed upon her to lie down upon the bed, where she continued to urge them to stay by her. She frequently uttered incoherent sentences, repeating, again and again, "the dead and the living cannot be one; God has forbidden it." And then again, "Rest to the wakeful — sleep to the sleep-walkers." These and such mysterious and broken sentences, she continued to utter until the clergyman arrived. Gerard Douw began to fear, naturally enough, that terror or ill-treatment, had unsettled the poor girl's intellect, and he half suspected, by the suddenness of her appearance, the unseasonableness of the hour, and, above all, from the wildness and terror of her manner, that she had made her escape from some place of confinement for lunatics, and was in imminent fear of pursuit. He resolved to summon medical advice as soon as the mind of his niece had been in some measure set at rest by the offices of the clergyman whose attendance she had so earnestly desired; and until this object had been attained, he did not venture to put any questions to her, which might possibly, by reviving painful or horrible recollections, increase her agitation. The clergyman soon arrived — a man of ascetic countenance and venerable age — one whom Gerard Douw respected much, forasmuch as he was a veteran polemic, though one perhaps more dreaded as a combatant than beloved as a Christian — of pure morality, subtle brain, and frozen heart. He entered the chamber which communicated with that in which Rose reclined and immediately on his arrival, she requested him to pray for her, as for one who lay in the hands of Satan, and who could hope for deliverance only from heaven.

That you may distinctly understand all the circumstances of the event which I am going to describe, it is necessary to state the relative position of the parties who were engaged in it. The old clergyman and Schalken were in the ante-room of which I have already spoken; Rose lay in the inner chamber, the door of which was open; and by the side of the bed, at her urgent desire, stood her guardian; a candle burned in the bedchamber, and three were lighted in the outer apartment. The old man now cleared his voice as if about to commence, but before he had time to begin, a sudden gust of air blew out the candle which served to illuminate the room in which the poor girl lay, and she, with hurried alarm, exclaimed:—

"Godfrey, bring in another candle; the darkness is unsafe."

Gerard Douw forgetting for the moment her repeated injunctions, in the immediate impulse, stepped from the bedchamber into the other, in order to supply what she desired.

"Oh God! do not go, dear uncle," shrieked the unhappy girl — and at the same time she sprung from the bed, and darted after him, in order, by her grasp, to detain him. But the warning came too late, for scarcely had he passed the threshold, and hardly had his niece had time to utter the startling exclamation, when the door which divided the two rooms closed violently after him, as if swung to by a strong blast of wind. Schalken and he both rushed to the door, but their united and desperate efforts could not avail so much as to shake it. Shriek after shriek burst from the inner chamber, with all the piercing loudness of despairing terror. Schalken and Douw applied every nerve to force open the door; but all in vain. There was no sound of struggling from within, but the screams seemed to increase in loudness, and at the same time they heard the bolts of the latticed window withdrawn, and the window itself grated upon the sill as if thrown open. One *last* shriek, so long and piercing and agonized as to be scarcely human, swelled from the room, and suddenly there followed a death-like silence. A light step was heard crossing the floor, as if from the bed to the window; and almost at the same instant the door gave way, and, yielding to the pressure of the external applicants, they were nearly precipitated into the room. It was empty. The window was open, and Schalken sprung to a chair and gazed out upon the street and canal below. He saw no form, but he saw, or thought he saw, the waters of the broad canal beneath settling ring after ring in heavy circles, as if a moment before disturbed by the submission of some ponderous body.

No trace of Rose was ever after found, nor was anything certain respecting her mysterious wooer discovered or even suspected — no clue whereby to trace the intricacies of the labyrinth and to arrive at its solution, presented itself. But an incident occurred, which, though it will not be received by our rational readers in lieu of evidence, produced nevertheless a strong and a lasting impression upon the mind of Schalken. Many years after the events which we have detailed, Schalken, then residing far away received an intimation of his father's death, and of his intended burial upon a fixed day in the church of Rotterdam. It was necessary that a very considerable journey should be performed by the funeral procession, which as it will be readily believed, was not very numerously attended. Schalken with difficulty arrived in Rotterdam late in the day upon which the funeral was appointed to take place. It had not then arrived. Evening closed in, and still it did not appear.

Schalken strolled down to the church; he found it open; notice of the arrival of the funeral had been given, and the vault in which the body was to be laid had been opened. The sexton, on seeing a well-dressed gentleman, whose object was to attend the expected obsequies, pacing the aisle of the church, hospitably invited him to share with him the comforts of a blazing fire, which, as was his custom in winter time upon such occasions, he had kindled in the hearth of a chamber in which he was accustomed to await the arrival of such grisly guests and which communicated, by a flight of steps, with the vault below. In this chamber, Schalken and his entertainer seated themselves; and the sexton, after some fruitless attempts to engage his guest in conversation, was obliged to apply himself to his tobacco-pipe and can, to solace his solitude. In spite of his grief and cares, the fatigues of a rapid journey of nearly forty hours gradually overcame the mind and body of Godfrey Schalken, and he sank into a deep sleep, from which he was awakened by someone's shaking him gently by the shoulder. He first thought that the old sexton had called him, but *he* was no longer in the room. He roused himself, and as soon as he could clearly see what was around him, he perceived a female form, clothed in a kind of light robe of white, part of which was so disposed as to form a veil, and in her hand she carried a lamp. She was moving rather away from him, in the direction of the flight of steps which conducted towards the vaults. Schalken felt a vague alarm at the sight of this figure, and at the same time an irresistible impulse to follow its guidance. He followed it towards the vaults, but when it reached the head of the stairs, he paused; the figure paused also, and, turning gently round, displayed, by the light of the lamp it carried, the face and features of his first love, Rose Velderkaust. There was nothing horrible, or even sad, in the countenance. On the contrary, it wore the same arch smile which used to enchant the artist long before in his happy days. A feeling of awe and of interest, too intense to be resisted, prompted him to follow the spectre, if spectre it were. She descended the stairs — he followed — and, turning to the left, through a narrow passage, she led him, to his infinite surprise, into what appeared to be an old-fashioned Dutch apartment, such as the pictures of Gerard Douw have served to immortalize. Abundance of costly antique furniture was disposed about the room, and in one corner stood a four-post bed, with heavy black cloth curtains around it; the figure frequently turned towards him with the same arch smile; and when she came to the side of the bed, she drew the curtains, and, by the light of the lamp, which she held towards its contents, she disclosed to the horror-stricken painter, sitting bolt upright in the bed, the livid and demoniac form of Vanderhausen. Schalken had hardly seen him, when he fell senseless upon the floor, where he lay until discovered, on the next morning, by persons employed in closing the passages into the vaults. He was lying in a cell of considerable size, which had not been disturbed for a long time, and he had fallen beside a large coffin, which was supported upon small stone pillars, a security against the attacks of vermin.

To his dying day Schalken was satisfied of the reality of the vision which he had witnessed, and he has left behind him a curious evidence of the impression which it wrought upon his fancy, in a painting executed shortly after the event I have narrated, and which is valuable as exhibiting not only the peculiarities which have made Schalken's pictures sought after, but even more so as presenting a portrait of his early love, Rose Velderkaust, whose mysterious fate must always remain matter of speculation.

THE JUDGE'S HOUSE

BRAM STOKER

HEN THE TIME FOR his examination drew near Malcolm Malcolmson made up his mind to go somewhere to read by himself. He feared the attractions of the seaside, and also he feared completely rural isolation, for of old he knew its charms, and so he determined to find some unpretentious little town where there would be nothing to distract him. He refrained from asking suggestions from any of his friends, for he argued that each would recommend some place of which he had knowledge, and where he had already acquaintances. As Malcolmson wished to avoid friends he had no wish to encumber himself with the attention of friends' friends, and so he determined to look out for a place for himself. He packed a portmanteau with some clothes and all the books he required, and then took ticket for the first name on the local time-table which he did not know.

When at the end of three hours' journey he alighted at Benchurch, he felt satisfied that he had so far obliterated his tracks as to be sure of having a peaceful opportunity of pursuing his studies. He went straight to the one inn which the sleepy little place contained, and put up for the night. Benchurch was a market town, and once in three weeks was crowded to excess, but for the remainder of the twenty-one days it was as attractive as a desert. Malcolmson looked around the day after his arrival to try to find quarters more isolated than even so quiet an inn as 'The Good Traveller' afforded. There was only one place which took his fancy, and it certainly satisfied his wildest ideas regarding quiet; in fact, quiet was not the proper word to apply to it — desolation was the only term conveying any suitable idea of its isolation. It was an old rambling, heavy-built house of the Jacobean style, with heavy gables and windows, unusually small, and set higher than was customary in such houses, and was surrounded with a high brick wall massively built. Indeed, on examination, it looked more like a fortified house than an ordinary dwelling. But all these things pleased

Malcolmson. 'Here,' he thought, 'is the very spot I have been looking for, and if I can only get opportunity of using it I shall be happy.' His joy was increased when he realized beyond doubt that it was not at present inhabited.

From the post-office he got the name of the agent, who was rarely surprised at the application to rent a part of the old house. Mr. Carnford, the local lawyer and agent, was a genial old gentleman, and frankly confessed his delight at anyone being willing to live in the house.

'To tell you the truth,' said he, 'I should be only too happy, on behalf of the owners, to let anyone have the house rent free for a term of years if only to accustom the people here to see it inhabited. It has been so long empty that some kind of absurd prejudice has grown up about it, and this can be best put down by its occupation — if only,' he added with a sly glance at Malcolmson, 'by a scholar like yourself, who wants it quiet for a time.'

Malcolmson thought it needless to ask the agent about the 'absurd prejudice'; he knew he would get more information, if he should require it, on that subject from other quarters. He paid his three months' rent, got a receipt, and the name of an old woman who would probably undertake to 'do' for him, and came away with the keys in his pocket. He then went to the landlady of the inn, who was a cheerful and most kindly person, and asked her advice as to such stores and provisions as he would be likely to require. She threw up her hands in amazement when he told her where he was going to settle himself.

'Not in the Judge's House!' she said, and grew pale as she spoke. He explained the locality of the house, saying that he did not know its name. When he had finished she answered:

'Aye, sure enough — sure enough the very place! It is the Judge's House sure enough.' He asked her to tell him about the place, why so called, and what there was against it. She told him that it was so called locally because it had been many years before — how long she could not say, as she was herself from another part of the country, but she thought it must have been a hundred years or more — the abode of a judge who was held in great terror on account of his harsh sentences and his hostility to prisoners at Assizes. As to what there was against the house itself she could not tell. She had often asked, but no one could inform her; but there was a general feeling that there was *something,* and for her own part she would not take all the money in Drinkwater's Bank and stay in the house an hour by herself. Then she apologized to Malcolmson for her disturbing talk.

'It is too bad of me, sir, and you — and a young gentleman, too — if you will pardon my saying it, going to live there all alone. If you were my boy — and you'll excuse me for saying it — you wouldn't sleep there a night, not if I had to go there myself and pull the big alarm bell that's on the roof!' The good creature was so manifestly in earnest, and was so kindly in her intentions, that Malcolmson, although amused, was touched. He told her kindly how much he appreciated her interest in him, and added:

'But, my dear Mrs Witham, indeed you need not be concerned about me! A man who is reading for the Mathematical Tripos has too much to think of to be disturbed by any of these mysterious "somethings", and his work is of too exact and prosaic a kind to allow of his having any corner in his mind for mysteries of any kind. Harmonical Progression, Permutations and Combinations, and Elliptic Functions have sufficient mysteries for me!' Mrs Witham kindly undertook to see after his commissions, and he went himself to look for the old woman who had been recommended to him. When he returned to the Judge's House with her, after an interval of a couple of hours, he found Mrs Witham herself waiting with several men and boys carrying parcels, and an upholsterer's man with a bed in a cart, for she said, though tables and chairs might be all very well, a bed that hadn't been aired for mayhap fifty years was not proper for young bones to lie on. She was evidently curious to see the inside of the house; and though manifestly so afraid of the 'somethings' that at the slightest sound she clutched on to Malcolmson, whom she never left for a moment, went over the whole place.

After his examination of the house, Malcolmson decided to take up his abode in the great dining-room, which was big enough to serve for all his requirements; and Mrs Witham, with the aid of the charwoman, Mrs Dempster, proceeded to arrange matters. When the hampers were brought in and unpacked, Malcolmson saw that with much kind forethought she had sent from her own kitchen sufficient provisions to last for a few days. Before going she expressed all sort of kind wishes; and at the door turned and said:

'And perhaps, sir, as the room is big and draughty it might be well to have one of these big screens put round your bed at night — though, truth to tell, I would die myself if I were to be so shut in with all kinds of — of "things" that put their heads round the sides, or over the top, and look on me!' The image which she had called up was too much for her nerves, and she fled incontinently.

Mrs Dempster sniffed in a superior manner as the landlady disappeared, and remarked that for her own part she wasn't afraid of all the bogies in the kingdom.

'I'll tell you what it is, sir,' she said; 'bogies is all kinds and sorts of things — except bogies! Rats and mice, and beetles; and creaky doors, and loose slates, and broken panes, and stiff drawer handles, that stay out when you pull them and then fall down in the middle of the night. Look at the wainscot of the room! It is old — hundreds of years old! Do you think there's no rats and beetles there! And do you imagine, sir, that you won't see none of them! Rats is bogies, I tell you, and bogies is rats; and don't you get to think anything else!'

'Mrs Dempster,' said Malcolmson gravely, making her a polite bow, 'you know more than a Senior Wrangler! And let me say, that, as a mark of esteem for your indubitable soundness of head and heart, I shall, when I go, give you possession of this house, and let you stay here by yourself for the last two months of my tenancy, for four weeks will serve my purpose.'

'Thank you kindly, sir!' she answered, 'but I couldn't sleep away from home for a night. I am in Greenhow's Charity, and if I slept a night away from my rooms I should lose all I have got to live on. The rules is very strict; and there's too many watching for a vacancy for me to run any risks in the matter. Only for that, sir, I'd gladly come here and attend on you altogether during your stay.'

'My good woman,' said Malcolmson hastily, 'I have come here on purpose to obtain solitude; and believe me that I am grateful to the late Greenhow for having so organized this admirable charity — whatever it is — that I am perforce denied the opportunity of suffering from such a form of temptation! Saint Anthony himself could not be more rigid on the point!'

The old woman laughed harshly. 'Ah, you young gentlemen,' she said, 'you don't fear for naught; and belike you'll get all the solitude you want here.' She set to work with her cleaning; and by nightfall, when Malcolmson returned from his walk — he always had one of his books to study as he walked — he found the room swept and tidied, a fire burning in the old hearth, the lamp lit, and the table spread for supper with Mrs Witham's excellent fare. 'This is comfort, indeed,' he said, as he rubbed his hands.

When he had finished his supper, and lifted the tray to the other end of the great oak dining-table, he got out his books again, put fresh wood on the fire, trimmed his lamp, and set himself down to a spell of real hard work. He went on without pause till about eleven o'clock, when he knocked off for a bit to fix his fire and lamp, and to make himself a cup of tea. He had always been a tea-drinker, and during his college life had sat late at work and had taken tea late. The rest was a great luxury to him, and he enjoyed it with a sense of delicious, voluptuous ease. The renewed fire leaped and sparkled, and threw quaint shadows through the great old room; and as he sipped his hot tea he revelled in the sense of isolation from his kind. Then it was that he began to notice for the first time what a noise the rats were making.

'Surely,' he thought, 'they cannot have been at it all the time I was reading. Had they been, I must have noticed it!' Presently, when the noise increased, he satisfied himself that it was really new. It was evident that at first the rats had been frightened at the presence of a stranger, and the light of fire and lamp; but that as the time went on they had grown bolder and were now disporting themselves as was their wont.

How busy they were; and hark to the strange noises! Up and down behind the old wainscot, over the ceiling and under the floor they raced, and gnawed, and scratched! Malcolmson smiled to himself as he recalled to mind the saying of Mrs Dempster, 'Bogies is rats, and rats is bogies!' The tea began to have its effect of intellectual and nervous stimulus, he saw with joy another long spell of work to be done before the night was past, and in the sense of security which it gave him, he allowed himself the luxury of a good look round the room. He took his lamp in one hand, and went all around, wondering that so quaint and beautiful an old house had been so long neglected. The carving of the oak on the panels of the wainscot was fine, and on and around the doors and windows it was beautiful and of rare merit. Here were some old pictures on the walls, but they were coated so thick with dust and dirt that he could not distinguish any detail of them, though he held his lamp as high as he could over his head. Here and there as he went round he saw some crack or hole blocked for a moment by the face of a rat with its bright eyes glittering in the light, but in an instant it was gone, and a squeak and a scamper followed.

The thing that most struck him, however, was the rope of the great alarm bell on the roof, which hung down in a corner of the room on the right-hand side of the fireplace. He pulled up close to the hearth a great high-backed carved oak chair, and sat down to his last cup of tea. When this was done he made up the fire, and went back to his work, sitting at the corner of the table, having the fire to his left. For a while the rats disturbed him somewhat with their perpetual scampering, but he got accustomed to the noise as one does to the ticking of a clock or to the roar of moving water; and he became so immersed in his work that everything in the world, except the problem which he was trying to solve, passed away from him.

He suddenly looked up, his problem was still unsolved, and there was in the air that sense of the hour before the dawn, which is so dread to doubtful life. The noise of the rats had ceased. Indeed it seemed to him that it must have ceased but lately and that it was the sudden cessation which had disturbed him. The fire had fallen low, but still it threw out a deep red glow. As he looked he started in spite of his *sang froid*.

There on the great high-backed carved oak chair by the right side of the fireplace sat an enormous rat, steadily glaring at him with baleful eyes. He made a motion to it as though to hunt it away, but it did not stir. Then he made the motion of throwing something. Still it did not stir, but showed its great white teeth angrily, and its cruel eyes shone in the lamplight with an added vindictiveness.

Malcolmson felt amazed, and seizing the poker from the hearth ran at it to kill it. Before, however, he could strike it, the rat, with a squeak that sounded like the concentration of hate, jumped upon the floor, and, running up the rope of the alarm bell, disappeared in the darkness beyond the range of the green-shaded lamp. Instantly, strange to say, the noisy scampering of the rats in the wainscot began again.

By this time Malcolmson's mind was quite off the problem; and as a shrill cock-crow outside told him of the approach of morning, he went to bed and to sleep.

He slept so sound that he was not even waked by Mrs Dempster coming in to make up his room. It was only when she had tidied up the place and got his breakfast ready and tapped on the screen which closed in his bed that he woke. He was a little tired still after his night's hard work, but a strong cup of tea soon freshened him up, and, taking his book, he went out for his morning walk, bringing with him a few sandwiches lest he should not care to return till dinner time. He found a quiet walk between high elms some way outside the town, and here he spent the greater part of the day studying his Laplace. On his return he looked in to see Mrs Witham and to thank her for her kindness. When she saw him coming through the diamond-paned bay-window of her sanctum she came out to meet him and asked him in. She looked at him searchingly and shook her head as she said:

'You must not overdo it, sir. You are paler this morning than you should be. Too late hours and too hard work on the brain isn't good for any man! But tell me, sir, how did you pass the night? Well, I hope? But, my heart! sir, I was glad when Mrs Dempster told me this morning that you were all right and sleeping sound when she went in.'

'Oh, I was all right,' he answered, smiling, 'the "somethings" didn't worry me, as yet. Only the rats; and they had a circus, I tell you, all over the place. There was one wicked looking old devil that sat up on my own chair by the fire, and wouldn't go till I took the poker to him, and then he ran up the rope of the alarm bell and got to somewhere up the wall or the ceiling — I couldn't see where, it was so dark.'

'Mercy on us,' said Mrs Witham, 'an old devil, and sitting on a chair by the fireside! Take care, sir! Take care! There's many a true word spoken in jest.'

'How do you mean?'Pon my word I don't understand.'

'An old devil! The old devil, perhaps. There! sir, you needn't laugh,' for Malcolmson had broken into a hearty peal. 'You young folks thinks it easy to laugh at things that makes older ones shudder. Never mind, sir! never mind! Please God, you'll laugh all the time. It's what I wish you myself!' and the good lady beamed all over in sympathy with his enjoyment, her fears gone for a moment.

'Oh, forgive me!' said Malcolmson presently. 'Don't think me rude; but the idea was too much for me — that the old devil himself was on the chair last night!' And at the thought he laughed again. Then he went home to dinner.

This evening the scampering of the rats began earlier; indeed it had been going on before his arrival, and only ceased whilst his presence by its freshness disturbed them. After dinner he sat by the fire for a while and had a smoke; and then, having cleared his table, began to work as before. Tonight the rats disturbed him more than they had done on the previous night. How they scampered up and down and under and over! How they squeaked, and scratched, and gnawed! How they, getting bolder by degrees, came to the mouths of their holes and to the chinks and cracks and crannies in the wainscoting till their eyes shone like tiny lamps as the firelight rose and fell. But to him, now doubtless accustomed to them, their eyes were not wicked; only their playfulness touched him. Sometimes the boldest of them made sallies out on the floor or along the mouldings of the wainscot. Now and again as they disturbed him Malcomson made a sound to frighten them, smiting the table with his hand or giving a fierce 'Hsh, hsh', so that they fled straightway to their holes.

And so the early part of the night wore on; and despite the noise Malcolmson got more and more immersed in his work.

All at once he stopped, as on the previous night, being overcome by a sudden sense of silence. There was not the faintest sound of gnaw, or scratch, or squeak. The silence was as of the grave. He remembered the odd occurrence of the previous night, and instinctively he looked at the chair standing close by the fireside. And then a very odd sensation thrilled through him.

There, on the great old high-backed carved oak chair beside the fireplace sat the same enormous rat, steadily glaring at him with baleful eyes.

Instinctively he took the nearest thing to his hand, a book of logarithms, and flung it at it. The book was badly aimed and the rat did not stir, so again the poker performance of the previous night was repeated; and again the rat, being closely pursued, fled up the rope of the alarm bell. Strangely too, the departure of this rat was instantly followed by the renewal of the noise made by the general rat community. On this occasion, as on the previous one, Malcolmson could not see at what part of the room the rat disappeared, for the green shade of his lamp left the upper part of the room in darkness, and the fire had burned low.

On looking at his watch he found it was close to midnight; and, not sorry for the *divertissement,* he made up his fire and made himself his nightly pot of tea. He had got through a good spell of work, and thought himself entitled to a cigarette; and so he sat on the great carved oak chair before the fire and enjoyed it. Whilst smoking he began to think that he would like to know where the rat disappeared to, for he had certain ideas for the morrow not entirely disconnected with a rat-trap. Accordingly he lit another lamp and placed it so that it would shine well into the right-hand corner of the wall by the fireplace. Then he got all the books he had with him, and placed them handy to throw at the vermin. Finally he lifted the rope of the alarm bell and placed the end of it on the table, fixing the extreme end under the lamp. As he handled it he could not help noticing how pliable it was, especially for so strong a rope, and one not in use. 'You could hang a man with it,' he thought to himself. When his preparations were made he looked around, and said complacently:

'There now, my friend, I think we shall learn something of you this time!' He began his work again, and though as before somewhat disturbed at first by the noise of the rats, soon lost himself in his propositions and problems.

Again he was called to his immediate surroundings suddenly. This time it might not have been the sudden silence only which took his attention; there was a slight movement of the rope, and the lamp moved. Without stirring, he looked to see if his pile of books was within range, and then cast his eye along the rope. As he looked he saw the great rat drop from the rope on the oak armchair and sit there glaring at him. He raised a book in his right hand, and taking careful aim, flung it at the rat. The latter, with a quick movement, sprang aside and dodged the missile. He then took another book, and a third, and flung them one after another at the rat, but each time unsuccessfully. At last, as he stood with a book poised in his hand to throw, the rat squeaked and seemed afraid. This made Malcolmson more than ever eager to strike, and the book flew and struck the rat a resounding blow. It gave a terrified squeak, and turning on its pursuer a look of terrible malevolence, ran up the chair-back and made a great jump to the rope of the alarm bell and ran up it like lightning. The lamp rocked under the sudden strain, but it was a heavy one and did not topple over. Malcolmson kept his eyes on the rat, and saw it by the light of the second lamp leap to a moulding of the wainscot and disappear through a hole in one of the great pictures which hung on the wall, obscured and invisible through its coating of dirt and dust.

'I shall look up my friend's habitation in the morning,' said the student, as he went over to collect his books. 'The third picture from the fireplace; I shall not forget.' He picked up the books one by one, commenting on them as he lifted them. '*Conic Sections* he does not mind, nor *Cycloidal Oscillations,* nor the *Principia,* nor *Quaternions,* nor *Thermodynamics.* Now for the book that fetched him!' Malcolmson took it up and looked at it. As he did so he started, and a sudden pallor overspread his face. He looked round uneasily and shivered slightly, as he murmured to himself:

'The Bible my mother gave me! What an odd coincidence.' He sat down to work again, and the rats in the wainscot renewed their gambols. They did not disturb him, however; somehow their presence gave him a sense of companionship. But he could not attend to his work, and after striving to master the subject on which he was engaged gave it up in despair, and went to bed as the first streak of dawn stole in through the eastern window.

He slept heavily but uneasily, and dreamed much; and when Mrs Dempster woke him late in the morning he seemed ill at ease, and for a few minutes did not seem to realize exactly where he was. His first request rather surprised the servant.

'Mrs Dempster, when I am out today I wish you would get the steps and dust or wash those pictures — specially that one the third from the fireplace — I want to see what they are.'

Late in the afternoon Malcolmson worked at his books in the shaded walk, and the cheerfulness of the previous day came back to him as the day wore on, and he found that his reading was progressing well. He had worked out to a satisfactory conclusion all the problems which had as yet baffled him, and it was in a state of jubilation that he paid a visit to Mrs Witham at 'The Good Traveller'. He found a stranger in the cosy sitting-room with the landlady, who was introduced to him as Dr Thornhill. She was not quite at ease, and this, combined with the Doctor's plunging at once into a series of questions, made Malcolmson come to the conclusion that his presence was not an accident, so without preliminary he said:

'Dr Thornhill, I shall with pleasure answer you any question you may choose to ask me if you will answer me one question first.'

The Doctor seemed surprised, but he smiled and answered at once. 'Done! What is it?'

'Did Mrs Witham ask you to come here and see me and advise me?'

Dr Thornhill for a moment was taken aback, and Mrs Witham got fiery red and turned away; but the doctor was a frank and ready man, and he answered at once and openly:

'She did, but she didn't intend you to know it. I suppose it was my clumsy haste that made you suspect. She told me that she did not like the idea of your being in that house all by yourself, and that she thought you took too much strong tea. In fact, she wants me to advise you if possible to give up the tea and the very late hours. I was a keen student in my time, so I suppose I may take the liberty of a college man, and without offence, advise you not quite as a stranger.'

Malcolmson with a bright smile held out his hand. 'Shake! as they say in America,' he said. 'I must thank you for your kindness and Mrs Witham too, and your kindness deserves a return on my part. I promise to take no more strong tea — no tea at all till you let me — and I shall go to bed tonight at one o'clock at latest. Will that do?'

'Capital,' said the Doctor. 'Now tell us all that you noticed in the old house,' and so Malcolmson then and there told in minute detail all that had happened in the last two nights. He was interrupted every now and then by some exclamation from Mrs Witham, till finally when he told of the episode of the Bible the landlady's pent-up emotions found vent in a shriek; and it was not till a stiff glass of brandy and water had been administered that she grew composed again. Dr Thornhill listened with a face of growing gravity, and when the narrative was complete and Mrs Witham had been restored he asked:

'The rat always went up the rope of the alarm bell?'

'Always.'

'I suppose you know,' said the Doctor after a pause, 'what the rope is?'

'No!'

'It is,' said the Doctor slowly, 'the very rope which the hangman used for all the victims of the Judge's judicial rancour!' Here he was interrupted by another scream from Mrs Witham, and steps had to be taken for her recovery. Malcolmson having looked at his watch, and found that it was close to his dinner hour, had gone home before her complete recovery.

When Mrs Witham was herself again she almost assailed the Doctor with angry questions as to what he meant by putting such horrible ideas into the poor young man's mind. 'He has quite enough there already to upset him,' she added. Dr Thornhill replied:

'My dear madam, I had a distinct purpose in it! I wanted to draw his attention to the bell rope, and to fix it there. It may be that he is in a highly overwrought state, and has been studying too much, although I am bound to say that he seems as sound and healthy a young man, mentally and bodily, as ever I saw — but then the rats — and that suggestion of the devil.' The doctor shook his head and went on. 'I would have offered to go and stay the first night with him but that I felt sure it would have been a cause of offence. He may get in the night some strange fright or hallucination; and if he does I want him to pull that rope. All alone as he is it will give us warning, and we may reach him in time to be of service. I shall be sitting up pretty late tonight and shall keep my ears open. Do not be alarmed if Benchurch gets a surprise before morning.'

'Oh, Doctor, what do you mean? What do you mean?'

'I mean this; that possibly — nay, more probably — we shall hear the great alarm bell from the Judge's House tonight,' and the Doctor made about as effective an exit as could be thought of.

When Malcolmson arrived home he found that it was a little after his usual time, and Mrs Dempster had gone away — the rules of Greenhow's

Charity were not to be neglected. He was glad to see that the place was bright and tidy with a cheerful fire and a well-trimmed lamp. The evening was colder than might have been expected in April, and a heavy wind was blowing with such rapidly-increasing strength that there was every promise of a storm during the night. For a few minutes after his entrance the noise of the rats ceased; but so soon as they became accustomed to his presence they began again. He was glad to hear them, for he felt once more the feeling of companionship in their noise, and his mind ran back to the strange fact that they only ceased to manifest themselves when that other — the great rat with the baleful eyes — came upon the scene. The reading-lamp only was lit and its green shade kept the ceiling and the upper part of the room in darkness, so that the cheerful light from the hearth spreading over the floor and shining on the white cloth laid over the end of the table was warm and cheery. Malcolmson sat down to his dinner with a good appetite and a buoyant spirit. After his dinner and a cigarette he sat steadily down to work, determined not to let anything disturb him, for he remembered his promise to the doctor, and made up his mind to make the best of the time at his disposal.

For an hour or so he worked all right, and then his thoughts began to wander from his books. The actual circumstances around him, the calls on his physical attention, and his nervous susceptibility were not to be denied. By this time the wind had become a gale, and the gale a storm. The old house, solid though it was, seemed to shake to its foundations, and the storm roared and raged through its many chimneys and its queer old gables, producing strange unearthly sounds in the empty rooms and corridors. Even the great alarm bell on the roof must have felt the force of the wind, for the rope rose and fell slightly, as though the bell were moved a little from time to time, and the limber rope fell on the oak floor with a hard and hollow sound.

As Malcolmson listened to it he bethought himself of the doctor's words, 'It is the rope which the hangman used for the victims of the Judge's judicial rancour,' and he went over to the corner of the fireplace and took it in his hand to look at it. There seemed a sort of deadly interest in it, and as he stood there he lost himself for a moment in speculation as to who these victims were, and the grim wish of the Judge to have such a ghastly relic ever under his eyes. As he stood there the swaying of the bell on the roof still lifted the rope now and again; but presently there came a new sensation — a sort of tremor in the rope, as though something was moving along it.

Looking up instinctively Malcolmson saw the great rat coming slowly down towards him, glaring at him steadily. He dropped the rope and started back with a muttered curse, and the rat turning ran up the rope again and disappeared, and at the same instant Malcolmson became conscious that the noise of the rats, which had ceased for a while, began again.

All this set him thinking, and it occurred to him that he had not investigated the lair of the rat or looked at the pictures, as he had intended. He lit the other lamp without the shade, and, holding it up, went and stood opposite the third picture from the fireplace on the right-hand side where he had seen the rat disappear on the previous night.

At the first glance he started back so suddenly that he almost dropped the lamp, and a deadly pallor overspread his face. His knees shook, and heavy drops of sweat came on his forehead, and he trembled like an aspen. But he was young and plucky, and pulled himself together, and after the pause of a few seconds stepped forward again, raised the lamp, and examined the picture, which had been dusted and washed, and now stood out clearly.

It was of a judge dressed in his robes of scarlet and ermine. His face was strong and merciless, evil, crafty, and vindictive, with a sensual mouth, hooked nose of ruddy colour, and shaped like the beak of a bird of prey. The rest of the face was of a cadaverous colour. The eyes were of peculiar brilliance and with a terribly malignant expression. As he looked at them, Malcolmson grew cold, for he saw there the very counterpart of the eyes of the great rat. The lamp almost fell from his hand, he saw the rat with its baleful eyes peering out through the hole in the corner of the picture, and noted the sudden cessation of the noise of the other rats. However, he pulled himself together, and went on with his examination of the picture.

The Judge was seated in a great high-backed carved oak chair, on the right-hand side of a great stone fireplace where, in the corner, a rope hung down from the ceiling, its end lying coiled on the floor. With a feeling of something like horror, Malcolmson recognized the scene of the room as it stood, and gazed around him in an awe-struck manner as though he expected to find some strange presence behind him. Then he looked over to the corner of the fireplace — and with a loud cry he let the lamp fall from his hand.

There, in the Judge's arm-chair, with the rope hanging behind, sat the rat with the Judge's baleful eyes, now intensified and with a fiendish leer. Save for the howling of the storm without there was silence.

The fallen lamp recalled Malcolmson to himself. Fortunately it was of metal, so the oil was not spilt. However, the practical need of attending to it settled at once his nervous apprehensions. When he had turned it out, he wiped his brow and thought for a moment.

'This will not do,' he said to himself. 'If I go on like this I shall become a crazy fool. This must stop! I promised the Doctor I would not take tea. Faith, he was pretty right! My nerves must have been getting into a queer state. Funny I did not notice it. I never felt better in my life. However, it is all right now, and I shall not be such a fool again.'

Then he mixed himself a good stiff glass of brandy and water and resolutely sat down to his work.

It was nearly an hour when he looked up from his book, disturbed by the sudden stillness. Without, the wind howled and roared louder than ever, and the rain drove in sheets against the windows, beating like hail on the glass; but within there was no sound whatever save the echo of the wind as it roared in the great chimney, and now and then a hiss as a few raindrops found their way down the chimney in a lull of the storm. The fire had fallen low and had ceased to flame, though it threw out a red glow. Malcolmson listened attentively, and presently heard a thin, squeaking noise, very faint. It came from the corner of the room where the rope hung down, and he thought it was the creaking of the rope on the floor as the swaying of the bell raised and lowered it. Looking up, however, he saw in the dim light the great rat clinging to the rope and gnawing it. The rope was already nearly gnawed through — he could see the lighter colour where the strands were laid bare. As he looked the job was completed, and the severed end of the rope fell clattering on the oaken floor, whilst for an instant the great rat remained like a knob or tassel at the end of the rope, which now began to sway to and fro. Malcolmson felt for a moment another pang of terror as he thought that now the possibility of calling the outer world to his assistance was cut off, but an intense anger took its place, and seizing the book he was reading he hurled it at the rat. The blow was well aimed, but before the missile could reach it the rat dropped off and struck the floor with a soft thud. Malcolmson instantly rushed over towards it, but it darted away and disappeared in the darkness of the shadows of the room. Malcolmson felt that his work was over for the night, and determined then and there to vary the monotony of the proceedings by a hunt for the rat, and took off the green shade of the lamp so as to insure a wider spreading light. As he did so the gloom of the upper part of the room was relieved, and in the new flood of light, great by comparison with the previous darkness, the pictures on the wall stood out boldly. From where he stood, Malcolmson saw right opposite to him the third picture on the wall from the right of the fireplace. He rubbed his eyes in surprise, and then a great fear began to come upon him.

In the centre of the picture was a great irregular patch of brown canvas, as fresh as when it was stretched on the frame. The background was as before, with chair and chimney-corner and rope, but the figure of the Judge had disappeared.

Malcolmson, almost in a chill of horror, turned slowly round, and then he began to shake and tremble like a man in a palsy. His strength seemed to have left him, and he was incapable of action or movement, hardly even of thought. He could only see and hear.

There, on the great high-backed carved oak chair sat the Judge in his robes of scarlet and ermine, with his baleful eyes glaring vindictively, and a smile of triumph on the resolute, cruel mouth, as he lifted with his hands a *black cap*. Malcolmson felt as if the blood was running from his heart, as one does in moments of prolonged suspense. There was a singing in his ears. Without, he could hear the roar and howl of the tempest, and through it, swept on the storm, came the striking of midnight by the great chimes in the market place. He stood for a space of time that seemed to him endless, still as a statue and with wide-open, horror-struck eyes, breathless. As the clock struck, so the smile of triumph on the Judge's face intensified, and at the last stroke of midnight he placed the black cap on his head.

Slowly and deliberately the Judge rose from his chair and picked up the piece of the rope of the alarm bell which lay on the floor, drew it through his hands as if he enjoyed its touch, and then deliberately began to knot one end of it, fashioning it into a noose. This he tightened and tested with his foot, pulling hard at it till he was satisfied and then making a running noose of it, which he held in his hand. Then he began to move along the table on the opposite side to Malcolmson, keeping his eyes on him until he had passed him, when with a quick movement he stood in front of the door. Malcolmson then began to feel that he was trapped, and tried to think of what he should do. There was some fascination in the Judge's eyes, which he never took off him, and he had, perforce, to look. He saw the Judge approach — still keeping between him and the door — and raise the noose and throw it towards him as if to entangle him. With a great effort he made a quick movement to one side, and saw the rope fall beside him, and heard it strike the oaken floor. Again the Judge raised the noose and tried to ensnare him, ever keeping his baleful eyes fixed on him, and each time by a mighty effort the student just managed to evade it. So this went on for many times, the Judge seeming never discouraged nor discomposed at failure, but playing as a cat does with a mouse. At last in despair, which had reached its climax, Malcolmson cast a quick glance round him. The lamp seemed to have blazed up, and there was a fairly good light in the room. At the many ratholes and in the chinks and crannies of the wainscot he saw the rats' eyes; and this aspect, that was purely physical, gave him a gleam of comfort. He looked around and saw that the rope of the great alarm bell was laden with rats. Every inch of it was covered with them, and more and more were pouring through the small circular hole in the ceiling whence it emerged, so that with their weight the bell was beginning to sway.

Hark! it had swayed till the clapper had touched the bell. The sound was but a tiny one, but the bell was only beginning to sway, and it would increase.

At the sound the Judge, who had been keeping his eyes fixed on Malcolmson, looked up, and a scowl of diabolical anger overspread his face. His eyes fairly glowed like hot coals, and he stamped his foot with a sound that seemed to make the house shake. A dreadful peal of thunder broke overhead as he raised the rope again, whilst the rats kept running up and down the rope as though working against time. This time, instead of throwing it, he drew close to his victim, and held open the noose as he approached. As he came closer there seemed something paralysing in his very presence, and Malcolmson stood rigid as a corpse. He felt the Judge's icy fingers touch his throat as he adjusted the rope. The noose tightened — tightened. Then the Judge, taking the rigid form of the student in his arms, carried him over and placed him standing in the oak chair, and stepping up beside him, put his hand up and caught the end of the swaying rope of the alarm bell. As he raised his hand the rats fled squeaking, and disappeared through the hole in the ceiling. Taking the end of the noose which was round Malcolmson's neck he tied it to the hanging bell-rope, and then descending pulled away the chair.

When the alarm bell of the Judge's House began to sound a crowd soon assembled. Lights and torches of various kinds appeared, and soon a silent crowd was hurrying to the spot. They knocked loudly at the door, but there was no reply. Then they burst in the door, and poured into the great dining-room, the doctor at the head.

There at the end of the rope of the great alarm bell hung the body of the student, and on the face of the Judge in the picture was a malignant smile.

THURNLEY ABBEY

PERCEVAL LANDON

HREE YEARS AGO I was on my way out to the East, and as an extra day in London was of some importance, I took the Friday evening mail-train to Brindisi instead of the usual Thursday morning Marseilles express. Many people shrink from the long forty-eight-hour train journey through Europe, and the subsequent rush across the Mediterranean on the nineteen-knot *Isis* or *Osiris*; but there is really very little discomfort on either the train or the mailboat, and unless there is actually nothing for me to do, I always like to save the extra day and a half in London before I say goodbye to her for one of my longer tramps. This time — it was early, I remember, in the shipping season, probably about the beginning of September — there were few passengers, and I had a compartment in the P. & O. Indian express to myself all the way from Calais. All Sunday I watched the blue waves dimpling the Adriatic, and the pale rosemary along the cuttings; the plain white towns, with their flat roofs and their bold "duomos," and the grey-green gnarled olive orchards of Apulia. The journey was just like any other. We ate in the dining-car as often and as long as we decently could. We slept after luncheon; we dawdled the afternoon away with yellow-backed novels; sometimes we exchanged platitudes in the smoking-room, and it was there that I met Alastair Colvin.

Colvin was a man of middle height, with a resolute, well-cut jaw; his hair was turning grey; his moustache was sun-whitened, otherwise he was clean-shaven — obviously a gentleman, and obviously also a pre-occupied man. He had no great wit. When spoken to, he made the usual remarks in the right way, and I dare say he refrained from banalities only because he spoke less than the rest of us; most of the time he buried himself in the Wagon-lit Company's time-table, but seemed unable to concentrate his attention on any one page of it. He found that I had been over the Siberian railway, and for a quarter of an hour he discussed it with me. Then he lost interest in it, and rose to go to his compartment. But he came back again

165

very soon, and seemed glad to pick up the conversation again.

Of course this did not seem to me to be of any importance. Most travellers by train become a trifle infirm of purpose after thirty-six hours' rattling. But Colvin's restless way I noticed in somewhat marked contrast with the man's personal importance and dignity; especially ill suited was it to his finely made large hand with strong, broad, regular nails and its few lines. As I looked at his hand I noticed a long, deep, and recent scar of ragged shape. However, it is absurd to pretend that I thought anything was unusual. I went off at five o'clock on Sunday afternoon to sleep away the hour or two that had still to be got through before we arrived at Brindisi.

Once there, we few passengers transshipped our hand baggage, verified our berths — there were only a score of us in all — and then, after an aimless ramble of half an hour in Brindisi, we returned to dinner at the Hôtel International, not wholly surprised that the town had been the death of Virgil. If I remember rightly, there is a gaily painted hall at the International — I do not wish to advertise anything, but there is no other place in Brindisi at which to await the coming of the mails — and after dinner I was looking with awe at a trellis overgrown with blue vines, when Colvin moved across the room to my table. He picked up *Il Secolo,* but almost immediately gave up the pretence of reading it. He turned squarely to me and said:

"Would you do me a favour?"

One doesn't do favours to stray acquaintances on Continental expresses without knowing something more of them than I knew of Colvin. But I smiled in a noncommittal way, and asked him what he wanted. I wasn't wrong in part of my estimate of him; he said bluntly:

"Will you let me sleep in your cabin on the *Osiris*?" And he coloured a little as he said it.

Now, there is nothing more tiresome than having to put up with a stable-companion at sea, and I asked him rather pointedly:

"Surely there is room for all of us?" I thought that perhaps he had been partnered off with some mangy Levantine, and wanted to escape from him at all hazards.

Colvin, still somewhat confused, said: "Yes; I am in a cabin by myself. But you would do me the greatest favour if you would allow me to share yours."

This was all very well, but, besides the fact that I always sleep better when alone, there had been some recent thefts on board English liners, and I hesitated, frank and honest and self-conscious as Colvin was. Just then the mail-train came in with a clatter and a rush of escaping steam, and I asked him to see me again about it on the boat when we started. He answered me curtly — I suppose he saw the mistrust in my manner — "I am a member of White's." I smiled to myself as he said it, but I remembered in a moment that the man — if he were really what he claimed to be, and I make no doubt that he was — must have been sorely put to it before he urged the fact as a guarantee of his respectability to a total stranger at a Brindisi hotel.

That evening, as we cleared the red and green harbour-lights of Brindisi,

Colvin explained. This is his story in his own words.

"WHEN I WAS travelling in India some years ago, I made the acquaintance of a youngish man in the Woods and Forests. We camped out together for a week, and I found him a pleasant companion. John Broughton was a light-hearted soul when off duty, but a steady and capable man in any of the small emergencies that continually arise in that department. He was liked and trusted by the natives, and though a trifle over-pleased with himself when he escaped to civilisation at Simla or Calcutta, Broughton's future was well assured in Government service, when a fair-sized estate was unexpectedly left to him, and he joyfully shook the dust of the Indian plains from his feet and returned to England. For five years he drifted about London. I saw him now and then. We dined together about every eighteen months, and I could trace pretty exactly the gradual sickening of Broughton with a merely idle life. He then set out on a couple of long voyages, returned as restless as before, and at last told me that he had decided to marry and settle down at his place, Thurnley Abbey, which had long been empty. He spoke about looking after the property and standing for his constituency in the usual way. Vivien Wilde, his *fiancée,* had, I suppose, begun to take him in hand. She was a pretty girl with a deal of fair hair and rather an exclusive manner; deeply religious in a narrow school, she was still kindly and high-spirited, and I thought that Broughton was in luck. He was quite happy and full of information about his future.

"Among other things, I asked him about Thurnley Abbey. He confessed that he hardly knew the place. The last tenant, a man called Clarke, had lived in one wing for fifteen years and seen no one. He had been a miser and a hermit. It was the rarest thing for a light to be seen at the Abbey after dark. Only the barest necessities of life were ordered, and the tenant himself received them at the side-door. His one half-caste manservant, after a month's stay in the house, had abruptly left without warning, and had returned to the Southern States. One thing Broughton complained bitterly about: Clarke had wilfully spread the rumour among the villagers that the Abbey was haunted, and had even condescended to play childish tricks with spirit-lamps and salt in order to scare trespassers away at night. He had been detected in the act of his tomfoolery, but the story spread, and no one, said Broughton, would venture near the house except in broad daylight. The hauntedness of Thurnley Abbey was now, he said with a grin, part of the gospel of the countryside, but he and his young wife were going to change all that. Would I propose myself any time I liked? I, of course, said I would, and equally, of course, intended to do nothing of the sort without a definite invitation.

"The house was put in thorough repair, though not a stick of the old furniture and tapestry were removed. Floors and ceilings were relaid: the roof was made watertight again, and the dust of half a century was scoured out. He showed me some photographs of the place. It was called an Abbey, though as a matter of fact it had been only the infirmary of the long-vanished Abbey of Closter some five miles away. The larger part of this building remained as it had been in pre-Reformation days, but a wing had been added in Jacobean times, and that part of the house had been kept in something like repair by Mr. Clarke. He had in both the ground and first floors set a heavy timber door, strongly barred with iron, in the passage between the earlier and the Jacobean parts of the house, and had entirely neglected the former. So there had been a good deal of work to be done.

"Broughton, whom I saw in London two or three times about this period, made a deal of fun over the positive refusal of the workmen to remain after sundown. Even after the electric light had been put into every room, nothing would induce them to remain, though, as Broughton observed, electric light was death on ghosts. The legend of the Abbey's ghosts had gone far and wide, and the men would take no risks. They went home in batches of five and six, and even during the daylight hours there was an inordinate amount of talking between one and another, if either happened to be out of sight of his companion. On the whole, though nothing of any sort or kind had been conjured up even by their heated imaginations during their five months' work upon the Abbey, the belief in the ghosts was rather strengthened than otherwise in Thurnley because of the men's confessed nervousness, and local tradition declared itself in favour of the ghost of an immured nun.

" 'Good old nun!' said Broughton.

"I asked him whether in general he believed in the possibility of ghosts, and, rather to my surprise, he said that he couldn't say he entirely disbelieved in them. A man in India had told him one morning in camp that he believed that his mother was dead in England, as her vision had come to his tent the night before. He had not been alarmed, but had said nothing, and the figure vanished again. As a matter of fact, the next possible dak-walla brought on a telegram announcing the mother's death. 'There the thing was,' said Broughton. But at Thurnley he was practical enough. He roundly cursed the idiotic selfishness of Clarke, whose silly antics had caused all the inconvenience. At the same time, he couldn't refuse to sympathise to some extent with the ignorant workmen. 'My own idea,' said he, 'is that if a ghost ever does come in one's way, one ought to speak to it.'

"I agreed. Little as I knew of the ghost world and its conventions, I had always remembered that a spook was in honour bound to wait to be spoken to. It didn't seem much to do, and I felt that the sound of one's own voice would at any rate reassure oneself as to one's wakefulness. But there are few ghosts outside Europe — few, that is, that a white man can see — and I had never been troubled with any. However, as I have said, I told Broughton that I agreed.

"So the wedding took place, and I went to it in a tall hat which I bought for the occasion, and the new Mrs. Broughton smiled very nicely at me afterwards. As it had to happen, I took the Orient Express that evening and was not in England again for nearly six months. Just before I came back I got a letter from Broughton. He asked if I could see him in London or come to Thurnley, as he thought I should be better able to help him than anyone else he knew. His wife sent a nice message to me at the end, so I was reassured about at least one thing. I wrote from Budapest that I would come and see him at Thurnley for two days after my arrival in London, and as I sauntered out of the Pannonia into the Kerepesi Utcza to post my letters, I wondered of what earthly service I could be to Broughton. I had been out with him after tiger on foot, and I could imagine few men better able at a pinch to manage their own business. However, I had nothing to do, so after dealing with some small accumulations of business during my absence, I packed a kit-bag and departed to Euston.

"I was met by Broughton's great limousine at Thurnley Road station, and after a drive of nearly seven miles we echoed through the sleepy streets of Thurnley village, into which the main gates of the park thrust themselves, splendid with pillars and spread-eagles and tom-cats rampant atop of them. I never was a herald, but I know that the Broughtons have the right to supporters — Heaven knows why! From the gates a quadruple avenue of beech-trees led inwards for a quarter of a mile. Beneath them a neat strip of fine turf edged the road and ran back until the poison of the dead beech-leaves killed it under the trees. There were many wheel-tracks on the road, and a comfortable little pony trap jogged past me laden with a country parson and his wife and daughter. Evidently there was some garden party going on at the Abbey. The road dropped away to the right at the end of the avenue, and I could see the Abbey across a wide pasturage and a broad lawn thickly dotted with guests.

"The end of the building was plain. It must have been almost mercilessly austere when it was first built, but time had crumbled the edges and toned the stone down to an orange-lichened grey wherever it showed behind its curtain of magnolia, jasmine, and ivy. Farther on was the three-storied Jacobean house, tall and handsome. There had not been the slightest attempt to adapt the one to the other, but the kindly ivy had glossed over the touching-point. There was a tall flèche in the middle of the building, surmounting a small bell tower. Behind the house there rose the mountainous verdure of Spanish chestnuts all the way up the hill.

"Broughton had seen me coming from afar, and walked across from his other guests to welcome me before turning me over to the butler's care. This man was sandy-haired and rather inclined to be talkative. He could, however, answer hardly any questions about the house; he had, he said, only been there three weeks. Mindful of what Broughton had told me, I made no inquiries about ghosts, though the room into which I was shown might have justified anything. It was a very large low room with oak beams projecting from the white ceiling. Every inch of the walls, including the doors, was covered with tapestry, and a remarkably fine Italian fourpost bedstead, heavily draped, added to the darkness and dignity of the place. All the furniture was old, well made, and dark. Underfoot there was a plain green pile carpet, the only new thing about the room except the electric light fittings and the jugs and basins. Even the looking-glass on the dressing-table was an old pyramidal Venetian glass set in heavy repoussé frame of tarnished silver.

"After a few minutes' cleaning up, I went downstairs and out upon the lawn, where I greeted my hostess. The people gathered there were of the usual country type, all anxious to be pleased and roundly curious as to the new master of the Abbey. Rather to my surprise, and quite to my pleasure, I rediscovered Glenham, whom I had known well in old days in Barotseland: he lived quite close, as, he remarked with a grin, I ought to have known. 'But,' he added, 'I don't live in a place like this.' He swept his hand to the long, low lines of the Abbey in obvious admiration, and then, to my intense interest, muttered beneath his breath, 'Thank God!' He saw that I had overheard him, and turning to me said decidedly, 'Yes, "thank God," ' I said, and I meant it. I wouldn't live at the Abbey for all Broughton's money.'

" 'But surely,' I demurred, 'you know that old Clarke was discovered in the very act of setting light to his bug-a-boos?'

"Glenham shrugged his shoulders. 'Yes, I know about that. But there is something wrong with the place still. All I can say is that Broughton is a different man since he has lived here. I don't believe that he will remain much longer. But — you're staying here? — well, you'll hear all about it to-night. There's a big dinner, I understand.' The conversation turned off to old reminiscences, and Glenham soon after had to go.

"Before I went to dress that evening I had twenty minutes' talk with Broughton in his library. There was no doubt that the man was altered, gravely altered. He was nervous and fidgety, and I found him looking at me only when my eye was off him. I naturally asked him what he wanted of me. I told him I would do anything I could, but that I couldn't conceive what he lacked that I could provide. He said with a lustreless smile that there was, however, something, and that he would tell me the following morning. It struck me that he was somehow ashamed of himself, and perhaps ashamed of the part he was asking me to play. However, I dismissed the subject from my mind and went up to dress in my palatial room. As I shut the door a draught blew out the Queen of Sheba from the wall, and I noticed that the tapestries were not fastened to the wall at the bottom. I have always held very practical views about spooks, and it has often seemed to me that the slow waving in firelight of loose tapestry upon a wall would account for ninety-nine per cent., of the stories one hears. Certainly the dignified undulation of this lady with her attendants and huntsmen — one of whom was untidily cutting the throat of a fallow deer upon the very steps on which King Solomon, a grey-faced Flemish nobleman with the order of the Golden Fleece, awaited his fair visitor — gave colour to my hypothesis.

"Nothing much happened at dinner. The people were very much like those of the garden party. A young woman next me seemed anxious to know what was being read in London. As she was far more familiar than I with the most recent magazines and literary supplements, I found salvation in being myself instructed in the tendencies of modern fiction. All true art, she said, was shot through and through with melancholy. How vulgar were the attempts at wit that marked so many modern books! From the beginning of literature it had always been tragedy that embodied the highest attainment of every age. To call such works morbid merely begged the question. No thoughtful man — she looked sternly at me through the steel rim of her glasses — could fail to agree with me. Of course, as one would, I immediately and properly said that I slept with Pett Ridge and Jacobs under my pillow at night, and that if *Jorrocks* weren't quite so large and ornery, I would add him to the company. She hadn't read any of them, so I was saved — for a time. But I remember grimly that she said that the dearest wish of her life was to be in some awful and soul-freezing situation of horror, and I remember that she dealt hardly with the hero of Nat Paynter's vampire story, between nibbles at her brown-bread ice. She was a cheerless soul, and I couldn't help thinking that if there were many such in the neighbourhood, it was not surprising that old Glenham had been stuffed with some nonsense or other about the Abbey. Yet nothing could well have been less creepy than the glitter of silver and glass, and the subdued lights and cackle of conversation all round the dinner-table.

"After the ladies had gone I found myself talking to the rural dean. He was a thin, earnest man, who at once turned the conversation to old Clarke's buffooneries. But, he said, Mr. Broughton had introduced such a new and cheerful spirit, not only into the Abbey, but, he might say, into the whole neighbourhood, that he had great hopes that the ignorant superstitions of the past were from henceforth destined to oblivion. Thereupon his other neighbour, a portly gentleman of independent means and position, audibly remarked 'Amen,' which dampened the rural dean, and we talked of partridges past, partridges present, and pheasants to come. At the other end of the table Broughton sat with a couple of his friends, red-faced hunting men. Once I noticed that they were discussing me, but I paid no attention to it at the time. I remembered it a few hours later.

"By eleven all the guests were gone, and Broughton, his wife, and I were alone together under the fine plaster ceiling of the Jacobean drawing-room. Mrs. Broughton talked about one or two of the neighbours, and then, with a smile, said that she knew I would excuse her, shook hands with me, and went off to bed. I am not very good at analysing things, but I felt that she talked a little uncomfortably and with a suspicion of effort, smiled rather conventionally, and was obviously glad to go. These things seem trifling enough to repeat, but I had throughout the faint feeling that everything was not square. Under the circumstances, this was enough to set me wondering what on earth the service could be that I was to render — wondering also whether the whole business were not some ill-advised jest in order to make me come down from London for a mere shooting-party.

"Broughton said little after she had gone. But he was evidently labouring to bring the conversation round to the so-called haunting of the Abbey. As soon as I saw this, of course I asked him directly about it. He then seemed at once to lose interest in the matter. There was no doubt about it: Broughton was somehow a changed man, and to my mind he had changed in no way for the better. Mrs. Broughton seemed no sufficient cause. He was clearly very fond of her, and she of him. I reminded him that he was going to tell me what I could do for him in the morning, pleaded my journey, lighted a candle, and went upstairs with him. At the end of the passage leading into the old house, he grinned weakly and said, 'Mind, if you see a ghost, do talk to it; you said you would.' He stood irresolutely a moment and then turned away. At the door of his dressing-room he paused once more: 'I'm here,' he called out, 'if you should want anything. Good night,' and he shut his door.

"I went along the passage to my room, undressed, switched on a lamp beside my bed, read a few pages of *The Jungle Book,* and then, more than ready for sleep, turned the light off and went fast asleep.

"THREE HOURS LATER I woke up. There was not a breath of wind outside. There was not even a flicker of light from the fireplace. As I lay there, an ash tinkled slightly as it cooled, but there was hardly a gleam of the dullest red in the grate. An owl cried among the silent Spanish chestnuts on the slope outside. I idly reviewed the events of the day, hoping that I should fall off to sleep again before I reached dinner. But at the end I seemed as wakeful as ever. There was no help for it. I must read my *Jungle Book* again till I felt ready to go off, so I fumbled for the pear at the end of the cord that hung down inside the bed, and I switched on the bedside lamp. The sudden glory dazzled me for a moment. I felt under my pillow for my book with half-shut eyes. Then, growing used to the light, I happened to look down to the foot of my bed.

"I can never tell you really what happened then. Nothing I could ever confess in the most abject words could even faintly picture to you what I felt. I know that my heart stopped dead, and my throat shut automatically. In one instinctive movement I crouched back up against the head-boards of the bed, staring at the horror. The movement set my heart going again, and the sweat dripped from every pore. I am not a particularly religious man, but I had always believed that God would never allow any supernatural appearance to present itself to man in such a guise and in such circumstances that harm, either bodily or mental, could result to him. I can only tell you that at that moment both my life and my reason rocked unsteadily on their seats.''

THE OTHER *Osiris* passengers had gone to bed. Only he and I remained leaning over the starboard railing, which rattled uneasily now and then under the fierce vibration of the over-engined mail-boat. Far over, there were the lights of a few fishing-smacks riding out the night, and a great rush of white combing and seething water fell out and away from us overside.

At last Colvin went on:

"LEANING OVER THE foot of my bed, looking at me, was a figure swathed in a rotten and tattered veiling. This shroud passed over the head, but left both eyes and the right side of the face bare. It then followed the line of the arm down to where the hand grasped the bed-end. The face was not entirely that of a skull, though the eyes and the flesh of the face were totally gone.

There was a thin, dry skin drawn tightly over the features, and there was some skin left on the hand. One wisp of hair crossed the forehead. It was perfectly still. I looked at it, and it looked at me, and my brains turned dry and hot in my head. I had still got the pear of the electric lamp in my hand, and I played idly with it; only I dared not turn the light out again. I shut my eyes, only to open them in a hideous terror the same second. The thing had not moved. My heart was thumping, and the sweat cooled me as it evaporated. Another cinder tinkled in the grate, and a panel creaked in the wall.

"My reason failed me. For twenty minutes, or twenty seconds, I was able to think of nothing else but this awful figure, till there came, hurtling through the empty channels of my senses, the remembrance that Broughton and his friends had discussed me furtively at dinner. The dim possibility of its being a hoax stole gratefully into my unhappy mind, and once there, one's pluck came creeping back along a thousand tiny veins. My first sensation was one of blind unreasoning thankfulness that my brain was going to stand the trial. I am not a timid man, but the best of us needs some human handle to steady him in time of extremity, and in this faint but growing hope that after all it might be only a brutal hoax, I found the fulcrum that I needed. At last I moved.

"How I managed to do it I cannot tell you, but with one spring towards the foot of the bed I got within arm's-length and struck out one fearful blow with my fist at the thing. It crumbled under it, and my hand was cut to the bone. With a sickening revulsion after my terror, I dropped half-fainting across the end of the bed. So it was merely a foul trick after all. No doubt the trick had been played many a time before: no doubt Broughton and his friends had had some large bet among themselves as to what I should do when I discovered the gruesome thing. From my state of abject terror I found myself transported into an insensate anger. I shouted curses upon Broughton. I dived rather than climbed over the bed-end on to the sofa. I tore at the robed skeleton — how well the whole thing had been carried out, I thought — I broke the skull against the floor, and stamped upon its dry bones. I flung the head away under the bed, and rent the brittle bones of the trunk in pieces. I snapped the thin thigh-bones across my knee, and flung them in different directions. The shin-bones I set up against a stool and broke with my heel. I raged like a Berserker against the loathly thing, and stripped the ribs from the backbone and slung the breastbone against the cupboard. My fury increased as the work of destruction went on. I tore the frail rotten veil into twenty pieces, and the dust went up over everything, over the clean blotting-paper and the silver inkstand. At last my work was done. There was but a raffle of broken bones and strips of parchment and crumbling wool. Then, picking up a piece of the skull — it was the cheek and temple bone of the right side, I remember — I opened the door and went down the passage to Broughton's dressing-room. I remember still how my sweat-dripping pyjamas clung to me as I walked. At the door I kicked and entered.

"Broughton was in bed. He had already turned the light on and seemed shrunken and horrified. For a moment he could hardly pull himself together. Then I spoke, I don't know what I said. Only I know that from a heart full and over-full with hatred and contempt, spurred on by shame of my own recent cowardice, I let my tongue run on. He answered nothing. I was amazed at my own fluency. My hair still clung lankily to my wet temples, my hand was bleeding profusely, and I must have looked a strange sight. Broughton huddled himself up at the head of the bed just as I had. Still he made no answer, no defence. He seemed preoccupied with something besides my reproaches, and once or twice moistened his lips with his tongue. But he could say nothing though he moved his hands now and then, just as a baby who cannot speak moves its hands.

"At last the door into Mrs. Broughton's room opened and she came in, white and terrified. 'What is it? What is it? Oh, in God's name! what is it?' she cried again and again, and then she went up to her husband and sat on the bed in her night-dress, and the two faced me. I told her what the matter was. I spared her husband not a word for her presence there. Yet he seemed hardly to understand. I told the pair that I had spoiled their cowardly joke for them. Broughton looked up.

" 'I have smashed the foul thing into a hundred pieces,' I said. Broughton licked his lips again and his mouth worked. 'By God!' I shouted, 'it would serve you right if I thrashed you within an inch of your life. I will take care that not a decent man or woman of my acquaintance ever speaks to you again. And there,' I added, throwing the broken piece of the skull upon the floor beside his bed, 'there is a souvenir for you, of your damned work to-night!'

"Broughton saw the bone, and in a moment it was his turn to frighten me. He squealed like a hare caught in a trap. He screamed and screamed till Mrs. Broughton, almost as bewildered as myself, held on to him and coaxed him like a child to be quiet. But Broughton — and as he moved I thought that ten minutes ago I perhaps looked as terribly ill as he did — thrust her from him, and scrambled out of the bed on to the floor, and still screaming put out his hand to the bone. It had blood on it from my hand. He paid no attention to me whatever. In truth I said nothing. This was a new turn indeed to the horrors of the evening. He rose from the floor with the bone in his hand and stood silent. He seemed to be listening. 'Time, time, perhaps,' he muttered, and almost at the same moment fell at full length on the carpet, cutting his head against the fender. The bone flew from his hand and came to rest near the door. I picked Broughton up, haggard and broken, with blood over his face. He whispered hoarsely and quickly, 'Listen, listen!' We listened.

"After ten seconds' utter quiet, I seemed to hear something. I could not be sure, but at last there was no doubt. There was a quiet sound as of one moving along the passage. Little regular steps came towards us over the hard oak flooring. Broughton moved to where his wife sat, white and speechless, on the bed, and pressed her face into his shoulder.

"Then, the last thing that I could see as he turned the light out, he fell forward with his own head pressed into the pillow of the bed. Something in their company, something in their cowardice, helped me, and I faced the open doorway of the room, which was outlined fairly clearly against the dimly lighted passage. I put out one hand and touched Mrs. Broughton's shoulder in the darkness. But at the last moment I too failed. I sank on my knees and put my face in the bed. Only we all heard. The footsteps came to the door, and there they stopped. The piece of bone was lying a yard inside the door. There was a rustle of moving stuff, and the thing was in the room. Mrs. Broughton was silent: I could hear Broughton's voice praying, muffled in the pillow: I was cursing my own cowardice. Then the steps moved out again on the oak boards of the passage, and I heard the sounds dying away. In a flash of remorse I went to the door and looked out. At the end of the corridor I thought I saw something that moved away. A moment later the passage was empty. I stood with my forehead against the jamb of the door almost physically sick.

" 'You can turn the light on,' I said, and there was an answering flare. There was no bone at my feet. Mrs. Broughton had fainted. Broughton was almost useless, and it took me ten minutes to bring her to. Broughton only said one thing worth remembering. For the most part he went on muttering prayers. But I was glad afterwards to recollect that he had said that thing. He said in a colourless voice, half as a question, half as a reproach, 'You didn't speak to her.'

"We spent the remainder of the night together. Mrs. Broughton actually fell off into a kind of sleep before dawn, but she suffered so horribly in her dreams that I shook her into consciousness again. Never was dawn so long in coming. Three or four times Broughton spoke to himself. Mrs. Broughton would then just tighten her hold on his arm, but she could say nothing. As for me, I can honestly say that I grew worse as the hours passed and the light strengthened. The two violent reactions had battered down my steadiness of view, and I felt that the foundations of my life had been built upon the sand. I said nothing, and after binding up my hand with a towel, I did not move. It was better so. They helped me and I helped them, and we all three knew that our reason had gone very near to ruin that night. At last, when the light came in pretty strongly, and the birds outside were chattering and singing, we felt that we must do something. Yet we never moved. You might have thought that we should particularly dislike being found as we were by the servants: yet nothing of that kind mattered a straw, and an overpowering listlessness bound us as we sat, until Chapman Broughton's man, actually knocked and opened the door. None of us moved. Broughton, speaking hardly and stiffly, said, 'Chapman you can come back in five minutes.' Chapman was a discreet man, but it would have made no difference to us if he had carried his news to the 'room' at once.

"We looked at each other and I said I must go back. I meant to wait outside till Chapman returned. I simply dared not re-enter my bedroom alone. Broughton roused himself and said that he would come with me. Mrs. Broughton agreed to remain in her own room for five minutes if the blinds were drawn up and all the doors left open.

"So Broughton and I, leaning stiffly one against the other, went down to my room. By the morning light that filtered past the blinds we could see our way, and I released the blinds. There was nothing wrong in the room from end to end, except smears of my own blood on the end of the bed, on the sofa, and on the carpet where I had torn the thing to pieces."

COLVIN HAD FINISHED his story. There was nothing to say. Seven bells stuttered out from the fo'c'sle, and the answering cry wailed through the darkness. I took him downstairs.

"Of course I am much better now, but it is a kindness of you to let me sleep in your cabin."

COUNT MAGNUS

M.R. JAMES

Y WHAT MEANS THE papers out of which I have made a connected story came into my hands is the last point which the reader will learn from these pages. But it is necessary to prefix to my extracts from them a statement of the form in which I possess them.

They consist, then, partly of a series of collections for a book of travels, such a volume as was a common product of the forties and fifties. Horace Marryat's *Journal of a Residence in Jutland and the Danish Isles* is a fair specimen of the class to which I allude. These books usually treated of some unfamiliar district on the Continent. They were illustrated with woodcuts or steel plates. They gave details of hotel accommodation, and of means of communication, such as we now expect to find in any well-regulated guide-book, and they dealt largely in reported conversations with intelligent foreigners, racy inkeepers and garrulous peasants. In a word, they were chatty.

Begun with the idea of furnishing material for such a book, my papers as they progressed assumed the character of a record of one single personal experience, and this record was continued up to the very eve, almost, of its termination.

The writer was a Mr. Wraxall. For my knowledge of him I have to depend entirely on the evidence his writings afford, and from these I deduce that as a man past middle age, possessed of some private means, and very much alone in the world. He had, it seems, no settled abode in England, but was a denizen of hotels and boarding-houses. It is probable that he entertained the idea of settling down at some future time which never came; and I think it also likely that the Pantechnicon fire in the early seventies must have destroyed a great deal that would have thrown light on his antecedents, for he refers once or twice to property of his that was warehoused at that establishment.

It is further apparent that Mr. Wraxall had published a book, and that it treated of a holiday he had once taken in Britanny. More than this I cannot say about his work, because a diligent search in bibliographical works has convinced me that it must have appeared either anonymously or under a pseudonym.

As to his character, it is not difficult to form some superficial opinion. He must have been an intelligent and cultivated man. It seems that he was near being a Fellow of his college at Oxford — Brasenose, as I judge from the Calendar. His besetting fault was pretty clearly that of over-inquisitiveness, possibly a good fault in a traveller, certainly a fault for which this traveller paid dearly enough in the end.

On what proved to be his last expedition, he was plotting another book. Scandinavia, a region not widely known to Englishmen forty years ago, had struck him as an interesting field. He must have lighted on some old books of Swedish history or memoirs, and the idea had struck him that there was room for a book descriptive of travel in Sweden, interspersed with epi- sodes from the history of some of the great Swedish families. He procured letters of introduction, therefore, to some persons of quality in Sweden, and set out thither in the early summer of 1863.

Of his travels in the North there is no need to speak, nor of his residence of some weeks in Stockholm. I need only mention that some *savant* resident there put him on the track of an important collection of family papers belonging to the proprietors of an ancient manor-house in Ves- tergothland, and obtained for him permission to examine them.

The manor-house, or *berrgård*, in question is to be called Råbäck (pronounced something like Roebeck, though that is not its name. It is one of the best buildings of its kind in all the country, and the picture of it in Dahlenberg's *Suecia antiqua et moderna,* engraved in 1694, shows it very much as the tourist may see it to-day. It was built soon after 1600, and is, roughly speaking, very much like an English house of that period in respect of material — red-brick with stone facings — and style. The man who built it was a scion of the great house of De la Gardie, and his descendants possess it still. De la Gardie is the name by which I will designate them when mention of them becomes necessary.

They received Mr. Wraxall with great kindness and courtesy, and pressed him to stay in the house as long as his researches lasted. But, preferring to be independent, and mistrusting his powers of conversing in Swedish, he settled himself at the village inn, which turned out quite sufficiently comfortable, at any rate during the summer months. This arrangement would entail a short walk daily to and from the manor-house of something under a mile. The house itself stood in a park, and was protected — we should say grown up — with large old timber. Near it you found the walled garden, and then entered a close wood fringing one of the small lakes with which the whole country is pitted. Then came the wall of the demesne, and you climbed a steep knoll — a knob of rock lightly covered with soil — and on the top of this stood the church, fenced in with tall dark trees. It was a curious building to English eyes. The nave and aisles were low, and filled with pews and galleries. In the western gallery stood the handsome old organ, gaily painted, and with silver pipes. The ceiling was flat, and had been adorned by a seventeenth-century artist with a strange and hideous "Last Judgment," full of lurid flames, falling cities, burning ships, crying souls, and brown and smiling demons. Handsome brass coronæ hung from the roof; the pulpit was like a doll's-house, covered with little painted wooden cherubs and saints; a stand with three hour-glasses was hinged to the preacher's desk. Such sights as these may be seen in many a church in Sweden now, but what distinguished this one was an addition to the original building. At the eastern end of the north aisle the builder of the manor-house had erected a mausoleum for himself and his family. It was a largish eight-sided building, lighted by a series of oval windows, and it had a domed roof, topped by a kind of pumpkin-shaped object rising into a spire, a form in which Swedish architects greatly delighted. The roof was of copper externally, and was painted black, while the walls, in common with those of the church, were staringly white. To this mausoleum there was no access from the church. It had a portal and steps of its own on the northern side.

Past the churchyard the path to the village goes, and not more than three or four minutes bring you to the inn door.

On the first day of his stay at Råbäck Mr. Wraxall found the church door open, and made those notes of the interior which I have epitomized. Into the mausoleum, however, he could not make his way. He could by looking through the keyhole just descry that there were fine marble effigies and sarcophagi of copper, and a wealth of armorial ornament, which made him very anxious to spend some time in investigation.

The papers he had come to examine at the manor-house proved to be of just the kind he wanted for his book. There were family correspondence, journals, and account-books of the earliest owners of the estate, very carefully kept and clearly written, full of amusing and picturesque detail. The first De la Gardie appeared in them as a strong and capable man. Shortly after the building of the mansion there had been a period of distress in the district, and the peasants had risen and attacked several châteaux and done some damage. The owner of Råbäck took a leading part in suppressing the trouble, and there was reference to executions of ringleaders and severe punishments inflicted with no sparing hand.

The portrait of this Magnus de la Gardie was one of the best in the house, and Mr. Wraxall studied it with no little interest after his day's work. He gives no detailed description of it, but I gather that the face impressed him rather by its power than by its beauty or goodness; in fact, he writes that Count Magnus was an almost phenomenally ugly man.

On this day Mr. Wraxall took his supper with the family, and walked back in the late but still bright evening.

"I must remember," he writes, "to ask the sexton if he can let me into the mausoleum at the church. He evidently has access to it himself, for I saw him to-night standing on the steps, and, as I thought, locking or unlocking the door."

I find that early on the following day Mr. Wraxall had some conversation with his landlord. His setting it down at such length as he does surprised me at first; but I soon realized that the papers I was reading were, at least in their beginning, the materials for the book he was meditating, and that it was to have been one of those quasi-journalistic productions which admit of the introduction of an admixture of conversational matter.

His object, he says, was to find out whether any traditions of Count Magnus de la Gardie lingered on in the scenes of that gentleman's activity, and whether the popular estimate of him were favourable or not. He found that the Count was decidedly not a favourite. If his tenants came late to their work on the days which they owed to him as Lord of the Manor, they were set on the wooden horse, or flogged and branded in the manor-house yard. One or two cases there were of men who had occupied lands which encroached on the lord's domain, and whose houses had been mysteriously burnt on a winter's night, with the whole family inside. But what seemed to dwell on the innkeeper's mind most — for he returned to the subject more than once — was that the Count had been on the Black Pilgrimage, and had brought something or someone back with him.

You will naturally inquire, as Mr. Wraxall did, what the Black Pilgrimage may have been. But your curiosity on the point must remain unsatisfied for the time being, just as his did. The landlord was evidently unwilling to give a full answer, or indeed any answer, on the point, and, being called out for a moment, trotted off with obvious alacrity, only putting his head in at the door a few minutes afterwards to say that he was called away to Skara, and should not be back till evening.

So Mr. Wraxall had to go unsatisfied to his day's work at the manor-house. The papers on which he was just then engaged soon put his thoughts into another channel, for he had to occupy himself with glancing over the correspondence between Sophia Albertina in Stockholm and her married cousin Ulrica Leonora at Rabäck in the years 1705-1710. The letters were of exceptional interest from the light they threw upon the culture of that period in Sweden, as anyone can testify who has read the full edition of them in the publications of the Swedish Historical Manuscripts Commission.

In the afternoon he had done with these, and after returning the boxes in which they were kept to their places on the shelf, he proceeded, very naturally, to take down some of the volumes nearest to them, in order to determine which of them had best be his principal subject of investigation next day. The shelf he had hit upon was occupied mostly by a collection of account-books in the writing of the first Count Magnus. But one among them was not an account-book, but a book of alchemical and other tracts in another sixteenth-century hand. Not being very familiar with alchemical literature, Mr. Wraxall spends much space which he might have spared in setting out the names and beginnings of the various treatises: The book of the Phoenix, book of the Thirty Words, book of the Toad, book of Miriam, Turba philosophorum, and so forth; and then he announces with a good deal of circumstance his delight at finding, on a leaf originally left blank near the middle of the book, some writing of Count Magnus himself headed

"Liber nigræ peregrinationis." It is true that only a few lines were written, but there was quite enough to show that the landlord had that morning been referring to a belief at least as old as the time of Count Magnus, and probably shared by him. This is the English of what was written:

"If any man desires to obtain a long life, if he would obtain a faithful messenger and see the blood of his enemies, it is necessary that he should first go into the city of Chorazin, and there salute the prince. . . ." Here there was an erasure of one word, not very thoroughly done, so that Mr. Wraxall felt pretty sure that he was right in reading it as *aëris* ("of the air"). But there was no more of the text copied, only a line in Latin: "Quære reliqua hujus materiei inter secretiora" (See the rest of this matter among the more private things).

It could not be denied that this threw a rather lurid light upon the tastes and beliefs of the Count; but to Mr. Wraxall, separated from him by nearly three centuries, the thought that he might have added to his general forcefulness alchemy, and to alchemy something like magic, only made him a more picturesque figure; and when, after a rather prolonged contemplation of his picture in the hall, Mr. Wraxall set out on his homeward way, his mind was full of the thought of Count Magnus. He had no eyes for his surroundings, no perception of the evening scents of the woods or the evening light on the lake; and when all of a sudden he pulled up short, he was astonished to find himself already at the gate of the churchyard, and within a few minutes of his dinner. His eyes fell on the mausoleum.

"Ah," he said, "Count Magnus, there you are. I should dearly like to see you."

"Like many solitary men," he writes, "I have a habit of talking to myself aloud; and, unlike some of the Greek and Latin particles, I do not expect an answer. Certainly, and perhaps fortunately in this case, there was neither voice nor any that regarded: only the woman who, I suppose, was cleaning up the church, dropped some metallic object on the floor, whose clang startled me. Count Magnus, I think, sleeps sound enough."

That same evening the landlord of the inn, who had heard Mr. Wraxall say that he wished to see the clerk or deacon (as he would be called in Sweden) of the parish, introduced him to that official in the inn parlour. A visit to the De la Gardie tombhouse was soon arranged for the next day, and a little general conversation ensued.

Mr. Wraxall, remembering that one function of Scandinavian deacons is to teach candidates for Confirmation, thought he would refresh his own memory on a Biblical point.

"Can you tell me," he said, "anything about Chorazin?"

The deacon seemed startled, but readily reminded him how that village had once been denounced.

"To be sure," said Mr. Wraxall; "it is, I suppose, quite a ruin now?"

"So I expect," replied the deacon. "I have heard some of our old priests say that Antichrist is to be born there; and there are tales — "

"Ah! what tales are those?" Mr. Wraxall put in.

"Tales, I was going to say, which I have forgotten," said the deacon; and soon after that he said good night.

The landlord was now alone, and at Mr. Wraxall's mercy; and that inquirer was not inclined to spare him.

"Herr Nielsen," he said, "I have found out something about the Black Pilgrimage. You may as well tell me what you know. What did the Count bring back with him?"

Swedes are habitually slow, perhaps, in answering, or perhaps the landlord was an exception. I am not sure; but Mr. Wraxall notes that the landlord spent at least one minute in looking at him before he said anything at all. Then he came close up to his guest, and with a good deal of effort he spoke:

"Mr. Wraxall, I can tell you this one little tale, and no more — not any more. You must not ask anything when I have done. In my grandfather's time — that is, ninety-two years ago — there were two men who said: 'The Count is dead; we do not care for him. We will go to-night and have a free hunt in his wood' — the long wood on the hill that you have seen behind Råbäck. Well, those that heard them say this, they said: 'No, do not go; we are sure you will meet with persons walking who should not be walking. They should be resting, not walking.' These men laughed. There were no forest-men to keep the wood, because no one wished to hunt there. The family were not here at the house. These men could do what they wished.

"Very well, they go to the wood that night. My grandfather was sitting here in this room. It was the summer, and a light night. With the window open, he could see out to the wood, and hear.

"So he sat there, and two or three men with him, and they listened. At first they hear nothing at all; then they hear someone — you know how far away it is — they hear someone scream, just as if the most inside part of his soul was twisted out of him. All of them in the room caught hold of each other, and they sat so for three-quarters of an hour. Then they hear someone else, only about three hundred ells off. They hear him laugh out loud: it was not one of those two men that laughed, and, indeed, they have all of them said that it was not any man at all. After that they hear a great door shut.

"Then, when it was just light with the sun, they all went to the priest. They said to him:

" 'Father, put on your gown and your ruff, and come to bury these men, Anders Bjornsen and Hans Thorbjorn.'

"You understand that they were sure these men were dead. So they went to the wood — my grandfather never forgot this. He said they were all like so many dead men themselves. The priest, too, he was in a white fear. He said when they came to him:

" 'I heard one cry in the night, and I heard one laugh afterwards. If I cannot forget that, I shall not be able to sleep again.'

"So they went to the wood, and they found these men on the edge of the wood. Hans Thorbjorn was standing with his back against a tree, and all the time he was pushing with his hands — pushing something away from him which was not there. So he was not dead. And they led him away, and took him to the house at Nykjoping, and he died before the winter; but he went on pushing with his hands. Also Anders Bjornsen was there; but he was dead. And I tell you this about Anders Bjornsen, that he was once a beautiful man, but now his face was not there, because the flesh of it was sucked away off the bones. You understand that? My grandfather did not forget that. And they laid him on the bier which they brought, and they put a cloth over his head, and the priest walked before; and they began to sing the psalm for the dead as well as they could. So, as they were singing the end of the first verse, one fell down, who was carrying the head of the bier, and the others looked back, and they saw that the cloth had fallen off, and the eyes of Anders Bjornsen were looking up, because there was nothing to close over them. And this they could not bear. Therefore the priest laid the cloth upon him, and sent for a spade, and they buried him in that place."

The next day Mr. Wraxall records that the deacon called for him soon after his breakfast, and took him to the church and mausoleum. He noticed that the key of the latter was hung on a nail just by the pulpit, and it occurred to him that, as the church door seemed to be left unlocked as a rule, it would not be difficult for him to pay a second and more private visit to the monuments if there proved to be more of interest among them than could be digested at first. The building, when he entered it, he found not unimposing. The monuments, mostly large erections of the seventeenth and eighteenth centuries, were dignified if luxuriant, and the epitaphs and heraldry were copious. The central space of the domed room was occupied by three copper sarcophagi, covered with finely-engraved ornament. Two of them had, as is commonly the case in Denmark and Sweden, a large metal crucifix on the lid. The third, that of Count Magnus, as it appeared, had, instead of that, a full-length effigy engraved upon it, and round the edge were several bands of similar ornament representing various scenes. One was a battle, with cannon belching out smoke, and walled towns, and troops of pikemen. Another showed an execution. In a third, among trees, was a man running at full speed, with flying hair and outstretched hands. After him followed a strange form; it would be hard to say whether the artist had intended it for a man, and was unable to give the requisite similitude, or whether it was intentionally made as monstrous as it looked. In view of the skill with which the rest of the drawing was done, Mr. Wraxall felt inclined to adopt the latter idea. The figure was unduly short, and was for the most part muffled in a hooded garment which swept the ground. The only part of the form which projected from that shelter was not shaped like any hand or arm. Mr. Wraxall compares it to the tentacle of a devil-fish, and continues: "On seeing this, I said to myself, 'This, then, which is evidently an allegorical representation of some kind — a fiend pursuing a hunted soul — may be the origin of the Story of Count Magnus and his mysterious companion. Let us see how the huntsman is pictured: doubtless it will be a demon blowing his horn.' " But, as it turned out, there was no such sensational figure, only the semblance of a cloaked man on a hillock, who stood leaning on a stick, and watching the hunt with an interest which the engraver had tried to express in his attitude.

Mr. Wraxall noted the finely-worked and massive steel padlocks — three in number — which secured the sarcophagus. One of them, he saw, was detached, and lay on the pavement. And then, unwilling to delay the deacon longer or to waste his own working-time, he made his way onward to the manor-house.

"It is curious," he notes, "how on retracing a familiar path one's thoughts engross one to the absolute exclusion of surrounding objects. To-night, for the second time, I had entirely failed to notice where I was going (I had planned a private visit to the tomb-house to copy the epitaphs), when I suddenly, as it were, awoke to consciousness, and found myself (as before) turning in at the churchyard gate, and, I believe, singing or chanting some such words as, 'Are you awake, Count Magnus? Are you asleep, Count Magnus?' and then something more which I have failed to recollect. It seemed to me that I must have been behaving in this nonsensical way for some time."

He found the key of the mausoleum where he had expected to find it, and copied the greater part of what he wanted; in fact, he stayed until the light began to fail him.

"I must have been wrong," he writes, "in saying that one of the padlocks of my Count's sarcophagus was unfastened; I see to-night that two are loose. I picked both up, and laid them carefully on the window-ledge, after trying unsuccessfully to close them. The remaining one is still firm, and, though I take it to be a spring lock, I cannot guess how it is opened. Had I succeeded in undoing it, I am almost afraid I should have taken the liberty of opening the sarcophagus. It is strange, the interest I feel in the personality of this, I fear, somewhat ferocious and grim old noble."

The day following was, as it turned out, the last of Mr. Wraxall's stay at Råbäck. He received letters connected with certain investments which made it desirable that he should return to England; his work among the papers was practically done, and travelling was slow. He decided, therefore, to make his farewells, put some finishing touches to his notes, and be off.

These finishing touches and farewells, as it turned out, took more time than he had expected. The hospitable family insisted on his staying to dine with them — they dined at three — and it was verging on half-past six before he was outside the iron gates of Råbäck. He dwelt on every step of his walk by the lake, determined to saturate himself, now that he trod it for the last time, in the sentiment of the place and hour. And when he reached the summit of the churchyard knoll, he lingered for many minutes, gazing at the limitless prospect of woods near and distant, all dark beneath a sky of liquid green. When at last he turned to go, the thought struck him that surely he must bid farewell to Count Magnus as well as the rest of the De la Gardies. The church was but twenty yards away, and he knew where the key of the mausoleum hung. It was not long before he was standing over the great copper coffin, and, as usual, talking to himself aloud. "You may have been a bit of a rascal in your time, Magnus," he was saying, "but for all that I should like to see you, or, rather— "

"Just at that instant," he says, "I felt a blow on my foot. Hastily enough I drew it back, and something fell on the pavement with a clash. It was the third, the last of the three padlocks which had fastened the sarcophagus. I stooped to pick it up, and — Heaven is my witness that I am writing only the bare truth — before I had raised myself there was a sound of metal hinges creaking, and I distinctly saw the lid shifting upwards. I may have behaved like a coward, but I could not for my life stay for one moment. I was outside that dreadful building in less time than I can write — almost as quickly as I could have said — the words; and what frightens me yet more, I could not turn the key in the lock. As I sit here in my room noting these facts, I ask myself (it was not twenty minutes ago) whether that noise of creaking metal continued, and I cannot tell whether it did or not. I only know that there was something more than I have written that alarmed me, but whether it was sound or sight I am not able to remember. What is this that I have done?"

POOR MR. WRAXALL! He set out on his journey to England on the next day, as he had planned, and he reached England in safety; and yet, as I gather from his changed hand and inconsequent jottings, a broken man. One of several small notebooks that have come to me with his papers gives, not a key to, but a kind of inkling of, his experiences. Much of his journey was made by canal-boat, and I find not less than six painful attempts to enumerate and describe his fellow-passengers. The entries are of this kind:

"24. Pastor of village in Skåne. Usual black coat and soft black hat.
"25. Commercial traveller from Stockholm going to Trolehättan. Black cloak, brown hat.
"26. Man in long black cloak, broad-leafed hat, very old-fashioned."

THIS ENTRY IS lined out, and a note added: "Perhaps identical with No. 13. Have not yet seen his face." On referring to No. 13, I find that he is a Roman priest in a cassock.

The net result of the reckoning is always the same. Twenty-eight people appear in the enumeration, one being always a man in a long black cloak and broad hat, and the other a "short figure in dark cloak and hood." On the other hand, it is always noted that only twenty-six passengers appear at meals, and that the man in the cloak is perhaps absent, and the short figure is certainly absent.

ON REACHING ENGLAND, it appears that Mr. Wraxall landed at Harwich, and that he resolved at once to put himself out of the reach of some person or persons whom he never specifies, but whom he had evidently come to regard as his pursuers. Accordingly he took a vehicle — it was a closed fly — not trusting the railway, and drove across country to the village of Belchamp St. Paul. It was about nine o'clock on a moonlight August night when he neared the place. He was sitting forward, and looking out of the window at the fields and thickets — there was little else to be seen —

racing past him. Suddenly he came to a cross-road. At the corner two figures were standing motionless; both were in dark cloaks; the taller one wore a hat, the shorter a hood. He had no time to see their faces, nor did they make any motion that he could discern. Yet the horse shied violently and broke into a gallop, and Mr. Wraxall sank back into his seat in something like desperation. He had seen them before.

Arrived at Belchamp St. Paul, he was fortunate enough to find a decent furnished lodging, and for the next twenty-four hours he lived, comparatively speaking, in peace. His last notes were written on this day. They are too disjointed and ejaculatory to be given here in full, but the substance of them is clear enough. He is expecting a visit from his pursuers — how or when he knows not — and his constant cry is "What has he done?" and "Is there no hope?" Doctors, he knows, would call him mad, policemen would laugh at him. The parson is away. What can he do but lock his door and cry to God?

PEOPLE STILL REMEMBERED last year at Belchamp St. Paul how a strange gentleman came one evening in August years back; and how the next morning but one he was found dead, and there was an inquest; and the jury that viewed the body fainted, seven of 'em did, and none of 'em wouldn't speak to what they see, and the verdict was visitation of God; and how the people as kep' the 'ouse moved out that same week, and went away from that part. But they do not, I think, know that any glimmer of light has ever been thrown, or could be thrown, on the mystery. It so happened that last year the little house came into my hands as part of a legacy. It had stood empty since 1863, and there seemed no prospect of letting it; so I had it pulled down, and the papers of which I have given you an abstract were found in a forgotten cupboard under the window in the best bedroom.

THE PHANTOM COACH

AMELIA B. EDWARDS

THE CIRCUMSTANCES I AM about to relate to you have truth to recommend them. They happened to myself, and my recollection of them is as vivid as if they had taken place only yesterday. Twenty years, however, have gone by since that night. During those twenty years I have told the story to but one other person. I tell it now with a reluctance which I find it difficult to overcome. All I entreat, meanwhile, is that you will abstain from forcing your own conclusions upon me. I want nothing explained away. I desire no arguments. My mind on this subject is quite made up, and, having the testimony of my own senses to rely upon, I prefer to abide by it.

Well! It was just twenty years ago, and within a day or two of the end of the grouse season. I had been out all day with my gun, and had had no sport to speak of. The wind was due east; the month, December; the place, a bleak wide moor in the far north of England. And I had lost my way. It was not a pleasant place in which to lose one's way, with the first feathery flakes of a coming snowstorm just fluttering down upon the heather, and the leaden evening closing in all around. I shaded my eyes with my hand, and stared anxiously into the gathering darkness, where the purple moor-land melted into a range of low hills, some ten or twelve miles distant. Not the faintest smoke-wreath, not the tiniest cultivated patch, or fence, or sheep-track, met my eyes in any direction. There was nothing for it but to walk on, and take my chance of finding what shelter I could, by the way. So I shouldered my gun again, and pushed wearily forward; for I had been on foot since an hour after daybreak, and had eaten nothing since breakfast.

Meanwhile, the snow began to come down with ominous steadiness, and the wind fell. After this, the cold became more intense, and the night came rapidly up. As for me, my prospects darkened with the darkening sky, and my heart grew heavy as I thought how my young wife was already watching for me through the window of our little inn parlour, and thought of all the suffering in store for her throughout this weary night. We had been married four months, and, having spent our autumn in the Highlands, were now lodging in a remote little village situated just on the verge of the great English moorlands. We were very much in love, and, of course, very happy. This morning, when we parted, she had implored me to return before dusk, and I had promised her that I would. What would I not have given to have kept my word!

Even now, weary as I was, I felt that with a supper, an hour's rest, and a guide, I might still get back to her before midnight, if only guide and shelter could be found.

And all this time, the snow fell and the night thickened. I stopped and shouted every now and then, but my shouts seemed only to make the silence deeper. Then a vague sense of uneasiness came upon me, and I began to remember stories of travellers who had walked on and on in the falling snow until, wearied out, they were fain to lie down and sleep their lives away. Would it be possible, I asked myself, to keep on thus through all the long dark night? Would there not come a time when my limbs must fail, and my resolution give way? When I, too, must sleep the sleep of death. Death! I shuddered. How hard to die just now, when life lay all so bright before me! How hard for my darling, whose whole loving heart — but that thought was not to be borne! To banish it, I shouted again, louder and longer, and then listened eagerly. Was my shout answered, or did I only fancy that I heard a far-off cry? I halloed again, and again the echo followed. Then a wavering speck of light came suddenly out of the dark, shifting, disappearing, growing momentarily nearer and brighter. Running towards it at full speed, I found myself, to my great joy, face to face with an old man and a lantern.

'Thank God!' was the exclamation that burst involuntarily from my lips.

Blinking and frowning, he lifted his lantern and peered into my face.

'What for?' growled he, sulkily.

'Well — for you. I began to fear I should be lost in the snow.'

'Eh, then, folks do get cast away hereabouts fra' time to time, an' what's to hinder you from bein' cast away likewise, if the Lord's so minded?'

'If the Lord is so minded that you and I shall be lost together, friend, we must submit,' I replied; 'but I don't mean to be lost without you. How far am I now from Dwolding?'

'A gude twenty mile, more or less.'

'And the nearest village?'

'The nearest village is Wyke, an' that's twelve mile t'other side.'

'Where do you live, then?'

'Out yonder,' said he, with a vague jerk of the lantern.

'You're going home, I presume?'

'Maybe I am.'

'Then I'm going with you.'

The old man shook his head, and rubbed his nose reflectively with the handle of the lantern.

'It ain't o' no use,' growled he. 'He 'ont let you in — not he.'

'We'll see about that,' I replied, briskly. 'Who is He?'

'The master.'

'Who is the master?'

'That's nowt to you,' was the unceremonious reply.

'Well, well; you lead the way, and I'll engage that the master shall give me shelter and a supper tonight.'

'Eh, you can try him!' muttered my reluctant guide; and, still shaking his head, he hobbled, gnome-like, away through the falling snow. A large mass loomed up presently out of the darkness, and a huge dog rushed out, barking furiously.

'Is this the house?' I asked.

'Ay, it's the house. Down, Bey!' And he fumbled in his pocket for the key.

I drew up close behind him, prepared to lose no chance of entrance, and saw in the little circle of light shed by the lantern that the door was heavily studded with iron nails, like the door of a prison. In another minute he had turned the key and I had pushed past him into the house.

Once inside, I looked round with curiosity, and found myself in a great raftered hall, which served, apparently, a variety of uses. One end was piled to the roof with corn, like a barn. The other was stored with flour-sacks, agricultural implements, casks, and all kinds of miscellaneous lumber; while from the beams overhead hung rows of hams, flitches, and bunches of dried herbs for winter use. In the centre of the floor stood some huge object gauntly dressed in a dingy wrapping-cloth, and reaching half way to the rafters. Lifting a corner of his cloth, I saw, to my surprise, a telescope of very considerable size, mounted on a rude movable platform, with four small wheels. The tube was made of painted wood, bound round with bands of metal rudely fashioned; the speculum, so far as I could estimate its size in the dim light, measured at least fifteen inches in diameter. While I was yet examining the instrument, and asking myself whether it was not the work of some self-taught optician, a bell rang sharply.

'That's for you,' said my guide, with a malicious grin. 'Yonder's his room.'

He pointed to a low black door at the opposite side of the hall. I crossed over, rapped somewhat loudly, and went in, without waiting for an invitation. A huge white-haired old man rose from a table covered with books and papers, and confronted me sternly.

'Who are you?' said he. 'How came you here? What do you want?'

'James Murray, barrister-at-law. On foot across the moor. Meat, drink, and sleep.'

He bent his bushy brows into a portentous frown.

'Mine is not a house of entertainment,' he said, haughtily. 'Jacob, how dared you admit this stranger?'

'I didn't admit him,' grumbled the old man. 'He followed me over the muir, and shouldered his way in before me. I'm no match for six foot two.'

''And pray, sir, by what right have you forced an entrance into my house?'

'The same by which I should have clung to your boat, if I were drowning.

The right of self-preservation.'

'Self-preservation?'

'There's an inch of snow on the ground already,' I replied briefly; 'and it would be deep enough to cover my body before daybreak.'

He strode to the window, pulled aside a heavy black curtain, and looked out.

'It is true,' he said. 'You can stay, if you choose, till morning. Jacob, serve the supper.'

With this he waved me to a seat, resumed his own, and became at once absorbed in the studies from which I had disturbed him.

I placed my gun in a corner, drew a chair to the hearth, and examined my quarters at leisure. Smaller and less incongruous in its arrangements than the hall, this room contained, nevertheless, much to awaken my curiosity. The floor was carpetless. The whitewashed walls were in parts scrawled over with strange diagrams, and in others covered with shelves crowded with philosophical instruments, the uses of many of which were unknown to me. On one side of the fireplace, stood a bookcase filled with dingy folios; on the other, a small organ, fantastically decorated with painted carvings of medieval saints and devils. Through the half-opened door of a cupboard at the further end of the room, I saw a long array of geological specimens, surgical preparations, crucibles, retorts, and jars of chemicals; while on the mantelshelf beside me, amid a number of small objects, stood a model of the solar system, a small galvanic battery, and a microscope. Every chair had its burden. Every corner was heaped high with books. The very floor was littered over with maps, casts, papers, tracings, and learned lumber of all conceivable kinds.

I stared about me with an amazement increased by every fresh object upon which my eyes chanced to rest. So strange a room I had never seen; yet seemed it stranger still, to find such a room in a lone farmhouse amid those wild and solitary moors! Over and over again, I looked from my host to his surroundings, and from his surroundings back to my host, asking myself who and what he could be? His head was singularly fine; but it was more the head of a poet than of a philosopher. Broad in the temples, prominent over the eyes, and clothed with a rough profusion of perfectly white hair, it had all the ideality and much of the ruggedness that characterizes the head of Louis von Beethoven. There were the same deep lines about the mouth, and the same stern furrows in the brow. There was the same concentration of expression. While I was yet observing him, the door opened, and Jacob brought in the supper. His master then closed his book, rose, and with more courtesy of manner than he had yet shown, invited me to the table.

A dish of ham and eggs, a loaf of brown bread, and a bottle of admirable sherry, were placed before me.

'I have but the homeliest farmhouse fare to offer you, sir,' said my entertainer. 'Your appetite, I trust, will make up for the deficiencies of our larder.'

I had already fallen upon the viands, and now protested, with the enthusiasm of a starving sportsman, that I had never eaten anything so delicious.

He bowed stiffly, and sat down to his own supper, which consisted, primitively, of a jug of milk and a basin of porridge. We ate in silence, and, when we had done, Jacob removed the tray. I then drew my chair back to the fireside. My host, somewhat to my surprise, did the same, and turning abruptly towards me, said:

'Sir, I have lived here in strict retirement for three-and-twenty years. During that time, I have not seen as many strange faces, and I have not read a single newspaper. You are the first stranger who has crossed my threshold for more than four years. Will you favour me with a few words of information respecting that outer world from which I have parted company so long?'

'Pray interrogate me,' I replied. 'I am heartily at your service.'

He bent his head in acknowledgement; leaned forward, with his elbows resting on his knees and his chin supported in the palms of his hands; stared fixedly into the fire; and proceeded to question me.

His inquiries related chiefly to scientific matters, with the later progress of which, as applied to the practical purposes of life, he was almost wholly unacquainted. No student of science myself, I replied as well as my slight information permitted; but the task was far from easy, and I was much relieved when, passing from interrogation to discussion, he began pouring forth his own conclusions upon the facts which I had been attempting to place before him. He talked, and I listened spellbound. He talked till I believe he almost forgot my presence, and only thought aloud. I had never heard anything like it then; I have never heard anything like it since. Familiar with all systems of all philosophies, subtle in analysis, bold in generalization, he poured forth his thoughts in an uninterrupted stream, and, still leaning forward in the same moody attitude with his eyes fixed upon the fire, wandered from topic to topic, from speculation to speculation, like an inspired dreamer. From practical science to mental philosophy; from electricity in the wire to electricity in the nerve; from Watts to Mesmer, from Mesmer to Reichenbach, from Reichenbach to Swedenborg, Spinoza, Condillac, Descartes, Berkeley, Aristotle, Plato, and the Magi and mystics of the East, were transitions which, however bewildering in their variety and scope, seemed easy and harmonious upon his lips as sequences in music. By-and-by — I forget now by what link of conjecture or illustration — he passed on to that field which lies beyond the boundary line of even conjectural philosophy, and reaches no man knows whither. He spoke of the soul and its aspirations; of the spirit and its powers; of second sight; of prophecy; of those phenomena which, under the names of ghosts, spectres, and supernatural appearances, have been denied by the sceptics and attested by the credulous, of all ages.

'The world,' he said, 'grows hourly more and more sceptical of all that lies beyond its own narrow radius; and our men of science foster the fatal tendency. They condemn as fable all that resists experiment. They reject as false all that cannot be brought to the test of the laboratory or the dissecting-room. Against what superstition have they waged so long and obstinate a war, as against the belief in apparitions? And yet what superstition has maintained its hold upon the minds of men so long and so firmly? Show me any fact in physics, in history, in archaeology, which is supported by testimony so wide and so various. Attested by all races of men, in all ages, and in all climates, by the soberest sages of antiquity, by the rudest savage of today, by the Christian, the Pagan, the Pantheist, the Materialist, this phenomenon is treated as a nursery tale by the philosophers of our century. Circumstantial evidence weighs with them as a feather in the balance. The comparison of causes with effects, however valuable in physical science, is put aside as worthless and unreliable. The evidence of competent witnesses, however conclusive in a court of justice, counts for nothing. He who pauses before he pronounces, is condemned as a trifler. He who believes, is a dreamer or a fool.'

He spoke with bitterness, and, having said thus, relapsed for some minutes into silence. Presently he raised his head from his hands, and added, with an altered voice and manner,

" 'I, sir, paused, investigated, believed, and was not ashamed to state my convictions to the world. I, too, was branded as a visionary, held up to ridicule by my contemporaries, and hooted from that field of science in which I had laboured with honour during all the best years of my life. These things happened just three-and-twenty years ago. Since then, I have lived as you see me living now, and the world has forgotten me, as I have forgotten the world. You have my history.'

'It is a very sad one,' I murmured, scarcely knowing what to answer.

'It is a very common one,' he replied. 'I have only suffered for the truth, as many a better and wiser man has suffered before me.'

He rose, as if desirous of ending the conversation, and went over to the window.

'It has ceased snowing,' he observed, as he dropped the curtain, and came back to the fireside.

'Ceased!' I exclaimed, starting eagerly to my feet. 'Oh, if it were only possible — but no! it is hopeless. Even if I could find my way across the moor, I could not walk twenty miles tonight.'

'Walk twenty miles tonight!' repeated my host. 'What are you thinking of?'

'Of my wife,' I replied, impatiently. 'Of my young wife, who does not know that I have lost my way, and who is at this moment breaking her heart with suspense and terror.'

'Where is she?'

'At Dwolding, twenty miles away.'

'At Dwolding,' he echoed, thoughtfully. 'Yes, the distance, it is true, is twenty miles; but — are you so very anxious to save the next six or eight hours?'

'So very, very anxious, that I would give ten guineas at this moment for a guide and a horse.'

'Your wish can be gratified at a less costly rate,' said he, smiling. 'The night mail from the north, which changes horses at Dwolding, passes within five miles of this spot, and will be due at a certain cross-road in about an hour and a quarter. If Jacob were to go with you across the moor, and put you into the old coach-road, you could find your way, I suppose, to where it joins the new one?'

'Easily — gladly.'

He smiled again, rang the bell, gave the old servant his directions, and, taking a bottle of whiskey and a wineglass from the cupboard in which he kept his chemicals, said:

'The snow lies deep, and it will be difficult walking tonight on the moor. A glass of usquebaugh before you start?'

I would have declined the spirit, but he pressed it on me, and I drank it. It went down my throat like liquid flame, and almost took my breath away.

'It is strong,' he said; 'but it will help to keep out the cold. And now you have no moments to spare. Good night!'

I thanked him for his hospitality, and would have shaken hands, but that he had turned away before I could finish my sentence. In another minute I had traversed the hall, Jacob had locked the outer door behind me, and we were out on the wide white moor.

Although the wind had fallen, it was still bitterly cold. Not a star glimmered in the black vault overhead. Not a sound, save the rapid crunching of the snow beneath our feet, disturbed the heavy stillness of the night. Jacob, not too well pleased with his mission, shambled on before in sullen silence, his lantern in his hand, and his shadow at his feet. I followed, with my gun over my shoulder, as little inclined for conversation as himself. My thoughts were full of my late host. His voice rang in my ears. His eloquence yet held my imagination captive. I remember to this day, with surprise, how my over-excited brain retained whole sentences and parts of sentences, troops of brilliant images, and fragments of splendid reasoning, in the very words in which he had uttered them. Musing thus over what I had heard, and striving to recall a lost link here and there, I strode on at the heels of my guide, absorbed and unobservant. Presently — at the end, as it seemed to me, of only a few minutes — he came to a sudden halt, and said:

'Yon's your road. Keep the stone fence to your right hand, and you can't fail of the way.'

'This, then, is the old coach-road?'

'Ay, 'tis the old coach-road.'

'And how far do I go, before I reach the cross-roads?'

'Nigh upon three mile.'

I pulled out my purse, and he became more communicative.

'The road's a fair road enough,' said he, 'for foot passengers; but 'twas over steep and narrow for the northern traffic. You'll mind where the parapet's broken away, close again the sign-post. It's never been mended since the accident.'

'What accident?'

'Eh, the night mail pitched right over into the valley below — a gude fifty feet an' more — just at the worst bit o'road in the whole county.'

'Horrible! Were many lives lost?'

'All. Four were found dead, and t'other two died next morning.'

'How long is it since this happened?'

'Just nine year.'

'Near the sign-post, you say? I will bear it in mind. Good night.'

'Gude night, sir, and thankee.' Jacob pocketed his half-crown, made a faint pretence of touching his hat, and trudged back by the way he had come.

I watched the light of his lantern till it quite disappeared, and then turned to pursue my way alone. This was no longer matter of the slightest difficulty, for despite the dead darkness overhead, the line of stone fence showed distinctly enough against the pale gleam of the snow. How silent it seemed now, with only my footsteps to listen to; how silent and how solitary! A strange, disagreeable sense of loneliness stole over me. I walked faster. I hummed a fragment of a tune. I cast up enormous sums in my head, and accumulated them at compound interest. I did my best, in short, to forget the startling speculations to which I had but just been listening, and, to some extent, I succeeded.

Meanwhile the night air seemed to become colder and colder, and though I walked fast I found it impossible to keep myself warm. My feet were like ice. I lost sensation in my hands, and grasped my gun mechanically. I even breathed with difficulty, as though, instead of traversing a quiet north country highway, I were scaling the uppermost heights of some gigantic Alp. This last symptom became presently so distressing, that I was forced to stop for a few minutes, and lean against the stone fence. As I did so, I chanced to look back up the road, and there, to my infinite relief, I saw a distant point of light, like the gleam of an approaching lantern. I at first concluded that Jacob had retraced his steps and followed me; but even as the conjecture presented itself, a second light flashed into sight — a light evidently parallel with the first, and approaching at the same rate of motion. It needed no second thought to show me that these must be the carriage-lamps of some private vehicle, though it seemed strange that any private vehicle should take a road professedly disused and dangerous.

There could be no doubt, however, of the fact, for the lamps grew larger and brighter every moment, and I even fancied I could already see the dark outline of the carriage between them. It was coming up very fast, and quite noiselessly, the snow being nearly a foot deep under the wheels.

And now the body of the vehicle became distinctly visible behind the lamps. It looked strangely lofty. A sudden suspicion flashed upon me. Was it possible that I had passed the cross-roads in the dark without observing the sign-post, and could this be the very coach which I had come to meet?

No need to ask myself that question a second time, for here it came round the bend of the road, guard and driver, one outside passenger, and four steaming greys, all wrapped in a soft haze of light, through which the lamps blazed out, like a pair of fiery meteors.

I jumped forward, waved my hat, and shouted. The mail came down at full speed, and passed me. For a moment I feared that I had not been seen or heard, but it was only for a moment. The coachman pulled up; the guard, muffled to the eyes in capes and comforters, and apparently sound asleep in the rumble, neither answered my hail nor made the slightest effort to dismount; the outside passenger did not even turn his head. I opened the door for myself, and looked in. There were but three travellers inside, so I stepped in, shut the door, slipped into the vacant corner, and congratulated myself on my good fortune.

The atmosphere of the coach seemed, if possible, colder than that of the outer air, and was pervaded by a singularly damp and disagreeable smell. I looked round at my fellow-passengers. They were all three men, and all silent. They did not seem to be asleep, but each leaned back in his corner of the vehicle, as if absorbed in his own reflections. I attempted to open a conversation.

'How intensely cold it is tonight,' I said, addressing my opposite neighbour.

He lifted his head, looked at me, but made no reply.

'The winter,' I added, 'seems to have begun in earnest.'

Although the corner in which he sat was so dim that I could distinguish none of his features very clearly, I saw that his eyes were still turned full upon me. And yet he answered never a word.

At any other time I should have felt, and perhaps expressed, some annoyance, but at the moment I felt too ill to do either. The icy coldness of the night air had struck a chill to my very marrow, and the strange smell inside the coach was affecting me with an intolerable nausea. I shivered from head to foot, and, turning to my left-hand neighbour, asked if he had any objection to an open window?

He neither spoke nor stirred.

I repeated the question somewhat more loudly, but with the same result. Then I lost patience, and let the sash down. As I did so, the leather strap broke in my hand, and I observed that the glass was covered with a thick coat of mildew, the accumulation, apparently, of years. My attention being thus drawn to the condition of the coach, I examined it more narrowly, and saw by the uncertain light of the outer lamps that it was on the last stage of dilapidation. Every part of it was not only out of repair, but in a condition of decay. The sashes splintered at a touch. The leather fittings were crusted over with mould, and literally rotting from the woodwork. The floor was almost breaking away beneath my feet. The whole machine, in short, was foul with damp, and had evidently been dragged from some outhouse in which it had been mouldering for years, to do another day or two of duty on the road.

I turned to the third passenger, whom I had not yet addressed, and hazarded one more remark.

'This coach,' I said, 'is in a desperate condition. The regular mail, I suppose, is under repair?'

He moved his head slowly, and looked me in the face, without speaking a word. I shall never forget that look while I live. I turned cold at heart under it. I turn cold at heart even now when I recall it. His eyes glowed with a fiery unnatural lustre. His face was livid as the face of a corpse. His bloodless lips, were drawn back as if in the agony of death, and showed the gleaming teeth between.

The words that I was about to utter died upon my lips and a strange horror — a dreadful horror — came upon me. My sight had by this time become used to the gloom of the coach and I could see with tolerable distinctness. I turned to my opposite neighbour. He, too, was looking at me, with the same startling pallor in his face, and the same stony glitter in his eyes. I passed my hand across my brow. I turned to the passenger on the seat beside my own, and saw — oh Heaven! how shall I describe what I saw? I saw that he was no living man — that none of them were living men, like myself! A pale phosphorescent light — the light of putrefaction — played upon their awful faces; upon their hair, dank with the dews of the grave; upon their clothes, earth-stained and dropping to pieces; upon their hands, which were as the hands of corpses long buried. Only their eyes, their terrible eyes, were living; and those eyes were all turned menacingly upon me!

A shriek of terror, a wild unintelligible cry for help and mercy, burst from my lips as I flung myself against the door, and strove in vain to open it.

In that single instant, brief and vivid as a landscape beheld in the flash of summer lightning, I saw the moon shining down through a rift of stormy cloud — the ghastly sign-post rearing its warning finger by the wayside — the broken parapet — the plunging horses — the black gulf below. Then, the coach reeled like a ship at sea. Then, came a mighty crash — a sense of crushing pain — and then, darkness.

IT SEEMED AS if years had gone by when I awoke one morning from a deep sleep, and found my wife watching by my bedside. I will pass over the scene that ensued, and give you, in half a dozen words, the tale she told me with tears of thanksgiving. I had fallen over a precipice, close against the junction of the old coach-road and the new, and had only been saved from certain death by lighting upon a deep snowdrift that had accumulated at the foot of the rock beneath. In this snowdrift I was discovered at daybreak, by a couple of shepherds, who carried me to the nearest shelter, and brought a surgeon to my aid. The surgeon found me in a state of raving delirium, with a broken arm and a compound fracture of the skull. The letters in my pocket-book showed my name and address; my wife was summoned to nurse me; and, thanks to youth and a fine constitution, I came out of danger at last. The place of my fall, I need scarcely say, was precisely that at which a frightful accident had happened to the north mail nine years before.

I never told my wife the fearful events which I have just related to you. I told the surgeon who attended me; but he treated the whole adventure as a mere dream born of the fever in my brain. We discussed the question over and over again, until we found that we could discuss it with temper no longer, and then we dropped it. Others may form what conclusions they please — I *know* that twenty years ago I was the fourth inside passenger in that Phantom Coach.

THE MAN ON THE STAIRS

ANONYMOUS

"**D**AMNED NONSENSE."

"Oh well, of course, Fanshawe, if you are going to take it like that — "

"And how else can any sensible man take it? Come now, Hatton," continued the exceedingly rubicund and ruffled Mr. James Fanshawe, beating a sharp tatoo upon the table, "Try to put yourself in my position. Yes, yes," anticipating an argumentative interruption, for Mr. Fanshawe was a gentleman who, even as his best friends allowed, loved to hear himself and no one else talk, whilst his enemies used to compare him to Tennyson's brook, "yes, yes, my dear fellow, we all know that you are simply crazy on spooks and table-turning and Sir Oliver Lodge and Conan Doyle, who wrote very sensible stories by the way until he took up this planchette business — Sherlock Holmes was quite good — but here I am, I have just bought a splendid old place, incidentally I should have thought it would have appealed to you, yet when I ask you to come down for the inside of a week or so you put me off with some fantastic yarn about Cheriton Manor being haunted and dangerous and — poof!" Mr. Fanshawe crushed the stub of his cigarette in the ash tray, and finished off his whisky and soda with the air of closing a tiresome discussion.

The time was about two-thirty on a late October afternoon. The scene, the smoking room of a well-known London club. In distant corners half-a-dozen members who had strolled in replete from lunch were lazily reading the papers until they fell asleep or found something better to do. Mr. Fanshawe, a natty well-paunched gentleman — one could never think of him under any other designation — in his late fifties, who looked like a retired city man, as indeed he was, amply filled a most comfortable armchair in a most comfortable corner in a window whence he could see all St. James Street wag by and benignly approve. Just then his usual placidity, perhaps rather a surface quality with him after all, was undeniably perturbed, and although he strove hard to keep his temper there appeared more than one sign of an imminent explosion. His friend Hatton, tall, angular and wiry, seemed of a different calibre, and at the moment there was an expression of earnestness upon his tired, lined face which gave it a shade of almost monkish melancholy, as he leaned forward to give more weight to his words.

"I know Fanshawe, I know. Of course it is bound to be a most terrible disappointment— "

"It's not a disappointment at all."

"But I am sure that after what I tell you, you will see the wisdom, the necessity, for leaving Cheriton during the winter months at all events."

"And why during the winter months?"

"Because then the manifestations are at their worst."

"Manifestations. Really, Hatton, if we were not such old friends—. How can you talk such infernal rubbish!"

"Infernal, yes, that is just what they are, only unfortunately not rubbish.'

"Do you actually mean to tell me you believe in all this rot of blue lights and clanking chains and that sort of stuff?"

"James, by everything that I hold sacred it is true." His voice shook slightly, and he spoke in low eager tones. The other voice seemed to gather loudness and vexation in reply.

"What is true? You haven't told me anything definite yet. Only vague warnings — it never does for a prophet to be too exact I know — what does it all amount to? And let me tell you, John," with a sudden fierce crackle of irritation, "and take it as you will, I call it damned bad taste, when we meet for the first time after nearly two years and I ask you down to my new place, just for a house warming among old friends, to come out with all this preposterous nonsense like a regular death's head at the feast. It is not as though I believed in it, mind you, I don't care two pence halfpenny for all your spiritualism and crystal gazing, and you know jolly well that I don't. Yet there are some crazy fools about. At any rate if you won't put your legs under my mahogany, there are others who will."

"I wish you wouldn't take it so hardly. If you will only listen to me quietly for a few moments I am sure I can make you see— "

"Listen to you quietly. What on earth else have I been doing this past hour and a half?" Mr. Fanshawe found it convenient to forget his own not inconsiderable share in the conversation. "As soon as I told you during lunch that I had bought Cheriton Manor you began, and you've kept on about it ever since."

"I only wish I had been in England, James, when you took up the idea of Cheriton, for then— "

"It would have been all the same if you had. Not counting what I gave for it I have spent more than two thousand on the house from first to last, for it was in a shocking state of neglect, had to be modernised right and left. It took a deuce of a time too and now I have got it ship-shape I am not going to be put off by any hanky-panky spiritualism. So that's that."

"I only wonder at the Dormers caring for it to go out of the family. I remember Lady Anne Dormer. But then she was an old, old woman when I was quite a small boy. Even she used to spend the late autumn and winter on the Riviera each year. She said it was health. My father said she couldn't get the servants to stay in the house during the dark months."

"There you go again. It's too bad. Do try to be sensible. Now look here won't you really come down to Cheriton next week as I ask you?"

"I'd rather not."

"What am I to understand by that? You seem to have arrived back home after all this time in a deuce of a funny mood anyhow. Are you going to drop all your old friends?"

"Don't say that. It hurts. If it were anywhere else, James, but to Cheriton, I would come to stay with you like a shot, and for as long as you liked."

"Well I am bound to say you seemed ready enough until I mentioned Cheriton Manor. Can't you see that it is all moonshine, this spook business? Take any old house like Cheriton wherever you like in town or country, preferably in the country, a place that for some quite good reason or the other has been shut up for years just as Cheriton has been, family can't keep it going, death duties, taxes, younger generation prefer to live in town, want excitement, it's all excitement now-a-days, and what, I ask you, is the result? Tales are bound to get round: a deserted house, mystery, haunted — bah! I hate the very word. We aren't living in the middle ages, although upon my soul I begin to think we must be. Apparently sensible level-headed men and women are quite cracked on this one subject. I suppose some of your modern up-to-date doctors would explain it — aftermath of the war, crowd neurasthenia — but I am wandering from the point. You accepted my invitation, John. A plain answer to a plain question. Are you going to back out?"

"I would rather not. I cannot stay at Cheriton Manor. You can't know the place and its reputation as well as I do. Don't forget that my old father was rector of Canons Roothing only seven miles away, and I lived there until I went up to King's. I am not talking at random. Believe me, James, I hate to offend you, and I know that I am offending you — oh yes, I am — more than you yourself are really aware of perhaps."

"Well, if you want it quite straight, I *am* annoyed, and I think I have a perfect right to be thoroughly annoyed. I won't disguise it from you. So you aren't coming? Yes or no."

"I would rather not."

"That is to say no." Fanshawe rose to his feet, and with an unmistakable sneer added, "You're afraid."

The other lifted his eyes and looked his friend straight in the face. "Yes, there are some things of which I am afraid," he said quietly. "Let me tell you— "

"Oh, no, thanks," interrupted Fanshawe with a harsh laugh his already high colour rising a little more, "I don't want to hear the yarn — keep it for the next Christmas annual. Tell it at the next séance you attend, the circle or what ever they call the mumbo-jumbo now." His voice rose higher, and more than one member in their vicinity looked up for a moment from his paper. "But don't let me hear any more of this rubbish, and for heaven's sake try to cultivate a little common sense. Let me tell you one thing, and I am quite serious about it, I'll give you or any other fellow who can show me a ghost in Cheriton Manor a hundred pounds down for each bogle he raises. There that's a firm offer, and a pretty safe one too, I'll wager. Ghosts, psha!" And then in a slightly smoother tone as he was moving towards the door he greeted a newcomer with a nod, "Afternoon, Markham, going to keep fine? I think so."

Hatton followed him for a moment with his eyes, and leaning back sighed heavily.

"My word, Hatton, old Fanshawe seems fairly put out about something. What's stung him now? And what's all this about a hundred pounds? I couldn't help hearing if the old buffer will raise his voice for the benefit of the whole smoking-room."

"Nothing much, Markham. We were only having a little discussion and Fanshawe can't bear to be contradicted."

"I know, any more than he can bear to lose at bridge. Well, I hope he recovers from his temper by Friday anyway, because I am motoring down to this new place of his, new old place I ought to call it, for by all accounts Cheriton Manor is as ancient as the hills and a little bit over."

"You are going down to Cheriton on Friday?"

"Yes, do you know it? Fanshawe has only just settled in, and mighty proud he seems of his new toy. According to what he says the place was in a shocking state when he found it. However, I've no qualms, I assure you. He knows how to make himself jolly comfortable, and his guests too, I will say that."

"It was what I was telling him about Cheriton Manor that rather upset him, I'm afraid."

"You know Cheriton then? And what is it like?" queried Markham, lighting a cigarette. "All gables and black and white? What were you heckling him about anyway? Drains?"

"No. I think perhaps I ought to tell you since you are going to stay there."

"Don't run away with the idea that Fanshawe does anything but patronize a poor younger son who can hardly make two ends meet. I am under no illusions, and I know very well why I am being asked down to Cheriton. Bridge, Hatton, bridge. I can play a pretty good hand, and there's nothing the old boy loves better than four after dinner. He says my play suits his, in plain words I have to do all the work for he's not above making a pretty foul bloomer now and again, and I just sit mum and say nothing but 'Bad luck that, sir, bad luck.' "

"You may laugh and joke just as he did. I can't help that. Since you are an invited guest it is my duty to tell you that Cheriton Manor is haunted — horribly haunted."

"Oh, how awfully interesting." And Markham dropped into a chair. "But I say you surely never let on to Fanshawe that there was a ghost, did you?"

"I warned him, as I am warning you now."

"Whew! That's torn it then. Cheriton Manor is the apple of the old man's eye, and you know what he thinks about ghosts."

"There certainly is a ghost, and a very fearful and malignant ghost."

"Of course I can't pretend to know much about that sort of thing. I met a man once who went in for table-turning and crystal-gazing a lot, but I've never come up against it personally."

"Do you know who are going to Cheriton besides yourself?" asked Hatton.

"Fanshawe was talking about quite a small party, only four, I expect for one bridge table. The real house-warming — the royal beano — will be later on, in December, I understand; this is only a preliminary canter."

"Could you possibly find out for me, then, who are going to be your fellow guests?"

"No I don't very well see how I could manage that. I can't ask the old chap point blank, can I? But why do you want to know?" He curiously queried.

"Because I should warn them too, just as I warned my old friend, and as I am going to warn you."

Markham relieved his feelings and his frank surprise by a soft whistle. Then with a glance at the elder man he said in a voice that was just a thought too obviously careless, "Oh, that'll be all right as far as I am concerned. Of course I'm glad to know and all that sort of thing, because if I hear the regulation footsteps in the corridor I certainly shan't bother to get out of bed. But you can trust me to look after myself."

"Then you are a sceptic too," said Hatton gravely.

"Oh, I wouldn't go as far as that. I daresay there's a lot of truth in what that chap says somewhere 'There are things in Heaven and earth,' but I simply don't let it worry me."

"To you, Markham, I may seem an old fool, a silly crank. But I want you to listen to me for a bit. I have travelled in many countries and seen many strange things. I have some knowledge of what we conveniently call the occult. There are forces, terrible forces of darkness and power, who can and do manifest themselves. For some reason, be it what it may, there is a concentration of these forces at Cheriton Manor. The family history of the Dormers — they are all dead now and one can speak freely — is simply damnable. For centuries they have been a legend throughout the countryside. The men were rakes and gamblers, duellists and murderers, and if report says true, something worse. The women were wantons and witches, wholly evil. A bad, bad stock. Cheriton was originally a religious house, and under Henry VIII Geoffrey Dormer, one of Cromwell's men, stabbed a monk at the altar as he was saying mass. His blood flowed into the chalice, and as he fell dying he cursed his slayers. They hanged the last abbot to an oak opposite his own church door. And Dormer got Cheriton as a reward for his zeal in the King's service. A Dormer was the wildest spirit of the Hell Fire Club at Medmenham. Buck Dormer was infamous even in Regency days. I remember his son's wife, Lady Anne. She was the toast of the gay Victorians. The tale went that she sold herself to the devil for a pretty face.

I used to see her, a raddled and wrinkled hag, and she was always glancing back over her left shoulder and clutching her companion, for she could never be left alone. The villagers said that she was looking to see when old Scratch would come to claim his bargain.''

"And which of these interesting — er — gentlefolk revisits his ancestral halls?"

"Black Dormer. He made his own sister his mistress, and when she was to be married to a neighbouring squire upon the wedding eve he cut her throat. They used to show the room where she was killed. A gloomy place enough. It opens on to the gallery at the top of the great stairs, and at midnight he walks down stairs, and in his hand his sword. Sometimes the blade is clean, but if there is blood upon the sword those who see him die within the year. He lived in the days of Charles I, and his portrait painted by Vandyke was one of the show pieces of the Manor. I expect it is in America now."

"Yes, but I imagine that even then you could hardly murder your relations promiscuously and get away with it. How did he escape?"

"It was supposed that the unfortunate bride was assassinated by thieves who had broken in on account of the family jewels, the pearls and diamonds she was to wear next day at the altar. The truth was only known when half a century after Dormer confessed it on his death-bed."

"But how about the family when they lived there? Did none of them ever see him?"

"More than once. There is an old saying though, "A Dormer never hurt a Dormer yet," and they felt safe enough. Black Dormer: I remember the Vandyke well. He was a handsome fellow with his blue eyes and flowing hair. They only called him 'Black' because his deeds were black, and his heart was black, black as hell."

"Does Fanshawe know all these bright spots of family history?"

"I can't tell. He would not listen to me, but I hope what I say will not be lost upon you, at any rate. Don't go to Cheriton Manor."

"We seem in for a pretty lively time. After all this black gentleman may not take it into his head to walk while we are there."

"You do not believe, I see. I have done my best. You don't believe any more than my old friend believed when he laughed in my face and offered a hundred pounds to the man who would show him a ghost in Cheriton Manor." John Hatton rose wearily. He was looking very old and tired. "I have no more to say, Markham. My last word is, don't go to Cheriton Manor."

Cyril Markham watched him with a puzzled expression. "Queer old bird," he thought, "I wonder how much of this ghost business he really believes. I'd forgotten for the moment, of course he's a Catholic, and so naturally he swallows anything. Let him yarn till all is blue, it'll take more than the spook of a gentleman who was a gay dog when Charles I walked and talked to keep me away from Fanshawe's port and his bridge, with the chance of making a bit. If one could only get hold of that hundred quid now . . ." He smoked a cigarette mediatively, when suddenly throwing it aside he made his way to the telephone booth in the club hall. "Primrose 0202."

About an hour or rather more later Cyril Markham was in the sitting-room of a small flat in the Finchley Road direction engaged in close conclave with his companion, a young man of six and twenty. Tall, undeniably handsome, he betrayed his profession by all those indefinable but unmistakable characteristics which stamp the actor. At the moment he was giving such close attention to the discussion under weigh that he actually forgot to sip his whisky and soda for quite ten minutes together.

"Let's get it clear from the beginning at any rate," he was saying in a singularly musical voice. "You are going down on Friday to this jolly old house which is jolly well haunted. The chap who owns it has betted a hundred of the best that nobody can show him the ghost, and you are proposing to meet his wishes in the shape of my humble self on a basis of fifty-fifty."

"You've got it slick. Now— "

"But, my dear fellow, the whole thing simply bristles with snags. I can't see on earth how we could work it. It sounds all right, but— "

"Isn't it worth a little trouble for fifty?"

"It's worth a damned lot of trouble. I could do very well with five, let alone fifty, just now. I was never so bloody hard up in my life."

"Well then, listen to me, and don't be a fool. I've planned it all out tophole. The ghost apparently stalks downstairs at midnight from a bedroom which opens out on to a gallery overlooking the hall. I know that Fanshawe is mighty proud of this hall — it is one of the features of the place, and it won't need much suggesting on my part to get him to arrange the bridge-table there. What you have to do is really very simple. In the first place you must have a cavalier costume and a sword. There's not any difficulty about that I suppose?"

"Oh no, Isaacs or Johnny Beecher will have the clothes all right."

"What about those togs you wore in 'Strafford'? That was a first-rate make-up, and all you have to do is to walk down the stairs at twelve o'clock."

"In another man's house. I don't half like it. I shall feel no end of a fool. Suppose he twigs?"

"Not he. I can feed him during the evening with a hint or two and a mysterious story. You know the kind of thing . . . Of course I don't believe in ghosts myself, but a funny thing happened to a cousin of mine . . ."

"Take care that a funny thing doesn't happen to a friend of yours." The young actor still hesitated. He looked gloomily at the lighted end of his cigarette. "How am I to get into the place anyhow?" he asked. "I'm not going to do any climbing through a window tricks or cat-burglar stunts. The local bobby is always mouching round these big places in the country. Nothing else to do I s'pose. I knew there would be a crab somewhere."

"Oh, do listen, I've got it all mapped out," interrupted the other. "I'm driving down on Friday, and you can come along with me as my chauffeur-valet. We'll take the togs with us in an extra suitcase, and during the evening you can easily slip up to my bedroom and change there, and just lie doggo until twelve o'clock when you do the cavalier act. It's simple as paint."

"It sounds damned risky to me."

"Of course there's a certain amount of risk. That's half the fun, isn't it? We can scout round on Saturday, you and I, and see the best way of working it. There's sure to be some room off the hall with French windows so you can step out when we've all had our big fright. And look here, if you don't like the lie of the land we'll just cry the whole thing off. But are you game if it can be worked?"

"Yes, I suppose so," was the somewhat unenthusiastic reply. "But if the old chap finds out and cuts up rough— "

"He won't, I tell you," interrupted Markham, "and if he does I'll stand the racket. What can he say or do? Only curse and swear a bit. He'd never give himself away by raising a dust. But you'll have to put some pep into it, Claude, no half-and-half business. After all it will only be like acting in some bally old period film." Claude Heseltine mixed himself another whisky and soda, a very amber-coloured fluid this time. When he had gulped down half his glass the scene wore a distinctly brighter aspect. After all what a glorious rag it would be! and fifty quid for it as well! At worst, as Markham said, the old chap daren't cut up too rough, surely. He wouldn't want to show himself up as an utter ass. Then later perhaps a par or two might be worked in the press. He knew that costume parts were his real line. A par with just a hint from Mrs. Rumour might lead to a decent shop in town. Another drink, and things began to look even more roseate.

"By Jove, Cyril, I believe there's something in it after all."

"Something in it, of course there's something in it. Fifty quid for you and fifty for me. It's just as easy as easy. Now look here . . ." and they settled down to talk.

SINCE CHERITON MANOR has been illustrated in *Rural Life* although it was a good while ago, I believe, I do not propose to attempt any description of the house, which in every respect justified the agents' *cliché* "a Tudor gem." As you motor along the rather solitary main road you find yourself echoing the phrase in all sincerity when you catch a glimpse through the trees of the gables and the famous twisted chimney-stacks. It is an ideal spot, a trifle remote perhaps, even a trifle too picturesque to seem quite real. Neither Cyril Markham nor his ultra-smart young chauffeur were by any means impressionable and their minds were undoubtedly pre-occupied with something other than aesthetic appreciation, yet even from their curt remarks as after the forty miles run the car turned in at the old lodge gates, and the Manor came more and more fully in sight from behind the autumn-tinted leafery it was plain they were both moved to an unusual admiration. Over and above his elegant blarney there was indeed a note of sincerity in the congratulations with which Markham greeted his host. "By Jove, sir, you've got a ripping place down here. I don't know when I've seen such a house. By gad, it's top-hole."

Mr. Fanshawe, very accurately dressed to play the role of country squire but yet having the air of not being quite at home in his sports-jacket and tweeds, had met him in the porch and listened with obvious gratification. With manly chest expanding like a pouter-pigeon, he replied just a shade too casually, "Yes, my dear fellow, I think that without boasting I may claim that Cheriton Manor has features. I'm glad you're here fairly early because I can show you round a bit. The others — you've met them both, Garraway and Peter Prothero — can't join us until just in time for dinner. They're coming along together. But, God bless my soul! I am forgetting my duties. What do you say to a cup of tea, or perhaps something stronger after your run, eh? and then a wash, and tea when you come down," Markham acknowledged that at the moment the "something stronger" certainly seemed to meet the situation. By this time they had reached the inner hall, the centre of the house, and if he was eulogistic when his host welcomed him, he waxed positively enthusiastic as he gazed around. The hall was indeed well worthy of all praise. Large and lofty, it was panelled in oak black with age, and vaulted with huge black rafters. In the wide open fire-place a great pile of logs blazed cheerily up the huge gaping chimney. Opposite, an oak staircase of exceptional width and stateliness, flanked at the foot with two great demi-wyverns supporters of shields bearing the Dormer arms and motto *Gare à qui nous touche,* led up to a wide gallery which ran along the whole length of one side, branching off into corridors right and left. There were some three or four doors, giving on to the gallery, and as with his back to the fire he basked in its generous warmth and sipped his drink "in mighty content," he saw his valet preceded by a footman who was carrying a medley of suitcases and rugs appear "above," as old plays have it, and pass through a centre door into the room beyond.

"Ah, yes, Markham," said his host following his guest's eyes, "I've put you in one of those rooms up there. The oldest part of the house, and not the least comfortable. Since there are only three of you I thought it might be more convenient, at least my housekeeper Mrs. Baxter suggested the arrangement."

"I am sure I shall be perfectly happy, thanks. And now perhaps I'd better be seeing about a wash, if you'll excuse me," and he began to mount the stairs.

"No hurry at all. Take your own time. Tea down here in the hall when you are ready for it. We shan't be dining until eight."

The bedroom, a vast apartment hung with faded tapestry not only boasted a monumental four-poster bed in which (needless to say) Queen Elizabeth had slept well-nigh to the undoing of her liege subject and host, but was also furnished with more grateful modernities in the shape of lounge chairs and a settee upon which reposed the valet, a cigarette in his mouth and a drink at his elbow. "Cheerio! I think we shall work the trick, Cyril, after all," was his greeting. "I don't know what it is, but there's an atmosphere about the place, which is a regular inspiration. I feel I'm going to make something of my part to-night."

"Ssh! you can never tell who may be hanging around. If anyone so much as guessed . . .''

"It's your turn to be funky now. I don't seem to mind a bit. In fact I'm awfully bucked. Have a drink, old man, and then you'll be all right."

"Well pour me out just one — whew — not too strong." Markham spoke from the depths of a face-towel. "Remember I've got to go and butter that old fellow."

"You're sure little Peter's going to play up all right to-night?"

"Rather. He's frightfully pleased. Here's luck to the ghost of Cheriton Manor."

"Here's how!" The actor raised his glass with a gesture. "That's a damned silly thing to have gone and done — spilt your drink all over the floor. Anyhow it's not part of your valet's job to swab your wasted whiskies."

"The glass slipped. It must have been a bit of soap stuck on my fingers. No harm done. Pour me out another whilst I mop up the mess. It won't show, it's only on the boards, not on a rug, thank goodness."

"Remember there are one or two points we have to fix."

"Righto! I shan't forget. Here's the key of the suitcase with the initials. Your grease-paints and clothes are in there. But for heaven's sake, be careful, don't leave anything about, and don't leave the case unlocked."

"Trust me. I won't even open it until about an hour before we begin."

"That's the best way. And now I've got to get down to the old man. Be up here at seven. I'll trot off early to dress and then we'll give it a final run over. So long." And the door closed behind Markham.

At tea which was taken in the hall, he found his host not only genial but expansive. It proved a simple job to administer a little judicious flattery and the first morsels were so greedily swallowed that the doses became stronger and more gross. Cheriton Manor was discussed from every point of view, but chiefly they praised Mr. Fanshawe's flair in finding such a place and his shrewdness in giving so low a price for the property, although the host carefully refrained from mentioning the exact figure it had cost him. "Really, now," said Markham, putting down his last cup, "you only want one thing to complete the picture — a family ghost."

Fanshawe frowned heavily.

"I hope I haven't offended you, sir."

"No, no," hurriedly rejoined the older man. "Not at all, not at all. You are a sensible fellow, and I am sure you do not believe in that kind of bunkum any more than I do. The fact is that — er — there *is* some sort of legend or other attached to Cheriton. I daresay the whole thing is pure invention. But between ourselves it is rather a sore point with me. I have always held that a man in my position, a hard-headed, sound business man, if I may say so, should be careful not to sanction — even in jest — any belief in these morbid traditions and stories of ghosts, which in their way are calculated to do very serious mischief. You may or may not be aware that to some extent I have actually come forward as an opponent of spiritualism, and indeed more than once I have expressed my views in letters to the public press. Now when I get down here and find that there is some silly gossip, especially among the older villagers, I make it a point of honour not to inform myself of the details of the legend. It might conceivably interest an antiquary, but thank goodness I have always had something better to do. Curious you should have mentioned it too, because just before I left London this last time I had a few words on the subject with an old friend of mine — you wouldn't know him — Sir John Hatton, a great traveller and a very good chap, except for his — well, what I must term his extraordinary superstitions. But then there's no accounting for fellows who have lived in the East, I always think. Seems to unsettle them somehow.''

"I quite see your point of view, sir,'' replied Markham slowly, in the tone of a man who is obliged to accept facts rather against his will, "the only thing which has made me think that there may be something in it after all is what happened once to an aunt of mine in a house in Cornwall— ''

"Come now, Markham, you'll be as bad as Hatton,'' interpolated his host. "No, never allow for a moment that the thing can be true. That's the right attitude to adopt. All the bogie stories in the world can be easily explained by a very few causes; ignorance, imagination, fraud, and liver, my boy, liver. Your aunt! I wouldn't accept what a woman said anyway.''

"I should have thought that it might have been interesting to know what the story about your own place was.''

"And that's how half the harm's done. Begin by listening to these yarns — oh, many of them very clever and plausible, I grant you — and end up by believing the whole bunch. Why, Hatton got quite warm the other day when I wouldn't stop to hear his romances. In fact between ourselves if I hadn't kept my temper and laughed him out of it we should have had quite a tiff. He always is a bit peppery — the East again. There he was, ready to reel off half the history of England, and Hatton, I said, now Hatton, look here if any man shows me a ghost in Cheriton Manor I'll pay him a hundred pounds. He didn't like that. But I mean it; show me a ghost here, Markham, and I'll hand you my cheque for a hundred pounds. Ha! ha! ha!''

"A jolly sporting offer, and one I won't forget when I'm hard up.''

"Stick to your bridge, my boy,'' retorted the older man clapping him cheerily upon the shoulder, "and you'll earn far more than ever you will by exhibiting ghosts I'll be bound. But now, come along, and we'll have a walk through the grounds. I like a stroll after tea, and it's quite dry under foot. We'll see the rest of the house to-morrow.''

As they moved towards the staircase Markham paused: "But that's a deuced fine portrait you've got there, sir. Surely a Vandyke?''

"Aha! I see you have an eye for a good painting. I took the pictures over with a good deal of the furniture when I bought the place. Of course most of the stuff was simply rubbish, but I found some first-rate bits as well. Especially the portraits. I've had a man down from town who understands these things, and he tells me that fellow over there is worth a very considerable sum; undoubtedly genuine.'' And Mr. Fanshawe chuckled ruminatively as he scrutinized his bargain.

Meanwhile Black Dormer gazed down in silence with his deep blue eyes upon the purse-proud merchant whose money had bought his heritage from the last of the race. How stately and handsome he looked! One might almost have thought that a smile of infinite scorn curled those full red lips set in the pale oval face. His auburn hair, those love-locks the Puritans so detested and abhorred, fell gracefully on his shoulders, and in his ears hung two milky orient pearls. He stood, beautiful and insolent. Over his white satin doublet was negligently thrown a cloak of murrey velvet, and beneath the delicate lace ruffles an ungloved hand with tapering jewelled fingers closed upon the pummel of his sword. Through the trees, at a distance, against a stormy sky could be seen Cheriton Manor, and over it upon a scroll ran the warning *Gare à qui nous touche.*

It was the portrait that gave Peter Prothero that evening the cue for a remark which considerably ruffled their hosts's urbanity. It wanted about ten minutes to dinner time and the four were sipping their cocktails in the hall, the host, fussy and very much of the *cicerone;* Garraway, a moonfaced and spectacled nonentity; Peter Prothero and Markham, who in the security of the latter's bedroom had less than an hour before been settling various details of stage management and production. Fixing his monocle in his eye the little pink-and-white cherubic young man stared for a few moments at the Vandyke, and said very distinctly and slowly, "So that's the chap who gives all the trouble, eh?"

"Chap who gives all the trouble? Really, Prothero, I don't quite follow you," a very puzzled Mr. Fanshawe paused, his glass half-way to his mouth.

"Why yes, your family ghost. Your Cavalier johnny who walks down the staircase at midnight. That's the story isn't it?" replied Prothero with weakly smiling amiability.

"Walks down the staircase — walks down *my* staircase at midnight! Upon my word, I never heard such nonsense in all my life!"

"Oh, I'm sorry. Have I said anything I ought not to? But of course you know the yarn, Mr. Fanshawe, all about Black Dormer, who cut his sister's throat— "

"Black Dormer!" Mr. Fanshawe having ejaculated the two words seemed incapable of further speech.

"But of course it's all rot, and oh! I'm afraid I've put my foot in it. I say, I'm frightfully sorry if I've— "

"I ought to tell you, Prothero, our host very much dislikes any discussion of these superstitions, and I am sure a ghost in his own house would quite seriously vex him," nervously piped Garraway in a clumsy effort to turn an awkward corner.

"Thank you, Garraway, thank you," said Mr. Fanshawe. "Yes I— "

"Believe me, sir, I spoke quite inadvertently. I had no idea. Only I have heard the legend of Cheriton Manor somewhere . . ."

"Half an hour ago, my lad, upstairs, you're doing it quite well," thought the impassive Markham watching the scene through half-closed eyes.

"And like a fool I blurted it out without thinking. I most sincerely apologize for my— "

"Not another word, Prothero," replied Fanshawe, who had quickly recovered his equanimity. "You could not have known my feelings with regard to these matters. You never came across my letters in the public press? No?'' In answer to a shake of the head from the seemingly penitent and rather crushed Prothero. "Ah, well, then. I have no belief at all in this spookery and superstition, and when I hear of manifestations in my own house I confess I am apt to feel a trifle warm. Nay, now no more apologies, please. Let us dismiss the subject, and turn to pleasanter topics. Another cocktail, Prothero, I insist. What did you think of this morning's leader in *The Times,* Garraway, eh? Very sensibly put; now I believe . . .''

"Dinner is served, sir,'' said a new voice breaking in at a most opportune moment.

DURING THE EVENING the cards had gone against Markham, and several times his host and partner had not been able to control an impatient movement on a sharp tchick of exasperation. The moon-faced Garraway was a much better player too than his foolish countenance and rather cod-fish eyes would have led one to expect. Damn it all! They were down. This next hand needed close attention. Another drink? please. Don't bother, he was dummy and he would help himself, and make it pretty strong. Ah! that was better. He returned to his seat which directly faced the stairs. As the time drew on, he was nervous. And yet what was there to be funky about? A damned good actor, Claude, a damned good actor. Ten to twelve already. God! how his hands were shaking. He hoped nobody would notice it. He thought that chap — what was his name, Garraway — had looked at him curiously more than once. Another spot then.

Markham splashed the soda into a generous half-tumbler of spirit, and as he turned he saw the Cavalier looking down on them from the gallery. He could not repress a start. By Jove, Claude had done the thing well. The figure advancing from the deeper shadows began slowly to decend the stairs. It wore a white satin doublet, and over one shoulder was carelessly thrown a cloak of some dark velvet. The hair hung in curls upon the shoulders; there were pearl-drops in the ears. But the face! How had Claude managed it, Markham wondered. It was a miracle of make-up. It was, if anything, a bit too realistic, a bit too ghastly, the face of a corpse. The very flesh looked green and spotted with decay; the eyes sunk deep in their sockets glistened and shone with evil menace beneath the shade of the huge brimmed beaver. The lips were shrivelled like old parchment, drawn tightly back from the grinning teeth. One hand, thin, carious, almost transparent, grasped a sword red to the hilt in blood. With horrible silent steps the figure slowly descended stair after stair. Suddenly there stole through the hall a chill blast of air, a stench foul with putrescence as the reeking breath of a charnel, and the three card-players looked up quickly from their game.

Fanshawe leaped to his feet and spun round with a hoarse animal cry of fear. When he saw the figure he staggered tugging for a moment at his collar, and crashed heavily to the floor in a fit. Garraway had collapsed face downwards over the table scattering the cards far and wide. With a still gliding motion the cavalier passed through the hall and seemed to melt into the shadows beyond. Gibbering and white with terror, Prothero was pointing with trembling hand at the Vandyke portrait. The figure had disappeared from the canvas, which showed a dark blank patch, and through the trees, against a stormy sky, Cheriton Manor — *Gare à qui nous touche.*

Shaking from head to foot, by a fierce effort Markham at a bound rushed up the stairs, crossed the haunted gallery and wrenched open the bedroom door. There upon the floor in the full blaze of the electric light lay the half-dressed body of Claude Heseltine. His arms were flung wide, his chin tilted up at a sharp angle, his eyes fixed and staring, and the horror upon his face was such as men thank God may rarely upon this earth be seen.

THE FAMILY OF THE VOURDALAK

ALEXIS TOLSTOY

IENNA. 1815. WHILE THE Congress had been in session, the city had attracted all the most distinguished European intellectuals, the fashion leaders of the day, and, of course, members of the highest diplomatic élite. But the Congress of Vienna was no longer in session.

Royalist émigrés were preparing to return to their country chateaux (hoping to stay there this time); Russian soldiers were anxiously awaiting the time when they could return to their abandoned homes; and discontented Poles — still dreaming of liberty — were wondering whether their dreams would come true, back in Cracow, under the protection of the precarious 'independence' that had been arranged for them by the trio of Prince Metternich, Prince Hardenberg and Count Nesselrode.

It was as if a masked ball was coming to an end. Of the assembled 'guests', only a select few had stayed behind and delayed packing their bags in the hope of still finding some amusement, preferably in the company of the charming and glamorous Austrian ladies.

This delightful group of people (of which I was a member) met twice a week in a chateau belonging to Madame the dowager Princess of Schwarzenberg. It was a few miles from the city centre, just beyond a little hamlet called Hitzing. The splendid hospitality of our hostess, as well as her amiability and intellectual brilliance, made any stay at her chateau extremely agreeable.

Our mornings were spent *à la promenade;* we lunched all together either at the chateau or somewhere in the grounds; and in the evenings, seated around a welcoming fireside, we amused ourselves by gossiping and telling each other stories. A rule of the house was that we should not talk about anything to do with politics. Everyone had had enough of *that* subject. So our tales were based either on legends from our own countries or else on our own experiences.

One evening, when each of us had told a tale and when our spirits were in that tense state which darkness and silence usually create, the Marquis d'Urfé, an elderly émigré we all loved dearly for his childish gaiety and for the piquant way in which he reminisced about his past life and good fortunes, broke the ominous silence by saying, "Your stories, gentlemen, are all out of the ordinary of course, but it seems to me that each one lacks an essential ingredient — I mean *authenticity;* for I am pretty sure that none of you has seen with his own eyes the fantastic incidents that he has just narrated, nor can he vouch for the truth of his story on his word of honour as a gentleman."

We all had to agree with this, so the elderly gentleman continued, after smoothing down his jabot: "As for me, gentlemen, I know only one story of this kind, but it is at once so strange, so horrible and so *authentic* that it will suffice to strike even the most jaded of imaginations with terror. Having unhappily been both a witness to these strange events and a participant in them, I do not, as a rule, like to remind myself of them — but just this once I will tell the tale, provided, of course, the ladies present will permit me."

Everyone agreed instantly. I must admit that a few of us glanced furtively at the long shadows which the moonlight was beginning to sketch out on the parquet floor. But soon our little circle huddled closer together and each of us kept silent to hear the Marquis's story. M. d'Urfé took a pinch of snuff, slowly inhaled it and began as follows:

Before I start mesdames (said d'Urfé), I ask you to forgive me if, in the course of my story, I should find occasion to talk of my *affaires de coeur* more often than might be deemed appropriate for a man of my advanced years. But I assure that they must be mentioned if you are to make full sense of my story. In any case, one can forgive an elderly man for certain lapses of this kind — surrounded as I am by such attractive young ladies, it is no fault of mine that I am tempted to imagine myself a young man again. So, without further apology, I will commence by telling you that in the year 1759 I was madly in love with the beautiful Duchesse de Gramont. This passion, which I then believed was deep and lasting, gave me no respite either by day or by night and the Duchesse, as young girls often do, enjoyed adding to my torment by her *coquetterie.* So much so that in a moment of spite I determined to solicit and be granted a diplomatic mission to the hospodar of Moldavia, who was then involved in negotiations with Versailles over matters that it would be as tedious as it would be pointless to tell you about.

The day before my departure I called in on the Duchesse. She received me with less mockery than usual and could not hide her emotions as she said, "d'Urfé — you are behaving like a madman, but I know you well enough to be sure that you will never go back on a decision, once taken. So I will only ask one thing of you. Accept this little cross as a token of my affection and wear it until you return. It is a family relic which we treasure a great deal."

With *galanterie* that was perhaps misplaced at such a moment I kissed not the relic but the delightful hand which proffered it to me, and I

fastened the cross around my neck — you can see it now. Since then, I have never been parted from it.

I will not bore you, mesdames, with the details of my journey nor with the observations that I made on the Hungarians and the Serbians, those poor and ignorant people who, enslaved as they were by the Turks, were brave and honest enough not to have forgotten either their dignity or their time-honoured independence. It's enough for me to tell you that having learned to speak a little Polish during my stay in Warsaw, I soon had a working knowledge of Serbian as well — for these two languages, like Russian and Bohemian are, as you no doubt know very well, only branches of one and the same root, which is known as Slovonian.

Anyway, I knew enough to make myself understood. One day I arrived in a small village. The name would not interest you very much. I found those who lived in the house where I intended to stay in a state of confusion, which seemed to me all the more strange because it was a Sunday, a day when the Serbian people customarily devote themselves to different pleasures, such as dancing, arquebus shooting, wrestling and so on. I attributed the confusion of my hosts to some very recent misfortune and was about to withdraw when a man of about thirty, tall and impressive to look at, came up to me and shook me by the hand.

'Come in, come in stranger,' he said. 'Don't let yourself be put off by our sadness; you will understand it well enough when you know the cause.'

He then told me about how his old father (whose name was Gorcha), a man of wild and unmanageable temperament, had got up one morning and had taken down his long Turkish arquebus from a rack on a wall.

"My children," he had said to his two sons Georges and Pierre, "I am going to the mountains to join a band of brave fellows who are hunting that dog Ali Bek." (That was the name of a Turkish brigand who had been ravaging the countryside for some time.) "Wait for me patiently for ten days and if I do not return on the tenth, arrange for a funeral mass to be said — for by then I will have been killed. But," old Gorcha had added, looking very serious indeed, "if, may God protect you, I should return after the ten days have passed, do not under any circumstances let me come in. I command you, if this should happen, to forget that I was once your father and to pierce me through the heart with an aspen stake, whatever I might say or do, for then I would no longer be human. I would be a cursed *vourdalak,* come to suck your blood."

It is important at this stage to tell you, mesdames, that the *vourdalaks* (the name given to vampires by Slavic peoples) are, according to local folklore, dead bodies who rise from their graves to suck the blood of the living. In this respect they behave like all types of vampire, but they have one other characteristic which makes them even more terrifying. The *vourdalaks*, mesdames, prefer to suck the blood of their closest relatives and their most intimate friends; once dead, the victims become vampires themselves. People have claimed that entire villages in Bosnia and Hungary have been transformed into *vourdalaks* in this way. The Abbé Augustin Calmet in his strange book on apparitions cites many horrible examples.

Apparently, commissions have been appointed many times by German emperors to study alleged epidemics of vampirism. These commissions collected many eye-witness accounts. They exhumed bodies, which they found to be sated with blood, and ordered them to be burned in the public square after staking them through the heart. Magistrates who witnessed these executions have stated on oath that they heard blood-curdling shrieks coming from these corpses at the moment the executioner hammered his sharpened stake into their hearts. They have formal depositions to this effect and have corroborated them with signatures and with oaths on the Holy Book.

With this information as background, it should be easier for you to understand, mesdames, the effect that old Gorcha's words had on his sons. Both of them went down on their bended knees and begged him to let them go in his place. But instead of replying he had turned his back on them and had set out for the mountains, singing the refrain of an old ballad. The day I arrived in the village was the very day that Gorcha had fixed for his return, so I had no difficulty understanding why his children were so anxious.

This was a good and honest family. Georges, the older of the two sons, was rugged and weatherbeaten. He seemed to me a serious and decisive man. He was married with two children. His brother Pierre, a handsome youth of about eighteen, looked rather less tough and appeared to be the favourite of a younger sister called Sdenka, who was a genuine Slavic beauty. In addition to the striking beauty of her features, a distant resemblance to the Duchesse de Gramont struck me especially. She had a distinctive line on her forehead which in all my experience I have found only on these two people. This line did not seem particularly attractive at first glance, but became irresistible when you had seen it a few times.

Perhaps I was still very naive. Perhaps this resemblance, combined with a lively and charmingly simple disposition, was really irresistible. I do not know. But I had not been talking with Sdenka for more than two minutes when I already felt for her an affection so tender that it threatened to become something deeper still if I stayed in the village much longer.

We were all sitting together in front of the house, around a table laden with cheeses and dishes of milk. Sdenka was sewing; her sister-in-law was preparing supper for her children, who were playing in the sand; Pierre, who was doing his best to appear at ease, was whistling as he cleaned a yagatan, or long Turkish knife. Georges was leaning on the table with his head in his hands and looking for signs of movement on the great highway. He was silent.

For my part, I was profoundly affected by the general atmosphere of sadness and, in a fit of melancholy, looked up at the evening clouds which shrouded the dying sun and at the silhouette of a monastery, which was half hidden from my view by a black pine forest.

This monastery, as I subsequently discovered, had been very famous in former times on account of a miraculous icon of the Virgin Mary which, according to legend, had been carried away by the angels and set down on an old oak tree. But at the beginning of the previous century the Turks had invaded this part of the country; they had butchered the monks and pillaged the monastery. Only the walls and a small chapel had survived; an old hermit continued to say Mass there. This hermit showed travellers around the ruins and gave hospitality to pilgrims who, as they walked from one place of devotion to another, liked to rest a while at the Monastery of Our Lady of the Oak. As I have said, I didn't learn all this until much later, for on this particular evening my thoughts were very far from the archaeology of Serbia. As often happens when one allows one's imagination free rein, I was musing on past times — on the good old days of my childhood; on the beauties of France that I had left for a wild and faraway country. I was thinking about the Duchesse de Gramont and — why not admit it? — I was also thinking about several other ladies who lived at the same time as your grandmothers, the memory of whose beauty had quietly entered my thoughts in the train of the beautiful Duchesse. I had soon forgotten all about my hosts and their terrible anxiety.

Suddenly Georges broke the silence. "Wife," he said, "at exactly what time did the old man set out?"

"At eight o'clock. I can clearly remember hearing the monastery bell."

"Well, that's all right then," said Georges. "It cannot be more than half past seven." And he again looked for signs of movement on the great highway which led to the dark forest.

I have forgotten to tell you mesdames, that when the Serbians suspect that someone has become a vampire, they avoid mentioning him by name or speaking of him directly, for they think that this would be an invitation for him to leave his tomb. So Georges, when he spoke of his father, now referred to him simply as 'the old man'.

There was a brief silence. Suddenly one of the children started tugging at Sdenka's apron and crying, "Auntie, when will grandpapa be coming back?"

The only reply he got to this untimely question was a hard slap from Georges. The child began to cry, but his little brother, who by now was surprised and frightened, wanted to know more. "Father, why are we not allowed to talk about grandpapa?"

Another slap shut him up firmly. Both children now began to howl and the whole family made a sign of the cross. Just at that moment, I heard the sound of the monastery bell. As the first chime of the eight was ringing in our ears, we saw a human figure coming out of the darkness of the forest and approaching us.

"It is he, God be praised," cried Sdenka, her sister-in-law and Pierre all at once.

"May the good God protect us," said Georges solemnly. "How are we to know if the ten days have passed or not?"

Everyone looked at him, terror struck. But the human form came closer and closer. It was a tall old man with a silver moustache and a pale, stern face; he was dragging himself along with the aid of a stick. The closer he got, the more shocked Georges looked. When the new arrival was a short distance from us, he stopped and stared at his family with eyes that seemed not to see — they were dull, glazed, deep sunk in their sockets.

"Well, well," he said in a dead voice, "will no one get up to welcome me? What is the meaning of this silence, can't you see I am wounded?"

I saw that the old man's left side was dripping with blood.

"Go and help your father," I said to Georges. "And you, Sdenka, offer him some refreshment. Look at him — he is almost collapsing from exhaustion!"

"Father," said Georges, going up to Gorcha, "show me your wound. I know all about such things and I can take care of it. . . ."

He was just about to take off the old man's coat when Gorcha pushed his son aside roughly and clutched at his body with both hands. "You are too clumsy," he said, "leave me alone. . . . Now you have hurt me."

"You must be wounded in the heart," cried Georges, turning pale. "Take off your coat, take it off. You must, I insist."

The old man pulled himself up to his full height. "Take care," he said in a sepulchral voice. "If you so much as touch me, I shall curse you."

Pierre rushed between Georges and his father. "Leave him alone," he said. "Can't you see that he's suffering?"

"Do not cross him," Georges's wife added. "You know he has never tolerated that."

At that precise moment we saw a flock of sheep returning from pasture raising a cloud of dust as it made its way towards the house. Whether the dog which was escorting the flock did not recognize its own master, or whether it had some other reason for acting as it did, as soon as it caught sight of Gorcha it stopped dead, hackles raised, and began to howl as if it had seen a ghost.

"What is wrong with that dog?" said the old man, looking more and more furious. "What is going on here? Have I become a stranger in my own house? Have ten days spent in the mountains changed me so much that even my own dogs do not recognize me?"

"Did you hear that?" said Georges to his wife.

"What of it?"

"He admits that the ten days *have been spent.*"

"Surely not, for he has come back to us within the appointed time."

"I know what has to be done."

The dog continued to howl. "I want that dog destroyed!" cried Gorcha. "Well, did you hear me?"

Georges made no move, but Pierre got up with tears in his eyes, and grabbed his father's arquebus; he aimed at the dog, fired, and the creature rolled over in the dust.

"That was my favourite dog," he said sulkily. "I don't know why father wanted it to be destroyed."

"Because it deserved to be," bellowed Gorcha. "Come on now, it's cold and I want to go inside."

While all this was going on outside, Sdenka had been preparing a cordial for the old man consisting of pears, honey and raisins, laced with *eau de vie*, but her father pushed it aside with disgust. He seemed equally disgusted by the plate of mutton with rice that Georges offered him. Gorcha shuffled over to the fireplace, muttering gibberish from behind clenched teeth.

A pine-log fire crackled in the grate and its flickering light seemed to give life to the pale, emaciated features of the old man. Without the fire's glow, his features could have been taken for those of a corpse.

Sdenka sat down beside him. "Father," she said, "you do not wish to eat anything, you do not wish to rest; perhaps you feel up to telling us about your adventures in the mountains."

By suggesting that, the young girl knew that she was touching her father's most sensitive spot, for the old man loved to talk of wars and adventures. The trace of a smile creased his colourless lips, although his eyes showed no animation, and as he began to stroke his daughter's beautiful blonde hair, he said: "Yes, my daughter, yes, Sdenka, I would like to tell you all about my adventures in the mountains — but that must wait for another time, for I am too tired today. I can tell you, though, that Ali Bek is dead and that he perished by my hand. If anyone doubts my word," continued the old man, looking hard at his two sons, "here is the proof."

He undid a kind of sack which was slung behind his back, and pulled out a foul, bloody head which looked about as pale as his own! We all recoiled in horror, but Gorcha gave it to Pierre.

"Take it," he said "and nail it above the door, to show all who pass by that Ali Bek is dead and that the roads are free of brigands — except, of course, for the Sultan's janissaries!"

Pierre was disgusted. But he obeyed. "Now I understand why that poor dog was howling," he said. "He could smell dead flesh!"

"Yes, he could smell dead flesh," murmured Georges; he had gone out of the room without anyone noticing him and had returned at that moment with something in his hand which he placed carefully against a wall. It looked to me like a sharpened stake.

"Georges," said his wife, almost in a whisper, "I hope you do not intend to. . . ."

"My brother," Sdenka added anxiously, "what do you mean to do? No, no — surely you're not going to . . ."

"Leave me alone," replied Georges, "I know what I have to do and I will only do what is absolutely necessary."

While all this had been going on, night had fallen, and the family went to bed in a part of the house which was separated from my room only by a narrow partition. I must admit that what I had seen that evening had made an impression on my imagination. My candle was out; the moonlight shone through a little window near my bed and cast blurred shadows on the floor and walls, rather like those we see now, mesdames, in this room. I wanted to go to sleep but I could not. I thought this was because the moonlight was so clear; but when I looked for something to curtain the window, I could find nothing suitable. Then I overheard confused voices from the other side of the partition. I tried to make out what was being said.

"Go to sleep, wife," said Georges. "And you Pierre, and you Sdenka. Do not worry, I will watch over you."

"But Georges," replied his wife, "it is I who should keep watch over you — you worked all last night and you must be tired. In any case, I ought to be staying awake to watch over our eldest boy. You know he has not been well since yesterday!"

"Be quiet and go to sleep," said Georges. "I will keep watch for both of us."

"Brother," put in Sdenka in her sweetest voice, "there is no need to keep watch at all. Father is already asleep — he seems calm and peaceful enough."

"Neither of you understands what is going on," said Georges in a voice which allowed for no argument. "Go to sleep I tell you, and let me keep watch."

There followed a long silence. Soon my eyelids grew heavy and sleep began to take possession of my senses.

I THOUGHT I saw the door of my room open slowly, and old Gorcha standing in the doorway. Actually, I did not so much see as *feel* his presence, as there was only darkness behind him. I felt his dead eyes trying to penetrate my deepest thoughts as they watched the movement of my breathing. One step forward, then another. Then, with extreme care, he began to walk towards me, with a wolflike motion. Finally he leaped forward. Now he was right beside my bed. I was absolutely terrified, but somehow managed not to move. The old man leaned over me and his waxen face was so close to mine that I could feel his corpselike breath. Then, with a superhuman effort, I managed to wake up, soaked in perspiration.

There was nobody in my room, but as I looked towards the window I could distinctly see old Gorcha's face pressed against the glass from outside, staring at me with his sunken eyes. By sheer willpower I stopped myself from crying out and I had presence of mind to stay lying down, just as if I had seen nothing out of the ordinary. Luckily, the old man was only making sure that I was asleep, for he made no attempt to come in, and after staring at me long enough to satisfy himself, he moved away from the window and I could hear his footsteps in the neighbouring room. Georges was sound asleep and snoring loudly enough to wake the dead.

At that moment the child coughed, and I could make out Gorcha's voice. "You are not asleep little one?"

"No, grandpapa," replied the child, "And I would so like to talk with you."

"So, you would like to talk with me, would you? And what would we talk about?"

"We would talk with how you fought the Turks. I would love to fight the Turks!"

"I thought you might, child, and I brought back a little yagatan for you. I'll give it to you tomorrow."

"Grandpapa, grandpapa, give it to me now."

"But little one, why didn't you talk to me about this when it was daytime?"

"Because papa would not let me."

"He is careful, your papa . . . So you really would like to have your little yagatan?"

"Oh yes, I would love that, but not here, for papa might wake up."

"Where then?"

"If we go outside, I promise to be good and not to make any noise at all."

I thought I could hear Gorcha chuckle as the child got out of bed. I didn't believe in vampires, but the nightmare had preyed on my nerves, and just in case I should have to reproach myself in the morning I got up and banged my fist against the partition. It was enough to wake up the 'seven sleepers', but there was no sign of life from the family. I threw myself against the door, determined to save the child — but it was locked from the outside and I couldn't shift the bolts. While I was trying to force it open, I saw the old man pass by my window with the little child in his arms.

"Wake up! Wake up!" I cried at the top of my voice, as I shook the partition. Even then only Georges showed any sign of movement.

"Where is the old man?" he murmured blearily.

"Quick," I yelled, "he's just taken away your child."

With one kick, Georges broke down the door of his room — which like mine had been locked from the outside — and he sprinted in the direction of the dark forest. At last I succeeded in waking Pierre, his sister-in-law and Sdenka. We all assembled in front of the house and after a few minutes anxious waiting we saw Georges return from the dark forest with his son. The child had apparently passed out on the highway, but he was soon revived and didn't seem to be any more ill than before. After questioning him we discovered that his grandpapa had not, in fact, done him any harm; they had apparently gone out together to talk undisturbed, but once outside the child had lost consciousness without remembering why. Gorcha himself had disappeared.

As you can imagine, no one could sleep for the rest of that night. The next day, I learned that the river Danube, which cut across the highway about a quarter of a league from the village, had begun to freeze over; drift ice now blocked my route. This often happens in these parts some time between the end of autumn and the beginning of spring. Since the highway was expected to be blocked for some days, I could not think of leaving. In any case, even if I could have left, curiosity — as well as a more powerful emotion — would have held me back. The more I saw Sdenka, the more I felt I was falling in love with her.

I am not among those, mesdames, who believe in love at first sight of the kind which novelists so often write about; but I do believe that there are occasions when love develops more quickly than is usual. Sdenka's strange beauty, her singular resemblance to the Duchesse de Gramont — the lady from whom I had fled in Paris, and who I saw again in this remote setting, dressed in a rustic costume and speaking in a musical foreign tongue — the fascinating line on her forehead, like that for which I had been prepared to kill myself at least twenty times in France; all this, combined with the incredible, mysterious situation in which I found myself ... everything helped to nurture in me a passion which, in other circumstances, would perhaps have proved itself to be more vague and passing.

During the course of the day I overheard Sdenka talking to her younger brother. "What do you think of all this?" she asked. "Do you also suspect our father?"

"I dare not suspect him," replied Pierre, "especially since the child insists that he came to no harm. And as for father's disappearance, you know that he never used to explain his comings and goings."

"I know," said Sdenka. "All the more reason why we must think about saving him, for you know that Georges. . . ."

"Yes, yes, I know. It would be useless to talk him out of it. We can at least hide the stake. He certainly won't go out looking for another one, since there is not a single aspen tree this side of the mountains."

"Yes, let's hide the stake — but don't mention it to the children, for they might chatter about it with Georges listening."

"We must take care not to let that happen," said Pierre. And they went their separate ways.

At nightfall we had still discovered nothing about old Gorcha. As on the previous night I was lying on my bed, and the moonlight again stopped me from going to sleep. When at last sleep began to confuse my thoughts, I again felt, as if by instinct, that the old man was coming towards me. I opened my eyes and saw his waxen face pressed against my window.

This time I wanted to get up but could not. All my limbs seemed to be paralysed. After taking a good long look at me, the old man disappeared. I heard him wandering around the house and tapping gently on the window of Georges's room. The child turned over on his bed and moaned as he dreamed. After several minutes silence the tapping on the window resumed. Then the child groaned once again and woke up. "Is that you grandpapa?" he asked.

"It is me," replied a dead voice, "and I have brought you your little yagatan."

"But I dare not go outside, Papa has forbidden it."

"There is no need to go outside; just open the window and embrace me!"

The child got up and I could hear him opening the window. Then somehow finding the strength, I leaped to the foot of my bed and ran over to the partition. I struck it hard with my fist. In a few seconds Georges was on his feet. I heard him mutter an oath. His wife screamed. In no time at all the whole household had gathered around the lifeless child. Just as on the previous occasion, there was no sign of Gorcha. We tried carefully to revive the child, but he was very weak and breathed with difficulty. The poor little chap had no idea why he had passed out. His mother and Sdenka thought it was because of the shock of being caught talking with his grandpapa. I said nothing. However, by now the child seemed to be more calm and everybody except Georges went back to bed.

At daybreak, I overheard Georges waking his wife and whispering with her. Sdenka joined them and I could hear both the women sobbing. The child was dead.

Of the family's despair, the less said the better. Strangely enough no one blamed the child's death on old Gorcha — at least, not openly. Georges sat in silence, but his expression, always gloomy, now became terrible to behold. Two days passed and there was still no sign of the old man. On the night of the third day (the day of the child's burial) I thought I heard footsteps all around the house and an old man's voice which called out the name of the dead child's brother. For a split second I also thought I saw Gorcha's face pressed against my window, but I couldn't be sure if I was imagining it or not, for the moon was veiled by cloud that night. Nevertheless I considered it my duty to mention this apparition to Georges. He questioned the child, who replied that he *had* in fact heard grandpapa calling and had also seen him looking in through the window. Georges strictly charged his son to wake him up if the old man should appear again.

All these happenings did not prevent my passion for Sdenka from developing more and more each day. In the daytime, I couldn't talk to her alone. At night, the mere thought that I would shortly have to leave broke my heart. Sdenka's room was only separated from mine by a kind of corridor which led to the road on one side and a courtyard on the other. When the whole family had gone to bed, I decided to go for a short walk in the fields to ease my mind. As I walked along the corridor I saw that Sdenka's door was slightly open. Instinctively, I stopped and listened. The rustling of her dress, a sound I knew well, made my heart pound against my chest. Then I heard her singing softly. She was singing about a Serbian king who was saying farewell to his lady before going to the war.

"Oh my young Poplar," said the old king, "I am going to the war and you will forget me.

"The trees which grow beneath the mountain are slender and pliant, but they are nothing beside your young body!

"The berries of the rowan tree which sway in the wind are red, but your lips are more red than the berries of the rowan tree!

"And I am like an old oak stripped of leaves, and my beard is whiter than the foam of the Danube!

"And you will forget me, oh my soul, and I will die of grief, for the enemy will not dare to kill the old King!"

The beautiful lady replied: "I swear to be faithful to you and never to forget you. If I should break my oath, come to me after your death and drink all my heart's blood!"

And the old king said: "So be it!"

And he set off for the war. Soon the beautiful lady forgot him . . . !

At this point Sdenka paused, as if she was frightened to finish the ballad. I could restrain myself no longer. That voice — so sweet, so expressive — was the voice of the Duchesse de Gramont. . . . Without pausing to think, I pushed open the door and went in. Sdenka had just taken off her knitted jacket (of a kind often worn by women in those regions). All she was wearing was a nightgown of red silk, embroidered with gold, held tight against her body by a simple, brightly coloured belt. Her fine blonde hair hung loose over her shoulders. She looked more beautiful than ever. She did not seem upset by my sudden entry, but she was confused and blushed slightly.

"Oh," she said, "why have you come? What will the family think of me if we are discovered?"

"Sdenka, my soul, do not be frightened! Everyone is asleep. Only the cricket in the grass and the mayfly in the air can hear what I have to say to you."

"Oh my friend, leave me, leave me! If my brother should discover us I am lost!"

"Sdenka, I will not leave you until you have promised to love me for ever, as the beautiful lady promised the king in your ballad. Soon I will have to leave. . . . Who knows when we will see each other again? Sdenka, I love you more than my soul, more than my salvation . . . my life's blood is yours . . . may I not be granted one hour with you in return?"

"Many things can happen in an hour," said Sdenka calmly. But she did let her hand slip into mine.

"You do not know my brother," she continued, beginning to tremble. "I fear he will discover us."

"Calm yourself, my darling Sdenka. You brother is exhausted from watching late into the night; he has been lulled to sleep by the wind rustling in the trees; heavy is his sleep, long is the night and I only ask to be granted one hour — then, farewell, perhaps for ever!"

"Oh no, no, not for ever!" cried Sdenka; then she recoiled, as if frightened by the sound of her own voice.

"Oh Sdenka, I see only you, I hear only you; I am no longer master of my own destiny; a superior strength commands my obedience. Forgive me, Sdenka!" Like a madman I clutched her to my heart.

"You are no friend to me," she cried, tearing herself from my embrace and rushing to another part of the room. I do not know what I said to her then, for I was as alarmed as she was by my own forwardness, not because such boldness had failed me in the past — far from it — but because in spite of my passion, I could not help having a sincere respect for Sdenka's innocence. It is true that I had used the language of *galanterie* with this girl at first (a language which did not seem to displease the society ladies of the time) but I was now ashamed of these empty phrases and renounced them when I saw that the young girl was too naive to comprehend fully what I meant by them — what you, mesdames, to judge by your suggestive smiles, have understood immediately. I stood before her, at a loss as to what to say, when suddenly she began to tremble and look towards the window, terror struck. I followed her gaze and clearly saw the corpse-like face of Gorcha, staring at us from outside.

At precisely that moment, I felt a heavy hand on my shoulder.

I froze. It was Georges. "What are you doing here?" he snapped.

Embarrassed by his tone of voice, I simply pointed towards his father, who was still staring at us through he window — but he disappeared the moment Georges turned to look at him.

"I heard the old man and came to warn your sister," I stammered.

Georges looked me straight in the eye, as if trying to read my innermost thoughts. Then he took me by the arm, led me to my room and left, without a single word.

THE NEXT DAY the family had gathered in front of the house, around a table laden with jugs of milk and cakes.

"Where is the child?" said Georges.

"In the courtyard," replied his wife. "He is playing his favourite game, imagining that he is fighting the Turks single-handed."

No sooner had she said these words, than to our amazement we saw the tall figure of Gorcha walking slowly towards us from out of the dark forest. He sat at the table just as he had done the day I arrived.

"Father, we welcome you," murmured Georges's wife in a hoarse voice.

"We welcome you, father," whispered Sdenka and Pierre in unison.

"My father," said Georges firmly, turning pale, "we are waiting for you to say Grace!"

The old man glared at him and turned away.

"Yes . . . Grace — say it now!" repeated Georges, crossing himself. "Say it this instant, or by St George. . . ."

Sdenka and her sister-in-law threw themselves at the old man's feet and begged him to say Grace.

"No, no, no," said the old man. "He has no right to speak to me in that way, and if he continues, I will curse him!"

Georges got up and rushed into the house. He returned almost immediately, looking furious. "Where is that stake?" he yelled. "Where have you hidden it?"

Sdenka and Pierre looked at each other.

"Corpse!" Georges shouted at the old man. "What have you done with my elder boy? Why have you killed my little child? Give me back my son, you creature of the grave!"

As he said this, he became more and more pale and his eyes began to burn with fury. The old man simply glared at him.

"The stake, the stake," yelled Georges. "Whoever has hidden it must answer for all the evils which will befall us!"

At this moment we heard the excited laughter of the younger child. We saw him galloping towards us on a wooden horse, or rather on a long aspen stake, shrieking the Serbian battle cry at the top of his voice. Georges's eyes lit up, as he realized what was happening. He grabbed the stake from the child and threw himself at his father. The old man let out a fearful groan and began to sprint towards the dark forest as if possessed by demons. Georges raced after him across the fields, and soon they were both out of sight.

It was after sunset when Georges returned to the house. He was as pale as death; his hair stood on end. He sat down by the fireside, and I could hear his teeth chattering. No one could pluck up the courage to question him.

By about the time the family normally went to bed he seemed to be more his usual self and, taking me to one side, said to me quite calmly: "My dear guest, I have been to the river. The ice has gone, the road is clear — nothing now prevents you from leaving. There is no need," he added, glancing as Sdenka, "to take your leave of my family. Through me, the family wishes you all the happiness you could desire and I hope that you will have some happy memories of the time you have spent with us. Tomorrow at daybreak, you will find your horse saddled and your guide ready to escort you. Farewell. Think about your host from time to time, and forgive him if your stay here has not been as carefree as he would have liked."

As he said this, even Georges's rough features looked almost friendly. He led me to my room and shook my hand for one last time. Then he began to tremble and his teeth chattered as if he were suffering from the cold.

Now I was alone, I had no thoughts of going to sleep — as you can imagine. Other things were on my mind. I had loved many times in my life, and had experienced the whole range of passions — tenderness, jealousy, fury — but never, not even when I left the Duchesse de Gramont, had I felt anything like the sadness that I felt in my heart at that moment. Before sunrise, I changed into my travelling clothes, hoping to have a few words with Sdenka before I departed. But Georges was waiting for me in the hall. There was no chance of my seeing her again.

I leaped into the saddle and spurred on my horse. I made a resolution to return from Jassy via this village, and although that might be some time hence, the thought made me feel easier in my mind. It was some consolation for me to imagine in advance all the details of my return. But this pleasant reverie was soon shattered. My horse shied away from something and nearly had me out of the saddle. The animal stopped dead, dug in its forelegs and began to snort wildly as if some danger was nearby. I looked around anxiously and saw something moving about a hundred paces away. It was a wolf digging in the ground. Sensing my presence, the wolf ran away; digging my spurs into the horse's flanks, I managed with difficulty to get him to move forward. It was then that I realized that on the spot where the wolf had been standing, there was a freshly dug grave. I seem to remember also that the end of a stake protruded a few inches out of the ground where the wolf had been digging. However, I do not swear to this, for I rode away from that place as fast as I could.

AT THIS POINT the Marquis paused and took a pinch of snuff.

"Is that the end of the story?" the ladies asked.

"I'm afraid not," replied M. d'Urfé. "What remains to be told is a very unhappy memory for me, and I would give much to cast it from my mind."

MY REASONS FOR going to Jassy (he continued) kept me there for much longer than I had expected — well over six months, in fact. What can I say to justify my conduct during that time? It is a sad fact, but a fact nonetheless, that there are very few emotions in this life which can stand the test of time. The success of my negotiations, which were very well received in Versailles — politics, in a word, vile politics, a subject which has become so boring to us in recent times — preoccupied my thoughts and dimmed the memory of Sdenka. In addition, from the moment I arrived, the wife of a hospodar, a very beautiful lady who spoke fluent French, did me the honour of receiving my attentions, singling me out from among all the other young foreigners who were staying in Jassy. Like me, she had been brought up to believe in the principles of French *galanterie;* the mere thought that I should rebuff the advances of such a beautiful lady stirred up my Gallic blood. So I received her advances with courtesy, and since I was there to represent the interests and rights of France, I made a start by representing those of her husband the hospodar as well.

When I was recalled home, I left by the same road I had ridden to Jassy. I no longer even thought about Sdenka or her family, but one evening when I was riding in the countryside, I heard a bell ringing the eight o'clock chime. I seemed to recognize that sound and my guide told me that it came from a nearby monastery. I asked him the name: it was the monastery of Our Lady of the Oak. I galloped ahead and in no time at all we had reached the monastery gate. The old hermit welcomed us and led us to his hostel.

The number of pilgrims staying there put me off the idea of spending the night at the hostel, and I asked if there was any accommodation available in the village.

"You can stay where you like in the village," replied the old hermit with a gloomy sigh. "Thanks to that devil Gorcha, there are plenty of empty houses!"

"What on earth do you mean?" I asked. "Is old Gorcha still alive?"

"Oh no, he's well and truly buried with a stake through his heart! But he rose from the grave to suck the blood of Georges's little son. The child returned one night and knocked on the door, crying that he was cold and wanted to come home. His foolish mother, although she herself had been present at his burial, did not have the strength of mind to send him back to the cemetery, so she opened the door. He threw himself at her throat and sucked away her life's blood. After she had been buried, she in turn rose from the grave to suck the blood of her second son, then the blood of her husband, then the blood of her brother-in-law. They all went the same way."

"And Sdenka?"

"Oh, she went mad with grief; poor, poor child, do not speak to me of her!"

The old hermit had not really answered my question, but I did not have the heart to repeat it. He crossed himself. "Vampirism is contagious," he said after a pause. "Many families in the village have been afflicted by it, many families have been completely destroyed, and if you take my advice you will stay in my hostel tonight, for even if the *vourdalaks* of the village do not attack you, they will terrify you so much that your hair will have turned white before I ring the bells for morning mass.

"I am only a poor and simple monk," he continued, "but the generosity of passing travellers gives me enough to provide for their needs. I can offer you fresh country cheese and sweet plums which will make your mouth water; I also have some flagons of Tokay wine which are every bit as good as those which grace the cellars of His Holiness the Patriarch!''

The old hermit seemed to be behaving more like an innkeeper than a poor and simple monk. I reckoned he had told me some old wives' tales about the village in order to make me feel grateful enough for his hospitality to show my appreciation in the usual way, by giving the holy man enough to provide for the needs of passing travellers. In any case, the word terror has always had the effect on me that a battle cry has on a war horse. I would have been thoroughly ashamed of myself if I had not set out immediately to see for myself. But my guide, who was less enthusiastic about the idea, asked my permission to stay in the hostel. This I willingly granted.

It took me about half an hour to reach the village. Deserted. No lights shone through the windows, no songs were being sung. I rode past many houses that I knew, all as silent as the grave. Finally I reached Georges's. Whether I was being sentimental or just rash, I don't know, but it was there I decided to spend the night. I got off my horse, and banged on the gate. Still no sign of life. I pushed the gate and the hinges creaked eerily as it slowly opened. Then I crept into the courtyard. In one of the outhouses I found enough oats to last the night, so I left my horse tethered there, still saddled, and strode towards the main house. Although all the rooms were deserted, no doors were locked. Sdenka's room had been occupied only a few hours before. Some of her clothes were draped carelessly over the bed. A few pieces of jewelry that I had given her, including a small enamel cross from Budapest, lay on her table sparkling in the moonlight. Even though my love for her was a thing of the past, I must admit that my heart was heavy. Nevertheless, I wrapped myself up in my cloak and stretched out on her bed. Soon I was asleep. I cannot recall everything, but I do remember that I dreamed of Sdenka, as beautiful, as simple and as loving as she had been when first I met her. I remember also feeling ashamed of my selfishness and my inconstancy. How could I have abandoned that poor child who loved me; how could I have forgotten her? Then her image became confused with that of the Duchesse de Gramont and I saw only one person. I threw myself at Sdenka's feet and begged her forgiveness. From the depths of my being, from the depths of my soul came an indescribable feeling of melancholy and of joy.

I lay there dreaming, until I was almost awakened by a gentle musical sound, like the rustling of a cornfield in a light breeze. I heard the sweet rustling of the corn and the music of singing birds, the rushing of a waterfall and the whispering of trees. Then I realized that all these sounds were merely the swishing of a woman's dress and I opened my eyes. There was Sdenka standing beside my bed. The moon was shining so brightly that I could distinguish every single feature which had been so dear to me and which my dream made me love again as if for the first time. Sdenka seemed more beautiful, and somehow more mature. She was dressed as she had been when last I saw her alone: a simple nightgown of red silk, gold embroidered, and a coloured belt, clinging tightly above her hips.

"Sdenka!" I cried, sitting up. "Is it really you, Sdenka?"

"Yes, it is me," she replied in a sweet, sad voice. "It is that same Sdenka you have forgotten. Why did you not return sooner? Everything is finished now; you must leave; a moment longer and you are lost! Farewell my friend, farewell for ever!"

"Sdenka; you have seen so much unhappiness they say! Come, let us talk, let us ease your pain!"

"Oh, my friend, you must not believe everything they say about us; but leave me, leave me now, for if you stay a moment longer you are doomed."

"Sdenka, what are you afraid of? Can you not grant me an hour, just one hour to talk with you?"

Sdenka began to tremble and her whole being seemed to undergo a strange transformation. "Yes," she said, "one hour, just one hour, the same hour you begged of me when you came into this room and heard me singing the ballad of the old king. Is that what you mean? So be it, I will grant you one hour! But no, no!" she cried, as if fighting her inclinations, "leave me, go away! — leave now, I tell you, fly! Fly, while you still have the chance!"

Her features were possessed with a savage strength. I could not understand why she should be saying these things, but she was so beautiful that I determined to stay, whatever she said. At last she surrendered, sat down beside me, and spoke to me of the past; she blushed as she admitted that she had fallen in love with me the moment she set eyes on me. But little by little I began to notice that Sdenka was not as I had remembered her. Her former timidity had given way to a strange wantonness of manner. She seemed more forward, more knowing. It dawned on me that her behaviour was no longer that of the naive young girl I recalled in my dream. Is it possible, I mused, that Sdenka was never the pure and innocent maiden that I imagined her to be? Did she simply put on an act to please her brother? Was I gulled by an affected virtue? If so, why insist that I leave? Was this perhaps a refinement of *coquetterie*? And I thought I knew her! What did it matter? If Sdenka was not a Diana, as I thought, she began to resemble another goddess at least as attractive — perhaps more so. By God! I preferred the role of Adonis to that of Actaeon.

If this classical style that I adopted seems a little out of place, mesdames, remember that I have the honour to be telling you of incidents which occurred in the year of grace 1758. At that time mythology was *very* fashionable, and I am trying to keep my story in period. Things have changed a lot since then, and it was not so long ago that the Revolution, having overthrown both the traces of paganism and the Christian religion, erected the goddess Reason in their place. This goddess, mesdames, has never been my patron saint, least of all when I am in the presence of other goddesses, and, at the time I am referring to, I was less disposed than ever to worship at her shrine.

I abandoned myself passionately to Sdenka, and willingly outdid even her in the provocative game she was playing. Some time passed in sweet intimacy, until, as Sdenka was amusing me by trying on various pieces of jewelry, I thought it would be a good idea to place the little enamel cross around her neck. But as I tried to do this, Sdenka recoiled sharply.

"Enough of these childish games, my dearest," she said. "Let us talk about you and what is on your mind!"

This sudden change in Sdenka's behaviour made me pause a moment and think. Looking at her more closely I noticed that she no longer wore around her neck the cluster of tiny icons, holy relics and charms filled with incense which Serbians are usually given as children, to wear for the rest of their lives.

"Sdenka," I asked, "where are those things you used to wear around your neck?"

"I have lost them," she replied impatiently, and hastily changed the subject.

"I do not know exactly why, but at that moment I began to feel a strong sense of foreboding. I wanted to leave, but Sdenka held me back. "What is this?" she said. "You asked to be granted an hour, and here you are trying to leave after only a few minutes!"

"Sdenka, you were right when you tried to persuade me to leave; I think I hear a noise and I fear we will be discovered!"

"Calm yourself my love, everyone is asleep; only the cricket in the grass and the mayfly in the air can hear what I have to say!"

"No, no, Sdenka, I must leave now . . .!"

"Stay, stay," she implored, "I love you more than my soul, more than my salvation. You once told me that your life's blood belonged to me . . .!"

"But your brother — your brother, Sdenka — I have a feeling he will discover us!"

"Calm yourself my soul; my brother has been lulled to sleep by the wind rustling in the trees; heavy is his sleep, long is the night and I only ask to be granted one hour!"

As she said this, Sdenka looked so ravishing that my vague sense of foreboding turned into a strong desire to remain near her. A strange, almost sensual feeling, part fear, part excitement, filled my whole being. As I began to weaken, Sdenka became more tender, and I resolved to surrender, hoping to keep up my guard. However, as I told you at the beginning, I have always overestimated my own strength of mind, and when Sdenka, who had noticed that I was holding back, suggested that we chase away the chill of the night by drinking a few glasses of the good hermit's full-blooded wine, I agreed with a readiness which made her smile. The wine had its desired effect. By the second glass, I had forgotten all about the incident of the cross and the holy relics; Sdenka, with her beautiful blonde hair falling loose over her shoulders, with her jewels sparkling in the moonlight, was quite irresistible. Abandoning all restraint, I held her tight in my arms.

Then, mesdames, a strange thing happened. One of those mysterious revelations that I can never hope to explain. If you had asked me then, I would have denied that such things could happen, but now I know better. As I held Sdenka tightly against my body, one of the points of the cross which the Duchesse de Gramont gave me before I left stuck sharply into my chest. The stab of pain that I felt affected me like a ray of light passing right through my body. Looking up at Sdenka I saw for the first time that her features, though still beautiful, were those of a corpse; that her eyes did not see; and that her smile was the distorted grimace of a decaying skull. At the same time, I sensed in that room the putrid smell of the charnel-house. The fearful truth was revealed to me in all its ugliness, and I remembered too late what the old hermit had said to me. I realized what a fearsome predicament I was in. Everything depended on my courage and my self control.

I turned away from Sdenka to hide the horror which was written on my face. It is then that I looked out of the window and saw the satanic figure of Gorcha, leaning on a bloody stake and staring at me with the eyes of a hyena. Pressed against the other window were the waxen features of Georges, who at that moment looked as terrifying as his father. Both were watching my every movement, and I knew that they would pounce on me the moment I tried to escape. So I pretended not to know they were there, and, with incredible self control, continued — yes, mesdames, I actually continued — passionately to embrace Sdenka, just as I had done before my horrifying discovery. Meanwhile, I desperately racked my brains for some means of escape. I noticed that Gorcha and Georges were exchanging knowing glances with Sdenka and that they were showing signs of losing patience. Then, from somewhere outside, I heard a woman's shriek and the sound of children crying, like the howling of wild cats; these noises set my nerves on edge.

Time to make for home, I said to myself, *and the sooner the better!*

Turning to Sdenka, I raised my voice so that her hideous family would be sure to hear me: "I am tired, my dear child; I must go to bed and sleep for a few hours. But first I must go and see whether my horse needs feeding. I beg you to stay where you are and to wait for me to come back." I then pressed my mouth against her cold, dead lips and left the room.

I found my horse in a panic, covered with lather and crashing his hooves against the outhouse wall. He had not touched the oats, and the fearful noise he made when he saw me coming gave me gooseflesh, for I feared he would give the game away. But the vampires, who had almost certainly overheard my conversion with Sdenka, did not appear to think that anything suspicious was happening. After making sure that the main gate was open, I vaulted into the saddle and dug my spurs into the horse's flanks.

As I rode out of the gates I just had time to glimpse a whole crowd gathered around the house, many of them with their faces pressed against the windows. I think it was my sudden departure which first confused them, but I cannot be sure: the only sound I could hear at the moment was the regular beat of my horse's hooves which echoed in the night. I was just about to congratulate myself on my cunning, when all of a sudden I heard a fearful noise behind me, like the sound of a hurricane roaring through the mountains. A thousand discordant voices shrieked, moaned and contended with one another. Then complete silence, as if by common assent. And I heard a rhythmic stamping, like a troop of foot soldiers advancing in double-quick time.

I spurred on my horse until I tore into his flanks. A burning fever coursed through my veins. I was making one last effort to preserve my sanity, when I heard a voice behind me which cried out: "Stop, don't leave me my dearest! I love you more than my soul, I love you more than my salvation! Turn back, turn back, your life's blood is mine!"

A cold breath brushed my ear and I sensed that Sdenka had leaped on to my horse from behind. "My heart, my soul!" she cried, "I see only you, hear only you! I am not mistress of my own destiny — a superior force commands my obedience. Forgive me, my dearest, forgive me!"

Twisting her arms around me she tried to sink her teeth into my neck and to wrench me from my horse. There was a terrible struggle. For some time I had difficulty even defending myself, but eventually I managed to grab hold of Sdenka by curling one arm around her waist and knotting the other hand in her hair. Standing bolt upright in my stirrups, I threw her to the ground!

Then my strength gave out completely and I became delirious. Frenzied shapes pursued me — mad, grimacing faces. Georges and his brother Pierre ran beside the road and tried to block my way. They did not succeed, but just as I was about to give thanks, I looked over my shoulder and caught sight of old Gorcha, who was using his stake to propel himself forward as the Tyrolean mountain men do when they leap over Alpine chasms. But Gorcha did not manage to catch up with me. Then his daughter-in-law, dragging her children behind her, threw one of them to him; he caught the child on the sharpened point of his stake. Using the stake as a catapult he slung the creature towards me with all his might. I fended off the blow, but with the true terrier instinct the little brat sunk his teeth into my horse's neck, and I had some difficulty tearing him away. The other child was propelled towards me in the same way, but he landed beyond the horse and was crushed to pulp. I do not know what happened after that, but when I regained consciousness it was daylight, and I found myself lying near the road next to my dying horse.

So ended, mesdames, a love affair which should perhaps have cured me for ever of the desire to become involved in any others. Some contemporaries of your grandmothers could tell you whether I had learned my lesson or not. But, joking aside, I still shudder at the thought that if I had given in to my enemies, I would myself have become a vampire. As it was, Heaven did not allow things to come to that, and so far from wishing to suck your blood, mesdames, I only ask — old as I am — to be granted the privilege of shedding my own blood in your service!

VARNEY, THE VAMPYRE

THOMAS PRESKETT PREST

HE SOLEMN TONES of an old cathedral clock have announced midnight — the air is thick and heavy — a strange, death-like stillness pervades all nature. Like the ominous calm which precedes some more than usually terrific outbreak of the elements, they seem to have paused even in their ordinary fluctuations, to gather a terrific strength for the great effort. A faint peal of thunder now comes from far off. Like a signal gun for the battle of the winds to begin, it appeared to awaken them from their lethargy, and one awful, warring hurricane swept over a whole city, producing more devastation in the four or five minutes it lasted, than would a half century of ordinary phenomena.

It was as if some giant had blown upon some toy town, and scattered many of the buildings before the hot blast of his terrific breath; for as suddenly as that blast of wind had come did it cease, and all was as still and calm as before.

Sleepers awakened, and thought that what they had heard must be the confused chimera of a dream. They trembled and turned to sleep again.

All is still — still as the very grave. Not a sound breaks the magic of repose. What is that — a strange, pattering noise, as of a million of fairy feet? It is hail — yes, a hail-storm has burst over the city. Leaves are dashed from the trees, mingled with small boughs; windows that lie most opposed to the direct fury of the pelting particles of ice are broken, and the rapt repose that before was so remarkable in its intensity, is exchanged for a noise which, in its accumulation, drowns every cry of surprise or consternation which here and there arose from persons who found their houses invaded by the storm.

Now and then, too, there would come a sudden gust of wind that in its strength, as it blew laterally, would, for a moment, hold millions of the hailstones suspended in mid air, but it was only to dash them with redoubled force in some new direction, where more mischief was to be done.

Oh, how the storm raged! Hail — rain — wind. It was, in very truth, an awful night.

THERE IS AN ANTIQUE chamber in the ancient house. Curious and quaint carvings adorn the walls, and the large chimney-piece is a curiosity of itself. The ceiling is low, and a large bay window, from roof to floor, looks to the west. The window is latticed, and filled with curiously painted glass and rich stained pieces, which send in a strange, yet beautiful light, when sun or moon shines into the apartment. There is but one portrait in that room, although the walls seem panelled for the express purpose of containing a series of pictures. That portrait is of a young man, with a pale face, a stately brow, and a strange expression about the eyes, which no one cared to look on twice.

There is a stately bed in that chamber, of carved walnutwood is it made, rich in design and elaborate in execution; one of those works of art which owe their existence to the Elizabethan era. It is hung with heavy silken and damask furnishing; nodding feathers are at its corners — covered with dust are they, and they lend a funereal aspect to the room. The floor is of polished oak.

God! how the hail dashes on the old bay window! Like an occasional discharge of mimic musketry, it comes clashing, beating, and cracking upon the small panes; but they resist it — their small size saves them; the wind, the hail, the rain, expend their fury in vain.

The bed in that old chamber is occupied. A creature formed in all fashions of loveliness lies in a half sleep upon that ancient couch — a girl young and beautiful as a spring morning. Her long hair has escaped from its confinement and streams over the blackened coverings of the bedstead; she has been restless in her sleep, for the clothing of the bed is in much confusion. One arm is over her head, the other hangs nearly off the side of the bed near to which she lies. A neck and bosom that would have formed a study for the rarest sculptor that ever Providence gave genius to, were half disclosed. She moaned slightly in her sleep, and once or twice the lips moved as if in prayer — at least one might judge so, for the name of Him who suffered for all came once faintly from them.

She has endured much fatigue, and the storm does not awaken her; but it can disturb the slumbers it does not possess the power to destroy entirely. The turmoil of the elements wakes the senses, although it cannot entirely break the repose they have lapsed into.

Oh, what a world of witchery was in that mouth, slightly parted, and exhibiting within the pearly teeth that glistened even in the faint light that came from that bay window. How sweetly the long silken eyelashes lay upon the cheek. Now she moves, and one shoulder is entirely visible — whiter, fairer than the spotless clothing of the bed on which she lies, is the smooth skin of that fair creature, just budding into womanhood, and in that transition state which presents to us all the charms of the girl — almost of the child, with the more matured beauty and gentleness of advancing years.

Was that lightning? Yes — an awful, vivid, terrifying flash — then a roaring peal of thunder, as if a thousand mountains were rolling one over the other in the blue vault of Heaven! Who sleeps now in that ancient city? Not one living soul. The dread trumpet of eternity could not more effectually have awakened anyone.

The hail continues. The wind continues. The uproar of the elements seems at its height. Now she awakens — that beautiful girl on the antique bed; she opens those eyes of celestial blue, and a faint cry of alarm bursts from her lips. At least it is a cry which, amid the noise and turmoil without, sounds but faint and weak. She sits upon the bed and presses her hands upon her eyes. Heavens! what a wild torrent of wind, and rain, and hail! The thunder likewise seems intent upon awakening sufficient echoes to last until the next flash of forked lightning should again produce the wild concussion of the air. She murmurs a prayer — a prayer for those she loves best; the names of those dear to her gentle heart come from her lips; she weeps and prays; she thinks then of what devastation the storm must surely produce, and to the great God of Heaven she prays for all living things. Another flash — a wild, blue, bewildering flash of lightning streams across that bay window, for an instant bringing out every colour in it with terrible distinctness. A shriek bursts from the lips of the young girl, and then, with eyes fixed upon that window, which, in another moment, is all darkness, and with such an expression of terror upon her face as it had never before known, she trembled, and the perspirations of intense fear stood upon her brow.

"What — what was it?" she gasped; "real, or a delusion? Oh, God, what was it? A figure tall and gaunt, endeavouring from the outside to unclasp the window. I saw it. That flash of lightning revealed it to me. It stood the whole length of the window."

There was a lull of the wind. The hail was not falling so thickly — moreover, it now fell, what there was of it, straight, and yet a strange clattering sound came upon the glass of that long window. It could not be a delusion — she is awake, and she hears it. What can produce it? Another flash of lightning — another shriek — there could be now no delusion.

A tall figure is standing on the ledge immediately outside the long window. It is its finger-nails upon the glass that produces the sound so like the hail, now that the hail has ceased. Intense fear paralyses the limbs of that beautiful girl. That one shriek is all she can utter — with hands clasped, a face of marble, a heart beating so wildly in her bosom, that each moment it seems as if it would break its confines, eyes distended and fixed upon the window, she waits, frozen with horror. The pattering and clattering of the nails continue. No word is spoken, and now she fancies she can trace the darker form of that figure against the window, and she can see the long arms moving to and fro, feeling for some mode of entrance. What strange light is that which now gradually creeps up into the air? red and terrible — brighter and brighter it grows. The lightning has set fire to a mill, and the reflection of the rapidly consuming building falls upon that long window. There can be no mistake. The figure is there, still feeling for an entrance, and clattering against the glass with its long nails, that appear as if the growth of many years had been untouched. She tries to scream again but a choking sensation comes over her, and she cannot. It is too dreadful — she tries to move — each limb seems weighed down by tons of lead — she can but in a hoarse faint whisper, —

"Help — help — help — help!"

And that one word she repeats like a person in a dream. The red glare of the fire continues. It throws up the tall gaunt figure in hideous relief against the long window. It shows, too, upon the one portrait that is in the chamber, and that portrait appears to fix its eyes upon the attempting intruder, while the flickering light from the fire makes it look fearfully life-like. A small pane of glass is broken, and the form from without introduces a long gaunt hand, which seems utterly destitute of flesh. The fastening is removed, and one-half of the window, which opens like folding doors, is swung wide open upon its hinges.

And yet now she could not scream — she could not move. "Help! — help! — help!" was all she could say. But, oh, that look of terror that sat upon her face, it was dreadful — a look to haunt the memory for a life-time — a look to obtrude itself upon the happiest moments, and turn them to bitterness.

The figure turns half round, and the light falls upon the face. It is perfectly white — perfectly bloodless. The eyes look like polished tin; the lips are drawn back, and the principal feature next to those dreadful eyes is the teeth — the fearful looking teeth — projecting like those of some wild animal, hideously, glaringly white, and fang-like. It approaches the bed with a strange, gliding movement. It clashes together the long nails that literally appear to hang from the finger ends. No sound comes from its lips. Is she going mad — that young and beautiful girl exposed to so much terror? She has drawn up all her limbs; she cannot even now say help. The power of articulation is gone, but the power of movement has returned to her; she can draw herself slowly along to the other side of the bed from that towards which the hideous appearance is coming.

But her eyes are fascinated. The glance of a serpent could not have produced a greater effect upon her than did the fixed gaze of those awful, metallic-looking eyes that were bent on her face. Crouching down so that the gigantic height was lost, and the horrible, protruding, white face was the most prominent object, came on the figure. What was it? — what did it want there? — what made it look so hideous — so unlike an inhabitant of the earth, and yet to be on it?

Now she has got to the verge of the bed, and the figure pauses. It seemed as if when it paused she lost the power to proceed. The clothing of the bed was now clutched in her hands with unconscious power. She drew her breath short and thick. Her bosom heaves, and her limbs tremble, yet she cannot withdraw her eyes from that marble-looking face. He holds her within his glittering eye.

The storm has ceased — all is still. The winds are hushed; the church clock proclaims the hour of one: a hissing sound comes from the throat of the hideous being, and he raises his long, gaunt arms — the lips move. He advances. The girl places one small foot from the bed on to the floor. She is unconsciously dragging the clothing with her. The door of the room is in that direction — can she reach it? Has she the power to walk? — can she withdraw her eyes from the face of the intruder, and so break the hideous charm? God of Heaven! Is it real, or some dream so like reality as to nearly overturn the judgment for ever?

The figure has paused again, and half on the bed and half out of it that young girl lies trembling. Her long hair streams across the entire width of the bed. As she has slowly moved along she has left it streaming across the pillows. The pause lasted about a minute — oh, what an age of agony. That minute was, indeed, enough for madness to do its full work in.

With a sudden rush that could not be foreseen — with a strange howling cry that was enough to awaken terror in every breast, the figure seized the long tresses of her hair, and twining them round his bony hands he held her to the bed. Then she screamed — Heaven granted her then power to scream. Shriek followed shriek in rapid succession. The bed-clothes fell in a heap by the side of the bed — she was dragged by her long silken hair completely on to it again. Her beautifully rounded limbs quivered with the agony of her soul. The glassy, horrible eyes of the figure ran over that angelic form with a hideous satisfaction — horrible profanation. He drags her head to the bed's edge. He forces it back by the long hair still entwined in his grasp. With a plunge he seizes her neck in his fang-like teeth — a gush of blood, and a hideous sucking noise follows. *The girl has swooned, and the vampyre is at his hideous repast!*

YOUNG RINGWOOD — fiancé of the late Clara Crofton — has heard strange tales about nocturnal happenings in the village church. He suspects that his beloved may have become a vampyre (through contact with Varney) and decides to see for himself . . . .

YES, IT WAS twelve o'clock, that mysterious hour at which it is believed by many that,

"Graves give up their dead,
And many a ghost in church-yard decay,
Rise from their cold, cold bed
To make night horrible with wild vagary."

Twelve, that hour when all that is human feels a sort of irksome dread, as if the spirits of those who have gone from the great world were too near, loading the still night air with the murky vapours of the grave. A chilliness came over Ringwood and he fancied a strange kind of light was in the church, making objects more visible than in their dim and dusty outlines they had been before.

"Why do I tremble?" he said, "why do I tremble? Clouds pass away from before the moon, that is all. Soon there may be a bright light here, and lo, all is still; I hear nothing but my own breathing; I see nothing but what is common and natural. Thank heaven, all will pass away in quiet. There will be no horror to recount — no terrific sight to chill my blood. Rest Clara, rest in Heaven."

Ten minutes passed away, and there was no alarm; how wonderfully relieved was Ringwood. Tears came to his eyes, but they were the natural tears of regret, such as he had shed before for her who had gone from him to the tomb, and left no trace behind, but in the hearts of those who loved her.

"Yes," he said, mournfully, "she has gone from me, and I love her still. Still does the fond remembrance of all that she was to me, linger in my heart. She is my own, my beautiful Clara, as she ever was, and as, while life remains, to me she ever will be."

At the moment that he uttered these words a slight noise met his ears.

In an instant he sprung to his feet in the pulpit, and looked anxiously around him.

"What was that?" he said. "What was that?"

All was still again, and he was upon the point of convincing himself, that the noise was either some accidental one, or the creation of his own fancy, when it came again.

He had no doubt this time. It was a perceptible, scraping, strange sort of sound, and he turned his whole attention to the direction from whence it came. With a cold creeping chill through his frame, he saw that the direction was the one where was the family vault of the Croftons, the last home of her whom he held still in remembrance, and whose memory was so dear to him.

He felt the perspiration standing upon his brow, and if the whole world had been the recompense to him for moving away from where he was he could not have done so. All he could do was to gaze with bated breath, and distended eyes upon the aisle of the church from whence the sound came.

That something of a terrific nature was now about to exhibit itself, and that the night would not go off without some terrible and significant adventure to make it remembered he felt convinced. All he dreaded was to think for a moment what it might be.

His thoughts ran to Clara, and he murmured forth in the most agonizing accents, —

"Anything — any sight but the sight of her. Oh, no, no, no!"

But it was not altogether the sight of her that he dreaded; oh no, it was the fact that the sight of her on such an occasion would bring the horrible conviction with it, that there was some truth in the dreadful apprehension that he had of the new state of things that had ensued regarding the after death condition of that fair girl.

The noise increased each moment, and finally there was a sudden crash.

"She comes! she comes!" gasped Ringwood.

He grasped the front of the pulpit with a frantic violence, and then slowly and solemnly there crossed his excited vision a figure all clothed in white. Yes, white flowing vestments, and he knew by their fashion that they were not worn by the living, and that it was some inhabitant of the tomb that he now looked upon.

He did not see the face. No, that for a time was hidden from him, but his heart told him who it was. Yes, it was his Clara.

It was no dream. It was no vision of a too excited fancy, for until those palpable sounds, and that most fearfully palpable form crossed his sight, he was rather inclined to go the other way, and to fancy what the Sexton had reported was nothing but a delusion of his overwrought brain. Oh, that he could but for one brief moment have found himself deceived.

"Speak!" he gasped; "speak! speak!"

There was no reply.

"I conjure you, I pray you though the sound of your voice should hurl me to perdition — I implore you, speak."

All was silent, and the figure in white moved on slowly but surely towards the door of the church, but ere it passed out, it turned for a moment, as if for the very purpose of removing from the mind of Ringwood any lingering doubt as to its identity.

He then saw the face, oh, so well-known, yet so pale. It was Clara Crofton!

"'Tis she! 'tis she!" was all he could say.

It seemed, too, as if some crevice in the clouds had opened at the moment, in order that he should with an absolute certainty see the countenance of that solemn figure, and then all was more than usually silent again. The door closed, and the figure was gone.

He rose in the pulpit, and clasped his hands. Irresolution seemed for a few moments to sway him to and fro, and then he rushed down into the body of the church.

"I'll follow it," he cried, "though it lead me to perdition. Yes, I'll follow it."

He made his way to the door, and even as he went he shouted:

"Clara! Clara! Clara!"

He reached the threshold of the ancient church; he gazed around him distractedly, for he thought that he had lost all sight of the figure. No — no, even in the darkness and against the night sky, he saw it once again in its sad-looking death raiments. He dashed forward.

The moonbeams at this instant being freed from some dense clouds that had interposed between them and this world, burst forth with resplendent beauty.

There was not a tree, a shrub, nor a flower, but what was made distinct and manifest, and with the church, such was the almost unprecedented lustre of the beautiful planet, that even the inscriptions upon the old tables and tombs were distinctly visible.

Such a refulgence lasted not many minutes, but while it did, it was most beautiful, and the gloom that followed it seemed doubly black.

"Stay, stay," he shouted, "yet a moment, Clara; I swear that what you are that will I be. Take me over to the tomb with you, say but that it is your dwelling-place, and I will make it mine, and declare it a very palace of the affections.''

The figure glided on.

It was in vain that he tried to keep up with it. It threaded the churchyard among the ancient tombs, with a gliding speed that soon distanced him, impeded, as he continually was, by some obstacle or another, owing to looking at the apparition he followed, instead the ground before him.

Still, on he went, heedless whither he was conveyed, for he might be said to be dragged onward, so much were all his faculties both of mind and body intent upon following the apparition of his beloved.

Once, and once only, the figure paused, and seemed to be aware that it was followed for it flitted round an angle made by one of the walls of the church, and disappeared from his eyes.

In another moment he had turned the same point.

"Clara! Clara!" he shouted. " 'Tis I — you know my voice, Clara, Clara."

She was not to be seen, and then the idea struck him that she must have re-entered the church, and he too, turned, and crossed the threshold. He lingered there for a moment or two, and the whole building echoed to the name of Clara, as with romantic eagerness, he called upon her by name to come forth to him.

Those echoes were the only reply.

Maddened — rendered desperate beyond all endurance, he went some distance into the building in search of her, and again he called.

It was in vain; she had eluded him, and with all the carefulness and all the energy and courage he had brought to bear upon that night's proceedings, he was foiled. Could anything be more agonising than this to such a man as Ringwood — he who loved her so, that he had not shrunk from her even in death, although she had so shrunk from him.

"I will find her — I will question her," he cried. "She shall not escape me; living or dead, she shall be mine. I will wait for her, even in the tomb."

Before he carried out the intention of going actually into the vault to await her return, he thought he would take one more glance at the churchyard with the hope of seeing her there, as he could observe no indications of her presence in the church.

With this view he proceeded to the door, and emerged into the dim light. He called upon her again by name, and he thought he heard some faint sound in the church behind him. To turn and make a rush into the building was the work of a moment.

He saw something — it was black instead of white — a tall figure — it advanced towards him, and with great force, before he was aware that an attack was at all intended, it felled him to the ground.

The blow was so sudden, so unexpected, and so severe, that it struck him down in a moment before he could be aware of it. To be sure, he had arms with him, but the anxiety and agony of mind he endured that night, since seeing the apparition come from the tomb, had caused him to forget them.

RINGWOOD RECOVERS. *The assailant is, of course, none other than Varney the Vampyre, protecting his bride. Meanwhile, the villagers — after a 'grand consultation at the ale-house' — have decided to take matters into their own hands . . . .*

"THE VAMPYRE, the vampyre," cried the blacksmith, "death to the vampyre — death and destruction to the vampyre."

"Hurrah!" cried another, "to the vaults — this way to Sir George Crofton's vault."

There seemed to be little doubt now, but that this disorderly rabble would execute summary vengeance upon the supposed nocturnal disturber of the peace of the district.

Ever and anon, too, as these shouts of discord, and of threatening vengeance, rose upon the night air, there would come the distant muttering of thunder, for the storm had not yet ceased, although its worst fury had certainly passed away.

Dark and heavy clouds were sweeping up from the horizon, and it seemed to be tolerably evident that some heavy deluge of rain would eventually settle the fury of the elements, and reconcile the discord of wind and electricity.

Several of the rioters were provided with links and matches, so that in a few moments the whole interior of the church was brilliantly illuminated, while at the same time it presented a grotesque appearance, in consequence of the unsteady and wavering flame from the links, throwing myriads of dancing shadows upon the walls.

There would have been no difficulty under any ordinary circumstances in finding the entrance to the vault, where the dead of the Crofton family should have lain in peace, but now since the large flagstone that covered the entrance to that receptacle of the grave was removed, it met their observation at once.

It was strange now to perceive how, for a moment, superstition having led them on so far, the same feeling should induce them to pause, ere they ventured to make their way down these gloomy steps.

It was a critical moment, and probably if any one or two had taken a sudden panic, the whole party might have left the church with precipitation, having done a considerable amount of mischief, and yet as it is so usual with rioters, having left their principal object unaccomplished.

The blacksmith put an end to this state of indecision, for, seizing a link from the man who was nearest to him, he darted down the steps, exclaiming as he did so, —

"Whoever's afraid, need not follow me."

This was a taunt they were not exactly prepared to submit to, and the consequence was, that in a very few moments the ancient and time honoured vault of the Croftons was more full o the living than of the dead.

The blacksmith laid his hand upon Clara's coffin.

"Here it is," he said, "I know the very pattern of the cloth, and the fashion of the nails. I saw it at Grigson the undertaker's before it was taken to the Grange."

"Is she there — is she there?" cried half a dozen voices at once.

Even the blacksmith hesitated a moment ere he removed the lid from the receptacle of death, but when he did so, and his eyes fell upon the face of the presumed vampyre, he seemed rejoiced to find in the appearances then exhibited some sort of justification for the act of violence of which already he had been the instigator.

"Here you are," he said, "look at the bloom upon her lips, why her cheeks are fresher and rosier than ever they were while she was alive; a vampyre my mates, this is a vampyre, or may I never break bread again; and now what's to be done?"

"Burn her, burn her," cried several.

"Well," said the blacksmith, "mind it's as you like. I've brought you here, and shown you what it is, and now you can do what you like, and of course I'll lend you a hand to do it."

Any one who had been very speculative in this affair, might have detected in these last words of the blacksmith, something like an inclination to creep out of the future consequences of what might next be done, while at the same time shame deterred him from exactly leaving his companions in the lurch.

After some suggestions then, and some argumentation as to the probability or possibility of interruption — the coffin itself, was with its sad and wretched occupant, lifted from the niche where it should have remained until that awful day when the dead shall rise for judgment, and carried up the steps into the church, from thence they passed into the graveyard, but scarcely had they done so, when the surcharged clouds burst over their heads, and the rain came down in perfect torrents.

The deluge was of so frightful, and continuous a character, that they shrank back again beneath the shelter of the church porch, and there waited until its first fury had passed away.

Such an even down storm seldom lasts long in our climate, and the consequence was that in about ten minutes the shower had so far subsided that although a continuous rain was falling it bore but a very distant comparison to what had taken place.

"How are we to burn the body on such a night as this?"

"Aye, how indeed," said another; "you could not so much as kindle a fire, and if you did, it would not live many minutes."

"I'll tell you what to do at once," said one who had as yet borne but a quiet part in the proceedings; I'll tell you what to do at once, for I saw it done myself; a vampyre is quite as secure buried in a cross-road with a stake through its body, as if you burned it in all the fires in the world; come on, the rain won't hinder you doing that."

This was a suggestion highly approved of, and the more so as there was a cross-road close at hand, so that the deed could be done quick, and the parties dispersed to their respective homes, for already the exertion they had taken, and the rain that had fallen, had had a great effect in sobering them.

And even now the perilous and disgusting operation of destroying the body, by fire or any other way, might have been abandoned, had any one of the party suggested such a course — but the dread of a future imputation of cowardice kept all silent.

Once more the coffin was raised by four of the throng, and carried through the church-yard, which was now running in many little rivulets, in consequence of the rain. The cross-road was not above a quarter of a mile from the spot, and while those who were disengaged from carrying the body, were hurrying away to get spades and mattocks, the others walked through the rain, and finally paused at the place they thought suitable for that ancient superstitious rite, which it was thought would make the vampyre rest in peace.

At last a dozen men now arrived well armed with spades and picks, and they commenced the work of digging a deep, rather than a capacious grave, in silence.

A gloomy and apprehensive spirit seemed to come over the whole assemblage, and the probability is that this was chiefly owing to the fact that they now encountered no opposition, and that they were permitted unimpeded to accomplish a purpose which had never yet been attempted within the memory of any of the inhabitants of the place.

The grave was dug, and about two feet depth of soil was thrown in a huge mound upon the surface; the coffin was lowered, and there lay the corpse within that receptacle of poor humanity, unimprisoned by any lid for that had been left in the vault, and awaiting the doom which they had decreed upon it, but which they now with a shuddering horror shrunk from performing.

A hedge stake with a sharp point had been procured, and those who held it looked around them with terrified countenances, while the few links that had not been extinguished by the rain, shed a strange and lurid glare upon all objects.

"It must be done," said the blacksmith, "don't let it be said that we got thus far and then were afraid."

"Do it then yourself," said the man that held the stake, "I dare not."

"Aye, do," cried several voices; "you brought us here, why don't you do it — are you afraid after all your boasting?"

"Afraid — afraid of the dead; I'm not afraid of any of you that are alive, and it's not likely I'm going to be afraid of a dead body; you're a pretty set of cowards. I've no animosity against the girl, but I want that we shall all sleep in peace, and that our wives and children should not be disturbed nocturnally in their blessed repose. I'll do it if none of you'll do it, and then you may thank me afterwards for the act, although I suppose if I get into trouble I shall have you all turn tail upon me."

"No, we won't — no, we won't."

"Well, well, here goes, whether you do or not. I — I'll do it directly."

"He shrinks," cried one.

"No," said another; "he'll do it — now for it, stand aside."

"Stand aside yourself — do you want to fall into the grave."

The blacksmith shuddered as he held the stake in an attitude to pierce the body, and even up to that moment it seemed to be a doubtful case, whether he would be able to accomplish his purpose or not; at length, when they all thought he was upon the point of abandoning his design, and casting the stake away, he thrust it with tremendous force through the body and the back of the coffin.

The eyes of the corpse opened wide — the hands were clenched, and a shrill, piercing shriek came from the lips — a shriek that was answered by as many as there were persons present, and then with pallid fear upon their countenances they rushed headlong from the spot.

EPILOGUE — *the final, total destruction of Varney the vampyre, and conclusion.*

"WE EXTRACT FROM the *Algemeine Zeitung* the following most curious story, the accuracy of which of course we cannot vouch for, but still there is a sufficient air of probability about it to induce us to present it to our readers.

"Late in the evening, about four days since, a tall and melancholy-looking stranger arrived, and put up at one of the principal hotels at Naples. He was a most peculiar looking man, and considered by the persons of the establishment as about the ugliest guest they had ever had within the walls of their place.

"In a short time he summoned the landlord, and the following conversation ensued between him and the strange guest.

" 'I want,' said the stranger, 'to see all the curiosities of Naples, and among the rest Mount Vesuvius. Is there any difficulty?'

" 'None,' replied the landlord, 'with a proper guide.'

"A guide was soon secured, who set out with the adventurous Englishman to make the ascent of the burning mountain.

"They went on then until the guide did not think it quite prudent to go any further, as there was a great fissure in the side of the mountain, out of which a stream of lava was slowly issuing and spreading itself in rather an alarming manner.

"The ugly Englishman, however, pointed to a secure mode of getting higher still, and they proceeded until they were very near the edge of the crater itself. The stranger then took his purse from his pocket and flung it to the guide saying, —

" 'You can keep that for your pains, and for coming into some danger with me. But the fact was, that I wanted a witness to an act which I have set my mind upon performing.'

"The guide says that these words were spoken with so much calmness, that he verily believed the act mentioned as about to be done was some scientific experiment of which he knew that the English were very fond, and he replied, —

" 'Sir, I am only too proud to serve so generous and so distinguished a gentleman. In what way can I be useful?'

" 'You will make what haste you can,' said the stranger, 'from the mountain, inasmuch as it is covered with sulphurous vapours, inimical to human life, and when you reach the city you will cause to be published an account of my proceedings, and what I say. You will say that you accompanied Varney the Vampyre to the crater of Mount Vesuvius and that, tired and disgusted with a life of horror, he flung himself in to prevent the possibility of a reanimation of his remains.'

"Before, then, the guide could utter anything but a shriek, Varney took one tremendous leap, and disappeared in the burning mouth of the mountain."